Song of Turand

Praise for
Song of Turand
Opening Aria
Legends from Turand

Somewhere between a true romance novel and *Game of Thrones* you will find *Song of Turand* with characters so real they seem as though you already know them and living in a world so real that you will swear you may have existed there yourself.

—Walt Hammond, Amazon reviewer

Part fantasy, part romance, part adventure, this expansive first novel of author Sandra Valencia takes you on your own adventure through vivid imagery and startling prose. Eerily, some of what she writes in this story parallels many events happening now.

—Barnes & Noble reviewer

When is the movie coming out? I can't believe how I feel like I am there and can visualize everything going on. What an absolutely incredible story.

—J. Peters, Mansfield, OH

Song of Turand

Opening Aria
Legends from Turand

Sandra Valencia

Book Design & Production:
Columbus Publishing Lab
www.ColumbusPublishingLab.com

Hardcover ISBN: 978-1-63337-662-5
Paperback ISBN: 978-1-63337-663-2
E-Book ISBN: 978-1-63337-664-9

Printed in the United States of America
1 3 5 7 9 10 8 6 4 2

Take comfort in the faith you have been given.
Guard it well.
Love is your strength.
Faith is your shield.

Foreword

Within these pages unfolds a story of transition. A nation must discover a way to meet the dark forces that suppress the lives of its people. Its people must search not for a new path but, instead, the strength to recapture the good they allowed to slip through their fingers. With so much lost, basic, primal needs must be satisfied before hope can be reborn or the spiritual renewal, craved by souls on a universal basis, can begin. To accomplish change, leaders must emerge and, through the strength of their character, seek recovery for their people—and themselves.

This story is a simple one. Yet, in its simplicity, it holds veracity—truths that we all must search to find—within these pages, within our own lives, whether we mirror the spiritual oppression of Turand or find ourselves threatened by similar destructive forces in our own world.

True love is honest, real beyond our imaginations.
Powerful enough to span the ages and the universe.
If only we open our souls to believe.

A Brief History

Turand, existing in a faraway world very much like Earth, is an expansive nation of many breathtakingly beautiful contrasts. Mountains soar heavenward to scrape sapphire skies. Warm turquoise seas kiss broad, white sand beaches. Vast stretches of emerald-carpeted land are bejeweled with innumerable varieties of flowers. Wide rivers and gurgling streams feed lofty guardian forests. Waterfalls of crystal clean waters dance over rocky cliffs and spill into great pools reflecting brilliant sunshine. Gentle breezes sweep broad plains. Occasional, ever-spring anomalies boast lush plant life and scenic riches with no regard for seasonal changes.

Turand is home to a nation of people vitally aware of the physical relationships between themselves and their world. They are also keenly in tune with the spiritual and sensual connections that bond them with each other. Since ancient times, Turandans have been deeply sensitive to the spirits that inhabit their souls. Gentle, yet vibrant, they are dedicated to intellectual and creative pursuits and the conservation of the land they love. Turand's people traditionally revere peace and detest violence.

The people of Turand recognize a single, universal God whom they call by the name Val, meaning "Father with Us." Servants of Val include priests and priestesses who nurture and cherish unique mystical gifts provided by Val. These religious guides are free to marry but must always

serve Val according to ancient teachings. Val's devoted priests and priestesses guide and teach Turandans to reach within themselves to touch the
flourishing spiritual essences that universally bind all peoples.

The Order of Val was established as Turand's elite society of anointed
priestesses known as Valiria. Valiria are extolled for their dedication to Val.
Valiria vow to serve Val first and foremost. Through passionate prayer and
meditation, they continuously revitalize their connection with Val, learn
more of His spiritual kingdom, and re-energize their internal spirits. Val
often enhances their unique insights with visions and dreams that provide
glimpses into the future. Valiria are blessed with a transcendent mysticism that allows them to read the life forces of those around them, thus
permitting them precious insight in order to guide and serve those souls.
To fulfill their commitment to faithful service, they willingly face dangers
with unparalleled grace, confidence, and peace.

Mystery is considered synonymous with Valiria. However, certain
specifics are known. All are blessed with the capability to meditate and call
upon Val's Healing Graces. Depending on Val's will, these graces either
heal completely or provide blessed comfort to those whose time it is to
die physically. Some Valiria are graced with a unique, heightened form of
this great gift that enables them to transfer these graces on a broad scale
in the event of calamity. Valiria are spiritually drawn to lavender, inspiring
peace and tranquility. They often wear flowing, hooded robes of lavender,
especially during events connected to their service. Upon acceptance of
their sacred vows and subsequent anointing into the Order of Val, they
are marked for life with the sign of the sun encased within a pyramid, Val's
symbol to Turand.

From the state of Valiria rises the High Priestess Valkana, whose presence must grace Turand in order to preserve the state of peace and vitality of that nation. Valkana, "Chosen One of Val," maintains a singularly
powerful link binding Val to his order of priestesses, priests, and Turand's

people. She bears sole responsibility for the spiritual maintenance of the sacred Temple of Val, located in Toraval. Valkana maintains all gifts received as Valiria but accepts responsibility for expanded degrees of those gifts. A Valkana's direct connectivity to Val is frequently manifested by a highly visible bluish-white aura that sheaths her in light.

Valkana is the teacher who leads and assesses those who choose to become priests and priestesses. A priest or priestess may profess vows and be anointed by a group of five Valiria. However, anointing and reception of vows can be performed by Valkana without any other priest or priestess. The sacred station of Valkana was instated during ancient times when the people of Turand were lost in an era of upheaval and intense violence.

Priests and priestesses exerted tremendous effort, risking their lives to spread the teachings of Val and of the gifts of peace he wished to bestow upon his people. His requirements were simple—that his people love and pray to him, that they love and serve one another, and that they reverently accept the teachers sent to provide spiritual guidance.

Upon Turand's conversion, Val swept into its midst the great age of peace. The first Valkana was introduced as Val's direct representative to his people. The presence of Valkana in Turand would be perpetuated through the faithfulness and prayers of the Turandan people. Her presence would ensure connectivity and continuity with Val's great rewards. When the physical life of one Valkana ended, a new Valkana would be selected by Val to act as chosen guide.

With the conversion, Turandans acknowledged a royal family bearing the ancestral name of Toscano. This family hailed from Toraval, in the central province of Toravalia. Inspired to a unique state of faith in Val, the Toscano family came to treasure his promises of prosperity and tranquility. Following generations of strife, the Royal House of Toscano, aided by the Knights of Jared and servants of Val, influenced and persuaded more and more of Turand's provinces to seek unity through Val. Their concerted efforts to spread Val's teachings resulted in Turand's centuries of peace and prosperity. Val also bestowed great blessings upon the Toscano family as a reward for the devotion shown to him and his people.

Following more than six centuries, a small movement of doubters began to encourage a new way of life based on a self-centered philosophy promoting instant gratification of wants and desires and the subsequent rejection of Val's teachings. Despite untiring efforts by Val's servants, the time came when too many Turandans shunned the ways of Val. An aged Valkana issued dire warnings from her deathbed. With the continued fall from true faith, Val would withdraw the blessing of Valkana from Turand. Without this presence, their nation would face untold dangers, calamities, and hardships. Great sorrows would usher in a spiritual dark age. Valkana would only be restored upon the return to spirituality demonstrated through prayers, faith, and service as required by Val.

A century has passed since the death of the last Valkana. Chaos plagues a nation once characterized by its pursuit of education, music, and art. Turand, once prosperous and happy, knows dissent and increasing poverty.

During the reign of Turand's previous king, Maxim, brutal invaders from the Sifiq Kingdom, a continental nation half a world away, overran the peaceful country. The Sifiq have plundered Turand and enslaved many Turandans to produce food supplies to ship to the Sifiq Kingdom. Their occupation has been bloody and violent, especially in their goal to eradicate the sacred Order of Val.

Part 1

Believe, My children, believe in me.
As darkness your hearts pierces,
Though evils your souls torture,
And troubles and turmoil bewilder,
My children, My children, have faith in me.
Into your midst, tormentors dare come,
Pain and hardship with them they bring,
With sorrows deep to sorely grieve you.
Falter you will, from all that is lost.
Your eyes will weep. Your hearts will ache.
Alone you will feel each day that you face
As departure from faith reveals its cost.
But believe, My children, believe in me.
Hold tight to your faith and hold it close.
For if you do, My comfort I'll send
But you must, My children, believe in me.
Set your eyes straight ahead; your path do not lose.
Lift high your heads, firm in your belief.
Breathe deeply of courage; Nerves do not quiver,
For mighty are you when your God you choose.

Song of Turand

My children, My children, have faith in me.
My signs shall I send as light to guide you.
Into your experience My help I'll dispatch,
Seek the lessons they bear,
Acknowledge My presence,
Accept so that, too, peace will come.
Allow me to hold you,
Your lives in My hands,
Trust in My love,
Let me speak to your spirits,
For to the greatest of loves
I promise to bear you.
Remember, My children, each child I love dearly.
Your love I ask, not only for me,
But for those gathered 'round you
And through love you will conquer,
My peace shall I give you, Great joy you'll discover,
But first, My children, believe in me...

From the Great Book of Val

Chapter 1

Garogan Province

Alexa lay asleep. Slumber had come easily for the first time since her return to Garogan Castle. Visions appeared. She found comfort in her mother's gentle smile, and she laughed to herself as her father attempted to surprise her with a new doll. She grimaced and dug fingernails into her palms as she faced their bloody, lifeless bodies. Victor's strong arms held her. He had somehow pulled her from her bedroom window and hidden them both from marauding Sifiq butchers.

Her nose burned, having been assaulted anew by the vile smells permeating the damp cell in Zenox Prison. She looked up at Gregor's dark, bearded face, unable to mask her disgust. His hair was black as ebony, thick and curling over the edge of his collar. In its waves were scattered hints of silver. His face was square, framed with a full, immaculately trimmed black beard. His eyes were so deep brown that they often appeared black, which so appropriately matched the blackness of his heart. Would she never be free of the remembered images that continued to haunt her even now that she had returned to Garogan?

Ten months earlier, Alexa had traveled to Toraval, the capital of Turand, in hopes of learning the fate of her betrothed. She had been mortified by rumors that he had been taken as prisoner to Zenox, which was reputed to be the most evil and deadly prison in the entire land. After arriving in Toraval, Alexa clearly felt Victor's life force as strongly as she felt his weakness and the danger surrounding him. She must save him. But how?

To find the answer, she knew she must risk going to the Temple of Val. Kneeling beneath its towering spires, she passed hours absorbed in deep meditation. That meditation had revealed Gregor, allowing her to know his face before she ever saw him with her own eyes. Gazing into those dark eyes, she had seen fires of both determination and conflict. She had seen him as king and as man. Alexa had also watched him take her hand into his. That moment in the vision left her fearful and bewildered, disquieted with the unwelcome certainty that this vision held the key, the solution to her quest to save Victor's life.

Early in the evening, Alexa walked to the palace. Upon her arrival, she stood beneath towering, arched doorways and whispered a fleeting prayer. Her image was tall and proud as she entered confidently, wrapped in the lavender cloak signifying her position in the Order of Val. Wearing the sacred garment in public could easily cost her life, yet she seemed unconcerned. The Sifiq had sworn death to all who professed faith in the ancient God of Turand. They ridiculed his teachings of love, tranquility, and peace, scoffing at the philosophy based on honor and loyalty. The fools of Val were the weaklings who had allowed them to take easy control of the once prosperous and peaceful kingdom of Turand.

Alexa strode through the palace as if she were the rightful ruler of those vast hallways. Her eyes were set straight ahead as she carried herself with grace and dignity. Some had thought to stop her; others had wanted to kill her and seize the prized robes. None dared, and all fell back away from her. They were stunned into inaction, prevented from approaching not only by her demeanor but by an impenetrable shield that was her unseen aura.

She neither stopped nor even slackened her pace until she finally stood before the throne of Turand. Lifting her chin in defiance, she reached up to slide the hood of the cloak back from her face. Gregor had been laughing with several members of his court when the awed silence struck him as well.

Alexa commanded with nothing more than her presence—and those magnificent green eyes. Those eyes were awe-inspiring—wide and almond-shaped, lined with lush, dark lashes. Her eyes—burning with the fires of emerald. One became so mesmerized that the rest of her face, lovingly framed by rich, golden-brown curls, ivory skin, and sensual, rose-colored lips, was almost unnoticed.

Gregor was stunned. He felt impaled by nothing more than her eyes. They pierced his soul and shook him to the very foundation of his being. Consciously, he cast off the powerful impact of her presence. He thought he had almost been bewitched—almost.

"I am Alexa Maraná," she replied to his unspoken question.

His wide, arched eyebrows shot up. "And why do you stand before the King of Turand, Alexa Maraná?" Perhaps her strange presence might provide a fresh source of amusement for Sifiq officers in his court.

"I come to seek private counsel with Turand's king."

Gregor was intrigued by her formality. Something in her presence washed away his initial desire to turn her into a subject of ridicule. However, there was nothing in the presence she exuded that allowed humor. She dominated his court hall, and, irrationally, he experienced a sudden, powerful desire to dominate her in return. "You are unknown to me, yet you seek private counsel?"

Alexa inhaled deeply. He wanted to toy with her, but she was in no mood to play games. Her stakes were too high. She summoned all her faith to sustain her courage. Her voice rang strong and clear. "Your Majesty, I have reviewed all of the new laws implemented in Turand. To date, none of those laws rescinds the right of members of the Order of Val to request private counsel with the king. Here is proof of my identity."

Her eyes never wavered from his as she extended her right arm and pulled back her sleeves. Just beneath the bend on the inside of her arm was the triangle surrounding the sun, the sacred symbol of Val.

"Can it be that you are so foolhardy?" The rude demand came from one of the king's attendants, obviously Sifiq by his dress. "Do you consider us so stupid as to believe that you are not only a Valkana but also Maraná? The Maraná family was banished years ago."

She withered the outspoken attendant with a look that he felt with physical impact. He stumbled backward and cringed. "You mean the Maraná family was slaughtered, do you not? And to further clarify your words of ignorance, I do not claim to be Valkana. I claim only to be Valiria, a member of the sacred Order of Val. And I assure you. I am the last of the Maraná. I survived the carnage."

Gregor mused to himself over the exchange. Thoughtfully stroking his beard, he was secretly impressed not only by her fearless response to his own inquiry but also pleased by the apparent discomfort she had caused Gor-Dan. Gregor despised Gor-Dan and tolerated him only out of necessity. The presence of Gor-Dan and others of his kind was necessary to preserve the continued illusion of cooperation.

"Alexa Maraná," Gregor said after a prolonged moment of assessment, "for my own amusement, I choose to honor the ancient laws and grant you private counsel." Gregor then stood and dismissed everyone from the great hall except his chief adviser, Stefan Sidano.

"I requested private counsel," she repeated when she saw Stefan remain. She was growing concerned by the effort required to control her breathing. She must not falter.

"Stefan is my confidant and my wisest, most trusted adviser. That which you say to me in his presence is indeed private and will go no further. Now, Alexa of the Order of Val, tell me what matter is of such importance that you risk your life to come before me." His words were spoken condescendingly.

Alexa refused to be intimidated. "I come to make a simple request. I ask for the life of Lord Victor Garogan that I may accompany him in peace back to his home province."

Gregor shook his head once in undisguised surprise. "Lord Garogan? You ask me to free Lord Garogan?" He tossed his head backward and emitted a laugh that reverberated from the high walls of the great court. The rich sound could have been one of great happiness had it not been filled with such cynicism.

"I do," she reaffirmed, relieved that her voice had not quivered the way her insides did.

As his laughter subsided, Gregor studied her intently. A part of him was amused by her sheer audacity. She was so young yet so daring. "And why should I consider such a thing? Lord Garogan is an enemy to the throne."

She paused a moment to form her response. "Victor has been enemy not to the throne but to those who defile it. Nevertheless, in Garogan Province, he poses no direct threat to you. I give my personal assurances that he will return there without incident."

"Do you really think it so simple, my dear? You have today made yourself a target with your lavender robes and mark of Val. Do you honestly believe you and Lord Garogan can survive the return journey?"

"With the personal assurance and protection of the King of Turand, yes." She gave no ground and continued to meet him eye to eye.

"What an incredible stand," Gregor thought. He could hardly believe her boldness. He glanced at Stefan, and they wordlessly communicated their mutual appraisal.

Long moments passed as Gregor considered her unwavering stance as well as her preposterous request. He continued to stroke his beard thoughtfully, shifting his gaze back to her. "I am compelled to ask this of you once more. Why is it that you risk so much to gain Garogan's freedom?"

Alexa tilted her head slightly backward in haughty regard. She breathed deeply. "He is an honorable man from an old, venerable family that long served the royal house of Turand." She paused briefly. "And he is my betrothed."

Gregor once again found it difficult to mask his surprise. A member of the Order of Val betrothed to Victor Garogan. Amazing. He wondered if she would believe the actions proven against her betrothed. Her order would have certainly condemned Garogan's plot. One glance at her obstinate countenance convinced him that any effort to convince her of the truth would most likely prove futile.

"My dear, I commend your courage despite its foolhardiness. Still, I cannot help but question the sanity of your actions this night. However, I am not an unreasonable man. I will consider your request. Stefan will show you to quarters where you may rest the night under protection of the throne. We will talk further in the morning. Good night."

Alexa was stunned by the abrupt dismissal. "But, Your Majesty..."

Gregor lifted his hand in dismissal and left the court hall without another word.

"Milady," Stefan's voice was gentle and respectful as he went to a second doorway and held it open for her. His hair was golden and his complexion fair. His eyes were brightly intelligent and his facial expressions intense as he regarded her with concern. His king's behavior had presented an unexpected quandary.

She hesitated, confused by the king's sudden departure.

"Milady," Stefan's voice was more insistent as it pierced the thoughts whirling through her brain. "His Majesty offers you safe lodging in a city that is quite unsafe for those who profess faith to Val. It is my sound advice that you graciously accept his hospitality."

Alexa gazed deeply into his bluish-gray eyes, closed her own, and touched his life force. Though he was in service to the king, she felt positive energy flowing within him. She opened her eyes and nodded slightly, allowing him to guide her.

⤸

She awoke suddenly, uncertain why. Sitting up in bed, she saw that moonlight streamed through the window across the room. She heard none of the night sounds one might expect. Gazing toward misty shafts of invading light, she lay down again.

"Gregor?" she whispered into the darkness before drifting back to sleep.

Toraval

At the palace in Toraval, Gregor tossed fitfully in her bed, punching pillows and drawing thick, feather-stuffed coverlets close around him. Finally, he reached for the pillow she had used that last night they had spent together. Tears stung his eyes as he sniffed faint traces of fragrance that lingered in the fabric.

"Alexa, my beloved Alexa. What have I done to you? What have I done?"

Gregor finally slipped into exhausted slumber. Instead of the dreamless sleep he so desperately needed, memories crowded in, and dreams tormented a soul troubled by the guilt and shame he bore.

"My dear Alexa Maraná. I wish you good morning." Gregor stood up from the table where he was finishing breakfast. His hand gestured that she should sit at his right. A place had already been set with brilliant white porcelain and gleaming silver in anticipation of her joining him.

"I bid you a good morning filled with Val's blessings." Alexa nodded, then walked to the indicated chair and allowed Stefan to seat her. Her greeting was formal and subdued, her eyes even more watchful than the night before.

Stefan seated himself at the end of the table opposite Gregor and accepted a cup of strong, fragrant tea from one of the servants. He chose to remain silent so as to study and analyze her words. He also carefully observed Gregor, whose eyes shone with an unusually intense determination that sparked distinct uneasiness.

"Tell me, Alexa Maraná," Gregor began slowly, gesturing with a nod of his head that she should eat from the plate in front of her. "Tell me about the Order of Val. I am exceedingly curious since everyone has believed all Valiria dead for years. How is it that you come to be Valiria?"

Alexa curled long, elegant fingers around the curved handle of a porcelain cup. She paused momentarily, then sipped the steaming brew. She swallowed, wondering at the reason behind Gregor's choice of questions.

"Your Majesty, I know not what you may have read or heard. Much is written in the Holy Book of Val, and much is passed along as sacred tradition. The Maraná family has always been strong in its faith. My mother's family, too, long shared this love for our God. Both families were always known for their commitment to serving the people of Turand in order to please Val. I chose to take vows at a very early age. So far as I know, I am the last anointed Valiria."

"So, your place in the Order of Val is to satisfy and preserve ancestral tradition?" His expression seemed genuinely curious.

"Not at all, my lord. I serve Val because I love him. He offers great peace and reward to those who love and honor him." Her reply was direct and honest.

"And what reward does Val offer you?" His probing was now fraught with malicious intent.

"He offers more than I can explain to you in words. The gifts he provides are beyond the understanding of someone outside the faith." Her expression was pointed.

"Help me to understand better. You come here to beg for the life of Victor Garogan. You reveal to my entire court that you are marked for life with the symbol of Val. You display remarkable, regal demeanor, yet you come without family or means. Right now, I fail to see any of these gifts that Val so generously shares with you."

Alexa's green eyes sparkled with fire. Her richly curved mouth formed a knowing smile. Again, he wished to play games with her. He wanted to taunt her, to bait her. She could feel his life force, and it was indeed powerful. Her great worry was that she could not read that force the way she usually did with others.

"Sire, I am alone because Sifiq marauders invaded the village where I lived. They viciously murdered friends and family. Yet Val provided means that saved my life and guides me wherever I go. My faith does not falter. He does not fail me. The gifts you question are mine, I assure you."

Gregor admired her confident reply but continued to press her. "Please explain what kinds of gifts. I have heard it told that Valiria are mystics with great powers. What powers does Val give you, Alexa Maraná?"

Alexa gazed down at her hands, still wrapped around the warm cup. "I have no powers, as you put it. Insight? Yes. A deeper understanding of nature's forces? Yes. But I have no powers. Only Val has true power."

He mulled over her response and how best to continue. "Do you consider yourself mystic? You seem to avoid that question."

Her eyes bored into his heart, his soul. He felt the very real, searing fire and resisted her, refusing to allow her to see the effect she created in him. She, in turn, remained outwardly tranquil, although unable to fathom the confusion stemming from her inability to read him. Finally, she lifted her shoulders in a shrug.

"Mystic? I meditate. Sometimes, during meditation or sleep, I see visions of what has been or what is to come. I have no control over what is shown to me. I see only that which Val chooses to reveal. I must discern his meaning. If that is considered mystical, then I suppose the answer you seek is yes."

She grew very quiet, turning undue concentration to a delicately formed piece of sweet bread on her plate. She had seemingly dismissed his presence, her eyes far away.

Having already eaten, Gregor was free to study her. As she pulled the bread apart and placed a bite in her mouth, his attention was drawn to her hands. Her fingers were long and elegant. He noted that she wore no jewelry, not even a ring to indicate her betrothal. For the first time, he noticed the rich hues of brown hair, highlighted with glints of gold and copper. She had pulled the long, waving mass away from her face with a thickly padded, burgundy headband. Shorter tendrils had escaped the restraint to curl around her face. Gregor was surprised by a nearly over-whelming temptation to float his fingers through those gleaming tresses, to touch their silken texture. He shook his head, forcing from his mind the peculiar thought.

"Alexa Maraná," he addressed her, continuing to use her full name as he broke the silence. "I ask of you again why I should free Lord Garogan."

She chewed and swallowed the bite in her mouth. She had expected his question, only not so soon. The king was indeed direct and persistent.

"Victor is a good man. You laughed last night. You scoffed, but you do not know him."

"I have no need to know him. I know what he has done and what he intended to do." The words were spoken as matter-of-fact.

"What is his crime, Sire? Loving his country? Wishing to free Turand's people from the oppression of ruthless invaders? Saving people who are being beaten, starved, and murdered? Are those really such terrible crimes?" Emotion surged with conviction as she spoke.

Gregor's eyes sparked with barely controlled anger before he tersely responded, "To save those in need is no crime. Nor do I consider it so terrible to wish to eradicate unwelcome invaders. However, when a man amasses weapons and plots to invade the palace for the purpose of assassinating the king and his household while they sleep—that I consider high crime."

She stared at him in disbelief. Victor would not—could not—plan such a vile act. To confront the king on equal ground? Yes, that was possible. To slink around in the night to kill as people slept? Impossible. That was not the Victor she knew and loved.

"I can see in your eyes that you believe I lie. You will have the opportunity to talk with him yourself. Ask him. Perhaps then you will know that I speak the truth." Gregor slapped his napkin on the table and rose abruptly.

He turned to walk away from the table but stopped to face her again. "Alexa Maraná, I require time to consider all implications of your request. In the meantime, you are expected to stay within the east wing of the palace. You are not a prisoner. I restrict your movement for your own safety until I decide my course of action."

Gregor strode angrily from the room. Stefan also rose from his place and left to follow the king. When Stefan caught up with him, Gregor had stormed into his private library. The king seethed with anger, his bronzed skin darker than ever, his dark brown eyes appearing almost black. His full lips were pulled into a taut line. Tension was evident throughout every inch of his tall, muscular body.

"Gregor, you must not allow the woman's request to trouble you so. She is obviously blinded by her love for him. You know the legend of Valiria as well as I. They are fiercely loyal. To be loved by a Valiria is to be gifted with unparalleled devotion." Stefan was seriously worried. He knew his friend too well and saw something in his face that he had never seen before.

"It is not her love for Garogan that troubles me. Nor is it even her request for his freedom," Gregor spat angrily. Fury burned within him. He never dreamed he could have so little self-control. His nerves were on edge. He felt shaken to the very core of his being.

"Gregor, please, you must explain. I don't understand. Why does she distress you so?"

Gregor turned to face Stefan, his eyes blazing with grim determination. "How can I explain to you that which even I do not understand? I only know that I must have her." He turned away again to stare beyond the multi-paned windows toward the Temple of Val in the distance. His insides churned. Suddenly, he pounded a fist against the dark wood frame of the window and muttered a curse.

"Gregor?" Stefan's voice was stunned by the king's reaction.

Tension filled the quiet room. When Gregor finally spoke, his words were barely audible. "I want her."

Stefan stepped backward, shocked, searching for something to say.

This was the worst possible time for Gregor to lose his focus. So many plans were approaching fruition. Stefan was unable to hide his astonishment. "Gregor…"

"Stefan, you heard me. I want her, and I intend to have her. I will have her. I cannot allow her to leave Toraval."

Early afternoon was bright with winter sunshine. Alexa sat on a carved stone bench in a small garden outside the breakfast room. Artfully trimmed evergreen shrubs lent color to the otherwise drab, leafless stems and limbs in the garden. The promise of spring colors was not yet even a hint.

Her eyes were closed as she raised her face to the sun. Its bright rays warmed cheeks that were rosy with the nip of the chilled air. She cleared her mind of all current distresses, knowing she must open herself to receive Val's strengthening forces in order to understand the direction he wished her to take. She sensed imminent great change. Part of her was frightened. As the sun bathed her face, she felt Val's comforting touch and resolved to accept his will. With her acceptance, peace inundated her.

Stefan chose not to disturb her immediately. He was baffled by the effect she had wrought on Gregor in a matter of so few hours. He closely observed her meditation. Yesterday, he knew she had hidden her fears. This morning, only a few hours earlier, she had been calm and steadfast. Now, meditative, peaceful. She was indeed lovely, but the court was often crowded with beautiful women, any one of whom would gladly welcome any attentions Gregor chose to bestow. What was so different about this woman sitting before him?

Suddenly, Stefan noticed a change. Fleeting. Perhaps only a second. Perhaps only something in his imagination. He quickly dismissed the soft light that seemed to bathe her form for just a moment. He scolded himself. Too much talk about Valiria and mysticism and such foolishness. Still…

She lifted heavy eyelids and blinked against the brilliance of the sunshine before shifting her attention to meet Stefan's gaze. "The king now summons me?"

"How did you know?" Stefan asked. Perhaps the mysticism was true. "Otherwise, I believe you would not have come for me."

Stefan smiled inwardly at his own overwrought imagination. Her reply had been so matter-of-fact—so logical. Why had he thought she had known because of mystic insight?

"Come." He guided her back to the palace. They walked down a long corridor, their footsteps echoing in the hollow passageway. Stefan showed her through a doorway leading to a private sitting room and then left her alone.

Self-control was not simple. Alexa inhaled deeply, unable to suppress the sense of impending disaster. She forced herself to concentrate on her surroundings. A large window was framed with blue velvet draperies. The rich blue repeated in the thickly padded sofa and chairs upholstered in damask. Two low, round tables stood on an intricately patterned woven carpet in front of the sofa. The walls, paneled in dark wood, held sconces containing candles that cast flickering shadows about the room. Flames burned low in the stone fireplace to her left. She turned back to the window, wishing freedom from this room that was too dark for her to feel comfortable.

The sound of the door opening interrupted her thoughts. She turned around to face Gregor. Two guards stood behind him, tightly gripping Victor, his arms bound behind him. Alexa gasped his name but dared say no more.

"Alexa Maraná, I bring to you the man whose freedom you seek. I offer you ten minutes alone with him." Gregor stepped aside. The guards shoved Victor forward and accompanied their king from the room.

Victor's eyes widened with shock at the unexpected presence of his betrothed. His first question was to himself. Surely he had been drugged and now suffered hallucinations. Her hand coming to rest against his cheek chased the thought from his mind, telling him that she was real as he turned cracked lips to place a kiss into her palm.

"My darling Alexa, in Val's name, why have you risked coming here? It is a blessing that you've not been slain!" His chastisement failed as her arms stretched up and around his neck. Sheer physical pain gripped him as bonds prevented his arms from pulling her into a tight embrace.

Tears slipped from his hazel eyes. His hair was dirty and shaggy, his beard scraggly. His clothes were stained and smelled of sour sweat. He had been provided no means for personal hygiene inside the filthy cell where he had spent the past three weeks. He had also been given little food, and his normally robust body was much thinner, his face gaunt. Yet, in spite of it all, she had shown not even the faintest hint of hesitation as she wrapped her arms around him.

"Victor, I love you. I had to come. I had to find a way to save you." Her eyes wept. Her lips quivered. She gently led him to the sofa where they could sit. "Victor, we have so little time, and so much needs to be said. Is it true they keep you at Zenox?"

He breathed in deeply. The fresh fragrance that always surrounded her filled his senses. He had thought never again to revel in that sweetness. "Dearest Alexa, yes, I stay in that despicable place. But that is of no real concern to me. How have you come to the king? Tell me why he allows us this time. I thought they came finally to execute me. I'm confused. What have you done?"

"Shush, my love. One thing at a time." She allowed herself to study him, his appearance shocking her. More than ever, she vowed to save him. "I came to the king for private counsel, as is my right."

"He obviously granted counsel. But why? It makes no sense. That worries me greatly, Alexa."

She hesitated. "They told me you planned to assassinate the king as he slept. Is that true?"

Victor faced her question squarely. How to answer without lying to her? She would recognize a lie immediately. He could not predict her reaction to the truth. "It was an option. I would have hoped never to be so desperate."

She accepted his evasive answer with invading sadness. The accusations were true. Still, how could she relinquish her faith in him? She owed him her life. He had planned to marry her, patiently honoring her virtue, knowing that her position as Valiria required her to remain virgin until marriage. He had adored her in all other ways. She was unwilling to withdraw her devotion.

"Garogan's people need you, Victor. You are their strength, their leader. The southern provinces cry out for your return. You must go back. I cannot tell you how, but I know that I'm the only one who can secure your freedom."

Victor sighed in fear and frustration. "Sweetest Alexa, what has that traitorous scum required of you? What bargain does he demand?"

Alexa smiled reassuringly. "He has yet to ask anything. Still, I have no idea what to expect from him. I can only rely on faith that Val will guide me."

Tears once again burned Victor's eyes. "Alexa, our people need you, too. I know you refuse to believe, but I am certain Val has marked you for the blessing of Valkana. Promise me you will do nothing to endanger yourself. I much prefer to lose my own life rather than sacrifice yours. You are my life's love. Perhaps you do not, but I fear our king's intentions."

"Victor, I have requested that I be allowed to accompany you home peacefully, without incident. If I can gain your release, you must swear to me that you will return immediately to Garogan. Please, Victor, swear it." Her eyes begged him, and, as always, he was unable to deny her anything she asked of him.

"I swear it." Their eyes held, and she leaned forward to place a brief kiss against his lips, the cherished moment interrupted by the turning of the handle on the door.

This time, Stefan entered. His face flushed scarlet with anger. Typically fluid movements were sharp and mechanical. "Take him. Guard him closely. He is to be permitted to bathe and provided clean clothing."

The guards grasped Victor's arms tightly and nearly dragged him from the room. Stefan turned an angry expression to Alexa. She met his hostility with maddening tranquility, hiding curious questions that formed in her mind. She was grateful that he was unable to see the uncertainty gnawing at her insides.

"The king summons you." Stefan's words were curt, his voice harsh. He said nothing more as he led her back through palace corridors until they reached the throne room.

As they entered, she was struck by an almost eerie quiet. She glanced toward the throne where Gregor sat, alone, awaiting her. He leaned to one side, resting his face on one hand, his elbow propped on the arm of his throne. His countenance appeared forbidding, his presence a tangible force in the room.

A straight-backed chair now sat in front of the throne. Gregor stood and nodded his head, indicating that she should sit. Until now, she had not realized how very tall he was. She knew she was unusually tall—taller than many men, yet he towered above her. He possessed broad shoulders and a powerful physique. His dark features presented a fearsome image, and she suddenly felt very small in his presence.

Settling herself in the chair, Alexa mentally prepared for the battle of wills certain to come. She met his appraising eyes with her own expression of confidence. He sat as they regarded each other with equal intensity.

"Majesty," she broke the uncomfortable silence, "I offer my gratitude for allowing me to see Victor. It is obvious that he has not been beaten or tortured. For that kindness, I am eternally thankful."

"I am probably a fool that I did not execute him immediately; however, no matter what you have heard or what you believe, I am no bloodthirsty monster. I derive no pleasure from pain inflicted on defenseless prisoners."

She perceived truth in his statement, and that perception astonished her. "King Gregor, I repeat my request. Please, allow Victor to return to Garogan in peace."

Gregor's eyes glittered maliciously in the subdued lamplight. "What assurance can you offer that Lord Garogan will return to his home province without creating more havoc or committing more violence?"

"He swore to me that if I secure his freedom, he will return directly." She prepared herself to verbally spar with him despite the nervousness that twisted her insides.

"And you believe him?" Skepticism saturated his response.

"Sire, Victor is a man of his word. He has never broken a promise to me. He swore he would return immediately. I am completely certain that he will not fail on his oath to me."

A tense pause ensued, broken only when Gregor cleared his throat to speak again. "I do not share your confidence, Alexa Maraná. Besides, there is nothing to guarantee he will return peacefully. What would you do should you find yourself in my place?"

Alexa mulled over his comments. Shivering in the chill room, she could not blame his reluctance. What assurance could she offer? Her mind raced through possible solutions, none of which might provide the necessary insurance the king sought. When at last she answered him, her voice was very soft. "I think of only one possibility. I offer myself as hostage in exchange for Victor's freedom."

Gregor cocked his head to one side, closing his eyes to conceal his initial moment of triumph. He had been entirely correct. She was willing to exchange her own freedom for that of her lover. He did well to hide his satisfaction. "I am not certain that holding you hostage is enough. Garogan would only devise a plan to free you."

"I assure you, Sire. He will return. He will not break his word to me." She pleaded now. "I promise you that I will stay. I offer you my personal word of honor. You know that members of the Order of Val are bound always to their word."

Gregor again stroked his beard, a habit that could have been endearing under different circumstances. He studied her closely. How much did she love Garogan? To what extreme would she go for him? Dare he push harder to gain that terrible, burning desire flooding his being? Placing his hands on the sculpted arms of his throne, he pushed himself upward. He stood above her–straight, tall, and intimidating.

"Alexa Maraná." Again, he pronounced her full name. "I am prepared to grant Garogan's freedom. However, the assurances you offer are far from sufficient. I have complete confidence that your word is a commitment of honor. I do not believe so strongly in Lord Garogan. He is strong, emotional, and capable of great violence. There are too many I am bound to protect."

"What else would you ask of me, Sire? I have nothing else to offer you." Tears threatened. There must be a way to convince him. Failure was an unthinkable option.

Gregor observed her carefully, willing himself not to touch her. "There is but one viable alternative that comes to mind."

"I will do anything within my power," she whispered, afraid to hope. "Are you certain?"

She stood to face him, swallowing hard. Why could she not anticipate him? Why did her senses fail now when she needed them most?

Despite increasing anxiety, her voice remained firm. "So long as there is no conflict with the practice of my faith, I will do anything."

"You will never lack my respect for your faith. In fact, I offer an alternative that will allow total freedom to actively practice your faith. I will release Victor Garogan on one set of conditions."

She was immediately wary. "The conditions?"

"That you agree to become my wife—and I do mean my wife. I have no need for a lifeless, unfeeling doll. I would expect you to be wife to me and queen to the people of Turand."

Alexa gasped, swaying from shock. His arms reached out to steady her. That first touch shocked him as much as it did her when visible sparks leapt from beneath his hands. She stared at him, emerald eyes darkening and glazing over with sorrow. She wanted to scream at him, to pound her fists against his chest. Yet he had offered her the fulfillment of her request.

She dropped her eyes to the floor. She had won the quest, but in the winning, she would lose the precious life she had dreamed would be hers. How could she ever explain to Victor? He would never understand. How could he when she herself could not explain the nauseating certainty that this was meant to be her new destiny?

She expelled a shuddering breath. Then, choking back a sob, she whispered, "I agree to your conditions."

Unmistakable triumph now flared in the dark king's eyes. "Are you certain? I remind you that I expect you to be my wife in all ways. I will accept nothing less. You must understand."

"Can you accept that I agree to do my best to be a good wife but that I need time to reconcile myself to what has just happened? And will you allow me to bid farewell to the only love I have ever known?" Her eyes implored him.

Gregor was unprepared for the possessive jealousy that shot through him. He also found it impossible to simply dismiss the hurt in her eyes.

"I will permit one final meeting for you to explain to him the terms of our agreement. I am not a cruel man. I understand there will be a time of adjustment for you, but I will not tolerate a long period of mourning. You must prepare yourself to face our people and give them the benefit and comfort of your station."

"As Queen or as Valiria?" she asked bitterly.

"As both."

"When is this all to be accomplished?"

"We shall wed two days hence."

She bit into her lower lip, wishing the pain would awaken her from this unbelievable nightmare. When she raised her eyes once again, she could only stare into the murky black depths of his. "Then, in two days, I shall become your bride."

Gregor released her arms abruptly and instructed Stefan to escort her back to her chambers. At the sound of his voice, she paused beneath the arched doorway. "Alexa Maraná, do you still believe your Lord Val offers you great rewards?"

She required only a moment's hesitation to search the farthest reaches of her soul. Her resolute response echoed throughout the chamber. "I do."

Chapter 2

Two days later, Stefan and four armed guards accompanied Alexa to Zenox Prison. Her nostrils burned from the foul odor of unwashed bodies mingling with the stench of human waste. Damp, stone walls were covered with thick fungus. Unidentifiable debris scattered across packed dirt floors. She stared straight ahead into the dimly lit tunnel as she was guided to Victor's cell. She stepped over the raised iron threshold into the cell. A tiny, grime-covered window allowed in only a hint of light. In semi-darkness, Victor awaited her.

"Alexa," he sighed, drawing her into his embrace. "Sweetest, how dare they bring you into a place like this?"

She rested her head against his shoulder, savoring this precious moment of closeness. Her head tilted back, and her eyes, now adjusted to the dim light, gazed into his. "You look so much better."

He emitted a cynical laugh. "Indeed. They've permitted me to bathe since I saw you at the palace. I was even allowed to shave and brush my hair. As if that is not surprise enough, I've even been given more generous portions of almost edible food."

"Victor, I love you." She pressed closer against him, feeling his arms tighten around her. His mouth sought hers, and she desperately welcomed his kiss.

His hand slipped up beneath her hair, cradling her head at the nape of her neck. "Tell me the truth, Sweetest. Why are you here like this? You're dressed much too beautifully to be in this god-forsaken hole. Is this our final goodbye before my execution?"

Her lips formed a tremulous smile. "Victor, do you remember the oath you made at the palace?"

"Oath? What are you talking about?" Her strange question puzzled him.

"You promised. No, you swore to me that if I could secure your release, you would immediately go home to Garogan without any trouble along the way. Do you remember? Can I believe in your oath to me?" Persistent desperation sounded in her voice.

"Sweetest, of course, I meant it. Have I ever failed you when I made a promise?"

A heavy sigh escaped from deep within her. Relief washed through her veins. "Victor, you are to be freed tomorrow morning, but you must keep your promise. You must not fail me now."

Victor's hands slipped up and down the satin sleeves of her gown. He could hardly believe his ears, yet here was the miracle of the woman he loved before him. The worried smile on her face touched his heart. He pulled her body against his once again.

"As soon as we return, I promise you one more thing. No more will I devote myself so completely to politics. We will finally be married."

Alexa buried her face against his shoulder, her fragile composure collapsing as a sob tore from deep within her soul. As it escaped, her entire body shook from its force. "Hold me, Victor. Please, my darling, hold me tight."

Victor acknowledged her plea, clutching her as tightly as he possibly could. With sudden, ominous dread, he realized something was terribly wrong. Loosening his embrace, he placed his hands on her shoulders and gently held her away from him. "Alexa, what? Tell me what has happened."

Tears streamed from her eyes. She struggled for control, forcing herself to breathe deeply despite the malodorous surroundings. "I—I shall not be leaving with you. I shall remain in Toraval."

"What?" Victor exclaimed. "Do you really expect me to leave you here? Does that monster king require you to stay as hostage in my stead? Alexa, this I do not accept! No! I refuse to leave you behind!" Anger spewed forth in every word.

"Victor, this was not the king's suggestion. It was mine. I had no other way to guarantee your return." Her voice turned soft. "You have no choice. You must go to lead our people. Besides, I hold your promise in my heart."

Victor grasped her hands, their coldness matching the icy chill in his soul. "Alexa, this is too much for me to bear. You know I must honor my promise to you, but the pain rips at my heart. I will return to Garogan, but never will I abandon you. I will return for you. I swear it."

"No, Victor. That you must not do." Her breasts rose and fell quickly, her breathing ragged with emotion.

"Of course, I must," he insisted. "How can you even imagine I wouldn't come back for you?" He stared at her, terrified by what he saw in her grief-stricken face. He drew in a fearful breath. "Alexa, tell me. You must explain why I am not to come back for you."

Alexa gazed over his shoulder, staring into nothing. She felt faint, yet aware that she dare not succumb to the weakness numbing her limbs. "If you come for me, Victor, I will be unable to return with you."

"In Val's great name!" he thundered. "Why not?"

"This afternoon, King Gregor and I shall be wed."

Victor staggered backward, her words as powerful a physical blow as any he had ever taken. "Oh, my God! No! Alexa, please! Tell me this isn't so!"

Tears flowed freely down her cheeks. Her eyes, glazed with grief, confirmed to him what her lips could not. "Hold me, Victor. Please, hold me one last time." She moved against him, crying as she listened to him whisper her name again and again, their bodies trembling in a final parting embrace.

~

The flames of nearly a hundred candles blazed inside the palace chapel. Richly hued tapestries hung from the walls, many depicting earlier times when Turand enjoyed the peace of a unified and prosperous nation. Polished wooden pews lined each side of the chapel, and a long purple carpet ran the length of the center aisle. In the front, a raised marble altar dominated the chamber. Tall, elaborate, golden candelabras stood on each side.

A priest, one of very few left in Toravalia, stood at the altar, ready to perform the ceremony. Priests, as well as priestesses, had died at the hands of the Sifiq. The royal family had convinced the Sifiq it would be easier to control the populace if a few of their religious leaders remained, so a handful of priests had been spared. The Sifiq accepted the arguments regarding the men but continued to persecute the female Valiria, believing they posed a more significant danger because of their legendary mystical powers.

Sympathy shone in the aging priest's eyes. He had spoken privately with Alexa just before she had gone to her chambers to rest and change for the ceremony. She reminded him that this would be little different from the arranged marriages of old. He could only admire her fortitude and determination to save Victor Garogan's life. He prayed Val would reward her selfless act of sacrifice.

Gregor stood before the altar. He towered above the other men accompanying him, many courtiers who were secretly bodyguards. His black hair was brushed backward, its length waving over the furred collar of his violet tunic. He had chosen to wear the crown of Turand this night. He inclined his head in a gesture of respect to the priest before turning noiselessly in the soft leather slippers in which his feet were clad. Expectant, he awaited the opening of the arched doors at the back of the chapel. Two pages soon obliged him, pulling the heavy oaken doors and holding them wide open.

Her image filled the doorway. Her face was shielded from view by layers of frothy lace veils. She wore a simple, white satin gown, the neckline scooped and unadorned. From the high waistline that began just beneath the fullness of her breasts, shimmering satin swept to the floor in graceful swirls. The lines of the dress repeated in the flowing sleeves. Intertwined ribbons of pale lavender and dark purple trimmed the hems at her wrists and ankles. She wore no jewelry except a necklace of diamonds and pearls that Gregor had given her that morning as a bridal gift.

From behind the altar, intricate musical chords of a harp filled the small chapel. The few invited guests stood as Alexa began to walk down the aisle. Her bearing was regal, her stride even and firm. Her head was lifted high, her shoulders squared and proud.

She stopped just in front of Gregor. The beribboned single rose she carried was placed in the hands of an attendant whom she did not know. Gregor's hands raised and lifted the layers of veil away from her face. His breath was a sharp intake. He could not have imagined she would look so beautiful. Her eyes gleamed with reflected candlelight. Her skin was silken smooth, and her lips were generous and beautifully shaped.

He had expected sullen resentment. Instead, he was presented with an expression of exceptional tranquility. For just a moment, his hands trembled. The very thought that she would now become his sent tremors shafting along his spine. He extended his hand, fingers outstretched, to receive her more delicate hand.

Alexa hesitated, staring down at the exquisitely shaped hand of the stranger about to become her husband, her destiny. As she finally placed her hand in his, images from the vision, shown to her days earlier, flashed through her mind. Her eyelids fluttered and closed for a moment, long lashes resting against her cheeks. So this was the meaning of the vision. This union was the will of Val.

Hours passed in a daze of confusion. Alexa barely remembered the ceremony that had bound her life to that of Turand's ruler. Many had sincerely wished them well. Over dinner, several Sifiq guests had become loud and crude, earning the king's distinct disapproval. To Gregor's credit, he recognized her terrible discomfort in the presence of the Sifiq and their disgusting behavior. He tightened his hand around hers protectively. She must have eaten, although she could not recall what. She was faintly aware that the taste of fine, sparkling champagne lingered in her mouth following a toast proposed by Stefan.

Still floating as if in a dream, she welcomed the silence of the wedding chamber. Two female attendants assisted her in changing from her wedding dress into a gossamer nightgown, the fabric glistening with silken threads. She held a delicately woven woolen shawl around her shoulders as the ladies brushed her hair into a waving mass that fell just below her shoulder blades.

The women left without a word. Alexa sat before the mirror, absorbed in her own image. She refused to allow herself to think that she should be waiting for Victor to come to her. Gregor was now her husband. She must live in accordance with her word. Her eyes closed, and she prayed. The remembered vision of her hand in Gregor's replayed in her mind. She had lived that vision this afternoon. Its transformation to reality was her only consolation that this marriage was Val's choice for her.

The sound of the opening door startled her. In the mirror, she watched her new husband enter in silence. He closed the door firmly and turned a heavy key in the lock. Gregor, his expression unfathomable, turned toward her. She had expected haughty triumph or smug, taunting satisfaction in his victory over her. Instead, there was more of a quiet expectation. Without speaking, he went to the bedside table and removed several jeweled rings from his fingers. Finally, he lifted the heavy gold medallion from around his neck and deposited it alongside his rings.

He raised his eyes to meet hers as she turned to face him. She rose from the delicate gilt chair, allowing her shawl to fall to the floor, and stepped toward him. Her chest expanded as she breathed, causing her firm breasts to rise against the fabric, revealing the outline of her nipples. Gregor's breath caught as he noticed how the thin, silky gossamer clung to her narrow waist and along the curve of her hips.

He lifted his hand to take a long, curling strand of hair between his index finger and thumb. He felt the luxurious texture and thought it even silkier than he had anticipated.

Slowly, he turned his back to her and went to sit on the bed. He slipped off shoes and stockings and then removed his black trousers, sliding them to the floor. He stood again, his long, strongly muscled legs now revealed. Alexa swallowed repeatedly, relieved that, at least momentarily, further evidence of his masculinity remained concealed by the length of his formal tunic.

His voice, rich in timbre, broke the silence. "I will require your assistance to undo the fastenings on the back of my tunic."

She took several steps toward him before stopping abruptly. "Gregor," she breathed nervously, "please, there is something I must ask of you." Her eyes beseeched understanding as words failed her.

"If your question regards Lord Garogan," he hissed, "I assure you he will be freed but not before this union is fulfilled."

Something in his eyes startled her, and she winced at the bitterness borne in his words. "I... My thoughts were not of Victor."

"Then, what?" he asked, his tone less abrasive as he sensed in her a different kind of distress.

Unable to meet his gaze any longer, she moved behind him. With trembling fingers, she began to undo the fastenings of his tunic. When the last fastener was undone, she allowed her head to tilt forward to rest against his broad back. He stood motionless, unsure of the reason behind her strange gesture.

Finally, she straightened and pulled apart the back of his tunic, allowing him to remove the garment. He turned to her, and she resisted the urge to run from him. His body was strong, his shoulders broad, his chest smooth and deep. His masculine form was both intimidating and frightening.

He took her chin in his hand and gently lifted her face. "If your thoughts were not of him, then what is it you wished to ask of me?"

Her heart skipped a beat. Stammering, she tried to explain. "I don't know how... Please—please, I only ask that you be gentle with me. I'm afraid."

"Afraid? Why? I have never been rough with women."

Instinctively, she recognized the direction of his thoughts. He believed that, because of their long relationship, she and Victor had been lovers. "You don't understand, do you?"

"What is it that I should understand?" he asked, somewhat impatiently.

"Gregor, I come to you a virgin."

Gregor inhaled sharply, convinced she spoke the truth only by the simple, direct way she told him. He should have known. She was Valiria, sworn to a virtue extolled throughout time. Inside, Gregor felt astounded not merely by the fact that she was untouched by any man but that he would be the only man ever to possess her.

He was unable to find words to respond to her. Instead, he placed warm hands against her cheeks and pulled her closer. His eyes caressed the beauty of her face. Temptation was too much to resist. He tilted her face to claim her lips. The kiss was gentle at first, but he slowly allowed his lips to increase their pressure. His mouth opened slightly, and his tongue tasted as he slowly began to probe past her lips. Her hesitation was evident as he continued to touch her only with his hands and lips, cradling her face as he deepened the kiss.

He then drew away, breaking the bond his mouth had formed with her. His hands began a sensual descent from her face along the line of her neck until they rested on her shoulders. Her body trembled as she returned his gaze. The passion she saw in his eyes frightened her even as it fascinated her. His long fingers slipped beneath the straps of her gown and slowly began to slide them from her shoulders. Guiding the fabric downward, his hands simultaneously caressed the length of her arms.

He deliberately controlled the fall of the gown, allowing it to reveal her body in stages until, at last, he permitted it to spill to the floor around her feet. He lowered himself along with it until he knelt before her. After a long moment of silence, he reached for her hands and rose again to his feet. Then, lifting her into his arms, he placed her on the bed.

Gregor lay down at her side and began to explore the sweeping curves of her body with warm, searching fingers. She shuddered as his touch grew intimate and more probing. He rose to claim her mouth in another long, searing kiss. His lips then moved against her neck, their hot dampness creating tremors that set fire to every nerve in her body.

She gasped when next he cradled her breast in his hand and brought his hot mouth to cover the roseate peak. He moved on to the next breast, repeating the process. Her body seemed to move of its own accord. She tried to marshal her thoughts, to remember how she had come to be here in his bed. However, his touch robbed her of coherent thought and filled her body with sensations she had never before imagined.

Gregor exhibited infinite patience even as his own arousal grew more insistent. Her body would be his soon enough. It was no longer enough just to possess her. He needed for her to want him, so he pressed on with his conquest, allowing his mouth marauding freedom as his fingers tracked along her body until they rested against the core of her femininity.

She twisted against him and felt the surge of his masculinity against her sensitized flesh. He grasped her hand, forcing her to touch him. Her fingers shook as they felt his heated skin. He pushed her hand down until he could wrap her fingers around the throbbing force that clamored to penetrate to the depths of her being.

As he moved above her and parted her legs, she cried out, a senseless, frightened animal sound. He touched her gently, sensitive to her fears and her inexperience. As she tried to pull back from him, he caught her hips and held her against him. She sobbed, her body betraying Victor in unexpected reaction to her husband's questing touch. Gregor pressed the warmth and weight of his body against the length of hers.

He whispered into her ear. "You must relax, my Alexa. It will be easier for you."

Tears wet her cheeks. His voice sounded so gentle, so reassuring.

Some unknown force brought her fingers to lace through his hair, and she pulled his mouth to hers. For a second, she noticed the roughness of his beard against her skin, but only for a second because the next thing she knew was the white-hot thrust as he claimed full possession of her.

Much later, she lay exhausted in his arms. The emotional events of the day had drained her. The past hours in his arms had left her soul in turmoil. Her body felt heavy—a peculiar warmth in her abdomen, a bruised tenderness between her legs. At long last, she slept. In the darkness, Gregor could barely make out her features as she slept. Secretly, he was glad because she would not see the tears wetting his face.

Chapter 3

Reluctantly, Alexa's eyes fluttered open. The effects of exhausted slumber left a lingering mist in her mind. A sound caught her attention, and she opened her eyes wider. Across the room stood Gregor, not yet clothed.

For several moments, she found it impossible to resist admiring his statuesque proportions. His body tapered from broad shoulders to his waist. Although too heavily muscled to be considered slender, his body was hard and beautifully defined. Dark hair shadowed his arms and the length of his legs. He turned slightly to remove a tunic from its hanger, and she blushed involuntarily upon glimpsing the full, virile scope of his masculinity.

She continued to watch as he dressed, burying in her heart the regret that she was not gazing at her dearest Victor. Tears pricked at her eyes with the realization that this very day, Victor would leave Toraval and her life.

It seemed as if Gregor sensed her gaze, and he turned to her. His face was unemotional, his eyes unreadable. "Good morning." He greeted her, then continued to dress without further acknowledgment.

Alexa sat up slowly, carefully covering her naked breasts with a blanket. "Good morning, Gregor." His name sounded strange as she pronounced it. Her equally simple greeting required intense effort as she mentally noted how tender felt so many intimate parts of her body.

Stony silence filled the room until she noticed a growing murmur that drifted up through a window that Gregor had left open. The chill morning air was fresh and penetrating. Alexa could not suppress a shiver as it touched bare skin. "What is it?" she asked curiously.

"I have no idea," he responded. "I looked out earlier, and a crowd had gathered in the central square. Do you intend to languish the day away in bed? If not, we can have breakfast and go investigate."

She cast him an unappreciative glance, hoping this was not the beginning of a life of unending barbs and veiled insults. "I will appreciate it if you would be so kind as to hand me a robe. The air is too cold for me to get up like this."

He picked up her robe from the vanity chair and placed it on the side of the bed. He watched her pointedly as though to taunt her over her nakedness. She lowered her face momentarily before deciding she must face the inevitable. Pushing the coverlet aside, she rose from bed and slipped the robe around her as quickly as she could. She then turned defiant eyes to meet his appraising gaze. Sharply, she addressed him. "I shall require assistance to dress. Am I to assume you intend to act as lady-in-waiting?"

A cynical smile was his response to her challenge. "I shall be most happy to assist you, dear wife."

She glared at him. Sarcasm was not what she needed, but her own determined nature prohibited easy surrender. "Then I will thank you to allow me a few moments in the bath to wash while you prepare my garments."

Undisguised surprise at her show of spirit lifted his eyebrows. She gave him no chance for rebuttal as she stomped into the adjoining bath and slammed the door. Her bravado ebbed, and she slipped to her knees. She hurt deeply. She wanted to scream out Victor's name. Worsening matters, she battled internal conflict as she recalled her vision. A prayer tumbled from her lips. "Merciful and loving Val, give me the strength and courage to accept your will. I need your wisdom to guide me through this ordeal. Please, Lord Val, help your humble servant."

Hastily finishing her prayer in silence, she drew fresh water to wash. She then rubbed a fragrant cream into already smooth skin, all the while preparing herself to face him again. She finally emerged from the bath with at least the image of self-control restored.

Gratefully, Gregor had finished dressing. Without a word, he carried her garments to her and handed them to her, one by one. She refused to flinch beneath his close perusal and continued until she was completely dressed. Turning her back to him, she waited patiently as his deft fingers closed the laces of her simple gown.

His touch was gentle, and she regretted how shrewish she had been with him. Knowing herself too well, she knew she could never survive in the face of such constant antagonism. She must attempt to set things on a civil level at the very least. "There is something I wish to tell you." He was just finishing the last closure at her neckline, and she felt the warmth of his fingers against sensitive skin. Slowly, she turned to him.

"And that would be?" He had been ready for her next challenge or, perhaps, an insult. Instead, he was caught off-guard by luminous green eyes searching his face for something; he knew not what.

"I apologize for my short temper this morning. You—you deserve better." She sighed in nervous exasperation, willing herself to continue. "You were so gentle with me last night. I only wanted to thank you."

Gregor was completely unprepared for her statement and equally lost for an appropriate reply. "I hurt you. Your anger is understandable."

A tiny smile played at the corner of her mouth. He honestly regretted the physical pain she had endured the night before. There could be no mistaking the lines of concern showing on his face. For the first time since she had met him, she considered the possibility that they might find some common ground. She reached out to take his hand without realizing that she did so. Reassurance filled her voice. "For me, some pain was inevitable. However, I do realize how considerate you were and how much you tried to minimize my discomfort. That is something I shall not forget."

He looked into her eyes, accepting the fragile truce she offered and regretting that he must so quickly change the tone. "Alexa, I sincerely regret this comes so soon, but we must go to the courtyard. Stefan sent word that he awaits us. Lord Garogan is with him. I believe it is essential for you to see that I intend to keep my word to you. I have two Garogan militiamen and six of my own private guards who will escort him to the border of Garogan Province."

His words did come too quickly for her, causing her to fight a sudden urge to cry. To face Victor on this particular morning threatened to destroy every shred of inner strength she had. She forced her gaze to remain steady. And she thought she saw a flash of pity in his eyes just as he turned from her to stride from the room, his clear expectation that she follow him.

They walked side by side from a palace doorway toward the central square. A tall, ornate fountain dominated the center of the entrance to the courtyard. It had been dry for generations, since long before the Sifiq had invaded Turand. Legend said that, so long as Turand was not blessed with the presence of Valkana, the fountain would remain dry. Today, people surrounded it, their faces showing amazement as they pointed toward the center basin. As Gregor and Alexa approached the fountain, people stepped back to provide their king and his bride an unimpeded path. They looked over the elaborately formed edge to see a simple trickle of water wetting the bottom of the fountain.

The two exchanged puzzled glances. Alexa spoke softly. "I don't understand. What is the fascination with a dry fountain?"

Gregor's eyes mirrored her puzzlement. "What is actually most interesting is that it is not dry. This fountain is dedicated to the tradition of the Valkana. It's my understanding that there has been no water at all in it for generations. This is the first time anyone here has ever seen water emerge from the fountain's underground source."

"I didn't know," Alexa replied. "Do you know why the sudden reappearance of the water?"

Gregor shrugged his shoulders. "You are Valiria. Perhaps you might explain it to me."

She lifted her shoulders, indicating her lack of understanding. With this her first trip to Toraval, she had no prior knowledge of the fountain. She had known only of the holy Temple of Val, and her greatest hope, aside from winning Victor's freedom, was to be allowed inside.

Gregor quietly greeted the citizens who surrounded them and then, nodding his head, indicated that he and Alexa should resume their original course. Entering the square, Gregor linked her arm into his as they approached a small group of men and horses by the gateway. His gesture was possessive, his posture straight and commanding.

"Gentlemen, His Majesty, the king, approaches," Stefan announced. All inclined their heads—all except Victor, whose face flushed with obvious rage. Hatred flared in his eyes as he glared, undaunted, at the imposing man before him.

"Lord Garogan, you will leave my capital today, peacefully and in accordance with the agreement you have made." Gregor's voice was commanding, his words firm.

"The day will come, Gregor, when a just price will be exacted for what you have done. You will pay dearly, and I sincerely hope to be the one to collect that payment."

"Victor!" Alexa gasped. She did not need the pressure of Gregor's hand on her arm to quiet her. The sheer loathing she saw in Victor's face shocked her.

"Garogan, you are to leave at once. You are not welcome in this city." Gregor stared back at him, his own anger barely under control.

The two men dueled with their eyes. Victor snorted his contempt, then shifted his attention to Alexa. The mere sight of her broke his heart. His muscles burned with tension as he fought the overwhelming urge to break free, to snatch her into his arms, and to flee. His voice softened. "Alexa, I will return for you. No matter how long it takes, I will come back for you."

Alexa was almost glad for Gregor's supporting arm, which had circled behind her waist. Otherwise, she surely would have collapsed. She gazed directly into Victor's face, summoning whatever remnants of self-control remained. "Victor, go. Please, never return. I am now Gregor's wife. My place is with him."

Victor staggered and leaned heavily against his horse. The underlying significance of her words sickened him. He wondered how long before he would become violently ill. Nausea threatened to overcome him at this very moment. She had slept with Gregor. She was telling him their intimacy was fulfilled, their marriage consummated.

He spun away from them and abruptly mounted his horse. He pulled up on the reins, and, just before he spurred his horse to leave, he spat at Gregor. "I will hate you until the day I die." Victor rode off, his escort following in a flurry of dust and flying hooves.

Alexa swayed, then leaned heavily against the body of the man who was now her husband. She wept quietly, her face hidden against his chest. A part of him seethed with resentment over her reaction. She belonged to him now, yet a gentler part of him permitted sympathy. Her entire life had just been turned upside down. Her destiny had taken an abrupt, uncharted course. Instead of shaking her in anger, he found himself embracing her, holding her as she cried. His eyes locked on Stefan, who solemnly shook his head and walked away.

～

Winter showed signs of fading into early spring. Azure skies were bright with sunshine and unmarked by any clouds. As she walked along a winding path, Alexa felt out of rhythm with the pace of the seasons. Her heart remained heavy with winter-like coldness.

Two weeks had crept by since she had become Gregor's bride. He had not come to her since that first night. During the long days that had passed, she spent early mornings struggling to keep up with her meditations. Later, she occupied her time by learning her new surroundings and the intricate workings of the palace. She usually ate breakfast alone. The heavier midday meal was most often eaten in the company of Stefan, her husband, and several of his advisers. Their conversation was animated and intellectual. She ate quietly, listening carefully to their exchanges of ideas.

Evenings were long and lonely. On only three occasions had Gregor joined her for light evening meals. Almost glad for his company, she had attempted conversation. Somehow, what began as neutral subjects always managed to turn in unpleasant directions, and Gregor would toss his napkin onto the table and stalk from the room. Each time, she was left wondering what she had said or done wrong.

Now, strolling outside, she felt freer despite the weight of her thoughts. Pulling her lightweight cloak more tightly around her, she stepped off the brick path and onto still dormant grass. She bent down to touch a tiny bit of color that had caught her attention. A delicate purple crocus was ready to blossom into spring's first herald flower. She looked up and into the garden, restraining tears that threatened to fall. Spring. A time for new life to emerge. Such an irony that she was beginning her own new life. If only she could understand why this new life must be with a stranger.

"Your thoughts are of him?"

Sitting back on her heels, she nearly lost her balance when the unexpected voice had roused her from deep reflection. Recovering quickly, she accepted the helping hand her husband offered. She looked directly into his eyes, uncertain how to anticipate him. Sighing, she shook her head. "Not really. I thought only of how my life changed so drastically in a matter of such a few days."

He reached out and lifted her chin with the tips of long fingers. She clearly had been close to tears, yet she now managed to exercise tight control as she faced him. "May I walk with you?"

She smiled ever-so-slightly, nodding assent. They strolled along the path for nearly half an hour before Gregor guided her to one of the many carved stone benches set within the vast, landscaped gardens. She trembled, knowing instinctively the direction any discussion must take.

He cleared his throat before speaking. "Alexa, I have been patient in permitting you time to adjust to the idea of our marriage. I told you in the beginning that I would not accept a prolonged period of mourning." She swallowed against the tightening in her slender throat and gazed beyond her husband's shoulder to stare at naked branches reaching heavenward.

"You promised to be my wife and serve my people as their queen. Are you prepared to assume the role upon which you agreed?"

Her eyes were unfocused, her thoughts slipping back in time to the evening she had offered herself in exchange for Victor's freedom. No matter what, she knew the time had come when she must fulfill her word. "What is it you ask of me?"

He studied her features. Her eyes were most prominent, a deep shade of emerald green framed by long, dark lashes and topped with distinctly curving brows. Her cheekbones were high, her mouth wide with full lips.

Her skin was flawless, a shade of ivory tinted with delicate tones of rose. She appeared exquisitely sad yet calm.

"Tell me something first. What kind of love is it that could make you sacrifice yourself as you have for Victor Garogan?"

She cast her gaze downward for a moment. When she again looked up at him, unreadable emotions shone in the depths of her eyes. "Gregor, I am not sure I can answer your question. Victor and I have known each other since childhood. For many years, we shared laughter, goals, dreams, and tragedy. There is much I owe him."

"A debt equal to the sacrifice of yourself?"

She shrugged, trying to grasp the intent behind his questions. "Victor and I were comfortable together. We understood each other."

His eyebrows arched in question. "Then, why were you never lovers? Why did he not marry you?" His questions were curious, with no hint of malice.

"The why behind the fact we never married? Victor was determined to initiate changes to improve life in Turand. That always came first. As to why we were never lovers? My vows as Valiria require strict adherence to the ancient rules of virtue. Coming to marriage as a virgin is part of that commitment."

He considered her reply for a moment. "Alexa, I need a queen who is willing to bring comfort and guidance to my people. I believe that even more difficult times lie ahead. I also need a wife who will stand by my side as I face what I believe are impending changes. My needs are immediate. It is time for you to sever the ties to your past and honor the promises you made to me."

She had known this moment must come. She had dreaded the idea, but, conversely, there was relief. She knew she could not continue to dwell in a past never to be recovered. And, too, she knew she must seek to understand Val's will by honoring the vows she had given.

"You need only let me know what it is you expect me to do. I will do everything I can to meet those expectations."

As he watched her face, intuitively, he knew she would apply herself to whatever task he asked of her. He would indeed have much to request of her in the near future. Having observed his new bride for two weeks, he found it difficult to reconcile the part of him that had inflicted this strange union upon her with the part of him that was truly decent and kind. He thought it much easier to assume a role of dominance rather than acknowledge the uncharacteristic weakness she had wrought in him.

"I shall expect you at breakfast in the morning, then. We can take time together to discuss some of the activities I would like you to organize and oversee."

That night, she changed into a rose-colored lace and satin nightgown. The plunging décolletage revealed the ample curve of her breasts through delicate lace. She sat before her vanity mirror, brushing golden-brown hair into a smooth, shining veil tumbling past her shoulders.

She perused the collection of atomizers on a mirrored tray on the vanity. Gregor had already seen that she was provided with an array of luxuries she had never known before. Choosing a light and lovely rose fragrance, different from the lilac scent she so loved, she found herself wondering if the scent would please him. He had not said he would come, but she was sure he would.

The hour grew late when she finally rose to pull back the covers on the bed. As she leaned over to plump the pillows, the door handle moved, and she looked up to watch Gregor enter. The mere sight of him prompted a heavy jolt in her stomach.

He looked surprised to find her awake. Saying nothing, he crossed the room to where she stood, pausing to run his fingers through her hair. "I must admit that you have the most beautiful hair I have ever seen."

She looked at him with a surprised smile, his compliment unexpected. "Thank you," she murmured. "May I help you with your things?"

Wordlessly, he turned for her to begin the task of unfastening his tunic. As he waited for her to finish, he realized she had already laid out a nightshirt and a robe for him. He turned questioning eyes to her. "It appears you expected me."

She reached up to the shoulders of the tunic and began to peel it away from his body. "I am your wife. You reminded me of that this afternoon. Part of my responsibility is to make certain your things are ready whenever you might have need of them."

He was impressed by the matter-of-fact way she answered him. She never stopped what she was doing, nor did she show any sign of undue detachment. In fact, she appeared quite concentrated on attending him. She took little time assisting him with the removal of his clothing. He watched her curiously as she neatly folded each garment and placed it on the wooden chest at the foot of her bed. Then, very slowly, she came to stand before him, seemingly untroubled by his nudity. Deliberately, she reached up with her index finger and traced a single line across the breadth of his chest, causing a torrent of shivers to race along the length of his spine.

Her eyes were wide and solemn as she studied his face with an intensity that unnerved him. "Gregor, you must help me. You must show me. I have no idea how to please you."

He swallowed, reeling inside as if thunderstruck by her words. Here she was, hostage in so many ways, offering herself to him for his pleasure. He wanted her more than he had ever wanted anyone or anything before in his life, but he suddenly found himself immobile, frozen into place.

Swiftly and with a great deal of surprise, she realized the effect her words had wrought on him. She moved closer to him, breathing deeply and chewing at her lip. With a sense of uncertainty, she began to touch him. To her surprise, she discovered a certain fascination with his body. As she traced the lines of his neck and shoulders, his arms, chest, and abdomen, she found herself awestruck by the symmetry and artistry of his masculine body.

He closed his eyes, shivering as her touch ignited sparks of sensation he was sure he had never before experienced. Her fingertips seemed afire as they stroked along the indented outline of the muscles in his arms. Then, with both hands, she initiated a fiery trail beginning just beneath his earlobes, feathering down his neck until again she touched his chest. Only now, she rested her palms against his sensitized skin and began a sensual descent along the entire length of his torso, much as he had done with her on their wedding night.

Finally, the innocent sensuality of her touch enflamed his passions almost more than he could bear. He bent forward, lifting her by her upper arms to face him once again. Regaining control of his own searing desires, he led her to the bed, where he guided her hands and lips as he assumed the role of master teaching the intricacies of fine art to a fledgling student. He found her to be an apt pupil, naturally sensuous, curious, and receptive. He allowed himself the luxury of escape into the web of fantasy that she wove around him.

The next morning, he awoke to find himself alone in her bed. Rolling over to look for her, he listened as, in the distance, a clock struck seven. He remembered she was usually in the chapel for meditation by seven. He lay back against the pillows, unwilling to examine the acute disappointment of not waking to find her beside him. Still, it was impossible to deny the overwhelming effect she had on him. He had never known a lover who inspired him as she had, nor had he ever had a lover who satisfied his wants the way she did. He wrestled to reconcile yet another facet of her impact on his life. Sighing heavily, he thrust the enigma of his bride into the deepest recesses of his mind while he rose to prepare for their breakfast meeting.

Chapter 4

Narrow streets closed in as fading afternoon sunlight was replaced by long, dark shadows filling the city. Alexa gathered her shawl more snugly around her face, glad she had worn old clothes that were less conspicuous than those her husband provided for her wardrobe. She had spent much longer than anticipated with the elderly woman left with no family while facing a lonely death.

A palace servant, who had known the woman since childhood, had brought her plight to the queen's attention. The servant had pleaded with Alexa to give her friend the dying pleasure of precious time with a true Valiria. Alexa's heart was moved, and she promised to do whatever she could to fulfill the simple request.

Arriving at the tiny home late in the morning, Alexa had prepared and served tea to the old woman. She had plumped pillows and done everything possible to make the lady's last hours more comfortable. Alexa patiently held the old lady's skeletal fingers within the warmth of her own hands while reciting passages from the Great Book of Val.

Occasionally, a question arose, the frail woman's mind much stronger than her quickly fading body. The woman's tired blue eyes had brightened as Alexa sang ancient songs of the Valiria. Haunting melodies carried her back to her youth when, although not dangerous as it was now, professing faith in Val had been unfashionable. However, those early years, rooted in faith, now eased her discomfort. Somewhere in the middle of a sweet hymn, the woman had smiled and died peacefully.

Alexa now hurried through the streets of Toraval. She knew being out so late, especially without bodyguards, was extremely foolhardy and dangerous. Her one consolation was the inner satisfaction of having ful-filled a small part of her mission, her purpose as Valiria. However, that sat-isfaction was tempered by the wry consideration of which was her greatest dread, meeting Sifiq soldiers on the street or facing her husband should he discover she had gone alone into the city.

Voices approached, and she quickly stepped into the shadows of a deserted shop entrance. She watched as several Sifiq soldiers strode by, their raucous dialogue leaving her holding her breath and trying to subdue agitated nerves. The presence of Sifiq never failed to leave her stomach tied in knots. She quickly mouthed a prayer for protection, ending on the supplication, "Val, be with me."

She waited several minutes before venturing out again in her flight toward the safe haven of the palace. She could already see the lights along the great walls surrounding the center of Turand's government, such as it was under Sifiq subjugation. However, it would take at least another ten minutes to safely negotiate the streets of Toraval and enter the concealing shadows of the woods just outside the palace complex.

Stepping down from a raised walk to cross a narrow side street, she gasped. Strong hands grabbed her by the arm and swung her around to face Gor-Dan, the Sifiq officer who had belittled her when she had first arrived at Gregor's court. She immediately cast her face downward and pulled her shawl more tightly around her.

"And what have we here?" His voice was maliciously taunting. "A lovely Toravalian wench on the street at dusk? May I guess at your destination?"

"Please, kind sir, I only return home after tending a dear friend who lay at death's door this night." She knew this Sifiq soldier was especially vicious and reputed to have a peculiar, sadistic penchant for violently taking Turandan women who crossed his path. Instinct warned her that, considering how often he shot hate-filled glares at her in the palace, he would relish the chance to force her into submission if he realized her identity.

"I care nothing about your dying friend. However, I believe you might find an interesting evening in my company." His voice was harsh and lewd, his hands grabbing her around the waist and roughly moving upward.

She stiffened as she felt him press his fingers into her flesh and close them around her breast. "Sir, please. I plead with you. Let me go."

He laughed heartily, the sound itself obscene. "Let you go when I have just found a fine source for my evening entertainment? I think not!"

Alexa swallowed hard, willing her racing mind to remain calm and focused. She knew she could deal with this situation. She had little choice. "I said, let me go!" This time, her voice was strong and demanding.

"Ah, a Toravalian with spirit! All the more satisfying when you bend to my will!" He yanked her against him and used one hand in an attempt to tug away her shawl, his intent to force a crushing kiss against her mouth. She twisted in his powerful embrace and brought her knee up between his legs.

He let go of her and bent over in pain, cursing vehemently at her. She knew she hadn't struck a blow strong enough to bring him down. Quickly swinging her shawl around, she whipped it neatly underneath his face and neck, grabbing it and pulling it tightly to choke him. She was glad she had worn boots because her second blow to his groin proved much more effective, dropping him to the ground.

She, who despised violence, knew her life hinged on her next actions. She struck one more solid, grinding blow with the heel of her boot directly

between his legs. He groaned with pain as she quickly stuffed a handkerchief into his mouth to silence him and tied her shawl around his face.

He writhed in agony as she rolled him onto the deserted side of
the street and forced his writhing body beneath the raised sidewalk. She
kicked him one last time in the side of the head, hoping to leave him sufficiently dazed to allow her to escape.

Fearful without the protective shield of her shawl, she rushed from
the spot. She was immensely grateful when she finally reached the woods
and sank behind a large boulder. Her chest heaved. Her head throbbed.
Forcing herself to breathe in and out, she finally calmed and regained
her composure. She was close to the palace. If she could only focus her
inner vision, she was confident she could avoid any Sifiq between here and
home. The trick would be avoiding her husband.

Upon rising to her feet, she realized with abrupt awareness that
she was hurting. Clutching her right breast, she felt the radiating soreness where Gor-Dan had squeezed and viciously pinched tender flesh.
There was also sharp pain in her lower leg. In the frenzy of struggle and
escape, she must have pulled a muscle or sprained an ankle. The pain was
excruciating.

Limping slowly, she threaded her way around underbrush and over
fallen trees. Tears of pain stung her eyes, and she prayed for fortitude. The
muscle in her leg tightened and burned. She needed to rest. Close to the
palace, she could go no further and huddled behind a huge boulder to rest.

She must have dozed because the sound of hooves on the road startled her awake. Holding her breath, she listened attentively for any hint of
someone approaching. She nearly cried out in relief when the distinctive,
resonant pitch of her husband's voice reached her ears. Alexa managed to
crawl the short distance to the road. Accompanied by several members
of his royal guard, he had already passed the spot where she had hidden.
Despite her dread of calling his attention, she had no other choice.

"Gregor! I'm here! Please help me!"

The horsemen halted. Gregor turned and guided his horse past his rearguard and quickly approached her. His face, lit only by moonlight, was a dark mask of fury. "What in Val's name are you doing out here? Have you lost your mind?" He dismounted hurriedly to kneel down, where she sat in the deep dust along the roadside.

"I was walking through the woods. I hurt my leg and couldn't make it back to the gateway," she explained, hoping to avoid the complete truth.

Impatiently, he shook his head. "We searched the palace over and couldn't find you. Here, let me help you." When he tried to help her up, she cried out in pain and leaned heavily against the unyielding wall of his body.

He was instantly more careful with her. "Do you think something is broken?"

"I don't think so," she responded softly. "I think I must have sprained something. It hurts terribly."

He signaled for two of his guards to dismount and assist him. He remounted. His guards then lifted her by the waist until he could settle her in front of him. She gritted her teeth against the pain in her breast as he wrapped his arms around her to take control of the horse's reins.

Once inside the palace, he was silent as he carried her up a back staircase to her suite. He gently set her down on the bed and removed her boots and stockings. He touched her injured leg and began to massage away the searing tension of a severe muscle spasm. She leaned back on her elbows, her jaw set against gradually easing pain.

"Thank you," she whispered, preparing herself to face the certain unleashing of his temper.

He got up and went to her bathroom to light wall sconces. He then walked to her armoire, removed a nightgown, and tossed it onto the bed. "You're filthy. Go clean up and change," he ordered.

Silently, she got up from bed, tentatively placing weight on her injured leg. It ached, but at least it supported her. She obediently went into the bath, closing the door behind her. Once inside, she unbuttoned the front of her blouse. Carefully, she removed it and then unfastened her skirt, letting it fall into a heap at her feet. Moving to the porcelain sink and filling it with water, she washed the grime from her hands and face. She then began to undo the fastenings of her undergarments, tossing them onto the floor with her other things.

She winced as she examined her breast with delicate fingers. Gor-Dan had squeezed hard enough that purple bruises now showed around her nipple. Soreness was deep and acute. She realized with dismay that Gregor had given her a very revealing lace gown that would do little to hide spreading discoloration.

"Do you intend to spend all night in there?" he called out impatiently.

"I shall be out in a moment," she answered, hastily brushing her hair down over the front of her shoulders. When she emerged, she quickly crossed her arms in front of her and limped back to bed. She leaned over to turn down the sheets, happy that her hair created a cascade to conceal her discomfort. Ignoring Gregor's brooding presence, she slipped into bed and pulled the covers high over her bosom.

Following tense and prolonged silence, he sat at the foot of the bed. His weight was sufficient to shift her uncomfortably. "Now, would you explain to me why you were outside the palace walls after dark?"

His dark eyes glittered menacingly, and she considered her reply carefully, deciding on evasive tactics. "I told you. I was in the woods. I hurt my leg. I sat down to rest awhile, and I think I fell asleep."

"Is that all?"

"What else would you have me tell you?" She suspected he knew about her venture into the city, but she refused to admit to anything unless absolutely necessary.

His chest heaved in a sigh of exasperation. "Shall we dispense with the games? Were you actually foolish enough to go into the city without an escort?"

Her face dropped. Still, she didn't answer.

"Alexa, do you have any idea of the danger in which you placed not only yourself but those of us who went out after dark to search for you? The Sifiq love to roam the city at night, and some are complete degenerates, spoiling for any chance to fight. And when they get their hands on a Turandan woman." His voice was a low rumble, anger and disgust barely under control.

"Gregor, I am so sorry," she sighed. "It got late before I realized the time. I was with an old woman who was dying. I just couldn't find it in my heart to leave her to die alone."

"In Val's great name, Alexa, why couldn't you at least let me know?" He jumped to his feet, raking his fingers through the flowing layers of his hair. "What were you thinking?"

She answered in a quietly subdued voice. "I suppose I wasn't thinking. Besides, I was certain you would forbid me to go. Gregor, she needed me."

He paced back and forth, furious with her. "I should expect such stupid behavior from you! Why must you be so headstrong?"

"Gregor, I took vows years ago to serve people like that old woman without regard for my own benefit or safety. I told you! She needed me!" she defended herself.

Her comments opened floodgates to mixed emotions surging just beneath the surface. Initial concern had given way to worry. Worry then changed to fear. When no one could locate her inside the palace, he had ordered guards to walk the gardens and the square that led to the temple. He had personally questioned his staff, his fears mounting when he discovered no one had seen her since morning. Cursing her stubbornness as his level of distress grew, he found himself forced to face an unwelcome truth. He was terrified by the idea that something might happen to her.

Pacing rapidly, he raged at her. His hands and arms flew through the air as though his verbal tirade required the reinforcement of physical gestures.

Through it all, she remained silent. He was justified in venting his fury at her. Her actions had provoked unnecessary concern and risk.

Finally, he returned to sit on the bed beside her. Lifting her chin to gaze into her eyes, he suppressed very real thoughts of how lost he was to her. He refused to admit such weakness. "Do you have any idea what might have happened had you run into Sifiq soldiers?"

She shut her eyes against the very fresh and repulsive memory. As she did, he pulled her close for a moment and whispered against her hair, "You must remember. You are Queen of Turand and the last Valiria left to Turand. Already you are loved and revered by all of Toraval. It is my responsibility to protect you. To do so, I need your cooperation."

As he settled her back, the sheet covering her slipped down, revealing fresh bruises on her upper arm. He saw them immediately. "What is this?" he questioned, reaching out to touch the marks. As he did, his arm brushed against her breast, causing her to cringe and gasp in pain.

His face grew even darker upon observing the shadows beneath the filmy lace of her gown. Then, holding her still by her left arm, he slid the strap of her nightgown down to inspect the blue discoloration on her breast. He then tilted her head backward, swearing under his breath, rekindled fury flaring in his expressive eyes. "Explain this."

She faced him squarely. No evasive answers could explain away the visible reminder of her encounter. "Unfortunately, you were right. I did run into a Sifiq soldier. Your delightful friend, Gor-Dan."

"What happened?" he growled, his need to know battling with a peculiar, sick feeling in the pit of his stomach.

"I had almost reached the woods when he stepped out from a blind corner and grabbed me. I recognized his voice. He said hideous, ugly things to me."

"I can only imagine," her husband sneered. "He has a disgusting reputation. So far, no one has been able to do anything to control him. He must have been especially thrilled to get his hands on you."

"He never recognized me. My face was covered by an old shawl."

"Tell me what happened."

"I brought my knee up between his legs. When he bent over and let go of me, I caught him tightly enough with my shawl that I was able to kick him again. I made certain he was subdued underneath a sidewalk before I escaped."

There was no doubting the disbelief on Gregor's face. "Do you mean to tell me that you brought Gor-Dan down by yourself?"

"I do not lie!" she retorted.

He shook his head in exasperation and ran tense fingers through his hair, pushing heavy locks back from his face. "Do you realize you may have created a serious political incident?"

"I realize only that I have a right to defend myself, and I am grateful that I was taught means to do so!"

Gregor rubbed his fingers up and down along his temple, unsure what to say or do. He knew she was bound to tell the truth. He also knew that he would surely have to face outrage from Sifiq officers as soon as Gor-Dan was found. Secretly, there was creeping admiration that his wife had accomplished with Gor-Dan what no one else had been able to do.

He sighed heavily. "Alexa, I once told you I needed no brainless statue for a wife. Right now, I believe I may have gotten much more than I bargained for." He got up, extinguished the lamps, and left her in darkness to ponder the significance of the night's events.

Predictably, Sifiq command officers stormed into the palace late the following morning to meet with Gregor. They demanded the king's personal attention to the brutality perpetrated on Gor-Dan. In truth, the officers despised Gor-Dan's arrogant behavior that was sordid even by Sifiq standards. However, his father's prominent position in their homeland gave them little choice but to tolerate his presence.

Alexa had arisen early, expecting the appearance of the Sifiq. With forced finesse and extraordinary poise, she entered her husband's office on the pretense of bringing tea and cakes. The Sifiq officers paused with their heated complaints as she served first her husband, then graciously offered them refreshments.

Gregor had been glad for her interruption and indicated she could stay despite disapproving scowls from the Sifiq. Noting her husband's approval, she moved to stand behind his high-backed leather chair.

"I do not wish to offend you, Milady," Colonel Kar-Dos, failing to mask his typical Sifiq disdain for women, directly addressed the queen. "This matter is unsuitable for discussion in the presence of a female."

"Kar-Dos, may I remind you that Turandan women are fully accepted members of our society? They are not relegated to roles as servants and objects of male satisfaction as in the Sifiq Kingdom. My wife is welcome to stay if she so pleases." Some part of Gregor took perverse pleasure in the obvious discomfiture of the Sifiq officers sitting across from him.

"Very well, Gregor," Kar-Dos ground out the words. "As I explained, my officer, Gor-Dan, was located in town. He suffered a brutal attack, and I demand that you find whoever is guilty and bring her to justice."

Gregor's eyebrows shot up in instant skepticism. "Her? Are you saying a woman attacked Gor-Dan? Is that not far-fetched? You and I have discussed many times the extent of Gor-Dan's, shall we say, conquests. We both know he is violent and sadistic. However, he is also a powerful and skilled warrior. Would you have me believe a woman successfully attacked and inflicted injury on a soldier like Gor-Dan?" Gregor scoffed, his voice heavily laced with skepticism.

Colonel Kar-Dos swallowed hard, his pale blue eyes mirroring embarrassment. "Let us say he was attacked in private areas."

"What, exactly, does that mean?" Gregor relished the rare opportunity to toy with Kar-Dos.

Kar-Dos glared pointedly at Alexa, whose face was an unemotional mask. "The woman apparently kicked him in his groin area. Several times according to Gor-Dan. He has suffered permanent damage. Some sort of rupture, according to our physicians."

"Ah, that is serious," Gregor said, barely able to conceal his satisfaction. "Still, how could this attack occur? Gor-Dan is an apt soldier. I find it impossible to believe a mere woman could subdue him."

Kar-Dos leaned forward at that moment, pausing to cast yet another angry glance at the queen still standing just behind Gregor. "Gor-Dan insists his attacker was no ordinary woman. He says it was some sort of she-devil or spirit that attacked him. He swears she looked like a normal woman until…"

"Until what?" Gregor prompted, leaning forward and lifting his brow in curious speculation.

"Gor-Dan stated that he and the woman were–were-coming to an arrangement for the evening when she attacked him. He said that she began to glow like a ghost or a spirit. The brighter the light around her glowed, the stronger she became."

Gregor let out a short laugh. "Let me understand this, Colonel. Gor-Dan was viciously attacked not only by a woman but by a glowing woman? What kind of preposterous story do you bring me?"

Colonel Kar-Dos harbored his own doubts about the account, but Gor-Dan had insisted. Although Gor-Dan was a rogue officer and challenging to manage, he was usually honest. Kar-Dos also had seen one thing that left him troubled. Beyond Gor-Dan's apparent physical agony, there had existed a burning terror deep in his eyes as he related the events.

"I understand your queen is Valiria. Perhaps she can shed some light, so to speak, on the matter. I know many Turandans still believe deeply in mysticism and other such rot." He clearly wanted to divert scrutiny from himself. The subordinate officers who accompanied him struggled to believe the story and did not envy the near-ridicule their commander faced.

Alexa gazed neatly through the colonel, making him want to squirm in the face of her perusal. "Colonel, mysticism has little to do with anything physical in this world, least of all a glowing female attacker of innocent Sifiq soldiers in the streets of Toraval. I would suggest you consider Gor-Dan's reputation. He probably encountered a woman desperate to defend her honor. He is far too proud to admit the truth for fear of total ridicule from his peers."

Kar-Dos stared at her. "What about all the stories about Valiria and their special powers? And where were you last night? I understand there was trouble because you were missing."

Gregor started to speak, but Alexa calmly answered before he had the chance. "Colonel, let us clarify any misunderstandings. Valiria have no special powers beyond unique insight to see deeply into most people around them. Truth becomes their *power* if you care to see it that way. Special powers, as you call them, are reserved for Valkana, and there has been no Valkana in Turand for a century now. Beyond that, the palace and gardens are quite large, and my husband and I often miss one another as we come and go. However, I spent the night in my suite."

"Are you certain?" Kar-Dos grew agitated at Alexa's calm, condescending tone of voice.

Gregor finally spoke. "I can assure you, Colonel, she was in her suite last night. She and I spent quite a long time there. Together."

Kar-Dos knew he could challenge Gregor no further. Although Gregor was a handful to manage at times, he was a necessary evil in order to continue the easy manipulation of the Turandans. The colonel rose abruptly from his chair. "Further discussion is pointless. I expect you to make every effort to find whoever or whatever is responsible for the attack on my officer." With that, he spun on his heel and left the office with whatever shreds of dignity remained to him.

Gregor sat quietly for several minutes with his elbows on his broad desk, his fingers laced together. Alexa glanced at him for just a moment before beginning to place cups and plates on a silver tray. Gregor studied her movements through half-closed eyes. Her body moved with sublime grace. Her face was serene, almost out of place, considering her encounter the previous night.

He finally cleared his throat as she prepared to leave his office. "Alexa, what was he talking about? This glowing personage?"

She met his gaze directly. "Truthfully, I have no idea. I saw no such light." She turned and left.

Later, Gregor related the details of the incident to Stefan, who immediately launched into a long lecture about the queen going out alone beyond the palace walls. Gregor stopped him with raised hands, informing Stefan that she had already promised never to repeat such an act. Gregor was much more interested in Stefan's opinion about the glowing spirit since Gregor knew what the Sifiq did not. His wife had, indeed, been the one to end Gor-Dan's sadistic sexual encounters inflicted on the women of Toraval.

Stefan's face was thoughtful as he recalled the day he had watched Alexa outside in the garden. He shook off the uneasy memory that still gave him gooseflesh. "In answer to your question, if she said she saw no light, I believe her." With that, Stefan left, leaving Gregor to ponder the strange account.

Several days later, Alexa shifted her weight on the thickly padded, high-backed chair in Thero's stark office. Oil lamps illuminated the small room behind the palace chapel. Volumes of books filled shelves that fully lined one wall. His modest desk held a quill and inkpot, paper, and a small, three-dimensional symbol of Val. He sat behind the desk, his hands clasped together as he waited for her to speak.

"I feel ashamed to admit it, but you're right. I have not failed in my daily prayers. Moreover, truly, I ask little for myself—only the strength and wisdom to understand Val's will. But, no, I have not performed my meditations. My heart has been too heavy, my mind too full of confusion."

His eyes were old, filled with kindness. "My dear, you are Valiria, a blessing to us during these times. Especially when so many thought your order had been completely destroyed. As Valiria, you cannot survive without the sacred meditations that forge your connectivity to Val. How long has it been now?"

"Gregor and I married almost three months ago. More than a month has passed since I have been able to clear my mind for meditations."

"Tell me, Alexa, how are things with you and Gregor? Is the animosity still so strong?"

She glanced at her hands. On her left, she wore the diamond and platinum ring that proclaimed her status as wife. On her right hand, she wore a golden ring he had given her on the day of her coronation. "We observe an odd sort of truce. At times, we converse on matters of state. I think so he can sound out his ideas. Those are the times when I see a different side of him. Sometimes I find it difficult to admit, but he is truly an intelligent man who is concerned about our people in his own way."

She paused to collect her thoughts. "Occasionally, I think we approach almost normal communications. But, mostly, he is cold, distant. I know I haven't been sensitive to whether or not he needs or even wants me to express myself at those times. Selfishly, I've been too centered on my own sorrows."

"Alexa, your honesty is important. You made a monumental decision to offer yourself in exchange for Victor's life. Now, you must reconcile yourself to the consequences. No matter how painful, you must put the past behind you. If there is any hope to ever have a decent relationship with your husband, you must first take charge of who you are. You must resume your meditations. It is the only way to reconnect yourself to Val, thus allowing him to guide you along this path. You know that. You must trust in Val's reasons for willing this marriage."

The sympathetic kindness in his voice and the undeniable truth of his words soothed her overwrought nerves. His counsel was a welcome beacon, casting light upon the dark and unknown shores before her. "Thero, would you join me now? Would you help me with the chants? I desperately need the cleansing that only meditation can bring."

He nodded his head. "It will be like a great gift to me. Many years have passed since last I accompanied a Valiria in meditations. Do you wish to go to the altar?"

She stood before him, nervous but excited. "Yes, please. I need this so very much."

An hour later, she still sat cross-legged behind the altar, her sweet, lilting voice chanting the final verses of her mantra. Thero had centered himself already. His heart filled with joy as his eyes opened. With the final notes of her song filling the chapel, he saw it. The duration was brief, but the blue-white aura that emanated from her entire body was unmistakable. In fulfillment of his promises, Val would once again send his priestesses to the people of Turand. As Alexa centered and opened her eyes, she was perplexed to see a single tear slide down along Thero's soft, red cheek.

The following morning, Alexa returned to the chapel to resume her regimen of daily meditations. Just as the old priest had promised, she began to recover her energy, her perspective. She finally discovered the strength to cope with her grief over losing Victor.

On the fifth day of meditations, her inner vision revived. She saw water tumbling down a stony hillside. The splashing, gurgling sounds were like a lullaby. She felt the sun warm upon her face. The fragrance of lilacs, favored flowers of the Valiria, floated around her. Peace began to descend upon her. Returning from her trance, she mouthed a prayer. She was totally reassured. Val would show her the way.

Chapter 5

Alexa sat quietly at the library writing table, reading for the fourth time the contents of the letter she had written to Adrina, Victor's sister. Her thoughts grew nostalgic as she recalled the many confidences and conversations they had shared over the years. They had enjoyed a friendship closer than most sisters, and Alexa sorely missed Adrina. The months since she had left Garogan seemed a lifetime.

Smiling and lost in thought, she jumped at the sound of the library doors banging shut. "Oh, Gregor! You startled me. I thought you were out with Stefan."

Gregor's expression was severe, darkening further as he pointedly glanced at the stationery and pen before her. "I was, but we returned early. I looked for you in your office. I thought you had meetings scheduled today."

"I had only one this afternoon, but I received a request that it be rescheduled. I had nothing else to do, so I came here." She observed him, noting he seemed agitated. "Do you require my assistance with something?"

"To whom are you writing?" he demanded brusquely.

"Is that what bothers you? You have only to ask. I wrote a letter to an old friend. Her name is Adrina."

"From Garogan Province?" he asked sharply.

"Of course. Practically everyone I know is from Garogan Province." She felt uncomfortable with his inquiries when he seemed so moody.

"And I suppose she knows Lord Garogan, as well?" He questioned sarcastically.

Alexa glared at him. She definitely disliked his present mood but refused to be deterred. "I should hope so. Victor is her brother."

Gregor was unprepared for her sharp reply. "Do you send a message to him as well?"

Alexa paused, reassessing circumstances since he was in a foul temper and ready to take it out on her. She had planned to show him the correspondence hoping to persuade him to let her send it. However, certain he would not believe that, especially in his current mood, she slid her letter from the table and handed it to him. "Here. I have nothing to hide. Read it."

"I don't wish to read it. Tear it up. You are to conduct no correspondence with anyone in Garogan." He issued the command as if it were a royal decree.

"Gregor, I will not tear it up, and I shall correspond with whomever I please," she answered, a willful expression hardening her features.

He strode across the room to the window, then turned back to her. "Do I understand you correctly? Do you dare to defy me?" His eyes glittered angrily, and she wondered what had happened to put him in such an ill-tempered disposition.

"I dare tell you that I intend to correspond with my friends if I so choose. When I agreed to become your wife, I never agreed to forsake all my friendships. I serve you well as wife and queen. You do not, however, take the place of my friends." She challenged him, pent-up loneliness and frustration spilling out.

"I remind you of your position in relation to mine," he spoke nastily.

Her response was haughty and unyielding. "You may be my husband and my king, but that makes you neither my master nor my God. I will send this letter, even if it means I myself ride to Garogan and back to see that it is delivered."

Her response was ridiculous. "And how do you propose to do that, dear wife? It is a long ride with many Sifiq soldiers along the way." He taunted her now, well aware of her fear of the Sifiq.

Her stance never wavered. "And how do you think I came to Toraval in the first place?"

He started toward her, impatient with her stubbornness and intent on taking the letter from her. Before he had taken two steps, she snatched up a silver coaster from the table and whipped it toward him, tumbling an elaborate candelabra from the table next to him.

He stopped abruptly, shocked by the swiftness of her throw. "How dare you try to hit me?"

Her own temper had risen. "If I had intended to hit you, Sire, I assure you I would not have missed such a large target."

Her retort caught him off-guard, and he stared at her in disbelief. Before he could think of an adequate response, she snatched another coaster from its revolving stand. "Let me demonstrate. Do you see that crystal vase? It's hideous!" Before he could respond, she sent another silver coaster flying through the air. The vase crashed onto the floor.

All her suppressed frustrations seemed to battle for instant release as she grabbed two more of the silver disks. "I hope you don't like those lion statuettes on the mantel, either. They're horrid!" With lightning-fast flicks of her wrist, she sent the two disks airborne. The porcelain figurines, one on either end of the mantel, flew off onto the floor and shattered into hundreds of pieces.

By the time she grabbed the last coaster, Gregor had jumped toward her and seized her wrists, his superior physical strength the only barrier between her and another round of crashing porcelain or crystal. "Stop it now!"

She dropped the coaster, and he let her go. They stood glaring at each other, she in wordless, defiant challenge and he in disbelief. That he would deny her contact with her friends infuriated her. He was shocked and frankly amused by her outburst. He was also quite impressed with her aim.

Gregor finally broke the silence, as well as some of the tension. "I take it you have played shots before?"

Sparks faded from her eyes, but she still clenched her jaw in obstinate defiance. "Once or twice."

He couldn't help but admire her refusal to be intimidated, but neither was he prepared to give in. "Hmmm," he stroked his beard as if in deep thought. "What if I challenge you to a round of shots? I win, I burn the letter. You win, you send it and write as many more as you like."

"Do you ask rhetorically, or are you brave enough to issue the challenge?"

For an instant, he thought he saw a flash of triumph flare in her eyes. What she didn't know was that he had always been exceptional at shots, a traditional Turandan target sport involving specially balanced clay disks. The disks were catapulted in the air as targets. Others, thinner and lighter in weight, were spun into the air to hit the targets. Standard matches required opponents to alternate five rounds of five shots each or continue until a player won outright.

"I issue the challenge." This could prove to be quite entertaining, he thought, since he had been undefeated in shots since he was ten. "How about now?"

She breathed in and exhaled slowly. "I accept your challenge. I will meet you at the foot of the stairs in fifteen minutes. Unfortunately, my gown is not exactly appropriate for a sporting event." With her chin high, she brushed past him, denying him any opportunity to speak.

Half an hour later, they stood outside the palace in a grassy field. A light breeze ruffled her hair as she stood confidently before him. She had changed into a fawn-colored split skirt and an ivory, long-sleeved, linen blouse. A crowd had gathered, the servants having gossiped in lively speculation over the mess in the library. Sifiq soldiers in the palace had overheard their comments and thought the face-off might offer welcome distraction from their more mundane duties. Stefan and other court attendants had joined the group, curious to discover the cause for so much commotion.

"Your Majesty," Gregor addressed his wife with exaggerated courtesy, "would you care to inspect the shot disks?"

She walked over to the narrow trough and picked up several in succession, balancing them on her hand and holding them up to scrutinize the shape and curve of the circles. After several minutes, she nodded her approval. "I wish to take a trial shot," she announced.

"Take two," he offered. The tone of his voice was intended to irritate her. Ignoring him, she took up one of the disks and nodded for the target disk to be catapulted into the air. She flicked her wrist and sent her shot into the air, watching with satisfaction as the target came crashing to the ground.

"Impressive, dear wife."

She cast him a disdainful glance and indicated to send up the second shot. She missed but remained oblivious to snickers from the Sifiq spectators on the far side of the target field.

Gregor smiled, his dark eyebrows arched in taunting satisfaction. "Ladies first."

She stepped back, her face a mask of intense concentration. One after another, she signaled the target disks up and took each one down in turn. Then, without even a hint of a smile, she spoke to her husband. "Your turn."

Gregor stepped up to his mark and took his first round even to hers.

There were no errors until the fourth round when Gregor missed his second shot. He scowled darkly, took aim, and missed the third as well. He stopped and breathed deeply, taking down the final two disks in the round.

By the time Alexa stepped up for her final turn, a gleam had stolen into her eyes. She needed only four successful throws to win. She signaled the shot and promptly missed the first. Gregor's sigh of relief was audible. She dropped her head for an extended moment, gathering her thoughts and concentration. She then signaled four shots in rapid succession, dropping all four from the sky.

Turning to face Gregor, her eyes sparkled with triumph at denying him even to play his final round. She expected him to be furious, but he looked first surprised, then expectant. "You know that now you must drink the Taca."

Taca was a dark, ale-like beverage. Turandan tradition required a shots winner to gulp down a full tankard at once. This would be especially sweet revenge since he knew she hated the brew.

She quickly masked a grimace before stalking over to the table where the Taca was being served. Gregor followed close behind and handed her a tankard, his eyes daring her to back down.

Again, she met his challenge. "At least it appears you Toravalians are somewhat less stout than the Garogans. Their tankards are half this size larger."

She gazed into the foaming brew, the aroma alone sufficient to turn her stomach. She gulped in several deep breaths of air, put the tankard to her lips, and tilted her head back, draining the liquid to both cheers and jeers from onlookers. Then, glaring at her husband for a long moment, she savored what she knew would be a very short victory celebration.

"I will go tend to my correspondence now." She pivoted on her heel and rapidly strode back to the palace.

Fifteen minutes later, on her knees in her bathroom with her head hanging over the porcelain toilet bowl, she heard her chamber door open. A fresh wave of nausea prevented her from remaining undetected. The door to the bath quickly opened to reveal Gregor's astonished expression.

"Get out," she hissed, choking on the vile taste in her mouth.

He crossed his arms and leaned arrogantly against the doorframe, his massive body practically blocking the entire doorway. "I looked for you in the library. Are you not feeling well?"

The hint of mockery was more than she could manage. "Get out and leave me alone," she shouted, rising slightly and grabbing a porcelain soap dish to hurl at him.

He sidestepped, neatly missing the projectile. "I would think you've had enough of throwing things, especially considering that is the cause of your current indisposition."

"I am not sick because of throwing things, thank you. I am ill because you are an unreasonable, insensitive…" before she could finish, she fell back to her knees again, heaving as though her stomach might turn inside out.

Gregor couldn't help but laugh. Her audacity, plus a healthy admiration for her skill, had restored his spirits. He removed a washcloth from a shelf and wet it with cold water. He then knelt beside her. "Here. Let me help you."

She wanted to scream at him, and he knew it. However, they both knew she didn't have the strength. He gently stroked from her face the sweat that trickled from her brow and down her cheeks. He then put his arms around her and slowly lifted her to her feet, pausing until a nauseating wave of dizziness passed. She asked him to help her to the sink basin, where she rinsed her mouth out.

Afterward, he led her to bed, tucking her in and wordlessly placing a white porcelain basin on the night table within easy reach. He then got a small hand towel, wet it thoroughly with cold water, and applied it as a cold compress to her forehead. Her face was deathly pale as she closed her eyes. Remembering his own first encounter with the dreaded Taca, he found it impossible not to commiserate. "Try not to fall asleep just yet. I'll be right back."

When he returned, he held a small glass of water into which he stirred a fine, white powder. He sat down and held it for her to drink. "The taste is vile, but I promise. You will recover faster."

As she swallowed the medicine, she looked sicker than ever. Her voice was low and hoarse. "Do you now try to poison me?"

He chuckled. "Never, my dear. I have every intention of demanding a rematch."

She groaned and turned her face away from him, pressing her fist against her mouth in an effort to hold back yet another urge to throw up.

⌇

The rich aroma of freshly baked breads and cooked meats assaulted her nose and threatened fresh revolt in her stomach as she slowly entered the breakfast room the next morning. Stefan had passed her on his way out, a curious look of appraisal on his face as he hastily wished her good morning.

Gregor sat, drinking his morning tea and reading some documents, when he noticed her arrival. "You look little better than when I left you yesterday afternoon. I'm surprised you even bothered to come down this morning."

"Good morning to you, too," was her grumpy response.

"I take it you feel almost as bad as you look," he commented cheerfully, pouring her a cup of hot tea himself instead of waiting for a servant to return from the kitchen.

She cast him a glare that bespoke total lack of appreciation for his comments, then turned undue attention to the rich brown brew in her cup. Studying it seriously, she wondered if she dared try to drink it.

"A thick slice of meat would be particularly good for you right now," Gregor suggested, a teasing glint in his eye.

She groaned and closed her eyes. "What perverted pleasure do you derive from tormenting me so?"

His features softened at her rebuke. "I take no delight in your malady. The meat would actually be good for you. Your stomach needs something solid inside. Why do you not return to bed?"

She shook her head, wincing at the pounding ache behind her eyes. "I have appointments scheduled this morning."

"No," he said gently. "I expected you would not feel well. I took the liberty of asking Stefan to cancel them."

She rolled her eyes and looked gratefully at him. "Thank you for that, at least."

He chuckled and, placing his napkin beside his plate, rose from the table. An aide stepped forward, taking the sheaf of papers from him. Gregor then offered her his hand. She looked at him questioningly, placed her hand in his, and then rose to her feet. He tucked her arm under his. "Let us walk awhile."

Slowly, they left the breakfast room and strolled down the hallway, neither noticing the gleaming rosewood paneling or the occasional portraits lining the walls to the library. Once outside the library doors, Gregor stopped and turned, placing his thumb beneath her chin to tilt her face upward. "I have an apology to make," he told her seriously. "You were right. I was in a foul mood yesterday. I had a rather nasty argument with some Sifiq officers. I was mad and frustrated. Then, when I realized you were corresponding with your Garogan friends, especially Lord Garogan's sister, I cannot say I was any happier. You unknowingly made yourself a convenient target for all my anger at once."

"I never meant to annoy you. Truthfully, I intended to tell you before I sent the letter." Her eyes locked on his. The darkness of those eyes concealed much. As of yet, she remained unable to penetrate his life force for a truer understanding of him.

Just when she thought she might glimpse a different aspect of his character, he turned and opened the library doors, guiding her in before him and then closing the doors. The room was illuminated by sunshine streaming in through several ceiling-high windows. He walked toward the writing table and picked up the letter she had written the day before.

"Here. This is your letter. Send it."

She looked at him intently. "You haven't read it, have you?"

"Why should I? It is not addressed to me. We made a bargain yesterday, and you won the right to send it." His expression had become grim, far different from the gently mocking countenance of just a few minutes ago.

"Read it." Her words were simply spoken.

"I prefer not to," he countered. He turned his back to her and went to stare out a window.

"Gregor." He ignored her.

"Gregor!" she said more insistently. "Listen to me."

The tone in her voice commanded his attention, and he faced her once again. He answered tensely. "Yes?"

Anxiously, she attempted to express the thoughts churning inside her mind. "Gregor, our marriage occurred without the normal foundation that supports two people combining to build a single life. Beyond that, our marriage is complicated by politics and by more outside factors than I can begin to name. If there is ever to be any hope for trust between us, we must start somewhere to build a level of confidence. Let this letter be that first step. Please. Read it."

Gregor stared at her, the words she had spoken reaching and touching a part of himself that he kept hidden. He wanted her to trust him. He needed her confidence in him. At the same time, he believed that real trust could never exist between them. Taking the letter back from her, he sat down.

My dearest friend Adrina,

I hope that when you receive this letter, you will be well and happy in the comfort and company of our friends. These long weeks past find me missing you terribly and wishing desperately for the chance to sit and talk as we always used to do. I know how worried you must be for me. Please set your mind at ease. I am healthy and certainly well treated. Truthfully, my position as queen affords me unexpected opportunities to minister to our people's needs, and I find in this great blessing. Furthermore, our king allows me great freedoms in the practice of our faith. Although I have yet to realize my dream of going to the holy Temple of Val, there is a lovely chapel inside the palace that offers peace and solace.

Adrina, my life here is very different from anything you or I might ever have dreamed of. However, I can assure you that my husband treats me with kindness and great gentleness. He shields me from the Sifiq, who make no effort to conceal their dislike for me. Gregor and I have our occasional disputes, but we also find common interests. He is intelligent and certainly more thoughtful and caring than any of us ever imagined. I promise you that the king is quite good to me and, honestly, somewhat indulgent, if not overly so. You would be proud, Adrina, to see the eight beautiful new gowns he had finished for me, complete with matching undergarments made from the most lovely silks and laces you have ever seen! It was quite a surprise and a shocking contrast to my practical riding skirts and blouses. You would certainly have no more complaints about my austere wardrobe.

Adrina, I know Victor will press you for news if he realizes this letter has come. You must tell him to accept that our lives have taken far different courses than we ever expected. Let him know that I accept that I am where I am supposed to be and find myself adapting very well. Tell him he must let go of the past and give him my sincerest wishes for a happy future.

I send you my love, Adrina.

As always,
Alexa

His eyes raised from the paper and took in every delicate line of her face. He caressed her brow, her cheek, her lips, without ever touching her. She had just touched his soul, and he wondered deep inside if he would ever touch hers.

"I can rewrite it if it does not meet your approval," she told him softly.

He cleared his throat, a suspicious lump impeding his speech. "There is no need. You may send it as is." He paused. "Alexa?"

"Yes?" she wondered at the gentle tone in his words.

"Thank you for what you wrote about me to your friend." He rose abruptly and left the library, leaving her alone to discern the reason for his sudden departure.

Following the shots competition, Alexa and Gregor slipped into a less strained routine. They met for breakfast and midday almost daily, although Stefan and some of Gregor's friends or other advisers usually joined them. On rare occasions, they met for the lighter evening meal. Still, they spent little time together.

While Gregor attended affairs of national concern or contended with the surly Sifiq, Alexa concentrated on other ways to fill her time. Although careful to avert unnecessary attention from her activities, she arranged discreet counseling sessions for those interested in spiritual development. Whenever possible, she organized picnics and educational events to provide a measure of fun and escape for Toraval's children.

Heeding the promise made to her husband, she avoided venturing out into Toraval. Instead, she made weekly appearances in the central square, comforting those seeking solace in the faith of the Old Ones, offering the soothing and healing touch of a Valiria priestess. All encounters were carefully disguised as ordinary occurrences as she sought avenues to practice her beliefs in the presence of disapproving Sifiq soldiers.

Even though she could now conduct personal correspondence freely, most of her days and evenings continued to be long and desolate. Since coming to Toraval, she had met no one with whom she had established any real friendship. Thero was the only person in whom she could confide at all. That she was serious in her role as Valiria could not alter the fact that she was a vital and intelligent young woman. She needed the stimulation of conversation and desperately missed the interaction she had always enjoyed with her friends. This was especially so considering her husband remained essentially a stranger to her.

Gregor continued to maintain his private suite separately from hers. Sometimes, she compared how different married life would have been with Victor. She did not doubt that their lively discussions and occasional verbal sparring matches would have continued. Undoubtedly, their nights would have been spent together so long as Victor was not away from Garogan City. The intrusion of such thoughts often left her melancholy as she lay alone and awake through so many nights.

On those nights when Gregor came to her suite, she did her best to please him. He said very little but never failed to be gentle and considerate with her. She realized early that the physical aspect of their marriage was the only time when they shared any harmony. She hated to admit the way he could arouse her body with the heat and expertise of his touch. However, neither had she surrendered any part of her soul to him, leaving even this part of their relationship short of complete fulfillment. Bewilderment filled her as she began to appreciate whatever intimacy they achieved, often wondering if, perhaps, it was just intense loneliness plaguing her.

On another of those many lonely afternoons, a servant knocked at her office door, bringing a message that the king requested her presence in the library. With a sigh, she cleared away the papers she had been reading and rose to go meet him. Just before opening the library's polished double doors, she heard voices beyond. She sighed in resignation, wondering which local official wanted her for some mundane appearance. Turning the brass handles, she entered.

Gregor glanced up and smiled as he stood talking with a visitor whose back was to her. For just a second, she thought her husband's smile looked genuinely welcoming.

"Alexa, we have a visitor for a day or two. I wanted to introduce you." The visitor turned, and Gregor continued, "Alexa, this is Lord Willem Zephirás. Willem, this is my new wife, Alexa."

Alexa's eyes grew wide in shocked disbelief. "Willem!" Her voice filled with unabashed excitement as she ran to the visitor and threw her arms around his neck. "Willem! I can hardly believe it's you!"

Willem's arms encircled her waist, and he picked her up off her feet. "Alexa! How are you?"

Alexa stepped back when he set her down, her eyes bright, her smile wide and joyous. "Oh, Willem, I'm well! How about you? And Katara! How is Katara?"

"We are both happy and well. Did you know that Katara is expecting a baby?"

"No! When?" Her face was alight with curiosity and happiness at the news.

"Soon. Very soon. In fact, I'm on my way home now, but I had some business here in Toraval. I sincerely hope that I arrive home before the baby comes. If I don't, Katara may never forgive me!"

Alexa laughed before suddenly realizing they had both forgotten Gregor's presence. She instantly slipped her arm through his and leaned against him, looking up into his face. "Tell me truthfully, Gregor. You were just playing a trick on me, weren't you? You knew all along that Willem is married to one of my best friends, didn't you?"

Gazing down into flashing emerald eyes, Gregor hoped he had managed to hide his dismay over her response. Seeing her face so full of pleasure and delight was such a novel experience for him. "I wish I had known. I might have been better prepared for your reaction."

"I should apologize, Gregor," Willem told him. "I had heard rumors, but I was hesitant to ask in case the rumors were false. Alexa was maid of honor at my wedding. She and my wife have been friends for years."

"Oh, Gregor, I wish Katara were here so you could meet her. She's incredible! She could make anyone laugh. Even the Sifiq, I think. She is the wildest, happiest, and funniest person I've ever known."

Alexa then launched into a non-stop string of questions, comments, and recollections as the three decided to go outside for a leisurely stroll through the gardens. Gregor found himself amazed as she continued to walk along with her arm linked in his. As his wife recalled something especially funny, she would often lean her face against his arm, trying to control her laughter. Occasionally, she laughed aloud in joyful abandon, the sound musical and happy. Her mood was cheerful and as full of sunshine as the summer's afternoon turquoise skies. He had never imagined her this way or the way her mood caused him to feel.

Later, in her suite, Alexa ran a brush through her hair as someone lightly rapped on her door. "Yes? Who is it?"

"May I come in?"

"Of course," she called out to her husband, wondering why he had knocked when ordinarily he would have just entered. She turned to watch him. "I was just finishing getting ready to come down for supper. Is something wrong?"

Gregor's dark features were pensive as he gazed at her. He could still feel her arm linked with his as he had watched her merry abandonment earlier in the afternoon. That sensation had created a lingering effect of enchantment. "No, not at all. I thought I might escort you downstairs to dinner."

For some unknown reason, his reply struck her as odd. However, she didn't question him. Instead, she smiled brightly. "If you would be kind enough to fasten my necklace, I will be ready."

She handed him the diamond and pearl necklace he had given her before their wedding and lifted her hair off her neck. Gregor had not expected such an intimate request from her, but he took the necklace and reached around her to fasten the diamond-studded clasp. His fingers, touching against the nape of her neck, sent a shiver along her spine, and she trembled slightly.

When she turned around, he straightened and settled the jewels against the velvet softness of her skin. He then smoothed a few strands that had strayed out of place when she had let down her hair. "I thought perhaps we could go after dinner to the family drawing room. That way, you and Willem can have extra time to visit together."

She smiled her pleasure. "That would be lovely, but you will join us, too, won't you?"

He nodded and smiled back. "Of course. I've known Willem for a long time, and I very much enjoy his company." He placed her hand on his forearm, and they walked together through the hallways and down the wide, curved staircase to an informal dining room.

Willem and Stefan were the only ones joining them for dinner. Alexa assumed the role of hostess, assuring that everyone enjoyed the light supper and accompanying fine wines. At the same time, she listened attentively to the men as they discussed a broad range of topics that covered everything from economics to history to weather. This dinner was a godsend for her. The company was relaxed, and when she did interject a thoughtful comment or opinion, the resulting interaction admirably satisfied her intellectual side.

Following dessert, Stefan excused himself, and Gregor invited Willem to have after-dinner drinks in the more relaxed atmosphere of the sitting room. The large room was already illuminated by several elegant oil lamps. A low fire burned in the marble fireplace, warding off a slight evening chill. Two enormous brocaded sofas faced each other, and two matching chairs stood at either end. The long, ornately carved wooden table in the center already held cut-crystal goblets containing golden liqueur. The furniture stood on an antique, floral-patterned carpet. Finished with warm wood paneling and family portraits on the walls, the room's overall effect was comfortable and inviting.

Willem moved to sit in one of the side chairs, and Gregor sat next to him at the end of the nearest sofa. Alexa shocked Gregor by gathering her satin skirts and settling comfortably on the floor beside his long legs. She reached forward, picked up two goblets, and handed one to each man. She then took the final goblet for herself. Gregor quickly regained his composure and offered a toast.

The conversation immediately reverted to the more personal and nostalgic recollections of earlier that day. Gregor contented himself with watching and listening to the easy, teasing banter his wife exchanged with Willem. He was particularly amused as she started to describe an incident in which Katara had tried to play a joke on Alexa and ended up being thrown by a horse into a muddy bog. Katara then caught her foot on something submerged inside the odiferous ooze and couldn't pull herself free. Alexa realized that the only way to free her friend was to wade into the bog herself.

Tears streamed from her eyes as Alexa related the details of how the mud was so slimy and smelly that she thought she might get sick. She finally reached Katara and managed to free her foot from some tangled roots deep beneath the surface. Their next challenge was to get themselves out. They kept sinking into the mire and, within minutes, were up to their shoulders in muck.

"Oh, Willem, I will never forget how happy I was to see you and Victor riding up and looking for us. I will always remember the expression on your face when you saw Katara." She lifted her eyes to Gregor, whose smile had melted away at the very mention of Victor's name. He had to force himself to ignore his discomfort at hearing her speak so freely of Victor.

She seemed not to notice as she continued, "Gregor, you really should have seen us. I was bad enough. My hair had come loose, and that muck was all stuck in it. But Katara! Her hair is the lightest shade of golden blonde you can imagine. The stuff covered her from the top of her head, and it was all over her face. And the stench!"

Willem shook his head, the remembered image fresh. "Gregor, your wife is not exaggerating. We managed to pull them out, but I can tell you.

We stayed as far away from them as we could. I have never smelled anything so disgusting in my whole life."

Without thinking, Alexa laid her arm on Gregor's muscular leg and now rested her head against it, shaking with laughter. She again raised her face to him. "It took me days to get all of that muck and grit out of my hair and ears and out from under my nails. We used gallons of lemon water to wash away the smell! I had to throw away my favorite riding boots and my clothes, too. It was impossible to get them clean!"

Gregor relaxed enough to laugh as he tried to picture the scenes her words painted. He secretly mused over the comfortable, easy way his wife now rested her chin on his leg. He was surprised to realize that his fingers played with a thick, curling tress of her hair. The entire day, from his viewpoint, had been so different from any since they had married. Her mellow behavior with him intimated at the kind of relationship he had always dreamed of finding in marriage.

As the conversation assumed a quieter tone, Alexa removed her slippers and raised up onto the sofa beside her husband. She curled up beside him, tucking her feet beneath her skirts. She felt more at ease than she had in months, and the cozy atmosphere allowed her a rare opportunity to experience the kind of companionship she had missed so much.

As Willem shifted subjects, Gregor settled back and wrapped his arm around Alexa's shoulders, the gesture natural and unaffected. Unconsciously, she snuggled closer and rested her head against him. As his chest rose and fell with the steady rhythm of his breathing, Alexa listened more closely to the beating of his heart than to the conversation. Her eyelids grew heavy, and she found it difficult to stay awake.

When she felt Gregor gently nudge her, she slowly lifted her head, instantly embarrassed that she had fallen asleep. She was relieved that Willem still sat across from her, a curious and amused smile on his face.

"Forgive me, Willem. I think I must have gotten too comfortable after the wine at dinner and the liqueur. You know I rarely drink."

Willem's smile was understanding and indulgent. "There's no need to apologize, Alexa. Actually, I think I'm quite ready to retire for the evening. I've been traveling for days, and I'm tired, too." He wished them both good night and allowed a servant, summoned by Gregor, to guide him to his rooms.

In the meantime, Alexa forced herself from the sofa and stretched, unable to stifle a yawn. She looked apologetically into her husband's face. "Gregor, please don't be angry with me."

He stood up and placed his hands around her waist. The short nap had left her face with an enticing vulnerability. "I see no reason why I should be angry. Why don't we just take you upstairs and put you to bed?" There was a soft, breathless quality to his voice as he released her and bent over to pick up her slippers.

She took them from him, but instead of putting them on, she carried them, dangling at her side. Neither spoke as they walked through the now quiet palace and climbed the stairs to her suite. When they reached her suite, he turned the key in the lock and pushed open the door.

She started to go in but paused to look up at him, wondering if he intended to spend the night. Filling her was a deep-rooted desire not to return to the loneliness that characterized too many of her days and nights. "Gregor, thank you for including me in your plans today. It has been such a lovely day."

No smile crossed his face. Instead, his expression appeared guarded, as though there was something he preferred that she not see. "It has been an unusually pleasant day," he agreed. "It pleases me that you enjoyed it so much. I may have to ask you to entertain Willem for a while tomorrow. Would you mind?"

"I would love to. Just let me know when." She wished more than ever that she could read his life force. There was a strange quality about his mood just now that she could not begin to penetrate.

"I will. We can discuss it in the morning. Good night."

"Good night," she said quietly.

He started to walk toward his own chambers, but as she was closing the door behind her, she heard him say her name.

"Yes?"

He turned to look at her with that same strange look. He paused and finally smiled. "Sleep sweet."

Hours later, in his own chambers, Gregor fervently wished that he could just fall asleep. Every sound magnified itself in his mind. He tossed uncomfortably, adjusting pillows, throwing covers off, and then pulling them back over him, one by one.

His body raged at him. He had never wanted to take her more than tonight, but something had stopped him. Downstairs, her closeness had jangled his nerves as he had sat listening to her talk with Willem. Her warmth against his leg had sent vibrating rivers of sensation flowing throughout his body. When she had leaned against him and fallen asleep, the fragrance around her had stimulated his other senses. He lay miserable and frustrated, berating himself for the weakness she created in him.

It was impossible to understand the barrage of feelings continuously assaulting him. From the very beginning, Alexa had fascinated him. Her demeanor had been so confident and strong when first she approached him in the throne room. She had shown no weakness, which now seemed even more startling as he began to recognize how far she would go to avoid Sifiq soldiers who were in and out of the palace. On the contrary, she had been relentless in pursuing her goal to free Victor Garogan. And when he had stated his proposition, she had lost her composure for only seconds before countering with her own conditions to be added to any such agreement.

He thought back on how she had looked when he had lifted her veils at the chapel altar. He would never forget her shyness when she told him of her virginity on their wedding night. Since then, she had been dutiful in performing her roles as both queen and wife. What was it about her that intrigued him so much that he had forced circumstances in order to marry her within days after meeting her? How could he have agreed to free Lord Garogan following the discovery of Garogan's abhorrent assassination plot?

Gregor rolled over again, groaning into the dark. His wife was, at best, an enigma and worse, he feared, a growing obsession. On the occasions they talked, he found her wit and intelligence impressive and admired her ideas even when they disagreed. He often avoided her simply because his desire for her exploded every time he saw or touched her. Tonight had brought rekindled chaos to both body and soul.

At breakfast the following morning, Alexa quickly noticed that Gregor was not himself. His face was taut, and he appeared withdrawn. Willem had excused himself after only a cup of tea, saying that he had some business to tend to before Alexa would accompany him to the palace museum. Wordlessly, she rose and walked behind her husband's chair. She felt him jump slightly when she placed her hands on his shoulders.

"Do you feel ill?" she asked.

"No, I just have a pounding headache," he muttered.

Automatically, she placed her hands on his forehead and began to stroke his forehead and alongside his temples. Then, placing her hands at the base of his neck, she began to massage tensed muscles. She was puzzled since he had seemed so relaxed the evening before. "Is there something I can get for you?"

Her sincere concern jabbed into his confused state of mind. She had every right to be impatient with him, yet she showed nothing but kindness. "No, I don't think anything will help."

"You should go upstairs and lie down for a little while. It might help," she suggested. "Since I don't have to meet Willem for another two hours, I can go up with you and try to massage some of these knots out of your neck."

Her thoughtful suggestion was almost more than he could tolerate. Unwittingly, she was the cause and making matters worse. "I have some things in my office that require my attention right now. As soon as I finish, I'll go up for a while." He rose abruptly, unaware how his rejection had stung her. "I will meet you and Willem for midday."

Later, as she and Willem strolled through the museum, her friend led her to a small settee to sit down. The sofa sat directly in front of an enormous painting that depicted the colorful panoramic view of a great valley in Garogan. "Alexa, I have a confession to make to you."

She stared questioningly into his blond features. "Confession? For what?"

"I stretched the truth yesterday when I told Gregor I had only heard rumors about your marriage." His blue eyes studied her face, and he wished he could read the play of emotions that fleetingly passed over it.

"I see. How did you find out?" She wasn't sure she wanted to know the answer.

"Victor came to visit us about a month after he left Toraval." Willem's voice was matter-of-fact, avoiding any emotion that might upset her.

She dropped her eyes and stared at the patterns in rose-colored marble floor tiles. "How was he?"

"I can truthfully say that I have never seen any man more distraught in my entire life. He was angry, hurt, and grieving."

"Did he tell you what happened?" she asked, continuing to stare at the floor.

"He told us he was being held as a condemned prisoner in Zenox Prison. He also said that Gregor forced you into marriage as the condition to set him free. Is that true?"

She detected anxiety in Willem's voice, a note that told her he resisted believing such a thing. She sighed. "Yes–and no. He did not force me to marry him. The truth is I volunteered to stay in Victor's place if Gregor would only rescind the execution order and release Victor from prison so he could go back to Garogan. Gregor argued a very valid point. Victor would only have come back, probably to free me and to carry out some new plot. Gregor's idea to marry me was to force Victor to leave and stay away."

"What do you mean by some new plot?" Willem questioned her. He needed to know the truth behind what had happened. Katara and Victor were cousins. Willem had known Gregor for years and had always considered him a friend. He was desperate to understand the facts.

"Victor was discovered plotting an assassination attempt. And not a pretty one. He had planned to murder Gregor and much of his staff while they slept." Her tone remained steady and unemotional.

Willem gasped softly. "Can that be true? That doesn't sound like the Victor I know."

"Nor I, but I asked him myself. His answer was not the one I wanted to hear. Willem, as much as I always loved Victor, I still find it so difficult to believe he could have involved himself in such a sordid plan." She raised her head and looked directly into Willem's eyes. Hers reflected deep sorrow.

"Am I being too personal to ask how things are with you and Gregor?" His question was just like Willem, direct and to the point.

She toyed with the wedding ring on her finger. "Did Katara put you up to this?"

"Yes. And no. Katara is brokenhearted for Victor, but she is also deeply worried about you. Besides that, I need to know for myself what Gregor's part is in all this."

Alexa never asked why. She sensed that he was making serious decisions that might significantly impact the future. "Willem, what can I tell you? Gregor and I are still adapting to our marriage. He is good to me in his own way. I know that my presence often creates quite a challenge for him. The Sifiq despise me, but Gregor never fails to shield me from their evil remarks and nasty comments."

"And what about Alexa? How does Alexa feel?"

Momentarily, she wrung her hands before clasping them together in her lap. "Alexa. Practicing, believing Valiria. Sometimes she's tired. Often, confused and lonely. She misses her friends. At the same time, she is grateful for a husband who provides her opportunities to practice her faith and also encourages her. Willem, honestly. I am doing much better than you might expect. It helps that I have come to respect Gregor as I watch and listen to him. He is most certainly not the traitorous villain those of us in Garogan thought him to be. That much I have come to believe."

"But, Alexa, where do your feelings come into this?" Concern laced his voice.

"I accept that I am where I am supposed to be," she replied cryptically.

"You mean you have reconciled yourself to this marriage?" Willem asked, disheartened that Gregor could have done this to her. Still, he had to wonder how last evening's cozy warmth could fit into this confused palette.

She looked at him and smiled. "Reconciled? Maybe, but I don't think so. I accept that my marriage is the will of Val. And, in due time, Val will help me to understand his reasons."

"The will of Val?"

She shook her head slightly. "Willem, it's too difficult to explain. Just know that your friendship with Gregor is important to him, and he deserves your continued friendship and loyalty. If there is one thing you can do for me, it is never to doubt your relationship with my husband."

Willem's smile was wry. "You felt my conflict all along, didn't you?"

She grinned, "Of course. What did you expect?"

"Does Gregor give you many problems?" he asked, still trying to convince her to open more of her feelings to him.

"I think Gregor causes himself more problems than he does for me. He pushes himself relentlessly. There are times when I sincerely worry about him. This morning, he had a terrible headache, but he insisted that he had work to do and couldn't take even a little time for himself. I believe he takes too little time to rest. Last night was a rare occasion for him, and I was so glad he seemed to relax so much."

"So, you think I need to relax more?" Gregor's voice echoed from the doorway leading into the museum. He walked in with his usual energy restored, a broad smile lighting his face. Upon reaching them, he leaned over and surprised Alexa by placing a kiss on her cheek. "I apologize for being a brute earlier. I feel much better now. Tell me, are you two solving all the woes of your king?"

Alexa smiled a bit nervously, wondering how long he had stood in the doorway listening to them before revealing himself. "I was being a good wife by complaining that you work too much."

He smiled at them both, his expressive brown eyes observant and questioning. "It sounded as if you were doing an admirable job. Shall we go have something to eat? I have promised to spend some time with Willem this afternoon."

Chapter 6

Days later, a cool summer rain tapped against the library windows. Alexa sat alone, reading passages from an ancient historical manuscript. Ordinarily, she thought history fascinating but tonight was finding it impossible to concentrate on more than one or two sentences at a stretch. When footsteps sounded behind her, she was almost glad as she rose to place the book back on its shelf.

When Gregor entered the library, his expression was remote and gloomy. He glanced over at her without uttering a word of greeting. The smile that had sprung to her lips faded. "Is something wrong?" she asked hesitantly.

He walked over to the fireplace and gazed absentmindedly into glowing embers, ignoring her inquiry. "I didn't expect to find you up so late. Especially not here."

"I couldn't fall asleep. I thought if I read a while, I might tire myself enough to go back to bed. You look tired. Is there something I can get for you?" Her voice was gentle with concern.

"I am tired. And frustrated. But, no, thank you. I believe there's nothing that will help my frame of mind just now."

She walked over to him and laid her hand upon his arm. "I won't distract you then. If you need anything, just let me know."

She started to leave when he stopped her, removing a folded and sealed letter from his pocket. "Here, I forgot to give this to you. It came today."

She took the piece of correspondence from him and stared intently at her name written on the linen stationery bearing Adrina's engraved initials. Her face transformed from gentle to severe. She started to toss the paper into the fire when Gregor took her wrist and stopped her.

"What are you doing? Why are you burning your letter without even opening it?" Her reaction was unexpected, and he wanted to know the reason behind it.

"This letter is not from Adrina," Alexa answered. "Burn it."

Gregor studied her face carefully and saw something there that sparked annoyance. "Who sent it?"

She met the intensity of his glare. "The handwriting is Victor's."

"I see. I would think you anxious to read what he has to say." Instant cynicism tinged Gregor's voice with ugliness.

"Obviously, I am not," she replied coolly, recognizing he was in yet another foul temper.

"Then perhaps I shall open it and read it to you," he sneered, starting to break open the red wax seal.

Alexa tried to snatch it back from him, but he held her at arm's length and flipped the page open. His mouth twisted as he read aloud Victor's words.

My dearest Alexa,

I have known nothing but heartbreak since the day I left you in Toraval. I feel as if I left you as a victim to be sacrificed. That thought torments me daily because I alone must bear the blame. I have seen the letters you wrote to Adrina. I can only suppose that His Majesty, the king, censors every word you write, and that is why you have sent me no messages.

I am hopeful that you have the chance to read this before anyone sees it. You know I wish to cause you no more grief than you already suffer. It is just that you must know that never will I forsake you. I miss you, my sweetest, and I pray each day that we can find a way to be reunited. No matter what has happened or what he has done to you, you must know that my love for you is as deep as ever.

I imagine that what you endure as his wife must be horrible. I know that, for me, the very idea of him even touching you rouses my fury. I sometimes wish that you had not loved me so dearly. Except that I always recall the sweetness of your kisses and the delight of your touch. Still, you should never have agreed to such hideous conditions for my freedom or even my life. At least had I been executed, you could be free of whatever it is he demands of you.

Alexa, I do love you. Know that I remain yours forever.

With all my love,
Victor

Her eyes glittered furiously as she stared into her husband's face. Her posture grew rigid. Her chin tilted upward, and she ground her teeth together. Her voice, when she finally spoke, was very soft. "I must admit that I never expected such perversity from you, nor can I even begin to understand why you would want to do such a thing to me."

He flinched, refusing to show any other outward weakness. He handed the letter back to her. "I want that man out of your life."

"No matter what either of us says or does, he will always be a very real part of who and what I am, Gregor. That is an unavoidable reality. However, I made a promise to you that I have kept without fail. I took sacred vows to be your wife, and I have been faithful to those vows. I do not deserve what you just did."

Gregor's face flushed with disgust as Victor again appeared like a specter haunting his marriage. "You say you are faithful to your wedding vows and yet still maintain that he is part of your life? How dare you insist that you keep your promises?"

"I consider everyone I ever cared about to be part of who I am. That does not make me an unfaithful partner in this marriage. I can at least point out details here and now that prove my level of integrity. Even in Victor's letter, he confirms I have sent him no messages. I could have deceived you when you asked who wrote the letter. Had you not stopped me, I intended to burn it without even reading it. What more proof do you need that I do not encourage him?"

Despite her effort to remain calm, Gregor heard the rising anger in her voice. Still, he was filled with unreasonable, inexplicable anger. There had been recent moments when he thought he might be able to reach her. When she had looked at the letter, he had seen a troubled shadow cross her face. That shadow must certainly evidence her continuing attachment to Victor, and Gregor felt compelled to lash out against whatever it was that still bound her to him.

"I will always remember what Garogan intended to do here. Believe me. His intentions to kill me are one thing. What I will never forget is that he intended to murder innocent people while they slept. You are my wife now, and I despise any connection you still have to him."

Her self-control began to fade. "You call me your wife," she responded, her voice dripping with angry sarcasm. "Right now, it seems that I am more hostage and prisoner than wife. A wife should at least merit some consideration and respect. Indeed, as prisoner, I enjoy this palace as a most luxurious and expansive cell. And I can always look forward to being placed on display as your queen or as Valiria whenever you wish to satisfy some political image. What about me? I am a human being with real needs of my own!"

"I see to it that your needs are well…"

Her voice turned shrill as she cut him off. "Well met? Because you keep me in a beautiful prison with beautiful clothes, and you neither starve nor beat me? I need more than that! You keep me from every friend I ever had! I have no friends here. If I'm lucky, you descend from your high and mighty position as king to allow me at the meal table, where I am essentially ignored while you spend your time in discussion with your own private circle of friends. I spend nearly every single evening alone. Alone! Oh, on occasion, you do decide to come to sleep with me. What does that make me? What kind of life do you think I have here? How much would you appreciate being so isolated from everyone and everything you ever held dear?"

Her verbal attack had been unexpected and replete with sarcasm. He reeled from the bitterness she had unleashed. He opened his mouth, but she launched into a fresh diatribe before he could utter a single word.

"Gregor, I have done everything possible to be a good wife to you, but I am dying a slow death of stagnation here. I'm tired of being a caged show animal! When Willem came, I began to think there finally might be hope for us to achieve a normal relationship. I have done nothing to deserve what you just did! Damn you, Gregor! Damn you!"

She crumpled the letter into a ball and flung it at him, striking him in the face. She spun around and ran from the library, leaving him stunned and rubbing the stinging mark left on his cheek. Quickly recovering from his shock, he ran after her. Upstairs, he crashed through the door to her suite. "Alexa!" He shouted angrily into the dark room.

Receiving no response, he proceeded into the bedchamber. He knew she was somewhere inside because he had heard the slamming of her door. "Alexa, answer me now!" he furiously demanded as he lit a lamp.

She did not respond, but he heard uncontrolled sobbing from behind the closed door of her bath. He grabbed the handle and, frustrated at finding it locked, shook the door violently. "Open the door now!" Again, there was no reply, only the sound of her weeping.

His frustration mushroomed, and he pounded his fists on the door. "Alexa, come out of there now, or I will break down the door! Do you hear me?"

"Go away, Gregor! Please! Have some mercy on me!" Her last words broke on a sob.

Gregor leaned his head against the door. Standing there, listening to her cry, he knew he had behaved despicably. Was she right in accusing him of being perverse? He had certainly shown no respect for her integrity that, in truth, he deeply admired. What was wrong with him that he could want her so and yet deliberately hurt her so badly? "Alexa, come out. Please." His voice had calmed.

"Go away. As long as I'm alone here, you nor anyone else can hurt me."

"I intend to stay here until you come out!" His voice raised again in frustration. She said nothing more, and, with each minute that passed, he grew angrier with himself than with her. Finally, he walked over and sat on her bed, determined to wait until she opened the door.

A clock striking the hour of three in the morning roused him. He had fallen into an uneasy sleep and now lay sideways on her bed. Opening his eyes, he muttered a curse as he realized the bathroom door was still shut. He got up slowly and pulled the bell chord to summon a servant from downstairs. He waited at the door and instructed the servant to go down and bring back the skeleton key to gain him entrance to the bathroom.

Quietly, he fitted the key into the lock and opened the door. His heart contracted with guilt when he realized she had laid her face on a folded towel on the cold marble floor and cried herself to sleep. Her robe was rumpled and gathered around her feet. Her arms were crossed and tucked tightly against her breast. Earlier, he had despised Victor. Now, he despised himself. He quietly approached her and squatted down by her side. Gently, he pushed away the heavy curtain of hair that hid most of her face.

Her eyes were puffy as she opened them. When she saw him, she turned her face into the towel and begged piteously, "Leave me alone. Please, Gregor. Just go away."

Ignoring her plea, he proceeded to pick her up from the floor. Wordlessly, he carried her in to lay her on the bed. He returned to the bathroom, wet a small towel with cold water, and took it back inside. He sat down beside her and placed the cold compress over her eyes. Rising again, he covered her with the sheet and blanket servants had pulled back earlier in the evening.

He grappled with guilt that left him with no words to say. Gregor feared the tumultuous feelings storming inside him. Regret inundated him, yet he had no idea how he could ever convince her. Alexa wished only to withdraw into herself, to escape to the inner dimension that would provide time and buffer while she struggled to reconstruct her perspective. Her faith remained intact. Still, she would need to reexamine her acceptance of this marriage as Val's will. One fact was irrefutable. It would be impossible for her to continue living her life this way.

⌇

For the first time in weeks, Gregor entered her chamber as she dressed for bed. He had avoided her since the incident involving Victor's letter. Fortunately, he and Stefan were absorbed in many covert plans that provided a convenient escape. Now, excessive fatigue lined his face. His shoulders drooped uncharacteristically. His manner had lost its coldness.

He avoided the delicate chairs she usually used; his frame was too large to be comfortable. Instead, he went directly to the bed and sat down. Without speaking, his face dropped into his hands. He appeared too tired to maintain the barriers they had constructed so well.

Alexa was perplexed. For perhaps the first time in their marriage, she crossed the room to stand in front of him, recognizing in him a desperate need for genuine compassion. Despite remaining unable to read his life force, she felt positive there was something sorrowful within him calling out for comfort. Finding herself incapable of hiding within the brittle shell of reserve into which she had withdrawn, empathy moved her. She knelt before him, cupping her hands beneath his.

Slowly, Gregor raised his head. His dark eyes appeared ravaged by some terrible inner battle. Still, remaining silent, he only gazed at her with incomprehensible emotion.

Alexa rose to her feet and slowly reached for his right hand to remove his rings. As if for the first time, she noted the length of his fingers—their exquisitely sculpted shape and form. She then took his other hand to remove the rings on it and was surprised to see he wore only the simple platinum band that matched her wedding ring. Without a word, he curved his finger downward to prevent her from removing it.

With deliberate, unhurried motions, she removed the heavy chain he wore around his neck before proceeding to remove his shoes, trousers, and tunic. Then, realizing he had no desire to take her this night, she took a finely woven nightshirt from an armoire and placed it beside him.

She padded softly into the bath and wet a cotton washcloth with cool water. When she returned, he had already donned the nightshirt and lay motionless on her bed. She climbed into the massive bed and settled beside him. Gently, she stroked the cloth across his forehead and his closed eyelids. He reached up to grasp her hand, taking the washcloth from her and dropping it onto the floor.

She debated whether she had misunderstood his intention as he pulled her down to lie beside him. He turned to face her, and his fingers caressed her hair with long, smooth strokes. He placed warm lips against her forehead. His strong arm pulled her body closer against his.

For the briefest moment, she could have sworn he trembled. As she awaited his now-familiar preamble to their intimacies, she heard the rhythmic sound of his breathing. Holding her tightly, he fell asleep.

When Alexa awoke, she was alone. Rolling over, the only sound that penetrated her mind was the ringing of temple bells in the distance. Sporadically and with no explanation, the bells in the twin carillon towers had recently begun to ring of their own accord. They were ringing again, and she responded to their call, her inner spirit understanding the bells acted as a summons.

Dressing quickly, she struggled to close the back of her burgundy gown. By the end of the week, she would have the services of two ladies-in-waiting. Gregor had informed her via a note only two days before. Right now, she wished they were already here.

Alexa opened the door, closing it quickly behind her. Unseen energy spurred her forward as she ran downstairs toward the breakfast room where she expected to find her husband. She burst into the room, her hastily arranged hair tumbling loosely around her face. She felt almost embarrassed upon seeing only Stefan at the table.

He looked at her flushed face and breathless form. "Is something wrong, Your Majesty?" Her unusual entrance was so unexpected that his typical aloofness was not so evident.

"Gregor? Has he been here? Has he already eaten breakfast?" Her breathless voice was insistent.

Stefan was surprised. Never once had she sought Gregor out. He wondered if something was wrong with her. "He came in only briefly for tea. May I be of some assistance?"

She studied him only a moment, confident of his high degree of integrity despite the dislike she sensed whenever she found herself in his presence. A breathy, worried quality touched her voice as she responded. "I only wish to speak with my husband. It's important. Do you know where he is?"

Stefan could not quite discern the expression clouding her face. Indeed, she appeared to have a pressing need to speak to Gregor. With some disdain, he could not help himself but wish she could be as cognizant of Gregor's needs.

"Stefan, please tell me where I might find him."

There was irresistible pleading—not only in her voice but also in those emerald eyes that had so bewitched his friend. Considering Gregor's mood this morning, it was surely a mistake telling her. "He planned to go walking in the gardens."

She rushed to the table, grabbed one of Stefan's hands, and looked directly into his astonished eyes. "Thank you, Stefan." Then, releasing his hand, she pivoted on her heel and literally ran out into the hallway.

Stefan stared at her departing figure and shook his head, wondering what in the world could be so urgent. He then summoned a guard to follow her at a discreet distance, a precaution Gregor had ordered to keep her safe outside palace walls.

Alexa's feet skimmed over brick and cobbled walkways leading to the gardens. Her eyes scanned the luxuriant foliage and landscaping. Completely unaware of the wondrous natural beauty late summer had brought to her surroundings, she sought only her husband. She grew more breathless as she hurried along wide, meandering paths. When she finally spotted him, she stopped abruptly, trying to calm herself. Her heart softened when she saw him leaning, motionless, against a tall birch tree. His great shoulders were slumped, his head hung low. A sense of desolation and loneliness deeply moved her as she watched him.

Very quietly, as her pounding heart slowed, she walked toward him. Something about him was impossible to resist. She reached out and placed her hand on his upper arm.

He started at her unexpected touch and turned. His expression was, at once, shocked and questioning.

"Gregor, may I speak with you?" Her voice was little more than a whisper.

He only nodded in response to her request.

She stepped in front of him and gazed upward into his brown eyes. For just a moment, she glimpsed that ravaged look she had seen the night before. The fleeting expression was quickly replaced with one of shuttered wariness. Raising her hands, she rested her palms against his cheeks. There existed none of the usual caution or reserve that usually marked their encounters. "I looked for you in the breakfast room. Stefan said you had come outside. I was worried."

He tilted his head ever-so-slightly to one side. "Worried? Why?"

Her hands dropped, but her eyes never left his face. "I'm afraid I cannot answer that, but..." Her words trailed off as she surrendered to the indescribable urge to embrace him. She felt his body register initial shock, but as her arms wrapped more tightly around him, she also felt the depth of need within him as he returned her embrace.

They stood that way for a long time, the silence broken only by the soft sounds of their breathing. Each seemed devoid of conscious thought. Their undemanding embrace was a mutual need, a strange kind of tonic that introduced a tentative healing factor into their strained, uncomfortable relationship.

He was the first to loosen the bond of that embrace to search her face for some sign of insincerity or deception. What he saw made his breath catch in his throat. Her eyes—those incredible emerald eyes—shimmered with a glaze of unshed tears. Rose-colored lips quivered. Deep in his heart, he was grateful. Though he saw no sign of the love he desired so much, he was satisfied that a threshold had been crossed. She finally saw him as a man with profound feelings of his own, and she had found it in her heart to care about those feelings. In some ways, it seemed so little, but it was so much more than he had ever really expected.

She leaned once more into the protective strength of his body. For a moment, he tensed, but then he relaxed in acceptance of the comfort he had craved so badly the night before. She, too, felt secure and comforted by arms that held her snugly within a tightening band. What she had neither seen nor heard was her personal guard dragging away the body of a would-be assassin.

Later that afternoon, as Alexa interviewed the two ladies-in-waiting who had arrived days earlier than expected, Gregor and Stefan sat in the king's private office. Both were shaken by how close the assassin had come to the king.

"Do we know yet if he is Turandan or Sifiq?" Gregor asked.

"No, he refuses to talk. I will personally interrogate him later. What troubles me most is how close he came to you before being discovered. Until now, the gardens have always been secure. Had Alexa not insisted on talking with you and had I not sent that guard out per your instructions…"

"Stefan, I have thought of little else the entire day."

"Gregor, you mustn't worry excessively. I have already instructed the guards to alter their intervals, and I have discreetly increased their numbers."

"I expected no less from you, my friend. However, my thoughts have actually drifted in a different direction."

"What, then?" Stefan watched Gregor closely, relieved that the excessive strain and tension of the morning had eased despite the attempted assassination.

"Stefan, when Alexa found me in the garden, I saw something I never expected to see. Tears were in her eyes but not tears of sadness. Instead, she seemed deeply relieved to find me."

"You should have seen her earlier when she burst into the breakfast room. She was in such a rush that her hair had fallen down, and her face was bright red. Never have I seen her so."

"I suppose what perplexes me most is when I asked why she had come looking for me. She seemed more puzzled than I. She claimed only to have been worried."

Gregor shut his eyes momentarily, remembering how he had felt when, for the first time in their marriage, she had been the one to come to him. The memory was one he would cherish forever, even as he forced himself to acknowledge that it may never happen again.

Stefan's blue-gray eyes reflected thoughtfulness. He moved closer to Gregor and clasped his shoulder in a gesture of intimate friendship. "You realize, my friend, that her insistence to find you likely saved your life."

Gregor's eyes met those of his friend. "Do you think her odd behavior was just coincidence?"

Stefan shook his head and shrugged his shoulders. This morning, for just a moment when she had stood before him at the table, he thought he had seen a hint of blue-white light around her face. This was the second time for him. "Who can say? After all, she is Valiria."

Chapter 7

Time passed. That morning in the gardens remained a cherished memory that Gregor reached inside himself daily to touch. That constant reminder was a moment of comforting escape as he and Stefan encountered ever-increasing vigilance from the Sifiq and greater pressures from the Turandans. As the king and his aide planned and negotiated with both factions, the atmosphere within Toraval grew heavier with malevolent tension and distrust.

Gregor and Stefan were nearly inseparable, spending long hours every day attending to the whims of the Sifiq. Gregor struggled to continue his masquerade as a puppet king whose main goal was to entertain his own selfish indulgences. His true intent was to provide the only bit of traditional continuity Turandans had left. Gregor and Stefan often found themselves exhausted by the efforts required to maintain the believability of their roles.

They also faced increasingly harsh conditions placed by the Sifiq on Turand's people. Gathering a precious, secret inner circle around them, they focused on developing strategies to offset and relieve some of the burdens created by the enemy's growing demands. Stefan was an undisguised blessing. As the king's primary spokesman, his brilliance and adept rhetoric allowed him to trick Sifiq leadership into allowing changes that brought the people slight but welcome relief.

All the while, the Sifiq grew more smug, confident of their brilliance in dealing with their conquered subjects. They were too arrogant to recognize the quiet, desperate game of manipulation.

Passing weeks provided Alexa much free time for meditations and prayers. Many evenings, she mulled over the blessings she had received when Tira and Tirani, her daughter, came into her service. Tira had served Gregor's mother years earlier. Both women were discreet in their devotion to Val's teachings, and Alexa often wondered if Gregor had known this when he arranged for them to come to the palace. It was a subject she hesitated to broach during the increasingly rare moments she saw her husband.

Often, she found it impossible not to worry about him. His dark brown eyes were more remote than ever, with the difference that, intuitively, she knew it was not because of tensions between them. She recognized that the burdens of his monarchy were becoming increasingly complicated. Although there was no way for her to know underlying details, she sensed that Gregor walked a tight wire, delicately balancing demands from the Sifiq with whatever actions he could take to alleviate the sufferings of their people. She observed his sacrifices in silence. Despite all she had sacrificed with the bargain he had forced upon her, she grudgingly admitted growing admiration and respect for her husband.

"Milady, your thoughts are so very serious." Tira's eyes glowed with inner light and wisdom.

Alexa smiled at the older woman. "Tira, in these short weeks since you've been here at the palace, you have come to know me too well."

"We face an uncertain future, Milady. Your husband and his chief adviser struggle to set our country right, and few people suspect what they do. They face dangers from every side. It is only natural you should be concerned." Tira lowered her tiny, wiry frame into a chair indicated by Alexa. Her silvery-white hair, pulled back into a thick bun, contrasted dramatically with her cinnamon coloring. Thin lips pulled into a smile of encouragement. Her face was full of sharp angles but radiated kindness.

"I admit my concern for him. He looks so weary of late. I'm glad that I have you and Tirani to keep me company so that I do not create any unnecessary demands on his time." Alexa's eyes were soft, her expression slipping away into thoughtfulness.

"Perhaps he needs for you to make some demands of his time," Tira suggested.

Alexa could not repress the laugh tinged with cynicism that escaped her. "He doesn't need me at all. I am most certainly a distraction in his life that creates more headaches than anything else."

"Why do you believe so?"

Alexa looked across the table at the tea service Tirani had just placed before her. She leaned forward to stir a bit of cream into the steaming liquid that had just been served. "I am Valiria. I hold no illusions that my husband is the only obstacle standing between me and death at the hands of the Sifiq."

"Do you believe he resents his role as protector?" Tira always spoke directly to Alexa, knowing that the difference in their ages allowed her broader freedom to speak her mind. Besides, she was well pleased that the younger woman, though queen, showed no arrogance because of her position. Instead, she was kind and respectful.

Alexa considered the question for a moment. She tensed slightly, wondering at the direction of Tira's probing questions. "I truly cannot say, Tira. He rarely shares his thoughts with me."

Tira studied her mistress's face and worried about the shadows lurking in the depths of those expressive green eyes. She decided to ask no further questions. Instead, she suggested they all three go to the palace chapel. Shared prayers and meditations would undoubtedly ease the ponderous mood.

Alexa gladly accepted the suggestion. Meditations during early morning hours. Prayers and lessons in the afternoons. She gratefully escaped into the world of faith that continuously revitalized her strength. Tira, secretly a teacher of the old ways, was capable of being a guide to the Valiria. Her own daughter had prepared to become a part of the holy order. The two provided Alexa with much solace and welcome spiritual support.

Days later, with Tira's questions still troubling her, Alexa found herself standing outside the massive oak door of her husband's private chambers. Nervous flutters filled her stomach. The hour was late, yet she was unsure if her husband was inside as she prepared to knock. She gathered her courage and rapped lightly.

"Who is there?" His voice sounded exceedingly tired.

"Gregor, may I come in?" She was embarrassed by the way her voice shook.

There was an extended pause before the door finally opened. "Alexa! Why have you not yet retired? You know you shouldn't roam the corridors at night." He could not hide his surprise as he allowed her to pass by him into his suite before he closed and locked the door.

She glanced around, not sure what to expect since she had never before entered his private chambers. Just beyond the sitting room where they stood, an arched doorway led to the bedroom. Her own bed was enormous, but his was twice as large. She returned her attention to the sitting room. There was little ornamentation. The walls were decorated with peaceful, hand-painted forest scenes. A tall, arched window was covered with dark green draperies trimmed with golden fringe at the top and the hem. On one side stood a wide desk littered with documents. An open book lay in the center. He must have been reading when she disturbed him.

She turned to meet his gaze and noted dark circles beneath his eyes. It was impossible to ignore the tension that drew his face into tired lines. He was more than fatigued. He was near exhaustion. Momentarily, words escaped her.

Heeding her inner voice, she slipped her arm through one of his, led him back to the chair at his desk, and urged him to sit. Once he settled into the chair, she quietly undid the fastenings of his tunic. Then, slipping her hands beneath the fabric, she began to massage the muscles in his neck and along his broad shoulders. Her fingers pressed and kneaded as she thought that, had she delayed only moments longer, his muscles seemed so tight they might have snapped.

Gregor tilted his head backward. Her touch was warm and welcome as her fingers delivered unanticipated and penetrating relief. He had no idea what had prompted her to come to him tonight. So far, she had not spoken. He didn't care. The only thing that mattered was the firm pressure melting away the pain pulling his shoulders and neck.

His eyes closed. The only sound he heard was the steady rhythm of her breathing. Occasionally, he stretched his neck to one side or the other as her probing fingers located particularly strained or sensitive spots. She tended to him for fully half an hour before she broke their silence.

"You push yourself too hard, Gregor. I know these times are especially difficult, but you must rest. You cannot continue this way."

He accepted her comments without protest. "How can I dispute what I know to be true? With circumstances as they are, I have no idea what else to do."

She moved around beside him and sank to her knees. Then, taking his hands, she smiled as she realized hers were barely more than half the size of his. She stared at his fingers, feeling less intimidated than if she met him eye to eye. "I can only guess at the extent of the crises you contend with right now. However, I had an idea that might offer at least a brief respite for you and your staff. It probably sounds a bit silly, but even the wretched Sifiq shouldn't object."

"Then tell me. What silly idea brings you to my chambers at such an hour?" He looked down at her bent head, feeling even too tired to indulge the sudden desire to place a kiss against her fragrant, silken hair.

"Next week is Stefan's birthday. I thought to ask your permission to plan a surprise birthday dinner. I even thought I could go to the kitchen and prepare a meal typical of the southern provinces. I love to cook, and I haven't done so since I came here. Besides, Stefan is your closest friend. I thought perhaps such an evening might be good for all of us."

He removed a hand from her hold and placed his fingers beneath her chin, tipping her face upward. Though exceedingly tired, he felt a brief charge of energy pulse through him as he gazed into her eyes. Slowly, he raised both his hands until he cradled her face between their finely sculpted length. Strong fingers slipped into the fullness of her waving hair. He smiled gently and kissed her forehead.

"With all the chaos lately, I had forgotten Stefan's birthday. The party is a fine idea. It will also provide a fine diversion now that the Sifiq have consented to allow a National Council."

His news was unexpected and fascinating. Anxiously, she wanted to know more but would save her questions until tomorrow. Tonight, she was keenly aware of her husband's need to rest. "Then, please, why do you not stop for tonight? I'll help you get ready for bed. We can talk more tomorrow if you wish."

He knew he should finish the reading left incomplete on his desk. However, his tiredness was overwhelming, and her insistent presence made it too difficult for him to ignore the invasive heaviness creeping through his limbs. He submitted wordlessly as she removed his clothing and found a nightshirt to slip over his head. Staggering slightly, he walked to his bed. When her arm snaked around his waist, he momentarily marveled at her strength as she supported him and helped him into bed. He was only vaguely aware of her pulling the covers over him.

He was unsure if he had succeeded when he tried to ask her to stay with him. However, moments later, he felt the comforting closeness as her body moved next to his. Her whisper felt like a caress in his ears. "Of course, my husband, I won't leave you. If you need me, I shall be right here beside you."

Slumber was a welcome visitor. Earlier this night, he had thought how he had never felt so stressed or so lonely. Finally, his spirits glided free of worldly bonds that fettered him. He would face the morrow strengthened and more rested than he could remember.

⌐

Alexa inspected every detail of the decorations and table settings in the formal dining room. Satisfied that all was perfect, she returned to the kitchens. She anxiously checked on the progress of the elaborate meal she had spent days planning. Even with the expert assistance of palace kitchen staff, many of the dishes had taken hours to prepare. Cooks had been shocked upon being advised that the queen herself would work in their kitchens. The very idea was unprecedented. They were even more astonished when they saw how competently she managed the dicing, chopping, mixing, and blending. Once she was satisfied the servants could complete the remaining steps, she left to dress for the affair.

Tira and her daughter awaited the queen in her suite. Alexa quickly bathed and allowed Tira to rub richly perfumed cream into her skin while Tirani battled to arrange the damp, swirling waves of Alexa's hair. At long last, Alexa burst into laughter at Tirani's frustrated expression.

"Tirani, please don't look so defeated. I have a friend in Garogan who, I swear, is the only one who knows the secret of how to tame my hair.

Unfortunately, she never shared that secret with me. Let's just dry this mess and apply a curling rod to control the ends. I shall wear a headband and let my hair fall loose."

"Are you sure, Milady? You know the fashion is to wear one's hair up." Tirani was reluctant to give up.

"Tirani, thank you for wanting to help. However, fashion and my hair are old adversaries. Besides, I do not believe Gregor will object."

"You do not believe Gregor will object to what?" That rich voice filled her chamber as he peeked around the corner into his wife's dressing room.

Alexa's spirits were unusually bright and merry. She tossed a brush toward the doorway, laughing as it bounced off the wall and onto the floor. "Rogue! You know you are never supposed to enter a lady's room while she's dressing for a party!"

"I surrender! I only heard my name and was curious to know what I'm not objecting to! By the way, did anyone ever inform you that it is a capital crime to assault the king?"

Tira listened carefully to a few more minutes of teasing repartee before Gregor agreed to leave them so the queen could finish getting ready. She smiled inwardly, thinking that their relationship had finally relaxed, even to the point of occasional laughter. She mused about this as she smoothed and arranged the folds of the queen's gown while Tirani quickly twisted the heated curling rod in and out of Alexa's hair.

Alexa's appearance was a breathtaking transformation. Her ivory skin glowed with natural color, and her eyes twinkled with nearly forgotten gaiety. Her brown hair, now swirling into curls dancing around her shoulders, gleamed with golden highlights. Her gown was also ivory, the heavy satin cascading from an empire-style waistline to the floor in sweeping folds. The sleeves were long and full, gathered into purple velvet cuffs trimmed with gold braid. The same velvet and braid trim accented the gown's demure, square neckline.

When all three women were satisfied with the results, Alexa breathed in deeply several times before leaving to act as hostess for the first real party the palace had seen in years. Tira and Tirani fell into place just behind her, following her to the grand marble staircase descending to the palace's main floor. Just as Alexa reached the top step, two friends directed Gregor's attention upward.

Gregor's face was, at first, frozen. Then, dark brown eyes sparkled with lights of appreciation. His smile grew wide and bright, the contrast striking as it curved between the blackness of his mustache and beard. His only conscious thought was unspoken. "Dearest Val, I have never seen anyone look so lovely!" He then bounded up the stairs, easily taking the risers two at a time.

Upon reaching the stair just beneath her, he took her hand and lifted it ceremoniously to his lips. He then stepped up beside her and slipped her arm onto his as he escorted her downstairs. That moment began an evening filled with delicious foods and beverages, witty conversation, and surprises, the first being Stefan's when he realized he had forgotten his own birthday. Although several Sifiq officers were present, not even they were able to diminish the lively atmosphere that had invaded the dining room. Once dinner was over, the Sifiq abruptly departed after learning that the entertainment would be traditional Turandan music.

Gregor had suggested bringing musicians to play for the party. The ensemble opened with a traditional song of salute to the birthday celebrant and then began playing a myriad of long-treasured songs. The music enticed many to dance away the evening. Gregor appeared especially inspired as he led his wife in the intricate steps of several traditional dances marked by scintillating rhythms pounded out on deep-throated drums. Guests watched in fascination as their king and queen moved in sensual unison, their eyes reflecting smoldering fires evoked by drums emulating the rhythms of beating hearts.

Later, to everyone's delight, Gregor stood and sang several well-known ballads that soon had many of the ladies wiping tears from their eyes. Until now, Alexa had never known how great was his love of music or what a wonderfully rich and resonant singing voice her husband possessed.

At the end of the evening, the ensemble began playing the introduction to their final piece, an ancient ballad about lovers torn apart by war. Alexa had long favored the song, which had always touched a note in her soul. She joined her husband, her clear soprano voice harmonizing exquisitely with his rich tenor. As their voices reached for notes long unsung, his dark eyes shone with appreciation and enjoyment. This again was that different side of his wife—bright, happy, charming. He would not have guessed similar thoughts passed through her mind as their voices faded away on the final musical notes of the evening.

That night, he came to her. Although she never knew when to expect him, she somehow had known that he would come this night and that something would be very different. He had always been tender with her. As he sought his own pleasure and ultimate satisfaction, he had never failed to consider hers. She had always submitted, following his lead as she tried to please him as best she could. However, she had known little of physical love and how it should be. His expert touch had never failed to arouse her, but neither had she ever completely opened herself to him.

This night, the transformation Tira had observed earlier overtook Alexa. She felt his kisses deeper and the heat of his touch more intense. Her nerves danced and tingled as his lips and hands quested over her smooth skin, exploring, caressing, and exciting her. She discovered a dormant need that seemed all-encompassing. Her lips feverishly sought his. With fingers splayed against his skin, her hands roved over the muscles rippling in his back and hips. Her fingers ached to tantalize him, to touch every inch of his vigorously masculine body.

Her body begged for him, her hips arching against him as never before. Clear thoughts popped into her agitated brain and vanished in bewildering confusion. All she knew for sure was an almost painful need to be part of him. Their union was swift, almost violent. She strained against him. Her blood felt like liquid fire surging and pounding through her veins. His body moved with hers. She writhed against him, her nails digging into his shoulders. Her hands slipped to his hips, urging him to her. Cries and sobs escaped from her, the animal-like sounds driving him further into impassioned frenzy.

An explosion such as she had never dreamed engulfed her completely. Wave after wave of nerve-jarring pulsations shook her entire body. Her heart raced as her lungs burned, threatening to burst as she gasped for air. Her fingers tangled in his hair, and she clutched his face against her neck. He held her tightly until her shuddering subsided, and then he tenderly kissed away tears streaking her face.

Disengaging her fingers from his hair, he settled her against the pillows, tucking the comforter around her bare shoulders. He then pulled her onto her side to lie against him. She still wept softly, occasionally pausing to place gentle kisses into the hollow at the base of his throat. Not only had their bodies loved this night. For the first time in their marriage, their souls had touched, bringing them both to simultaneous and overwhelming climax.

Chapter 8

Two weeks after the party, Gregor glanced out a library window and spotted Alexa alone on a bench in the palace gardens. He had already looked for her in her private chambers, chapel, and the kitchen. After Tirani's suggestion to check the library, he gazed outside. Something in her posture struck an uncomfortable chord in him, prompting him to go check on her.

Autumn had settled on Toraval, and the air already carried winter's sharp chill. Too soon in the season, trees had started to lose their brightly colored leaves. Drab colors in other shrubs and plants also heralded impending arrival of an early winter. As Gregor approached, he realized her shoulders were shaking. When he was close enough to see her profile, he realized that tears rolled down her cheeks. He reached out and turned her face toward his. Her eyes were red and puffy, her lips swollen where she had bitten into them. Raw pain shocked him. "Alexa, in the name of Val, what's wrong?"

She swallowed hard, shook her head, and turned her face away from him. At that moment, it was much too difficult to face him or anyone else. She only wanted to be alone with her grief.

"Alexa, please. Tell me. What's wrong?" He had seen her in distress many times before, especially during the early days of their marriage.

However, this was different, although he could not explain how. He only knew how much more content she had been lately. Now, suddenly, he was faced with this unexpected crisis.

Tears overpowered her. She seemed almost ready to speak when sobs choked back anything she might have tried to say. Gregor felt helpless to know what to say or do. He feared she would pull away if he attempted to hold her. Hesitantly, he sat on the bench beside her, picking up her icy fingers and rubbing them between his large hands.

Her sobs were daggers thrusting into his heart. Searching for possible reasons for her behavior, he knew the obstacles that separated them were a gulf he might never bridge. Still, their time together since Stefan's party had been amiable, almost happy. He wanted so much to love her but seriously doubted she would ever accept the heart and soul he wished so badly to offer. Even now, in her obvious state of despair, she turned away from him, rejecting his attempts to reach out to console her.

Frustration started to course through his veins as his imagination sought explanations. A sudden jolt of jealousy fired through his blood with the irrational thought that Victor was the source of this outburst. He struggled to tame raging doubts, but the harder she cried, the wilder his imaginings became. Finally, he forced himself to maintain self-control.

At long last, her sobs subsided, leaving her drained and hiccuping. She finally turned around to face him, her eyes watery and her face blotchy. She knew she looked awful and would have preferred for him not to see her this way. He had more than enough problems of his own.

"Alexa, tell me. I shall not rest until you explain what this is all about." Perhaps it would have been better not to ask, but he reminded himself of how attentive she had recently been as she tried to lift his spirits.

"It's so difficult to explain," she replied, her voice thick and hoarse. "The nightmare—I used to have it so often. It came again last night for the first time in so very long. When I awoke and realized today's date, I…" her voice faded.

"Whatever it is, Alexa, the pain is too much to bear alone. At least your husband is a man with strong shoulders." A small, wry expression curved her mouth into the faintest hint of a smile, encouraging him to continue. "Tell me about this nightmare."

A faraway expression haunted her eyes. Then she slipped uneasily into the past. "The nightmare is no more than the reliving of tragedy. I remember as well as if it were yesterday. A fall morning in Garogan. Summer's warmth still lingered in the air. My father carried huge baskets of freshly picked fruits into the kitchen. My mother and I were overseeing preparations to make preserves for the winter.

"We heard a sound like thunder. We looked out, and, in the distance, we saw smoke. Sifiq raiders were approaching. My father grabbed me and dragged my mother and me upstairs to my room. My mother shoved me into a hidden closet and locked me inside. I knew all along that she would never leave him.

"Other villagers had been running toward our house. I could already hear shouts and wailing, but the bedlam had just begun. It seemed only a matter of a few seconds before I heard cries from Sifiq horsemen mingle with the most horrific screams you could ever imagine. The smell of smoke terrified me. Suddenly, the closet door began to shake. Someone outside had discovered it and was jerking it open.

"I was more terrified than ever. All I could think of was the sound of chaos outside and the stories of women being raped and then butchered by the Sifiq. You cannot imagine my shock when Victor grabbed me by the arm and yanked me to my feet. He dragged me to the window. Somehow, we managed to escape onto the roof. To this day, I believe our escape was a miracle because flames were already flaring up along the sides of the house.

"The rest of what I remember seems like so many confused images racing through my mind. My only clear memory is of Victor dragging me along with him. I'm not even sure how he found a cellar door out of sight of the Sifiq, but he jumped in and pulled me down into the darkness. He barred the door, and we huddled in the dark for what seemed like a lifetime.

"I can still hear his voice whispering against my ear. He told me one fairy tale after another, his whispered words against my ear deadening the sounds of murder, death, and destruction from above. He sang nursery rhymes to me. I tried to pray, but every word or thought got lost in that ungodly noise.

"We stayed in that cellar for nearly two days until all the crying and moaning stilled. Victor refused to let me out until he was sure it was safe. When we did emerge, part of me wanted to die. Everywhere I looked were bodies or parts of bodies. Men, women, children. Animals. Slaughtered. Slashed. Speared. Mutilated. The stench of death and so much spilled blood sickened me so badly that I fell to my knees and vomited.

"Victor held me the entire time. When I was finally able to stand, we walked toward what had been my home. Most of it had burned. This morning, when I awoke, I was standing there again. The horrific sight of my parents' bodies stretched out on the ground. The gruesome injuries that had killed them." She fell silent, staring at the ground yet seeing only fresh images of long-ago tragedy.

Unable to restrain himself any longer, Gregor gathered her into his arms and held her close. He understood so much more now, so much he had never dared to guess. Her discomfort in the presence of the Sifiq. The occasional melancholy that transformed her features when someone spoke of her parents. Even her loyalty and devotion to Victor Garogan. Clearly, Victor had saved her life and stayed by her through what must have been an excruciating period of mourning and recovery. Together, they had faced and survived life-threatening danger and then embarked upon rebuilding her life. This had been the love he had severed to satisfy his own willful wants.

No longer did she cry. Meekly, she accepted Gregor's closeness. Her face was buried against his chest, much the same as the day Victor had been set free. Neither spoke. Each was lost within themselves, each scarred for a lifetime by evils wrought by the Sifiq.

$$\backsim$$

"How long have we been riding?" Alexa's voice still sounded subdued but expectant. The days since the anniversary of her parents' deaths had been difficult, but everyone around had exerted combined efforts to distract her from painful memories.

Gregor, desperately needing to get away from the tense environment of the palace, decided to take a five-day break to visit his family's summer home. The property was almost a seven-hour ride by carriage. However, the trip should be worthwhile since Lindaval was an isolated area with unusual spring-like weather the year around. Now, he smiled indulgently at his wife. "We should arrive in the next half-hour."

At first, she had objected to the trip. For every objection she raised, Gregor or Stefan had posed a response she could not argue. Each man fully recognized that Gregor and Alexa both needed a respite from the rigors and intrigue that currently typified palace life.

When they finally rolled to a stop, one of the bodyguards accompanying them opened the door of the royal carriage. Gregor stepped out first. He then helped Alexa down from the coach. The light in her eyes and the smile that transformed her face more than justified the time he would spend away from Toraval.

The summer home was large but much more inviting than the gray stone walls of the palace. Stucco and stained wooden beams formed the outside walls here. Sparkling clean windows reflected the waning light of the afternoon sun. Intricate wainscoting ornamented the enormous covered patio that ran the entire length of the front of the house. Potted plants were set everywhere on pedestals of varying heights, and the leafy green foliage was a treat to eyes already growing accustomed to the charcoal hues of winter.

"Let's go inside," Gregor suggested, cupping her elbow in his hand and guiding her up the broad steps to the soaring double-door entrance.

"When can I look around? It's so lovely outside!" The delight in her voice was fresh and still new to him.

"Tomorrow morning. Darkness comes very quickly, and it will be darker than any night you have ever seen." He grinned at her obvious disappointment. "If you will only trust me tonight and give me no trouble, I promise to show you something quite special tomorrow."

"Trouble? What kind of trouble?" she asked, puzzled by his choice of words.

"Never mind. Our things are already upstairs. Why don't you go up to supervise the unpacking? Oh, and by the way, I have put you in what used to be my mother's rooms. You are welcome to anything you might like." He wagged a finger of caution at her. "And remember. Behave yourself."

Morning was glorious at Lindaval. Alexa awoke just after dawn, feeling refreshed and looking forward to a day more than any since before her journey to Toraval. Feeling surrounded by an incomparable peace, she began her meditations early.

After completing her final prayers, she acquainted herself with the room and its contents. Gregor's mother had left a unique essence of grace in this room. There were miniature hand-painted oils framed in fil-igree. On the nightstand by the bed stood a silver frame with an oil por-trait of a small boy. She studied the little boy's face beneath the golden light of an oil lamp. The impish smile and bright eyes most certainly belonged to her husband. She grinned to herself as she glimpsed a bit of him as a child.

She decided to unpack a small case containing a few personal items and placed them inside a drawer of the massive rosewood dresser domi-nating one wall. Arranging the last of her undergarments inside, she felt something cold and hard tap against the wooden back of the drawer. Closing her fingers around it, she pulled out an elaborate chain that gleamed with the patina of old gold. Dark purple silk braid entwined with the chain. The crystal pendant was smooth and beautifully cut. She sucked in her breath, amazed by her find. She wrapped the piece in a satin scarf and secured it inside a small travel case. Someday, she would find the courage to ask Gregor about it.

Later, she dressed and pulled her hair back with a tortoise-shell head-band. There was relief in leaving the formalities of court behind her. Here, she could dress more comfortably and according to Gregor's instructions. He had been quite serious when he had explained she would need only split skirts for riding, lightweight blouses, and a warm riding jacket. He had laughed when she asked if she should bring riding boots or if she should just go barefoot.

Gregor already awaited her when she arrived downstairs. Glancing up to watch her descend the spiral staircase, he smiled. "I do believe I can dispense with questions about how you slept. You look very fresh and rested this morning." His compliment held undeniable admiration.

She almost skipped down the final steps and over to hug him. "I can't wait to go outside! I heard so many birds singing in the tree by my windows!"

He chuckled lightly. Rarely had he seen her like this—the way she was indeed meant to be. Lovely, bright, cheerful, sparkling. What an inspiration it had been to bring her here.

After breakfast, he wrapped a light shawl around her shoulders to ward off the still-cool morning air and donned a knitted jacket of his own. He then led her outside to another expansive, enclosed patio at the back of the house. Instructing her to close her eyes and trust him not to let her get into trouble, he slipped a hooded blindfold over her head.

"What's this for, Gregor? What are you doing to me?"

He laughed aloud, a musical sound that seemed to resonate around her and through her. "I'm preparing to lead you to your first surprise of the day. Are you ready?" When she nodded yes, he guided her carefully outside the patio and along a path through a vast, maze-like, informal garden. "All right, you may stop."

She turned her head from side to side and sniffed as best she could at the morning air. She lifted the hood slightly and inhaled deeply. "Impossible! It's too late in the year! Gregor, can that scent be lilac?"

He pulled the blindfold off and gently spun her around by the shoulders. Before her were great, sweeping shrubs and trees filled with the sweet fragrance of hundreds of lavender and white cones of lilac blossoms.

"I don't believe this! How can it be?" she exclaimed, pulling a branch laden with flowers to her nose and sniffing appreciatively.

Gregor smiled broadly, his bronzed features alight with pleasure. Dark brown eyes glowed as he watched her skip from one bush to another, breathing in the perfumed air as if she would never again have such an opportunity. "Lindaval is an anomaly. This place enjoys perpetual spring. Mornings and evenings are cool. Days are warm and usually sunny. My mother had these unique species planted. They were her favorites."

"Oh, Gregor, it's been so long since I've been able to indulge in the fresh fragrance of live lilacs. They didn't grow well at Garogan City."

Suddenly, she paused as an odd thought came to her. "Your mother had these planted? It's strange that her favorite flower is mine, too. What was she like?"

Gregor hesitated. They had never spoken of his parents. Right now, he didn't want to let past loss and sorrow dampen his plans for this day.

Sensing his withdrawal, she instinctively knew that it was his wish to avoid her question. The time just wasn't right. She turned away from him and floated over to another giant lilac to enjoy its soft hues and rich scent. "You've never spoken much about your family. Maybe later you'll tell me about your parents? Mmmm, this one is exceptional! Come smell for yourself!"

He came over and sniffed the flowers, intensely glad to let shadows of the past recede from his mind. "Are you ready for your second surprise?" he asked. At least the first had been successful. He hoped the second would be best.

Unexpectedly, she threw her arms around his neck. "I don't know if I'm ready or not! This is already so much more than I expected!"

Gregor's eyes closed, and he savored this precious moment. The sweetness of her abandon and her show of affection were an incredible balm to a spirit weary with talk of war and violence in addition to the problems haunting their marriage. Moments like this were all he had ever wanted.

"Gregor?" She nearly sang out his name as she stepped away, breaking his magic moment and drawing him unwillingly from his private reverie.

"Are you ready?" he asked again, struggling to recover his composure.

"Of course."

"Then let's go."

They walked to the stables, where two grooms already awaited them with saddled horses. Each horse carried packs, which Gregor explained, held their lunches.

As they rode away from the house and grounds, they trotted along in amiable silence. Each was content to study the scenery stretching before them. Occasionally, they broke into a canter, then slowed their horses again. Finally, after about forty minutes, Gregor halted his horse and dismounted. He tethered the animal near shade and easy grazing. He then lifted his wife down from her mount, secured the second horse, and produced the blindfold once more.

"Again?" she asked, mock dismay in her voice as she allowed him to adjust the dark fabric over her eyes.

"Yes, again. And this time, hold on tight and step carefully. Do as I say because I also have to carry our packs for later." His voice was revealing, his pleasure immense.

Within moments, she understood the reason behind his words of caution. The ground was rough and rocky. She stumbled, but he held her securely. She could hear him pulling back limbs as he helped her move forward just before letting go of branches that swooshed and crackled in the air. Suddenly, she paused. The sound of rushing water was part of a musical symphony now quite near. She felt warm, wet vapors rising to dampen her face.

"Stop. Don't move," Gregor whispered from just behind her left ear. She felt the closeness of his body as he lifted the blindfold from her a second time.

She opened her eyes and gasped. "For the love of Val! Gregor! I've never seen any place so beautiful in my entire life!"

She stood rooted to the spot, taking in every detail. Wide, smooth areas were green and cushiony with thick, moss-like groundcover. Green spaces stretched like ribbons of carpet running around the great pool of water. Steam rose from the pool, evidencing the hot springs feeding it from below. At the far end, a rocky wall that sheltered the area was shrouded in heavy mist. A narrow fall of cooler water tumbled and splashed down its face, causing brilliant morning sunshine to refract into literally dozens of dancing, prismatic displays of color.

She spun around to face him, her eyes sparkling with astonished delight. Her cheeks blushed with entrancing rose color from the short, rough walk from where they had left their horses. Her mouth spread into a full, uninhibited smile. He had never seen her look so lovely before or so completely happy.

Gregor controlled a rising desire to pull her into his arms and kiss her, wanting this day to be more than simple seduction, more than a passionate interlude. He wanted them to be together without the pressures and responsibilities of court or reminders of how she had come to live there. Wanting to escape, however briefly, the painful memories that lingered at the palace, he reached out and caught her hand in his to lead her to the water's edge.

"Here, sit down and take off your boots."

"My boots? Why?" she asked, lowering herself to the soft, spongy ground. Lights danced merrily in her eyes as she allowed herself to be carried by his uniquely high spirits.

He left her long enough to retrieve one of the packs he had dropped. He removed a blanket and spread it out. He also took out several towels and laid them on the blanket. He then sat down and pulled off his boots and stockings. He grinned at her, got up, and waded ankle-deep into the water. Not wanting to be left out, she lifted her skirts and followed.

"Mmmm. This feels wonderful. It's so warm," she sighed, wiggling her toes in the heated water.

"Are you brave enough to go in all the way to bathe?" His eyes were gently mocking as he grinned wickedly at her.

"Bathe? Here? But what about my clothes?" She glared at him, long-forgotten humor reacting with amusement to his taunting expression.

She laughed out loud when he started stripping away his clothing, tossing it into an untidy heap by the blanket.

Admiration filled her as he gingerly stepped further and deeper into the water. She watched his male form as if seeing him for the first time. His springy hair feathered backward to the base of his neck, a shining black mass with just a few shimmers of silver threading through it. His shoulders were broad, with the musculature of his arms and torso as well defined as if carved by a master sculptor. His buttocks were firm and rounded, his legs long and powerful. As he looked over his shoulder to invite her in, his eyes shone with an almost boyish glint of mischief.

Gasping involuntarily, she experienced a moment of shock as she realized how very handsome he was and wondered why she had never noticed before. She shook off the disturbing thought, hesitated, then decided she may as well give in and join him. Modestly, she turned around to disrobe. Their shared intimacies as man and wife were forgotten as she blushed, knowing he studied her every movement.

When she turned back to step into the water, she held her lacy camisole to shield her nudity. His eyebrows lifted in amusement, but he said nothing. As she waded into deeper water, she finally abandoned all pretenses and tossed the garment onto the blanket. When she gained enough courage to look up at him, his expression was tender and understanding. She had half-expected him to be teasing or taunting. Instead, he offered his hand, and she stared at it for a long moment before sliding hers into its firm grip.

Wordlessly, he led her further into the water. Beneath their feet, large stones were flat and smooth. Occasionally, they felt tingling jets as heated water shot from beneath the rocky floor. Glancing up at him, she was amazed by the relaxation seeping into her limbs as the warmth caressed her body.

"Tell me truthfully. Do you like it here?" His voice was expectant, her approval very important to him.

"Oh, Gregor, what can I say? I love it! I've never experienced anything like this!"

As they lounged around the pool, time seemingly stood still. Gregor showed her places to sit to maximize the massaging effects of the hot streams of water. He explained how several sources of water fed the springs and created the unique trees and other flora that surrounded this private oasis. He savored the image of her brilliant smile, shining eyes, and golden hair clinging damply around her face and shoulders.

Reluctantly, he finally suggested they leave the pool to share the lunch waiting by the edge of the blanket. As they stepped carefully toward the water's edge, Alexa slipped, lost her balance, and fell heavily against her husband. Gregor had turned around to help her out. Instead, he caught her in his arms, pulling her body against him.

Her initial gasp, caused by the sudden fall, was forgotten almost instantly as their eyes locked. Gone was the sparkle of humor and merry abandon. Instead, emerald eyes burned with fires utterly new to him. His eyes swiftly glazed with a passion that pierced through all the protective armor she had erected, penetrating to her very soul.

Slowly, deliberately, he pulled her from the water, never loosening his embrace. As she tried to walk, her legs shook, seemingly unable to support her weight. She wondered fleetingly if her weakness resulted from time spent in the water or from the incredible heat emanating from his body. Sensing what was happening, she felt the sharp rise of his passion. The difference this time was that, just as the night of Stefan's party, she could feel her body not simply responding but issuing its own demands. The sounds of birds and tumbling water and leaves rustling in the breeze faded to near silence. Her awareness encompassed nothing except the man who was gently guiding her down onto the blanket.

With no conscious thought, she reached upward to his face. Her fingers traced the arch of his brow, the line of his beard, the curve of his lips. Her gaze intensified as she then allowed her hands to glide downward along the column of his neck, out across his shoulders. Her eyes momentarily followed the motion of her hands, noting the lines that she caressed.

He moved to lie on his side, drawing her with him. Ivory skin beneath his touch was smooth and supple, cooling as clinging droplets of water evaporated into the air. He closed his eyes to concentrate fully on her touch that traced sensuous paths along his face, his neck. No woman had ever touched him as she did now. Neither had any woman ever awakened the fiery passion that threatened to consume him so entirely as her slender fingers explored and caressed further and further across the firm planes and angles of his body.

A sigh escaped from deep within him as she placed the palm of her hand against his hair-roughened abdomen, his muscles contracting as her hand slowly glided along the expanse of his lower torso. His breathing grew rapid and shallow. Passion surged, and he laced his fingers in hers, guiding them to touch him even more intimately. She wrapped her fingers around the surging force of his masculinity, robbing him of coherent thought.

Her name tumbled forth. With hands and lips, he reciprocated her caresses. The heated dampness of his mouth tasted hers before trailing a line of fiery kisses along her neck toward the full globes of her breasts. Her head fell back as she moaned softly in a rising tide of ecstasy. She trembled violently beneath the sensuous, rippling wave of sensations created by heated kisses that tantalized her.

After what seemed a lifetime of sweet torture, his hands moved beneath her hips. His possession was breathtaking for both of them. Their bodies strained as though they could not be close enough. Her hands roved wildly over the sinuous muscles of his back. She cried out his name, urging him to greater heights of passion. The moment arrived when both were caught in the force of simultaneously exploding, pulsating shock waves that roared and flooded through every vein and fired across each and every nerve.

For a very long time, they lay in each other's arms. She kept her face against his chest; his chin rested on her head. Minutes passed as pounding hearts and heaving lungs struggled to achieve normal rhythms. Finally, they dozed beneath the warming rays of the sun.

Sleep was short. As they awoke, neither deigned to speak, fearing to break the spell that glowed around them. They helped each other dress in silence, both their hands still trembling. Quietly, they sat and ate their meal of freshly baked bread, cheese, fresh fruit, and wine. There was unspoken regret as they finally packed their things away and returned to their horses. After securing the packs to their saddles, Gregor started to help Alexa mount her horse.

She stopped him, her eyes searching his face. What she saw struck a previously unknown chord inside her. His dark brown eyes glistened, glazed with tears. His face had transformed completely in the aftermath of the day they had spent together. She attempted to speak, needing to talk with him. A flood of fresh and fragile emotions threatened to consume her. Words tumbled in disarray inside her head. Finally, she reached out, placing a hand against his cheek. "Gregor?" His name was little more than a whisper.

He straightened and cradled her face between his hands, his eyes intently studying her passion-softened features. "Tell me," he murmured gently.

"Gregor, I..." she paused, not knowing what she had wanted to say. "Gregor, thank you for an absolutely perfect day." She moved closer and rested her head against his chest. She memorized the rhythm of his beating heart as he held her, thinking how tender the sound of his voice as he breathed her name against her hair.

They rode back to the manor in contemplative silence. Each was immersed in a private myriad of thoughts and questions. They would need time to talk, to explore this new turn in their relationship. Neither was quite sure what had happened today alongside the water's edge. Alexa knew only that she had never been more confused in her life. Gregor dared to hope he might yet touch the cherished dream he guarded within the depths of his heart.

Upon approaching the manor house, they stopped their horses. A detachment of royal guards waited with saddled horses at the stable while others lounged on the grand front veranda. Stefan was with them. Gregor glanced at Alexa, his countenance at once becoming grim, his lips tightening in regret. Something was terribly wrong. They pressed their horses forward again, hurrying across the lawn to the front of the house.

"Stefan!" Gregor called out, dismounting quickly and then moving around his horse to help his wife down from hers. "What happened? Why have you come?"

"I'm sorry that I must interrupt you here, my lord. May we go inside?" Stefan's request was undoubtedly urgent.

Gregor purposefully strode forward and up the steps into the house. Alexa followed him with Stefan close behind her. Once inside, Alexa took Gregor's jacket before he went through the foyer to the sitting room with Stefan. She removed her coat, handed everything to a servant who had appeared from upstairs, then hurried to the sitting room.

Upon joining the two men, who stood before the window in deep conversation, it was apparent the circumstances that had brought Stefan were exceedingly serious. Stefan's face was weary and tense. Gregor's expression was equally tense yet resolute. Seeing that she had entered the room, Gregor asked Stefan to leave them so that he could explain that he must return immediately to Toraval.

Gregor's steps were slow yet firm as he walked toward her. His eyes clouded with sadness, and his voice carried an unmistakable tone of regret. Their day had been perfect. His anticipation of spending tomorrow with her had filled him with fresh hope. Now, he had no choice but to relinquish his private dream. He was king, and his responsibilities required that he leave tonight for his capital city. He didn't touch her. He could not bear to do so.

"I must return to the palace tonight. Lord Manaran arrived this morning from Fosan Province. He demands to speak with me immediately about matters that could impact Council. As if that weren't enough, the Sifiq received word their ships are due to arrive in the north within six weeks for troop rotation. This is the moment we have awaited. I must go."

"I understand. I shall prepare to accompany you." She was calm. Finally, Val's changes had begun.

"No, it isn't safe to travel at night. I will leave guards here who will return with you. Stay a day or two longer if you like." His heart ached at the very idea of leaving her behind.

"You know that I'm an excellent horsewoman," she reminded him, not wanting to remain alone. "I can make the trip with you."

He couldn't avoid smiling. "I have no doubt; however, I think it best that the country's two monarchs travel separately right now. The guards can concentrate on defending only one of us at a time if the need arises."

She bit into her lip, her expression pensive, and nodded understanding. "Then I shall return tomorrow. Let me get something for you to eat before you leave."

He watched her turn and leave the room. For a fleeting moment, Gregor wanted to damn Council, the Sifiq, and every other tie that bound him to the throne of Turand. He only wanted to hold her and convince her to accept the love that had flared into an inner blaze, consuming more and more of his soul. He shook his head against an impossible dream. His destiny had been determined at birth. He left to find Stefan.

Alexa stood on the bottom step as guards fell into place to escort Gregor back to Toraval. They would not arrive until well after midnight. Gregor guided his horse to stand in front of her. He sat tall and proud, command an unmistakable air about him. "I want you to be careful when you return tomorrow. My guards have their orders. Listen to them."

She barely contained a smile. He sounded so anxious for her safety when he was the one who faced real danger, planning a wild, late-night ride back to Toraval. Spontaneously, she stretched her hand out to him. He took it, leaning forward to place a kiss into her palm.

"Be safe, my husband." Never would she have imagined it could be so difficult to stand and watch while he rode away from her.

"Good afternoon, Carlo. Please see that His Majesty's belongings are taken to his suite and then have my things placed in mine."

Alexa had whisked through the doors of the palace without ceremony and with all the intensity of a winter storm. Her heavy skirts and long cloak swished behind her as she administered instructions to the servants for the disposition of the things she had brought back with her from Lindaval. She then turned to the housekeeper, who had appeared to check on the noises echoing through the grand entrance hall. "Lena, is my husband here? Did he arrive safely last night?" Her voice was brusque and demanding.

Before the startled woman could reply, another voice sounded from a corridor leading to the west wing of the palace. "I believe I can answer both of those questions immediately."

The housekeeper glanced beyond Alexa's shoulder, relieved to see the king approaching. The queen, usually a reclusive figure, had seemed almost agitated. Lena quickly took charge of servants and baggage and directed everyone from the entrance.

Breathing in a muffled sigh of relief, Alexa turned in acknowledgment of her husband's voice. Secretly glad to see Gregor safely returned to Toraval, she received his kiss on her cheek in formal greeting. When she spoke, her voice carried a different tone than he had ever heard before. "I was so concerned when you left last night."

Before he could respond, Stefan appeared to announce that the midday meal was prepared and ready to serve to their guests. A tightly controlled, formal expression quickly replaced the frustration that flashed across Gregor's face. "Alexa, you must be hungry after such a long trip. Will you join us?"

She looked up into his eyes, hiding continuing bewilderment that she was still so unable to read his life force. "May I have a few minutes to go upstairs to wash my face and hands?"

"Of course."

"I won't be long." She started to climb the stairway but hesitated before speaking very quietly. "Gregor, before I go, I know how occupied you are just now. I only wondered if we might find some time to talk later. Privately."

He managed a gentle smile. "Of course. Now hurry. We have ungracious guests who will be unbearable if we keep them waiting."

Later, she understood exactly what he had meant. Lord Manaran was a rotund, middle-aged man who was actually quite pleasant and a splendid conversationalist. Manaran's trip to Toraval had indeed been urgent. He had brought intelligence regarding the Sifiq fleet in transit to ports in two neighboring northern provinces.

Contrasting sharply with her husband, Lady Manaran was thin, shrewish, and demanding almost to the point of being obnoxious. She spoke incessantly of problems she noted in the palace and how her provincial capital was much more stimulating in comparison. To make matters worse, several cousins attended her, and all were irritating whiners. They complained about the spices in the food, the lack of entertainment, and how they were sure the time they had spent indoors since their arrival would lead to illness. Alexa and Gregor exchanged glances several times, communicating without words their dwindling patience.

When the meal was over at last, Alexa rose and, much against her better judgment, offered to stroll with the Manaran ladies through the palace museum and library. She was immensely glad when all of the ladies declined her invitation, stating they would prefer to rest. However, her relief was short-lived when Lady Manaran informed her that her party had requested a ride in the countryside the following day. Since the king had voiced no objections, she would look forward to meeting the queen early the next morning.

Once all the guests had left the dining room, Alexa turned horrified eyes to her husband. "Please tell me they're not serious."

"I am so sorry," Gregor apologized sincerely. "Stefan and I have endured one interruption after another from them. I cannot believe Lord Manaran has maintained his sanity all the years that he has been married to that woman. If you do not wish to go, then don't. You are, after all, mistress of this domain."

Alexa sighed and shrugged her shoulders. "I'll go. Perhaps you can finish your business with Lord Manaran, and they'll leave quickly."

Gregor stifled a chuckle. "That sentiment is not exactly what I would expect from a queen, let alone a Valiria."

"Even queens and Valiria have limitations on what foolishness they can tolerate," she retorted.

Fatigue from the day's long journey found Alexa yawning early and barely able to stay awake. She excused herself to her guests and wished them a good night. Her husband rose to escort her upstairs for the first private moments they had managed since her return. As they stood outside the door to her private chambers, he was apologetic.

"Please understand that I must return to attend them. I know you wanted to talk, but you can see what I've had to contend with. I told Lord Manaran that I require some private time tomorrow afternoon. Tell me you can wait until then."

She smiled up at him. Part of her desperately needed to speak with him now, to discuss and probe the very new and disconcerting feelings welling up inside her. Another part of her remained afraid, as yet fearful of severing her ties to the past. "Tomorrow afternoon will be fine. We'll talk then."

He reached up to stroke her face, then leaned forward to kiss her cheek. "Thank you for understanding. Sleep sweet."

Later, she stirred as she heard faint sounds in the room. When she felt the bed move, she realized her husband had decided to retire to her room. "Gregor?" Her voice was thick with sleep.

"I'm sorry. I didn't intend to awaken you," he whispered, settling his huge frame into the comfortable warmth of her bed.

"What time is it?"

"Almost two in the morning," he answered, his voice weary but gentle. "Go back to sleep."

She turned over and, surrendering to some undefined inner need, snuggled close against him. Her hand sought his beneath the blanket, and she curled her fingers around his. Desire simply to be near him was unexpectedly strong. "Will you hold me until I fall asleep again?"

He turned on his side to face her and wrapped an arm around her, pulling her closer. Her request, given in such a vulnerable state of sleepiness, struck him as exquisitely sweet. He smiled into the darkness as the soft, even sound of her breathing lulled him to sleep.

The following morning, Stefan found Alexa in the library at seven, already dressed for an early morning excursion. "I expected to find Gregor here. I knocked at his door, but there was no answer."

She glanced up at Stefan, smiled, and beckoned him to sit in the chair opposite her. "I left him asleep in my room. He looked so peaceful that I had no heart to disturb him."

Stefan showed no evidence of surprise. "I'm glad he's resting. These next several weeks promise to be very trying. Did you need me for something?"

"Stefan, I sent breakfast to Lady Manaran and her attendants with advice to meet us in the stable at eight-thirty. I admit that I exercised my prerogative as queen to determine the time. I'm not looking forward to this little event. However, I am glad that you'll be with us." She paused, debating whether or not to ask the questions on her mind. "Stefan?"

"Milady?"

She tilted her head slightly and looked directly into Stefan's eyes. As always, she felt the intensity of his loyalty and devotion to Gregor and read that he was unquestionably an honest man. She needed to clarify certain matters if she ever hoped to understand her husband any better.

"Stefan," she began tentatively, "what happened to Gregor's parents?"

This time, Stefan's face reflected surprise. "Is that not a question you should ask of the king?"

"I did. It seemed the moment wasn't right for him to discuss it, so I changed the subject. Please, Stefan, help me understand."

Her request was a plea laced with sincerity he could not ignore, although he would have preferred that Gregor explain. He paused uncomfortably. "Gregor's mother died when he was almost twelve. She was a very loving woman, and they were very close. It was several years later that we learned her death resulted from poisoning—by the Sifiq." He watched her face for reaction and saw the grimace that crossed her features.

"Why? Why did they kill her?"

"Your Majesty, they needed a monarch of traditional royal blood. They also needed to be able to control that monarch. They knew that Turandans would be easier to manage if they had tangible ties to past traditions and beliefs. By killing Queen Anlía, as well as threatening to do the same to Gregor, the Sifiq effectively gained control over Gregor's father. Not realizing that King Maxim would do nothing to endanger his only child, they also decided to ensure their control over the king by administering regular doses of drugs. Those drugs eventually killed him. His death was long and agonizing beyond belief. Gregor and I swore a secret pact that someday we would find a way to defeat the Sifiq by using their arrogance against them. I pray that day is at hand."

Alexa sat quietly, considering what she had just learned. "So, Gregor lost his family at the hands of the Sifiq just as I did."

"As I understand, you at least have one or two living cousins. Gregor has no one at all."

The whining sound of Lady Manaran's voice drifted down the stairs, and consternation replaced the pensive expression on Alexa's face. "I suppose we should go to the stables now. Otherwise, we will most certainly have to listen to them complain the rest of the day about how I made them get up so early and then arrived late to meet them."

⤸

A young groom firmly grasped the reins of Gregor's stallion as the king lifted his foot into the stirrup to mount. Gregor stopped suddenly, his attention attracted by the sound of pounding hooves. What he saw brought no sense of relief. The rapidly approaching riders were almost two hours late returning and in obvious distress.

Stefan rode at the front and practically jumped from his mount as soon as it stopped. He barked out orders to grooms and mounted guards waiting to leave with Gregor. The grooms helped the ladies dismount while the guards went to aid those who had accompanied the morning's riding party. Several were wounded, and their temporary bandages were soaking through with blood.

Assured the other riders were being attended to, Stefan sucked in a deep breath and turned to face Gregor. His face hurt from cold and the blow he had been struck, but that was nothing compared to the pain of what he now must tell his friend.

"Stefan, in Val's great name, what happened? Where is Alexa?"

Stefan's chest heaved as he struggled to catch his breath. When he finally spoke, his words carried the weight of a death knell. "They took her, Gregor. She's gone."

Chapter 9

Garogan Province

The hooves of more than twenty horses beat asynchronous rhythms across the bridge leading to Garogan Castle. Alexa glanced up at the familiar turrets and wind-tossed pennants lining the castle's outer walls. Massive ramparts of gray stone were punctuated by tiny windows used initially by archers. When Turand had entered long centuries of peace, glass was installed, which now caught sunlight and flashed it back across the countryside. Immense, double wooden doors stood wide open with sentries posted on each side.

Even though her body felt heavy with fatigue, Alexa's posture was straight as she moved in rhythm with her horse. Since the Garogan raiders had captured her, they had ridden with little rest for three days, the typical duration of the trip shortened by more than a day because of the driving pace.

As they rode through the castle entry and into the center court-yard of the fortress, people from the adjoining town began spilling into the area, excited as they followed the group of riders. The Queen of Turand had arrived at last. The Valiria, the last of her kind and the one they claimed as their own, had finally returned home. The crowd was hushed and respectful, awed by the regal and commanding presence she now exuded.

A guard came to steady her mount. Another offered assistance as she climbed down from the horse. She staggered slightly, the ground feeling strange and unstable beneath her feet. People moved aside, creating a pathway to the entrance of the main castle edifice. A group of finely attired men and women appeared from inside and walked toward the dismounted riders. Excitement permeated the gathering.

With her heart pounding, Alexa watched the entourage approach. A figure emerged from the group, his stride long and rapid. As he came closer, his arms extended, Victor's hazel eyes glazed with tears. A smile spread his mouth. Within seconds, Alexa found herself wrapped in the familiar haven of his embrace.

His arms formed a strong band around her. She felt his well-remembered strength and heard the beat of his heart. He loosened his embrace and lifted a hand to her chin, tilting her face upward. She received his kiss of welcome without protest. In the haze of overwhelming fatigue, the only shadow of a thought that crossed her mind was that these arms were not quite the refuge she had expected.

Joyous cheers jarred her rambling mind. She opened her eyes to gaze directly into his. How much she had loved those eyes! Still, the eyes now burning in her memory were so much darker, so much more penetrating. What was this confusion rushing through her? With shouts of welcome from the Garogan citizenry ringing in her ears, Alexa swayed weakly, then collapsed against Victor's muscular body.

⌒

Alexa rolled over in bed. Images of Lindaval's great hot springs teased her mind. She saw so vividly the white mist rising against the stone backdrop as colder water spilled into the pool of heated spring water. Tumbling waters occasionally caught rays of sunshine and refracted rainbows of brilliant color. She felt the strength of Gregor's arms around her as she leaned back against the warmth of his body. She listened to his laughter, that rich sound joyous and newly shared with her.

She sat up abruptly, her dream cut short too quickly by an unexpected sound. She shook off the sleepiness dulling her senses and glanced around. The opening of the door must have disturbed her. Adrina. Her dear friend had entered to check on her.

"Finally! You're awake!" Adrina's lilting voice was overjoyed when she sat on the edge of the bed and swept Alexa into a giant hug. "We have waited so long to have you back with us! I cannot tell you how much I've missed you."

"I've missed you, too, Adrina." Alexa returned the hug with loving enthusiasm.

"You've slept nearly twelve hours! We were beginning to worry since no one has ever known you to sleep so long at a time." Adrina studied the face of her childhood friend, certain she perceived a change. But what?

"The ride was terrible! It was so long, and Victor's men barely gave me time to eat, let alone rest."

"The return ride was too dangerous, Alexa. The Sifiq have increased their patrols along the roads to Garogan. Our men had no choice if they were to avoid any skirmishes. You have no idea how much effort Victor put into those plans. He was determined to avoid any interference with your return. He has been so completely miserable since—since…" she stammered.

"Since I married King Gregor?" Alexa finished the sentence for her.

"Please, Alexa, you need not worry," Adrina quickly interjected, the subject now broached. "Victor commissioned many scholars to study all the laws, and we're certain you can be released from this awful union."

Alexa lowered her eyes briefly before sliding her legs toward the right, away from Adrina and off the bed. She stood and stretched sleep-induced stiffness from her limbs, then walked to the glass-paned double doors that led to a tiny balcony. She pushed aside heavy lavender draperies to gaze out. Mid-morning sunshine drenched the autumn countryside. The lushness of the Garogan district stretched out in colorful panorama before her. Nostalgia filled her as she remembered how she had loved staring out these doors when this had been her room.

Garogan, the largest of Turand's three southern provinces, was fertile, rolling countryside until it reached the southernmost boundaries that touched the sea. Its people were typically robust in physical appearance and iron-willed in the extreme. Even the Sifiq avoided Garogan Province as much as possible, their soldiers often disappearing into the night. Any reprisals resulted in the subsequent disappearance of three times as many victim soldiers.

"Adrina, where is Victor now?"

Alexa still faced the outside, and her question carried a note of demand that Adrina had never heard before. "He meets with Lord Anderon from Tasa Coast Province." Adrina watched the solitary figure by the window. Yet again, she nervously considered some indefinable difference in her friend.

Alexa stared outside for several extended, silent moments before turning around to face Adrina. "I would like to dress now and get something to eat."

"I'll help you. Your clothes are all still here. The truth is that Victor has never allowed anyone to come here except me so that I might dust a little." She chattered on and on as she set about helping Alexa draw her bath and then dress and arrange her hair.

Later, outside in a beautifully tended garden, Alexa sat in meditative silence. She was sipping the last of her tea when she heard the firm stride of footsteps behind her. There was no need to turn around. She knew from memory the rhythm of those footsteps.

"Alexa, my sweetest! Welcome home!" Victor's greeting was joyful. He hurried to her side and dropped onto one knee. He grasped her right hand and lifted it tenderly to his lips. "There exist no words that even begin to tell you how happy I am that you are finally home where you belong." His eyes roved hungrily over her features, his inner desires instantly kindling as he ached to love away from her every vestige of Gregor's possession.

She gazed back at him. Now that she had rested, it was easier to remember his features. His hair was straight, parted to one side, and an intense shade of chestnut brown. His hazel eyes sparkled with vitality. His nose was prominent and straight, his mouth not very wide but with lips richly curved. She reached out to place a palm against his cheek and smiled.

"I think I had almost forgotten how beautiful you are," he whispered, leaning forward to graze her lips with his. He then stood and pulled a wrought-iron chair out to sit beside her.

Alexa continued to smile. Her heart and soul had ached abominably for him and Garogan after she had first married Gregor. Now, finally, she had returned to the place once intended to be home for all her life. For just a moment, that seemed like forever ago.

"You're so quiet. My men told me the trip back was uneventful. The only problem they encountered was a certain high-spirited woman who gave them a terrible struggle outside Toraval. I told them you probably thought they were Sifiq coming to capture you."

She half-laughed. She had indeed fought them. Hard. "Victor, why would you risk so many lives to bring me back?"

Luminous green eyes seared into his soul as he reached out to grasp both her hands. Tenderly, he kissed each fingertip before answering. "Alexa, my sweetest, have you forgotten that I promised to bring you home? I could no longer suffer the thought of your being trapped at Toraval."

She studied the expression on his face. Knowing him so well, she had no doubt there was more than his explanation revealed. What was it that he withheld from her? "You should never have taken such a risk. You endangered too many lives."

Still smiling, he accepted her softly spoken rebuke as an attempt to express her concern. "It is done now. We must be grateful that all went well. Alexa, please listen. I have great news to share with you. I just spoke with Lord Anderon and members of both provincial councils. We have researched old laws and discovered clauses that will allow us to declare your wedding to Gregor an invalid union based on the extreme circumstances he forced on you. Council members are drawing up the proper documents as we speak. Within two days, all can be completed and approved by a priest who came with Lord Anderon. Alexa, you and I can finally be married."

She stared at him in utter disbelief. "How can this be? I know of no such law."

He stood, pulling her up with him. "We can discuss the details later. Come. The day is so beautiful. I thought we might walk for a while."

Hand in hand, they strolled through the castle gardens and outside the gates. The autumn afternoon was sunny, and the temperature perfect for a long, comfortable amble along the frothy, rushing stream flowing close to the castle. Alexa stopped several times, closing her eyes and tilting her face upward to bathe in the warm rays of the sun. Victor watched her intensely, his breath catching as he reveled in sheer happiness at having her home again.

Beginning to walk again, he would slide his arm around her waist, hugging her close to his side and chuckling as they recalled humorous memories from the past. Occasionally, one of them would run off in front and, as if playing charades, would reenact some of their funnier experiences with exaggerated gestures, causing the other to laugh to the brink of tears.

Finally, they came to an outcropping of rocks that once provided a favorite place for them to sit, talk, and dream. Large stones formed a crescent around a grassy area and shielded them from anyone who might be watching from the castle. Victor sat down and patted the ground, inviting her to join him. She hesitated, then gathered her skirts before lowering herself beside him. He leaned back against the stone, sliding an arm around her and snuggling her close to him. Sighing heavily, he savored her almost forgotten sweet fragrance as she rested her head against his shoulder.

"If only I could tell you how painfully lonely I've been since I left you in Toraval," he began, his voice quiet and low. "Alexa, I never knew such pain could exist until I left you there."

"Victor, please let's not discuss it now. So much has happened. So much is changed." She questioned how she felt. Still, the remembered feel of Victor's embrace was so comforting. The sound of his voice was so familiar, so welcoming. Garogan had been home for many years and Victor the center of all her dreams.

"Sweetest, I have lived for the day when I could beg you to forgive me for what I let happen to you. I have been tormented day and night. I love you, Alexa. I love you so much." His eyes darkened, emotions of regret, sorrow, and desire mingling in their depths. To Victor, it almost seemed as if they had never been separated. Even though he knew he could not yet claim her as his own, it no longer mattered that she was still Gregor's wife. She had been his love first, and she had been promised to him.

He brought his lips to hers, pouring months of wanting into the very real presence of her in his arms. His hand slid along her arm, moving to her trim waist to pull her on top of him. She tried to push away from him, but he held her firmly with one strong arm, allowing his free hand to slide upward, cupping the enticing fullness of her breast.

She finally managed to plant a hand against the hard surface of the rock and pushed herself away from him. She gasped for breath, fearful of her sudden, raging sense of confusion. What turmoil churned inside her? Was she not home at last?

"Alexa. Sweetest, please." He reached for her, wanting her back in his arms. His eyes begged her to let him hold her, to kiss her. His soul cried out for the satisfaction only she could give.

"Victor, I cannot. This is wrong. You know that Gregor is still my husband." She jumped to her feet and, hugging her arms tightly around herself, turned away from him to stare into the distance.

Victor weakly rose on shaky legs to go and stand behind her. He resisted the desperate urge to touch her, afraid that he would be unable to restrain the tide of wanting that surged through him. "Please, Alexa, forgive me. I would never deliberately hurt you. You know that. I can only plead that I've been too long away from you. As much as I dreamed of having you back, touching you again overwhelms me."

When she turned back to him, he saw her face lovely and troubled at the same time. "Sweetest, we can finally put an end to this nightmare. You have no idea how much time and effort I've put into the research that led to that obscure clause I mentioned at the castle. I'll show you later, but those ancient documents mean we can end your marriage. Just think. In two days, you can be free of Gregor. Then we can start anew to plan our own lives."

"After all that has happened, the very idea seems unimaginable." She spoke very softly.

"Alexa, you have suffered so much at his hands. I know the real responsibility for what happened belongs to me. I only want to make you mine as you were intended to be. Then I can spend the rest of our lives making it up to you."

He grasped her hands tightly, causing her wedding ring to cut into her finger. She winced at the pressure and started to tug her hand free from his. As they both looked downward, sunshine sparkled and danced off the diamonds in the ring.

"You can take off that damned sign of his possession now. Throw it in the river if you like. You are finally free of him."

She stared at the ring and began to twist the band nervously on her finger with the fingers of her right hand. She looked up once more into Victor's eyes, shimmering with tears. Strangely, her own eyes remained dry. He had said she was free of Gregor now. Slipping the ring upward, she paused to look at the gleaming stones and wondered if she would ever really be free again. Firmly, she slid the band back into place. "You don't understand, Victor. The ring is where it belongs. I am Gregor's wife."

Staring at her in stunned, wordless dismay, Victor opened his mouth to speak, but no words came forth. Jerking his head to the side, he sucked in a deep breath. He paced back and forth several times, his mind refusing to grasp what she had just said. When he finally stopped to stare at her, his face flushed scarlet, and his eyes snapped in anger. "Alexa! In Val's name, what are you saying?"

Alexa faced him squarely. The figure she presented was solemn. "Victor, I made sacred vows before the altar of Val. Gregor made promises to me that he kept. Now, I must keep mine. Nothing can change that."

"That is absurd! He forced you to marry him! I told you what we found. Even a priest concurs with the interpretation! There is no doubt the marriage can be declared invalid." He railed at her, his voice loud with angry frustration.

"And who is this priest? One of Lord Anderon's intimidated servants?" she countered. Although the glare she received was furious, she remained undaunted, even though instinct warned her to be cautious.

"Well? Are you sure there's no other reason to risk so much to bring me back? "

"Alexa, what has gotten into you? I love you! There's nothing in the world more important to me than having you back." He reached for her, but she avoided him.

"Victor, I must be sure of the truth. Do you still believe I'm Valkana? Tell me truthfully that your motive was not to reunite with your stolen love, to promote her as Valkana, and rally people beneath that banner to embark on civil war." She stunned herself, bewildered by the unknown source of her accusation.

Victor stared at her, his chest heaving and perspiration forming on his brow in his struggle for self-control. She had loved him so deeply, and, in truth, he adored her. Still, he had not succeeded in hiding from her other less honorable needs for the emotional symbol she would represent as the love who had sacrificed herself, only to be restored to him. Moreover, he was dumbfounded by her apparent refusal to annul the marriage to Gregor.

As he stood watching her in approaching twilight, he envisioned Gregor's possession of her. Victor could almost see him touching her body and kissing her mouth. How many times before had the pitching nausea forced him to his knees, leaving him weak, sweating, and heaving. Something in Victor's mind snapped, and he grabbed her, shaking her as if she were a rag doll. "Alexa! Listen to me! You will be free of him! I swear it by all that I hold holy! You've been drugged and have no idea what you say! Listen to me!"

Expressive emerald eyes turned icy. Blood throbbed through her veins. "Victor, I tell you again. I made promises that I am honor-bound to keep. Understand me well. I am Queen of Turand and wife to King Gregor. He kept his promise to me to set you free. I must keep mine."

Victor gripped her upper arms so tightly that his fingers bruised her flesh, yet she faced him fearlessly. She was unprepared when he jerked her against him, covering her mouth with his. He forced his kiss on her, bruising her further as he reinstated his claim on her. Clasping her tightly with one arm, his free hand slid upward along the firm curves of her hips. Once again reaching her breast, he closed his hand with such squeezing pressure that he hurt her. He wanted her badly, and his rising passions left no doubt of how ready he was to take her.

Angry and unmoved by the burning desires so evident in him, she shut her eyes against the onslaught of his demands and stiffened in his arms. His use of superior physical strength only served to make her response to him more unyielding. Abruptly, he thrust her away in disgust. She had been devoid of the sensual response he had always received from her. How could this be happening? What had Gregor done to her?

Alexa stood opposite him, more confused than he. Something had just happened between them that neither could have ever foreseen. Her voice, when finally she spoke, was cold and scathing. "That is something I might once have expected from Gregor. To his credit, he has never once treated me as you just did."

Horrified, Victor reached his limit of endurance. He grabbed her again by the arm. "I have no idea what he has done to you, but you will be mine again. No matter what it takes, my darling Alexa. What you need is time." With that, he dragged her back to the castle. He then forced her up the stairs until he shoved her into her room, locking her inside.

Alexa grasped the bedpost beside her, pulling herself up from the floor where she had stumbled and fallen. She breathed in deeply several times, willing her hands to stop shaking. Her mind raced at breakneck speed, analyzing this most unexpected turn in her life and its significance for her future.

In near-total isolation, days crept by slowly. Adrina brought her meals up, leaving the trays behind without speaking. Alexa understood the intention. Valiria were typically claustrophobic, possessed by an inherent need for freedom of movement, for the outdoors. There were times when she wept piteously, her confinement overwhelming.

Sleep came with difficulty. Images from the past confused and tormented her. She recalled her life before she left on her fateful journey to Toraval. Unfolding as if on a stage, memories played through her mind with the plans, dreams, and love she once shared with Victor. Such an incredible love! They had been nearly inseparable whenever he was home. They had spent untold hours in the outdoors. Beneath the shade of tall trees, they had laughed and teased and planned for their future together. They had kissed and caressed, yearning for the day when they would be able to fulfill the heated desires burning within them.

Alexa considered the many times they had discussed a wedding date. She never doubted, even now, how much Victor had wanted to marry her. That was why she had never been able to understand all of his excuses for not finalizing a date. There had always been a critical council meeting, plots against the Sifiq to plan, or strategy sessions with the New Knights of Jared.

Her mind wandered. When Victor had resurrected the order, she had smiled indulgently, believing it to be one more way of demonstrating his love. In ancient times, the Knights of Jared had been an elite society dedicated to the protection and defense of the Valkana and the Valiria who served Turand's people. Those knights had also been the forces that had supported the royal family. With wisdom and guidance from the Order of Val, they had been instrumental in leading Turand into the great age of peace and enlightenment.

Now, with so many solitary hours of contemplation, she recognized his deeper purpose. With the power of his rhetoric, he had influenced many to join the revival of the order, convincing new members their goals were noble and their plans critical to Turand's recovery. His followers embraced his image, feeding his ego. Without hesitation, they would follow him into war.

Despite her newfound comprehension, Alexa instinctively knew that, although Victor was ambitious and craved power, he was not simply evil. He was a complex man with great good in him. Otherwise, she never could have loved him. He cared deeply about the suffering and oppression that had stretched across provincial borders into Garogan. He had taken many personal risks to help and protect others. And, she admitted, he still loved her. The complication was that she no longer believed his love to be pure for the sake of love alone. For Victor, everything fed something else. Neither his love for her nor his concern for their people could be considered altruistic. He sought higher position and recognition. Every action he took and every person he loved must fulfill a dual purpose.

Other times, her mind drifted to Toraval. Her vision in front of the Temple of Val was the first sign of the tremendous upheaval about to occur in her life. Memories of all she had lived through in Toraval played time and again through her mind. The tumultuous feelings that had raged inside her. The joy of seeing Victor that first time, of touching him, of simply knowing he was alive. Her shock when Gregor had proposed his terms for Victor's release. The subsequent despair she faced had seemed insurmountable.

Bewilderment had filled her upon seeing the realization of her vision. That first moment when Gregor took her hand, she knew their marriage was the will of Val. She puzzled and contemplated over how and why God would have given her so many years to love and dream with Victor, only to alter her destiny so drastically within only a few short days.

Reflection brought with it images of her husband. So many contradictions. His dominance, stubbornness, and temper—all countered by the tenderness and concern he always demonstrated during their intimate moments alone.

Discarding the memory of Victor's departure was impossible. She had been incapable of controlling the tears and sobs that wracked her body. Although he could have been so angry, Gregor had wrapped his arms around her, holding her until she no longer cried. Despite wanting to resist him, she had found herself unable to flee his embrace. When she stumbled, weak and spent from emotional trauma, he had lifted her into his arms and carried her into the palace. His shoulder had provided a resting place for her weary head until he settled her in the bed they had shared on their wedding night.

She remembered in detail the months that followed. So many, many days had passed when they exchanged only polite greetings or formal discussions when Gregor had been cool and distant. There had been occasional heated confrontations, but there had also been times when they had honestly conversed. Those moments had provided precious insight into the ideals and thoughts behind another very complex man.

Memories crowded in on her. The wedding. Willem's visit. The night of Stefan's party. She blinked tears from her eyes, thinking that night had ushered in transition. Slow. Quiet. Subtle. Neither had spoken much the following day. Neither had known quite what to say. Each was still vigilant, anxious, tentative. Conversations gradually increased in frequency, opening them to discover more shared interests and opinions than either might have guessed.

Alexa, isolated in her rooms in Garogan, touched her memories with near reverence. Especially the short-lived trip to Lindaval just before her abduction by the Garogan raiders. With the clarity of retrospect, she realized it had been there that this perplexing bond to her husband truly had been forged.

Their return to Toraval had been too soon, forced by events beyond their control. And, still hesitant, each had accepted barriers preventing them from giving voice to the feelings and thoughts released that afternoon at Lindaval. Instead, they remained too fearful, allowing the tide of impending history to wedge them apart so they could escape acknowledgment of emotions clamoring for recognition.

"Your thoughts reveal a troubled heart."

Alexa, startled, looked around. Adrina spoke the first words she had heard in days. "Does Victor send you to discover if imprisonment has spurred a change of mind, or do you speak from your own heart?"

Adrina flinched, her eyes immediately revealing hurt. Her longtime friend had never spoken harshly to her. "He would be angry to know I am here."

Alexa searched Adrina's face, feeling simultaneously relieved and guilty when she neither saw nor sensed any hint of deception. Standing, she offered outstretched hands to Adrina. The other woman hesitated only moments before embracing Alexa, their closeness bringing great comfort. "Please forgive me for my ill temper," Alexa whispered.

Adrina smiled gently and guided Alexa over to the bed, where they both sat cross-legged as they had done so many times over the years. "You were so far away when I entered that you did not hear me. What were you thinking?"

"Oh, Adrina, how can words describe my thoughts? So much more than thoughts are feelings and remembered images."

"Can it possibly be true that you rejected Victor's arrangements to annul your marriage to the king? I find that so hard to believe."

Alexa gazed into her friend's light brown eyes and her sweetly rounded face. Adrina felt torn between love for her brother and the close friendship the two young women had always shared. "I know what I told Victor confounds you. I know Victor must have told you about—about his final days in Toraval."

She nodded sadly. "Victor told me how shocked he was when they dragged him from his prison cell to the palace where you awaited him. He repeatedly told us how he had never felt so afraid or so proud or so loved in his life. All he talked about was how strong and how beautiful you were.

"When he told me about the day you went to his prison cell to tell him what you planned to do, he looked like he was dying inside. He said you both cried and that he had never even known such agony could exist before that day."

"Adrina, I know he was stunned. You must understand how desperate I was to see him free—to know he would be safe. I gave my word of honor that he would be freed. I loved Victor far more than my own freedom."

Adrina heard the truth yet still discerned some undefinable difference. "You once believed you would love him always. Is that no longer so?"

The question penetrated Alexa's mind like a spear as she considered all the implications the answer might hold. "Adrina, there is a part of me that will love Victor forever. We shared so much more than most people ever do. That can never change."

"But?"

"The woman I have become travels a different path. The ideals and dreams that I shared with Victor remain as strong as ever. My determination to achieve peace and freedom for our people grows daily. Only my path has changed."

"Your path? What about your heart?" Adrina's question was direct and provoking but not malicious.

Alexa expelled a heavy sigh. "And my heart? Who can say?"

"My friend, you must help me understand. Gregor has been our enemy instead of the loyal king we needed. Would you have me believe that you have come to love him instead of Victor?" Adrina shook her head in confusion, her eyes searching for comprehension.

Alexa smiled, more to herself. "You don't know him as I do. I've lived with him for almost a year now. I've watched him and listened to him. You must believe me when I tell you he is a good man. He is committed to a free Turand. His circumstances have necessitated a different approach that none of us could have ever imagined."

Adrina studied the faraway expression in her friend's eyes, worried about what she saw and wanting very much to deny its significance. "You still haven't answered my question. Do you love the king?"

Alexa's eyes dropped as she stared at her hands. Moments ago, her heart had leapt at the thought of Gregor. Why were her lips unable to speak words of love? Had Victor been right? Was there indeed something wrong with her?"

"Alexa?"

"Adrina," Alexa replied at last, "there is much locked away in my heart and soul that is too painful for me to discuss just now. Please forgive me."

Adrina shook her head in consternation. "Alexa, you need clarity. You hold too many conflicts within that require reconciliation. Our friendship is a gift from Val that I have no desire to violate. Still, Victor is my brother. I believe your heart to be different, but you need to decide the reasons for yourself. Right now, I fear more for Victor's happiness as well as for your life. You know if you agree to the annulment, Victor will marry you immediately. Your life will be safe and redirected to its original path. We both know that Victor wants to make you happy more than anything else, no matter all the politics.

"If you decide to continue your refusal to denounce the marriage, you face great danger. Think carefully, dear friend. Choose wisely. If you decide your heart belongs to the king, you turn your back on all who ever cared for you and loved you. If you choose Victor, you accept a man who will do everything possible to make you happy, and your life will be safe. Whatever your course, events are now such that you must decide quickly. And you must prepare to accept the consequences."

Adrina rose from the bed. She paused to place her hand on Alexa's shoulder, then left without another word.

Early the following day, Alexa stood on the balcony and stared out over the countryside. Fading splendors of autumn were lost on unseeing eyes. Sleep had been fitful. Images, past and present, had teased and taunted her all through the night. Adrina's words echoed in her mind. At times, she wondered if all the events of the past months might be driving her insane.

She was finally back. Garogan. Home. Only a few short months ago, she had longed for the inviting warmth and familiarity of the south of Turand. Dreams had ushered in long-forgotten memories of times spent with her friends and, most significantly, with Victor. Even now, she found it impossible to deny the bond they shared.

Yet, she could not forget the ring circling her finger or the vows she had made. Other than the fact she had given her word, there should be no compelling reason for her to remain loyal to her husband. He had turned her entire life upside down and torn her away from the man she had loved.

Still, the vision given by Val was hauntingly clear. Besides that, Gregor had been more than just kind to her. She thought again of the gradual transformation over the past two months. They had become more than civil, more than polite. Seeds of friendship, however tentative, had taken root. Then, there had been Stefan's birthday. And Lindaval.

A knock sounded at the door. Alexa turned, staring dumbly. Another knock came, a little louder, and the door slowly began to open. She was surprised to see Victor standing there.

"May I enter?" His voice was solemn.

She nodded in response. Wordlessly, she watched as he left the door slightly ajar and approached her, finally placing his hands on her shoulders. "Oh, my sweetest, I am so sorry you've had to endure this confinement. My heart has ached." He pulled her close, relieved when she did not resist.

She rested her head against the firmness of his shoulder and felt his arms tighten around her. She inhaled his well-remembered scent and felt his breath warm and soft against her neck.

"I came to take you down to breakfast. Later, if you like, we can go outside for a walk."

Pulling away from him, she gazed into the golden depths of his eyes and saw sadness mingled with hope. Finding no words to answer him, she only nodded in agreement.

Later, she finally addressed him as they finished a generous breakfast of eggs, smoked meat, sweet rolls, and fresh fruits. "Victor, tell me. What is happening? Why did you allow me to be locked away so long? You know..."

"How difficult confinement is for Valiria to bear? Yes, I know, but we thought it best for you."

"Why?"

"We believe you were likely drugged at the palace. You weren't yourself. The physicians recommended at least ten days of isolation to ensure your system could be purged. Not a week has passed. I could stand it no longer. I knew you must be desperate." His eyes studied her closely as his hand reached out to cover hers.

Her eyelids closed as she breathed in deeply, dazed by a weakness new to her. "What now?" she whispered.

"First, I have with me all the transcripts of the laws we discovered. You need to see them yourself. Alexa, read them carefully. You will see that a forced marriage such as yours can be invalidated not only under the laws of the nation but under the sacred laws of Val as well."

His voice grew strident with the same convincing tone he used in many of his speeches. As he explained, he opened a portfolio filled with documents and placed the papers in front of her.

She read slowly, absorbing the legal content and the powerful impact it could deliver to her life. There existed no doubt. If these documents were indeed authentic, all she had to do was attest to the circumstances of her marriage, and, upon affixing her signature, she could be free.

"Well?" The tone of his voice conveyed his anxiety.

She gazed solemnly at the papers strewn before her. "I'm not sure what to say. Are you positive these are genuine?"

"Absolutely, Sweetest. There is no doubt." Victor's heart skipped a beat as he studied her reaction. He needed her so badly. He hesitated to push her. Instead, he rose from his chair and, grasping her hand, drew her to her feet.

She allowed him once again to embrace her. Without resistance, she accepted his kiss. Victor's lips parted from hers, a gentle smile lighting his face. "Let's go outside."

He led her to the front entrance, stopping to drape a lightweight woolen cape around her shoulders. In a loving gesture, he lifted the hood over her head. Donning a coat of his own, he held her close to his side as they walked out into the crisp morning air. Bright sunshine assaulted her eyes. Fresh, fragrant air filled her lungs and lifted her spirits. Victor grinned adoringly, his heart rejoicing that she was home at last. With his arm around her waist, he held her firmly and possessively. They walked together as they had done so many times before.

Conversation was sparing. She was too relieved to be outside again, the glories of the fall day reviving her, body and soul. His occasional endearments were poignant reminders of hours and days spent together throughout the years. Several times, he stopped, and they kissed.

When finally they returned to the castle, nearly the entire day had slipped by without either being conscious of how much time had elapsed. She was caught in a near meditative state. She appeared content, and happiness filled him as he luxuriated in her closeness after so much time apart.

Reentering the castle, they discarded their wraps. Victor still held onto her hand, unwilling to turn her loose. They went to the kitchen and sat together while servants placed plates of fruits, cheeses, and rolls in front of them.

Finally, Victor suggested she go upstairs to rest. He escorted her up but, before opening the door to her rooms, found he could no longer resist his need for her. His hands stroked her hair as his eyes devoured the loveliness of her face. His arms caught her, imprisoning her in a desperate embrace. He couldn't hold her tightly enough. When his mouth crushed hers, all his grief of losing her to another man surged forth.

She pressed tightly against him and returned his kiss with all the ardent love she had ever known for him. Her kiss was just as he remembered. Victor needed every shred of self-restraint to avoid carrying her through that door into the privacy beyond, where he wanted desperately to make love to her. Forcing himself to break the union of their kiss, he was immensely satisfied to see her reaction. Tears brimmed in her eyes, and her lips quivered.

"Sweetest Alexa, I never stopped loving you, and I never will. Tomorrow. Tomorrow morning we will go to the chapel, and you can sign the papers. We will free you from him so we can be married at last. I love you."

She smiled wordlessly, touching trembling fingertips to his cheek and tracing the line of his jaw. Yes, so long ago, she had loved him enough to sacrifice everything for him. Now, she recalled how precious he had always been to her. Her lips parted again as she sought not only his kiss but also reconnection to the safe refuge he had always been for her.

She then slipped inside her room, closing the door behind her. Upon entering, she slowly walked around, touching smoothly varnished wooden furniture, richly textured velvet drapes, and matching bedspread. She fingered carved wooden frames surrounding delicate oil paintings. This had been her haven, her home. At long last, she could make it so again.

Much later, Alexa requested a simple dinner of soup, freshly baked rolls, and milk to be brought to her room. Fatigue filled her, and tomorrow promised to be an unprecedented and momentous occasion. First, she wished to meditate and then rest.

After eating, she changed into her nightgown before sitting on the bed to prepare for her meditation. Whispering a prayer for protection, she then began her chant and entered a deep trance. Her soul floated free and unfettered. Great peace invaded her being as Val's presence surrounded her, his words filling her mind. Later, when she tried to center herself to emerge from the trance, Val maintained his hold on her. Somewhere, Alexa was vaguely aware of her body floating before settling gently on the bed. Val was bestowing the gift of healing sleep as she had not known in years. She smiled her gratitude as he left her.

Alexa slept peacefully for hours before dreams invaded. Victor's image hovered close, just beyond her reach. Behind him stood her husband. His dark eyes were glazed and grief-stricken, his face etched with deep lines of sorrow. She wanted to go to him, to comfort him. Victor blocked her way.

Splashing water sent swirling mist into the air around her. Heated stones were smooth beneath her feet. Sunshine warmed her skin. Her husband's face searched for her from the water's edge. She was sure she called out his name, but he seemed not to hear her.

She began to toss in her sleep. Something inside her ached. Victor's face hovered once more in front of her. She spun round and round,

listening, seeking. Searching eyes found Gregor, sitting astride his great stallion, his eyes scanning the land before him. She turned again, saw the bowstring pull back, heard the ping as the arrow released.

"No! Gregor, no!" She bolted upright in bed, gasping his name into the darkness of night. Finally, she understood. Despite having her eyes squeezed tightly shut, she saw him so clearly. Mounted on his majestic horse. Tall, erect, in total command. His thoughtful countenance as he studied book after book of history and strategy. His face, bronzed and handsome. His lips, full and sensual. His eyes, dark and passionate. She envisioned him so distinctly.

"Gregor…" His name tore from the depths of her soul. "Gregor. Oh, Gregor, I love you." She lay back, weeping into the cushioned softness of her pillow. How could she have doubted? How had she not known? Val had brought them together, knowing how much alike they were, how much they needed one another. She pressed the back of her fist against her lips, reverently kissing her wedding ring and what it now represented to her. Stunned, she finally fell asleep again, whispering his name.

When morning arrived, she rose early. Sitting in an old rocker rescued from the burned ruins of her childhood home, she rocked back and forth, the motion calming her. She knew this morning would be difficult, and she was uncertain what to expect. She had no concept of time, no idea of how long she had sat rocking when Adrina entered the room.

"Alexa! What in the world? You haven't even begun to dress! Victor, the priest, and Lord Anderon have already left for the chapel. We'll be late!"

Alexa stopped rocking and lifted her eyes to meet those of her friend. Emerald fires blazed, and Adrina shuddered. "I'm not going to the chapel."

"What?" Adrina gasped in shock. "In Val's great name, why not? Alexa!"

Alexa's expression remained tranquil, resolute. "I said I am not going to the chapel, Adrina. My marriage to Gregor is a sacred union. I will not consent to the annulment."

Adrina's face revealed utter disbelief. "You cannot be serious! Not after yesterday! I saw you with Victor. It was as if you had never been apart! What has happened to you?"

Alexa smiled. "Today, I finally comprehend Val's will."

"What does Val's will have to do with this? Alexa, you cannot be serious! Victor loves you! He needs you desperately! Especially now! War is imminent. You know that. You were so happy yesterday."

Alexa rose from the rocker, approached Adrina, and grasped her shaking hands. The expression on her face was serene. "Adrina, I cannot explain to you more than the fact that my vows to Gregor are sacred commitments I intend to keep—because I wish to do so."

Adrina's face flushed with continued disbelief that mixed with fear. "Alexa, I am sorely afraid of how Victor will react when he hears this. I told you before. Please reconsider. You jeopardize your life."

Alexa stepped away from Adrina before turning her back to stare outside at the broad, sunlit meadows and the shadowy forest beyond. Her insides quivered as she anticipated further confinement. She looked around again at Adrina's bewildered face.

"Adrina, I accept that my decision places my life in grave danger. If not from Victor's jealous anger, then I entertain no doubts that Lord Anderon will demand my execution as a traitor."

"Then why risk your life when you could surely be happy again with Victor! You could!"

Alexa shook her head, smiling enigmatically. "No, Adrina, I could never find happiness again with Victor. That will never be."

"I don't understand. How can you just refuse after all that has happened? You cannot do this! Not to Victor! And, yes, Lord Anderon will surely call for your execution!" Adrina's voice trembled, and tears slid down scarlet cheeks.

"Adrina, if it is Val's will, then I shall face execution and death as Queen of Turand and loyal wife to King Gregor." Her words were spoken with conviction, the finality in her voice like a leaden weight descending on Adrina's heart. Alexa smiled serenely as she reached out to squeeze Adrina's hand one final time. She then returned to the old chair, where she sat and began to rock slowly to her own inner rhythm.

Adrina backed out of the room, her eyes never leaving the face of the old friend, who was now more like a stranger. How in the world would she explain this to Victor? What would she say?

Chapter 10

Toraval

Centuries earlier, the nation's laws had mandated a biennial conference of representatives from each of Turand's twenty provinces. This would be the first National Council scheduled in more than two decades, and preparations for the session dragged. Delegates argued incessantly over every detail of the agenda, even seating arrangements.

"Ladies! Gentlemen! We shall recess until tomorrow. Consider this. Either you reach agreement by tomorrow noon, or I shall exercise my right as monarch to dictate the details of conduct for how this council will proceed." Gregor's voice reverberated throughout the council chamber, his frustration and anger evident as he stood and exited the hall.

Stefan also rose, but he faced the surprised delegates. His voice was quiet and imposing. "This is the first time during this entire session that all of you have simultaneously paid attention to our king. King Gregor has taken enormous risks with the Sifiq to reinstate Council. Yet too many of you have done nothing but bicker among yourselves like irresponsible, petty authorities instead of the premier leaders of the great provinces you represent."

Seeing that he had gained their attention, he pressed on. "Our king has patiently and dutifully attended these preliminary sessions at great personal cost while we still try to determine with complete certainty the fate of our queen. I ask for your compassion and your cooperation. If Council is to occur as scheduled, it is essential that you lay aside all these personal and egotistical arguments that have impeded final arrangements. We must achieve this primary goal before we can proceed for the benefit of all Turand. I expect a more reasonable and cooperative meeting tomorrow. If not, the king's command will be implemented. Good evening."

Stefan presented a dignified and powerful image as he purposefully strode from the chamber, followed by his aides. The delegates who remained behind were startled, some ashamed. Others harrumphed at Stefan's audacity. Most respected the manner in which he spoke and the validity of his remarks. There was little conversation as they assembled their portfolios and prepared to leave the conference tables.

Having instructed his aides to go on to dinner before preparing for the next day's session, Stefan headed straight for the palace library. He knew his friend well and never once doubted where he would find him. He stopped only long enough to receive and read a sealed dispatch handed to him by a servant.

The polished double doors stood slightly open. A single oil lamp had been lit and shed golden light into the room. Two large upholstered chairs faced the great stone fireplace. Although the library held a heavy chill, no fire burned in the grate.

Stefan paused before approaching the chair to his right. Gregor sat back against the high chair. His longish hair layered backward untidily, evidence of his occasional habit of running nervous fingers through the thick locks. His eyelids were closed, his countenance sorrowful. His elbows perched on the arms of the chair, his hands clasped together as if in prayer.

Stefan exhaled slowly, calming himself as he placed an outstretched hand gently on Gregor's shoulder. His grip was a firm, comforting gesture.

"My patience suffers greatly, Stefan. It requires too much effort to control my temper in the face of such ridiculous foolishness."

"Perhaps I can offer a somewhat positive note after such a trying day."

Gregor sighed heavily. "Are you going to tell me you have shamed them into submission?"

Stefan noted that Gregor neither moved nor opened his eyes. "I believe I can assure you that tomorrow will go much more smoothly. But, more importantly, I just received a dispatch. Alexa is safe—at Garogan Castle."

Gregor squeezed his eyes tightly together. So this is how he would lose her. She was home now. Victor certainly would have discovered that he could legally arrange an end to the marriage. Gregor's stomach lurched. Victor would not wait to take her as his wife.

"Gregor?" Stefan ached at the grief he saw etched into Gregor's face.

"Stefan, please leave me. I need time alone with my thoughts."

As Stefan closed the library doors, the unmistakable sound of sobs followed him, haunting him as he walked to his suite for the night.

"Honorable delegates, I commend you for your wisdom and your expediency in the completion of our agenda for this auspicious National Council. We shall meet again when National Council convenes, and I trust we will achieve new direction for Turand."

The many representatives applauded their king's words of farewell. Most were, at long last, optimistic that they might begin to regain some of what had been lost despite continued Sifiq domination. Some were skeptical yet willing to contribute their efforts because the alternative was to continue the constant drain of spirits as well as resources. There were also those who were noncommittal, secretly backers of the rebellious approach favored by the Garogan and Tasa Coast provinces.

No matter their political agenda, not a single man or woman present could deny the strain clearly showing on Gregor's face. Dark circles puffed beneath his eyes. His mouth was taut, his face tense and drawn. The disappearance of his queen demanded a heavy toll.

Complicating circumstances was knowledge shared by a few of those present. Secretly, a guerrilla army had been assembled, armed, and trained. Many were Turandans who had been imprisoned by the Sifiq and supposedly executed. While preparations for the upcoming National Council were winding down, that army was hidden in the largest ports in northern Turand.

Sifiq advisers and soldiers in Toraval were busy preparing to head to the coast. There, they would exchange places with fresh troops and return home. In their arrogance, they paid little heed to this National Council business, considering it an amusing game for the benefit of the Turandans to appear more important than they were. They were confident that Gregor was their ally, his selfish greed key to their continuing occupation. Besides, Turandans were too weak to offer much resistance. Most important to the Sifiq were the ships arriving in the north to take them home while bringing replacement Sifiq soldiers to control this conquered land.

A small contingent force would remain while the main body would journey northward. As they left, none dreamed that Turandans were preparing traps that would sink Sifiq ships too far from shore for the replacement soldiers to swim to safety. Guerrilla fighters would be entrenched, awaiting the arrival of the unsuspecting occupation army.

Lord LeAndro Karanan, a distinguished man in his late fifties, approached Gregor to request private audience, which the king granted immediately. Leaving the others, Lord Karanan draped his arm around Gregor's broad shoulders. "My friend, the weight of our world rests on you this day. Tell me how you have managed to cope with it all."

Gregor glanced sideways into his godfather's wise, mature face. "Papino, you seem quite calm yourself, especially considering your home province will bear the initial brunt of war."

The two men entered a private drawing room and closed the door. Gregor moved to a large cabinet, opened the doors, and withdrew crystal snifters and a bottle of brandy. The two men shared a drink, each cognizant of the significant course upon which they were embarking.

"Have you any news of the queen?" Lord Karanan's question was concerned and sympathetic.

Gregor turned away from him, fighting the choking lump in his throat. "She's at Garogan Castle," he replied flatly.

"I thought that would be so. What else have you learned?" He probed gently, aware not only of the potential political ramifications but of his godson's apparent emotional distress.

Gregor shook his head ever-so-slightly. "Nothing. Absolutely nothing more than that."

Lord Karanan was unable to hide his surprise. "With her in Garogan, I would have expected immediate announcement not only of her return but of the dissolution of your marriage. I find it quite curious that Lord Garogan hasn't already proclaimed their marriage."

"As do I. Alexa is gone almost two weeks now, and there have been no such declarations. They haven't even officially confirmed her return."

"Gregor, I must leave now. I wish to be near home with all that looms before us. I shall pray for you and for our country. And, if you should need, I can leave part of my private guard to accompany you should you decide to ride to Garogan."

Gregor's face reflected his appreciation. "You read my mind, dear Papino."

The two men embraced. "If she were my wife, that is precisely what I would do. All I ask is that you be very careful. Right now, Turand needs you more than ever."

~

My beloved husband,

I write to you with great hope that, somehow, my words will reach you. I know our relationship has been far from that which a husband and wife should share. My disgust for you ran so deeply that it blinded me to the truth. So much did I lose in those early months when you had stolen me from the life I had planned, forcing me away from the love I believed was mine.

Now, all has changed. As a political prisoner, I have time to relive all that has happened. Time to ponder realities obscured by misguided passions. I long to see your face - even as your image burns clearly in my memory. Alas, I fear I shall die before I can satisfy this heart's desire.

Dearest Gregor, it is unbelievable sorrow to know that I may never be able to tell you how much I have come to love you. Gregor, I have seen so much pain, so much grief in my lifetime. Most of it was the result of Royal Decrees. I had no way of knowing those edicts were not the work of the Royal Family. I could not have known the suffering and control your father was forced to endure at the hands of the Sifiq. None of us knew. All we knew was that your father, our king, stood side by side with the enemy and watched as our people became more and more oppressed. Later, it appeared to us that you did the same.

Time to ponder. Time to face truth and destiny. If, through some miracle, these words reach you after my death, you must know that, honestly, I love you.

Gregor, my shame sickens me. I am dismayed at how wrong I was to have believed in Victor and his New Knights of Jared. I loved Victor. I risked all to be part of his dreams, his ideals. As you well know, I even sacrificed all that he might have his life to continue to give spark to those dreams and ideals. The words - his words! The power of his rhetoric! How he moved my soul! I know neither when nor how, but he changed, and I never saw."

She glanced up from the paper and gazed out the window above the desk where she sat. Tears brimmed in her eyes, threatening to spill over in a fresh flood of anguish. "Gregor..." His name escaped from her lips as a tormented whisper ripped from her soul. Floodgates crashed open, and tears splashed from her cheeks onto the paper, smudging final words she had begun to write.

She rose and began to pace the limited confines of her rooms, her prison. At last, she sank to the floor beside her bed. Resting her head on her arms, she waited for this fresh wave of despair to subside.

"Alexa? Alexa!" She awoke to the sound of her name as someone gripped her by her shoulder, shaking her firmly but gently. Her brain was full of gray haze. Her body was stiff and chilled. "Alexa, wake up!"

Her eyelids fluttered before opening reluctantly. Sandy dryness scraped and burned her eyes. "Victor," she whispered hoarsely.

"Here, let me help you." He supported her with his arm firmly tucked around her waist and lifted her from the cold stone floor. She swayed slightly as he then guided her onto the bed.

She sat without protest, unwilling to expend more energy trying to stand. Her body wavered for a few moments before she was able to gain complete control. "Thank you, Victor. I'm all right now."

"All right?" he scoffed. "Look at you! Never in your life have you been able to endure being enclosed this way! None of your kind ever could! What will it take to bring you to your senses? Why will you not admit that you've been drugged? Alexa, for your own good, you must denounce your position. Your life is in danger, and you behave as if you don't give a damn!"

His newest verbal attack was immediate and bitter. In reaction, Alexa's head shot up. Unexpected strength flowed throughout her body. Anger and challenge burned fiercely in the depths of her green eyes. "Denounce my position? I am Gregor's wife! How am I to deny that fact?"

Victor's body shook with shivers that ran the length of his spine. His hazel eyes glittered with renewed fury and hatred as he stared back at her. His lips tightened in disgust as he wondered how many times she had lain in Gregor's arms. His heart contracted painfully as, yet again, the momentary image of Gregor possessing her raced through his mind, his entire psyche newly aghast at the idea of her being Gregor's wife. Still, he managed to compose himself, and he dropped down before her on one knee.

Victor gazed into her troubled face. When he finally spoke, the tone of his voice was soothing. "Alexa, I know you're his wife. I also know why. You cannot deny the extreme circumstances of your marriage. You know as well as I that he manipulated you into this marriage. Alexa, Sweetest, he shamelessly used marriage as a way to violate you."

She swallowed against the tightness in her throat. If she closed her eyes, she could remember vividly the unbelievable stress she had endured that day. "That was a long time ago, Victor. Everything has changed." Her voice was barely more than a whisper.

Victor's patience wavered. "I do not accept that you are willingly the queen of that bastard!" he spat out.

"He is not a bastard! And you have no choice but to accept. I am Gregor's wife and his queen!"

"How can he have poisoned you so? You of all people! Alexa, you are blessed with the spirit of the Old Ones. You alone in our generation—in our century—can bring down the power of the Sifiq! You have that power! How can you turn your back to your people and to the good to which you are sworn?" Victor jumped to his feet and paced angrily in front of her.

She also stood, strengthened in ways she did not yet comprehend. "Victor, you see nothing any longer beyond your own quest for power and position. I will be no man's tool to use for gaining personal power."

He reached out and grabbed her arms, shaking her in exasperation. Abruptly releasing her, he stared into her face. His voice dropped to an intense and demanding whisper. "Alexa, face reality. Why do you think you're still alive? How long do you think I can prevent your execution? How long?"

Her voice was calm and firm when she answered. "Victor, the past is gone. I loved you so much that I gave up everything to gain your freedom. I believed in you that much! Now you threaten me with execution. From my viewpoint, you and your New Knights of Jared are no different from the Sifiq. You are an insult to the tradition of Jared and a farce!"

Her head snapped back from the force with which he slapped her.

"You fool! Don't you see? I must play the game! How else am I to achieve the goal of freeing our people?"

"Play the game?" she countered, ignoring the trickle of blood from her swelling lip. "Play the game? By abduction? By torturing? By killing slowly and painfully?"

"Have they not done so to our people? Even to your own family? Have you forgotten?"

She grimaced. "I will never forget. But neither will I compromise my own dignity and integrity. I refuse to degrade myself to the level of those deathmongers. I will not become a hypocrite by committing such atrocities. I refuse to become that which I hate most!"

Victor's chest heaved as he faced her, uncertain about how to respond. He needed her desperately. He loved her. Yes, he still did. Even more, he needed her powers, her abilities—those gifts she had not yet acknowledged. Without them, he would never succeed in assuming leadership of the country. He decided on a new course.

"Alexa, I am sorry. Please, Sweetest, forgive me. I beg you. My heart aches with all that has happened. I hurt every time I think of what you lived through for my sake. I do understand—more than you think. You gave your word to be his wife to secure my release from Zenox Prison. You must understand. Your word was forced from you, but you're far away from the capital now. You're finally safe, and he can no longer hurt you. No one will ever blame or criticize you. You can renounce him and all he ever did to you. People will praise your courage and your devotion to me. You were my betrothed, and you gave yourself in exchange for my life. Such a cry to unite our people! You are returned from Gregor's clutches and reunited with me. No one will ever again think of you as his wife."

Alexa's expression was pensive as she listened to the convincing power in his voice. She remembered other times when the passion in his words had been her anchor and her inspiration. "No one?" she questioned, her emerald eyes locked on his.

"No one," he confirmed confidently, convinced he was finally reaching her.

"No one. Except me. I will forever think of myself as Gregor's wife."

Victor stared at her in disbelief and drew a deep breath of exasperation. When he spoke again, his voice trembled slightly. "My dearest Alexa, what has that monster done to you?"

Alexa gazed into Victor's eyes. She smiled as her mind drifted momentarily to the night before her abduction. Gregor had come to her bedchamber, but he had not made love to her. Touching her had seemed all he needed. His touch had been so different, at once tender and firm—almost questioning in the silent darkness. Perhaps he had sensed the change she was so reluctant to admit.

"Well?" Victor's demand was more like a plea interrupting her reverie.

Her reply was simple, profound. "He loved me."

Victor had been totally unprepared for her response. Bile rose, bitterly burning his throat. Minutes ticked by in silence as the two glared at each other. He faltered first, turning to stalk from the room.

Hearing the desolate sound as he locked the heavy door from the outer corridor, she whispered to herself, "He loved me. I only pray that I have not learned too late that I love him."

Chapter 11

Inside the palace library, Gregor leaned over a long mahogany table, intently studying the plans of Garogan Castle. His mind recorded every minute detail in the drawings strewn before him. He was determined to memorize every corner, every door, every turn into every passage. His plan must be perfect. Too much was at stake, more than he could bear to lose. He paused briefly, straightening his back. Every inch of his body ached with fatigue. He massaged his temples to ease the painful throbbing in his head. Never in his life could he remember being so tired.

"Gregor, my friend, you must rest." The voice belonged to Stefan Sidano, the only real friend he had ever known.

"Of course, Stefan, I will. I only hoped to devise a better scheme if I studied these drawings a while longer. Tomorrow is the beginning of what may prove an impossible task. I know I need some rest."

Stefan assessed his friend with growing concern. Gregor's face was pale. Dark circles rimmed his eyes. His black hair was disheveled from the many times he had pushed his fingers through it. "Gregor, please stop for now and get some sleep. You'll feel stronger, and surely you'll think more clearly tomorrow."

Gregor placed his palms flat against the table and rested his weight there. His eyes mirrored the depths of his worry as he took one long, last look at the architectural plans. He raised those dark eyes, filled with questions and pleading, to his friend. "Stefan, why do you think they've made no proclamations? Surely they must be eager to announce Alexa's return to Garogan Province. Garogan is the center of their power. As the last openly declared Valiria, she commands the people's imagination. Many even believe she may be Valkana. The people love her. They would surely rally behind her."

Stefan was contemplative. Gregor's observations were all true, and the situation was perplexing. "I have no concrete answers."

Secretly, he suspected the reason no communiqué had been forthcoming, but he felt this was not the time to voice his suspicions. Stefan's post as Gregor's chief adviser allowed him great freedom. He studied everyone and rarely missed even the most fleeting expressions. In fact, he prayed his speculations were true. Moreover, his spies were in Garogan, trying to ferret out more information at this very moment. His hesitation to discuss the matter had been that Gregor's distress might cause him to react irrationally.

Gregor's voice was filled with anxiety. His eyes revealed simple hope. "Your opinion?"

"May I speak candidly?" Stefan badly wanted to avoid answering his king. However, it was impossible to ignore Gregor's desperate desire for some sort of reassurance.

"Stefan, you know there is never a need for such formalities between us. You are my friend—the one person I trust."

Stefan sighed thoughtfully. Gray eyes expressed appreciation for Gregor's confidence. "My opinion." He stopped, inhaling deeply. "The revolutionary movement loses appeal and momentum. Recent changes begin to improve general conditions. People realize something is happening—that we must strengthen ourselves before we can hope to unify against the Sifiq. Garogan remains the strongest and most dangerous revolutionary stronghold. Alexa was close to the movement because of her relationship with Lord Garogan. Now that she has returned, she has not openly championed their cause. Instead, she remains curiously silent."

"And why do you think she is silent?"

Stefan shrugged his shoulders noncommittally. "I cannot be certain. She gave her word of honor when she committed to be your wife if you freed Lord Garogan. You kept your side of the bargain. Alexa is faithful to the ancient traditions of Val. She would be unlikely to break such a promise as she made."

He paused, carefully considering his next words. "I believe no communiqué has been forthcoming because Alexa refuses to renounce your marriage."

Gregor grew more pensive. "Why? In Garogan, she can renounce the marriage and be hailed a heroine. Her word was given to the people before it was given to me. She was also promised in marriage to Garogan years ago, and it was her love for him that brought her here. There, she is free to return to him."

After a long moment, Stefan could offer only that which he suspected to be true. "Perhaps she does not wish to end the marriage."

"Can that be so, my friend? The past year has not been happy for her. She was not here by her own volition." His rich voice filled with anguish as he struggled to cope with guilt.

Stefan moved beside Gregor and placed a hand on his friend's shoulder. "True. She did not come or stay by desire. However, something has changed recently. She has been different. Not resigned, my friend, but tranquil. Content even. Surely you must have noticed."

"Or imagined it? Have you ever wanted something so very badly that you were afraid of seeing it there simply for the wanting?" Briefly, Gregor recalled the night before the abduction. He had held her. She, too, had embraced him, and it seemed she had settled herself as close to him as she possibly could. He shook his head slightly, pushing away the bittersweet memory.

"Have you considered the possibility of wanting something so much that you could make it happen?" Stefan countered.

"Is such a thing possible?"

Stefan smiled. "You do really love her."

Gregor was never surprised by any observation Stefan made. Especially not now. "For all the good it does me. Yes, I love her. Not only do I love her, I almost fear this obsessive need I have for her. From the very beginning, I coveted her unique magnetism. The moment I saw her, I wanted her as my queen. I knew the people would adore her, and I think I hoped to draw some of that adulation to myself. I never dreamed that circumstances would explode the way they did. Inside, I was wanton in my desire for her. When she offered herself in exchange for Garogan..." He sighed heavily. "I was shameless when I offered marriage as the condition for his freedom. Only now that I face losing her do I begin to realize how much I have come to love her. I find myself the fool caught in his own trap."

"Gregor, you're no fool. I am uncertain how to convince you, but I can tell you something that perhaps I should have told you sooner. When we were surrounded in the countryside, Alexa struggled and fought so hard that I feared she would be hurt. Only when the Garogans threatened me and the other riders did she stop. Before they left with her, she demanded to speak to me for just a moment. I was surprised when they allowed her to do so. She appeared so incredibly strong. She asked not that I tell you but that I make you understand that she had no part in this—that she was leaving because she had no other choice."

Gregor gazed at Stefan in utter astonishment. His breathing quickened as his heart began to throb violently within his chest. He felt his entire body tremble. His hands grasped Stefan's arms tightly. "Tell me truthfully, Stefan. Please tell me this is not just an attempt to console me."

Stefan's eyes did not waver as he regretted not telling Gregor sooner. "I speak only the truth, my friend. If we want to bring her back, you must go to rest now."

～

Dark brown eyes misted as Gregor slid sensitive fingertips along the silken fabric of Alexa's nightgown. He stood inside her dimly lit suite, sensing remnants of her presence and knowing it had been self-inflicted punishment to enter her chambers instead of his own. He needed sleep. A bitter laugh filled the room. He wrapped strong fingers around the tall post of her canopied bed and leaned his forehead against the cool wood. Sleep was not his most pressing need; he desperately needed his wife.

Long moments passed in silence. Weariness was overwhelming, and he finally slid beneath the thick coverlets on her bed. He tossed about restlessly, unable to find a comfortable position. In the distance, he heard temple bells sounding their midnight toll. Bells that had been silent for generations had started to ring sporadically just after their marriage. Mysteriously, they had begun to ring at midnight ever since her abduction. He could no longer resist the flow that wet his face and pillow. Gregor turned on his side and wrapped his arms around her pillow, burying his face into its deep softness and inhaling faint lilac scent. His heart screamed in agony for her as his lips whispered her name into unrelenting, lonely darkness.

～

Alexa moved away from the window, her contemplation disturbed by the rattle of the lock in the door. She dreaded that Victor might return. Her face still hurt from the fresh blow he had struck her the night before. She watched in silence as Adrina entered with a tray containing a soup tureen, rolls, fruit, and tea that she placed on a stand. Alexa turned and resumed her gaze out the window, aware that Adrina had come to stand directly behind her.

"Why do you not face me?" Adrina's voice was unusually demanding. Alexa allowed a tense moment to pass before replying in a calm, controlled voice that sharply contrasted with Adrina's. "There is little left for me to say. I know the path before me, and I accept wherever it leads."

Adrina's body trembled with anger, and she reached out, spinning Alexa around to face her. Usually calm and reserved, Adrina was furious as she slipped into a vehement outburst. "I cannot believe what you're doing! Why? How can you treat Victor this way? I don't know what you told him. Whatever it was, you have devastated him! You brutally broke the heart of a man who loves you more than anything in this world! I don't understand you at all. I simply cannot believe you could have loved him so much only to turn your back on him now!"

Alexa reached out to touch Adrina, only to watch her jerk away in disgust. Alexa chose to remain silent.

"Alexa, why won't you answer me? Is it possible you might be ashamed? Victor saved your life! He gave you everything—his home after yours was destroyed! His protection, his love! Now, you throw it all back in his face! You repay him with betrayal. How can you do this to him?"

Alexa finally answered. "Adrina, I am forever grateful to Victor for all he gave me. I remind you that I also made my own terrible sacrifices to save his life. All that is behind us now, supplanted by the will of Val, to whom I have sworn my ultimate loyalty."

"What does Val have to do with this?" Adrina nearly shrieked.

Alexa inhaled a deep breath. "Oh, Adrina. If only I could explain."

"I only want you to explain one thing. What did you say that hurt my brother so much?"

"I only told him the truth," came the simple answer. "I love my husband."

Adrina, in shock, drew her hand back and slapped Alexa full in the face. Her eyes grew wide with disbelief as she watched fresh blood ooze from Alexa's already cut lip. Alexa winced against the burning sensation in her bruised face and felt the soreness creeping toward the corner of her eye. Still, she showed no sign of submission.

"Adrina, leave me. The divide between us is now too deep. Go." Her words were a commanding dismissal. Turning back around, Alexa stared out the window once more.

꩜

Days later, Adrina returned to the rooms where Alexa remained a prisoner. A chambermaid, carrying fresh linens, accompanied her. The maid quickly removed blankets and sheets from the bed and took used towels from the attached bathroom. Everything else was left in the expectation that Alexa could make her own bed and put away the remaining linens.

Adrina waited in silence while the servant completed her tasks and left. "You don't look well," Adrina said, her voice aloof.

"How long have I been in Garogan now?" Alexa asked, seeming to ignore the question as she set about placing fresh sheets on her bed.

"Nearly four weeks. I believe twenty-five days, to be more exact. Why?"

"Then I've been away from home for almost five weeks. I've been kept in virtual isolation most of that time. No wonder my appearance doesn't meet your approval. You know how unhealthy it is for Valiria to be imprisoned this way. Add that to my lovely visit last evening with Lord Anderon. All I can say is that I am more surprised I look as well as I do."

Adrina paid closer attention to Alexa, whose face had been partially concealed by her long hair. Dark blue and purple bruises showed on both her cheeks. Her left eye was particularly dark and swollen, resulting from one of Lord Anderon's more convincing arguments being laid over blows already meted out by Victor and Adrina. Alexa's mouth was also badly swollen, resulting from the many times she had been struck in the face. Despite painful disappointment in her old friend, Adrina felt deep remorse for the violence being inflicted on Alexa.

"I attended a birth last night, so I had no knowledge of Lord Anderon's visit."

Alexa flashed a fiery, spirited glance at Adrina. "Adrina, understand this. No matter what any of you says or does to me, nothing changes. I love my husband. I love him, and even if Lord Anderon carries through on his threat of execution, I shall die screaming that you will never destroy my love for Gregor."

Adrina cringed at the soft-spoken fury Alexa's words flung at her. "Alexa, you must believe me. I never imagined things could get so out of control. Victor took off at breakfast yesterday and has yet to return. He is completely morose and withdrawn.

"Making matters worse, Lord Anderon has instructed his retinue to begin preparations to return to the capital of Tasa Coast Province. He plans to take you with him. For execution."

"Take me from Garogan? I think not, Adrina. I may be a prisoner, but I can still make myself heard to someone, somehow. If you can manage to find enough backbone, give Victor a message. Tell him if he is man enough to scheme with Anderon to execute me, then tell him to prove how much a man he is by executing me here, in Garogan. At least be merciful enough to let me die in a place of my own choosing." Alexa's voice was sharp, her expression contemptuous.

"Alexa…" Adrina started to speak but choked. Alexa had never spoken so caustically to her. In fact, Adrina could never recall a time when Alexa had sounded so bitter or so angry.

Alexa dismissed a fleeting wish for time to mend all this heartache, all these broken treasures of friendships. Patience drained from her. "Adrina, say nothing. If you can honor whatever remnants might exist of a once-beloved friendship, get my message to Victor. For now, I prefer to be alone in the comfort of my memories." Alexa picked up the stack of neatly folded towels and walked into the bathroom, closing the door behind her.

⌒

Somewhere in the distance, clock chimes rang out the midnight hour. Alexa dozed, sleep her only escape from weeks of imprisonment in the place she had once called home. Words from another place and another spirit whispered to her.

"Faithful child, it is time to seek the true path intended for you. The time is upon you when you must leave Garogan. Focus and connect to all that is within you. I will be here always to guide you. Trust your heart and your intuition, for they not only show you the way. They will take you to rewards that are gifted by God. Awake, my child. You must go."

She awoke with the words echoing in her mind. The hours ahead were undoubtedly dangerous, but she knew no fear. Val was with her. She accepted that his will must prevail. If she remained firm in her conviction, she would yet find happiness.

Climbing from bed, she dressed in several layers of clothing to ward off the night's cold air. With nimble fingers, she succeeded in working a hole into the center of a blanket by using a sharp metal plate pried loose from the fireplace screen. She worked quickly, thankful for bright moonlight streaming through the window.

She slid stockinged feet into her shoes and put her head through the hole in the blanket, converting it to a cape. Standing motionless in the center of the room, she considered what to do next. Finally, with a firm stride, she walked to the door and closed both hands over the handle. She didn't try to open it. She knew it was securely locked. Instead, closing her eyes tightly, she focused all energy into her hands, feeling the vibrations move through the handle and into the inner mechanism. Within seconds, a clicking noise sounded. Smiling, she directed a brief prayer of thanks to Val and proceeded to open the door noiselessly.

She glanced in both directions, relieved that the hallway was deserted. Years of living here had left imprinted on her memory every door and every turn. Hugging the walls, she cautiously began making her way to the back stairwell leading to the central kitchen. She listened carefully for any waking sounds. Remembering the voice that had spoken to her, she again closed her eyes and reached out with her inner senses. Finally satisfied that all was clear, she descended the stairs.

Once in the kitchen, she hurried to the back door. It took a great deal of effort, combined with a steady hand, to slide back the heavy bolt that secured the door. As soon as she stepped outside, she crouched behind a thick clump of evergreen shrubs, gratefully gulping in fresh air, feeling invigorated by early winter scents and invading relief at being freed from her prison.

Several long moments passed by as she studied the way to the stables. She knew she would need a horse to accomplish her escape and would have to cross the grounds in a zigzag pattern to minimize her exposure in the open. Her lips moved in a prayer for protection. Fully an hour later, she reached the stables after huddling behind a bench for what seemed like forever while two sentries decided to take a break in their rounds.

At last, she managed to enter the stalls housing Victor's prized riding horses. Inside, she breathed in the scents of leather, saddle soap, horses, and sweet hay. She almost sighed aloud, catching herself before disturbing any of the sleeping animals. Once more, she drew from her inner resources, projecting a calming force to the animals, keeping them in their peaceful state.

Darkness was thick, seemingly impenetrable. She desperately required light to locate a saddle and select a suitable horse for her flight. With hands crossed over her heart, she murmured a prayer. "Please, dearest Val, if this is to be my path, help me. Please show me the way."

Slowly, her eyelids lifted. The inside of the stable was now dimly lit, and she quickly found her way to a lightweight saddle and one of Victor's finest geldings. Never once did she think to look for the source of the light. Never once did she realize it emanated from her own body.

The horse she selected responded to her gentle caresses by nuzzling her with his velvety nose. He seemed to understand her need for silence. Not once did he emit even the slightest sound. She led him from the back of the stable. The gate from this part of the castle enclosure was massive, but it was also quieter and less visible than the main entrance. Each step closer without discovery was one step closer to a reunion with her husband.

She would never know how she managed to slip through the gate with the horse following on its lead. She concentrated on each step, fearing it had taken too long to reach this point in front of the castle. Rose-colored fingers were stretching across the heavens, heralding dawn's arrival. Her escape was now almost certainly in jeopardy. No matter which way she rode, she would be in clear view of sentries posted along the castle walls and in turrets placed at intervals around the perimeter.

She hugged the wall as long as she dared. The closest cover was a stretch of trees directly in front of the compound. She would need to cross down a gently sloping meadow and wade across a rocky stream before she could reach the shielding cover of the ancient forest.

Suddenly, muted sounds of excited voices reached her ears. Someone had discovered her escape. Positive she heard Victor's voice shouting commands, Alexa threw the front half of the blanket back over her shoulders to allow greater freedom of movement for her arms. Lifting her foot into the stirrup, she hoisted herself up into the saddle. Quickly, she glanced upward at the wall, then scanned the forest edge to decide her fastest, safest path.

Unexpected movement caught her attention. She stared hard, the dark of night fading now into misty gray. Her heart sank, and she gulped back sudden fright at the thought of being trapped between Garogan's great castle and a rogue band of Sifiq marauders. An instant later, her heart leapt in her breast. There could be no doubting that tall, statuesque physique mounted atop a magnificent stallion. "Gregor." His name tumbled from her lips.

Shouts from within the castle walls sounded closer. She could not afford to hesitate a moment longer. Digging her knees into the sides of her mount and slapping his flank, she urged him into a mad gallop down the dew-wet meadow. She slapped her horse again, spurring him on faster. From somewhere behind her, she heard Victor's shouted warning for her to stop. When she was almost at the stream's edge, an arrow whistled by her ear.

The gurgling stream separating her from the edge of the forest was too wide to jump and was filled with large stones. She was forced to slow her horse to cross for fear he might stumble. Her breathing grew rapid. Blood pounded through her veins. Ahead, seeing her flight from the castle, Gregor approached along the tree line at full gallop. Stefan and a detachment of royal guards followed close behind him.

Remembered visions flashed through her mind as her horse stepped back onto dry ground. She glanced over her shoulder and saw Victor raise his bow, aiming his arrow directly at Gregor. Victor's marksmanship was renowned for its deadly accuracy. She urged her horse into a desperate run. Gregor's horse protested as he abruptly reined in the animal, trying to avoid colliding with the animal Alexa rode. Alexa jerked her mount sideways at the last possible second, simultaneously lunging toward her husband as she screamed, "Gregor! No!"

Stefan halted his horse, watching in horror as Gregor tumbled backward from his horse. Jumping to the ground, Stefan broke into a run and ordered men to control snorting, stomping, confused horses. Then, reaching Gregor, he grabbed him by the shoulders. Dazed by the fall, Gregor shook off his friend, scrambled to his knees, and frantically crawled around a horse being led to block him from archers standing ready on the castle wall.

"Alexa! Alexa!" He desperately called out her name as he rushed to her side.

Stefan grabbed him again, holding him back. "Slowly, Gregor! Gently!"

Both men now knelt beside her. Stefan signaled for help. Victor's arrow protruded from her upper back, having struck her to lodge sideways against her shoulder blade. With Gregor holding her face off the ground and Stefan bracing her, another set of hands firmly grasped the slender shaft and broke it off. Carefully supporting her with her face down where she had fallen, they were able to get a better grip to pull the remainder of the arrow from her shoulder. His men worked quickly, thrusting whatever cloth they could find into Stefan's hands to stanch the bleeding.

Gently, they turned her over, and Gregor cradled her head in his arms. Tears coursed without shame down his cheeks. At that point, Stefan realized that she also bled profusely from a gash on the side of her head. He quickly loosened his sash and tugged it from around his waist, using it to apply pressure to the wound.

Gregor could only stare into her ashen face, unable to believe the swelling and dark bruises along her cheeks or her cut and swollen mouth.

She had been beaten, and the knowledge tore at him. He held her gently, fervently willing her to live. "Alexa, please don't die. Please, my love, you can't die."

Her eyelids fluttered, opening slowly, revealing eyes near shock and glazed with pain. For just a second, recognition flared. "Gregor," she whispered, "you came for me. You came." Somewhere, far away, she heard the faint beating of a heart. She felt warm, wet splashes on her cheek. Was it only a dream? Could that really be Gregor's resonant voice calling her name? She then faded into the welcome void of unconsciousness.

Gregor clutched her close against his chest, hopelessness overtaking him as he started rocking slowly back and forth. Never in his life had he known such total panic and such terrible, overwhelming fear as he did at that moment.

"Please, Gregor. Be still. We must stop the bleeding if we're to have any hope of saving her life." Stefan saw that he was too lost in sorrow to hear him. "Gregor! You must help us if we're to save her!" This time, Stefan's sharp declaration pierced through the shock in the king's mind, snapping him back to reality.

"Dare we move her?" Gregor asked, regaining control only through the greatest of effort. He thrust all fears deep inside, realizing that conscious restraint was his best ally in this most critical battle for her life.

"We must get her back to Toraval. Tira and Tirani will know best what to do."

Gregor's liquid brown eyes gazed up at Stefan, pleading for reassurance. "Do you think she can survive the trip?"

Stefan looked straight into the king's frightened face. "Truthfully, I don't know. I only believe it to be our best chance for her."

"Then get ready. We must leave immediately." He rose to his feet. "First, move those horses out of my way!" His command was sharp and furious.

Gregor glared straight up at the castle wall, directly at Victor's motionless figure. He then stooped down and gathered his wife's unmoving body into his arms, lifting her effortlessly from the ground. He stood, feet planted firmly, holding her so Victor could see her, swathed in bloody bandages. His powerful voice rang out, "Garogan, see what your hatred has wrought!"

As Victor collapsed to his knees, Gregor and his men disappeared beyond the protective barrier of the forest. With great urgency, they organized themselves for the return to Toraval in a desperate attempt to save their queen.

Chapter 12

Flickering candlelight. Eerily dancing shadows on the walls. The sweet fragrance of fresh lilacs rushed from Lindaval to the capital city and into tall vases inside the queen's chambers. The occasional chink of fine silver against delicate porcelain. Hushed whispers. Quietly chanted prayers.

The palace physician held little hope for her recovery while Tira and her daughter worked tirelessly, applying every shred of knowledge they possessed of Val's healing powers. They prayed for Val to send his Healing Graces to help them. Alexa had lain unconscious for four days since Gregor had returned with her to Toraval. She had suffered a severe concussion from the gash on her head. Victor's arrow had torn flesh and broken bone. Infection had set in before the king could bring her back to the palace.

Tira had spent hours searching inside glass gardens and nearby woodlands for the exact herbs and barks they would need. Tirani had then washed and chopped and pressed, brewing them into powerful potions to promote energy and healing. Patiently, they held Alexa's head up, spooning tiny amounts of the brews into her mouth, taking care that she did not strangle. They had then fashioned poultices to press against the wound on her shoulder.

Alexa lay still, her chest barely lifting as she breathed shallowly. Without that faint rising motion, she was so motionless as to appear dead. Her face was deathly pale, her skin nearly transparent. A unique masque of peace had settled upon her. Tira and Tirani rarely left her side, watching her extraordinary expression, noting her stillness, and feeling something strikingly different about her presence.

Gregor visited the chamber frequently. He never touched her. To gaze down at her face, so bruised yet incredibly lovely, was indescribably painful. Her mad dash had undoubtedly saved his life. Alexa's whispered words constantly perplexed and tormented him. For the first time in his life, he truly regretted the responsibilities he bore as king. War had finally come to Turand. Dispatches from the north called for additional supplies. Surprise, detailed planning, and strategies were succeeding. The Sifiq were on the run following years of cruel occupation.

The impending National Council tempered even this bit of good news. Every province had sent delegates. Garogan Province had demanded to exercise its right to send Victor as their chief delegate to Toraval. Gregor seriously questioned his ability to face Victor without violent reaction.

Complicating matters was the clearly written Law of Council Standards. If a presiding king were married, the law mandated that his queen be present for the sessions. Exceptions could be made only for a woman whose time was at hand to deliver a child or if she were ill with some sort of contagion. Times and circumstances were too critical for this National Council to fail in its mission. Leadership roles must be established. Failure meant sure and rapid descent into all-out civil war. Dissent and outrage would be encouraged by factions opposed to the king. They had returned four days earlier. Only four days remained before Council would convene.

On the fifth night following their return, Gregor decided he could no longer bear to stay away from her. Allowing Tirani to administer a final dose of medicinal tea, he dragged a wing-backed chair into Alexa's room and positioned it close beside his wife's bed. When he had needed her, she had come to him. Perhaps she might need him. Hope made for a lonely companion.

Sometime after midnight, Gregor was still unable to sleep. He leaned forward, elbows resting on his knees, his fingers laced together in unspoken supplication. His head bent forward. Long, black lashes dropped down, forming a dark fringe on his upper cheeks. His profile was strong, his nose gently curved outward from his face, his brow prominent, his jawline darkened by the blackness of his beard. His mouth was closed, revealing even from the side the sensual fullness of his lips. His face was softly illuminated from behind by the orange glow of the fire burning in the fireplace.

Heavy eyelids lifted, blinking slowly. Semi-darkness confused her. Her mind was awash in a sea of mist and shadows. Alexa struggled to focus—to recall what had happened and to understand where she was. She turned her head on her pillow. The sight of her husband's face, so extraordinarily somber, afflicted her heart. She swallowed several times, then wet her lips with the tip of her tongue. When she first tried to speak, she made no sound. She tried again. "Gregor?"

His name was little more than the rasping of dry fall leaves tossed across the stone walks winding through the gardens. At first, he thought he had only imagined hearing something. Weary eyelids lifted, and he turned sorrowful eyes toward her.

"Gregor?" she whispered hoarsely again.

A slow, disbelieving smile softened and spread his mouth. He turned to face her and moved from his chair to kneel beside her. "Alexa, at last. You're awake. Praises be to Val."

Her eyes begged him to come closer. "I must tell you. You must know." She swallowed hard against the soreness in her throat that made speaking difficult.

He wondered what could possibly be so important for her to convey to him. "Tell me," he whispered back, leaning over to press delicate kisses upon her forehead and against her eyelids.

"Gregor, they found a law. Victor had papers drawn to annul our marriage. I didn't let them. I couldn't." Her voice faded. Speaking had required too much effort. Her eyelids fluttered and closed.

Gregor stared at her, the words she had said finding and filling a deep, aching niche in his soul. Tears slid from his eyes, and he leaned forward again, this time pressing a kiss against her lips. He allowed the contact to linger, drawing immense, satisfying solace from the gift those lips had just imparted.

After several long minutes, he rose and left the room to inform Tira that Alexa had awakened briefly and that she had spoken to him. Tira showed no reservations despite his status as king. She threw her arms around him in a joyous hug.

"You can rest at last, Sire," she told him. "We will not lose her now."

⤿

Embers glowed with golden brilliance in the fireplace grate, only slightly diminishing the pre-dawn darkness. Alexa awoke, her eyes opening wide. She gazed into nighttime shadows, her memory clear but her body feeling leaden. Although aware she had suffered grievous injuries, she also realized that Val had sent his Healing Graces to her. During what had appeared to be a deathlike coma, Alexa had learned what needed to be done and had accepted Val's will yet again. She hoped that she could perform his will as now revealed to her.

She heard a sound and turned her head on her pillow. Close to the side of her bed was a tall chair from her sitting room. Gregor slept in the chair, his head propped sideways against a pillow. A blanket lay across his lap. His arm draped over the side of the chair, and his hand hung limply alongside.

Alexa blinked against the sudden threat of tears, a fullness in her heart rising and spilling forth. She flexed her fingers, noting the stiffness running the length of her arm. Slowly, she pulled her hand up from beneath the covers and then moved it to the edge of the bed. She reached out, first stroking, then gently enclosing Gregor's long fingers in her hand. Just touching him infused her with a strong desire to be closer to him.

He had prayed for her recovery. In the distant reaches of his weary mind, Gregor dreamed of her. When she had spoken to him so briefly, he had known an invasion of relief that had finally eased his mind enough that he could fall asleep. Now, she appeared so exquisite, standing before him as he marveled at the smooth, delicate feel of her hand within his.

His eyelids blinked open, sudden awareness prompting him awake. It took several moments for the cobwebs of sleep to clear from his exhausted brain. He turned his head slowly. The pillow against which he had rested slipped and plopped onto the floor. In the hazy darkness, his black hair and beard seemed darker than ever, making his wide smile appear even brighter. His voice was hardly more than a husky whisper. "You've finally come back to us."

Alexa swallowed several times, her throat irritated by dryness. "Tell me I'm not dreaming. Am I truly home?"

Gregor rose and shifted positions to sit on the bed by her side. With the back of his right hand, he tenderly stroked the smoothness of her cheek and then pushed tangled strands of hair away from her face. Val help him. He could think of not a single word to say to her.

Their eyes reached out from wounded souls. Alexa's arms stretched upward, and he leaned forward, allowing her to encircle his neck. His arms wound around her, and he straightened, drawing her up against him. At first, he held her tentatively, but then his arms tightened to hold her close. In the early morning hours, they clung to one another, Gregor quietly joyful while Alexa surrendered to the secure refuge of her husband's embrace.

Minutes ticked away in compelling silence until, reluctantly, he eased her back to lie down, smiling against her neck as she resisted letting him go. Once again, she broke the silence. "Gregor, please help me sit up. I need something to drink."

Silently, he lifted her again long enough to arrange several pillows behind her. When he had her comfortably settled, he walked over to her dresser to pour water into an engraved crystal glass that had formed a cap over the matching glass decanter. With infinite patience, he tilted the cup gradually as she sipped the refreshing liquid.

She smiled her thanks. "What time is it?"

"I imagine around five in the morning." He wondered what possible interest she could have in the time. Time held so very little importance for him at that moment. All that mattered was that she had returned to him.

He sat close to her, and her gaze was gentle as she reached out to caress his mussed hair. "I must ask you to do something very special for me, Gregor. Will you?" She took his hands into hers and held them close to her heart.

"Of course. Anything you ask. You have my promise."

"My husband, you're exhausted, and I'm so worried about you. I want you to find Tirani. Send her in to stay with me. Then, I want you to go to your own bed, and I want you to rest." She raised two fingers and pressed them to his lips, silencing his protest before it was born. "Don't argue. You promised. Tirani will stay with me until you return."

He gazed at her, sighing heavily and swallowing the argument that had arisen. He was tired. Extremely so, especially now when he knew he could surrender to his weariness without fear that she might die while he slept. Silently, he dropped a kiss on her brow and rose to fulfill her simple request.

With a surprised and overjoyed Tirani left to care for Alexa, Gregor went to his chambers and tucked himself beneath the heavy blankets on his bed. Just before sinking into welcome slumber, he whispered a prayer. "Oh, great and loving Val, I prayed with all my might that you would heal her. I now pray doubly hard in gratitude that you have restored her to me." Peace and exhaustion overpowered him, and he finally slept.

Later in the morning, Tira's slim fingers worked diligently at trying to remove some of the more stubborn tangles from Alexa's thick, curling hair. She had spent a long time brushing and smoothing the unruly mass, finally managing to tame it to a more presentable image.

Alexa smiled patiently. "I am uncertain why you put so much effort into my hair when surely it will be a mess again. I'm tired already, and I shall need to sleep through much of the day. There is much for me to do."

Tira's expression alone questioned her.

"Tira, would you ask Tirani to join us? I must speak with both of you about a matter vitally important."

Moments later, mother and daughter sat at Alexa's bedside, attentive to every word.

"Tira, Tirani has often discussed with me her dreams to take the vows of the Order of Val. There can be much sacrifice and, in these times, serious peril in professing to be Valiria. Have the two of you discussed this? Do you approve?" It was evident that Alexa was still very weak, but she was determined to accomplish a mission.

Tira spoke, her words carrying great strength. "It has been my honor to serve our Lord Val and his servants, the Valiria. Long ago, I even hoped to take vows myself. I could wish nothing better for my daughter."

Tirani's smooth, light, cinnamon-colored skin glowed, her hazel eyes alight with anticipation. How impossible it seemed that their queen, not nearly recovered, would consider her circumstance with such high merit.

"Tirani, once more, I ask you. Are you completely certain you wish to take vows to become Valiria?"

Tirani's reply was firm. "Absolutely."

Alexa sighed in satisfaction and leaned back into her pillows. She closed her eyes to rest.

Tira observed her closely before clearing her throat to speak. "Milady, we face a major obstacle. You know that to become Valiria, a candidate must meet the approval of no fewer than five avowed Valiria or by Valkana. Unfortunately, we are unable to fulfill this ancient mandate. I fail to understand how Tirani can possibly make her vows."

Alexa smiled without opening her eyes. "I ask you to entrust details to me. For now, I need for the two of you to attend to some very crucial details for me."

"Anything you ask, Milady," Tirani vowed, her trust in the queen complete and unwavering.

"Tirani, I want you to prepare a mild sleeping potion. I also want you to see that Gregor gets it with his evening meal. He mustn't realize what you're doing. Perhaps you can arrange for him to come here early to be with me, and he can take the potion with tea. Then I want you to prepare Raija tea and place it in a carrying bottle. Bring a flask of wine and a bottle of virgin oil. Pack both bottles together with ten new candles. Then I want you to lie down to rest for a while."

Tirani, puzzled by the instructions, left immediately to carry them out.

"Tira, I wish for you to rest, too. You need not attend me because I, too, will sleep. First, you must seek out Stefan. Find him and tell him that I must speak with him privately, between eight and nine o'clock. You must convince him of the urgency and the necessity for complete discretion. No one must know, especially not Gregor."

"I will do as you ask, Milady, but I do not understand."

"You will. Trust me. Now go. I must rest."

⌒

A light tap sounded on the door to Alexa's chamber. "Please, Stefan, enter."

The door opened, revealing the surprised face of her husband's adviser. "You sounded so certain it was I who knocked. What if you had been mistaken?"

She smiled, mildly amused. "I suppose I would have looked rather foolish. However, Tira and Tirani are taking care of some requests I made, and Gregor just left. Besides that, your life force is quite distinctive. And I expected you."

Stefan's eyebrows arched in silent inquiry. "You sent for me regarding some urgent matter?"

Alexa glanced downward at her hands. Breathing in deeply, she prepared herself for whatever his reaction might be. "Stefan, I am in desperate, urgent need of your assistance."

"Please explain, Your Majesty. Whatever I can do, I shall." He noticed how pale her skin was, her cheeks gaunt following her prolonged unconsciousness. What struck him as odd was that she was fully dressed in a dark violet gown, the once-fitted bodice loose because of the weight she had lost.

"Stefan, I know that you and Gregor struggle with arrangements for the opening day of Council. Is this not so?"

Stefan nodded, saying nothing. He quickly noted the sound of authority in her voice that contrasted so sharply with the fragility of her appearance.

She continued, "You negotiate to excuse my absence from Council, but you encounter stubborn opposition. Since ancient times, the laws have required the presence of Turand's queen if the king is married. The opposition you face wants the law enforced because they believe I cannot be present. With the current state of my recovery, both you and Gregor know that it will be nearly impossible for me to attend. Is this not so?"

Stefan stared at her. "You describe exactly the problem we face, Milady, but we do have allies who will support our request for an exception."

She impatiently shook her head. "You know the laws governing the proceedings as well as I. The only exceptions are for a queen who has an infectious disease or is near delivery of a child. Even if Gregor's allies agree, you know that not one of the southern provinces will concur."

"For someone who has been away and then so seriously ill for so many days, you have a remarkable grasp of the current political crisis."

Alexa's tone softened, yet her insistence intensified. "Stefan, that is why your assistance tonight is of such critical importance. As I am now, I will certainly fail to stand by Gregor through inauguration ceremonies, not to mention Council. I beg of you, Stefan. Help me. I must not fail Gregor. Not now. I must be there with him."

"What would you have me do, Milady?" Stefan showed outward calm. His controlled demeanor concealed inner conflict. A cynical part of him could not help but wonder if her escape from Garogan had been staged. Their timely arrival had placed Gregor perfectly within Victor's sights. She had been galloping full tilt, inadvertently taking the arrow meant for the king. Yet, she had screamed out a warning, and her leap toward him that day had most assuredly saved the king's life. He looked deeply into her eyes now. Though still sunken, they sparkled with determination.

"Stefan, I sense your internal conflict. Yes, I took Victor's arrow by accident, but I swear to you that I had escaped. They were planning my execution. When I saw Victor take aim at Gregor, my only thought was to save my husband's life. My thoughts are much the same now. This time,

I need your help. Stefan, you must trust me. You must help me to help him." She paused, both gauging his reaction and praying for his comprehension. "Stefan, I have risked my life and may now do so again. Help me, Stefan. Please love him as much as do I."

Stefan could not avoid staring at her. Her perception of his private thoughts was disconcerting. Her expression was pleading. Her voice echoed commitment combined with clarity of thought. And she unmistakably had said that she loved Gregor.

"Stefan?" His deliberation was too prolonged for her level of patience.

He gazed at her intently. "What would you have me do?"

She breathed in a long, deep breath, then released a sigh heavy with relief. She spoke rapidly and quietly. "You and Gregor know the palace and the city of Toraval better than anyone, do you not?"

Stefan nodded, his blue-gray eyes intrigued as he tried to fathom her intentions.

"I believe there is a secret tunnel that leads from within the palace, directly under the central square and into the Temple of Val. You know where the tunnel is and how to negotiate it. I need you to escort me there. Tonight. Tira, Tirani, and Thero will accompany us. Will you do this for me, Stefan? Will you do this for Gregor?" Her eyes appraised his reaction. She must convince him.

"Your Majesty…"

She interrupted. "Stefan, I ask you to forgo the formalities. Call me Alexa."

"Alexa," he addressed her in accordance with her request. "It will be difficult to reach the tunnel entrance without being seen. There is too much activity in the palace just now. And what happens if Gregor comes to check on you and finds you gone?"

"I promise you, Gregor will be fine. In fact, as we speak, he enters his chamber, unable to resist the sleep that beckons him."

"What have you done to him?" Stefan demanded abruptly, suddenly frightened for his friend.

She glanced up sharply. "You know better than I that my husband is so exhausted he's near collapse. I have arranged only a safe sleeping potion that will allow him not only to sleep but will restore his energies. By tomorrow, he will feel very well rested. You must believe me, Stefan. I could never do anything to harm him."

"Why is it so important that you go to the Temple of Val tonight? The temple has been sealed and empty for years."

Alexa sought words to convince him. "Stefan, if only you can find it within yourself to trust me for a little while, you'll understand. The hour grows late. I must be there no later than one hour before midnight. Stefan, Gregor needs you more than ever right now. I need you. You must believe me when I tell you that, if I don't go there tonight, all your months of planning and efforts exerted to bring this Council to fruition and to bring peace to Turand—all will have been in vain. You must guide me there."

She argued her request powerfully, sincerity ringing in every word. "Are you ready?" he asked. "We must leave immediately."

Her shoulders slumped, her effort to influence him a leaden weight of anxiety now lifted. She drew in a calming breath. "Check my sitting room. The others await us."

Half an hour later, the unlikely companions stood outside an enormous set of barred double doors. The tunnel began just beyond a false wall in an unused corridor behind the palace wine cellar. Arriving without attracting notice had not been easy. Stefan had gone ahead and commanded servants to tend other duties that would take them away from the route to the tunnel. Several times, he had physically supported Alexa. As strongly as she had delivered her arguments, he found it difficult to believe how physically weak she was.

Stefan and Thero pushed on the bar to loosen it in its braces. Then, the two men carefully raised the heavy beam, gratefully accepting Tirani's assistance to lift it clear before quietly lowering it to the dirt floor.

The doors posed yet another problem. Rusted iron hinges threatened to creak with ungodly noise that would echo through the palace cellars and reach the upper floors. Alexa surprised them by pulling a flask from the velvet bag Tira carried. She removed the glass stopper and poured some of the bottle's contents onto the ancient hinges. Then, placing her hands over first one hinge and then the next, she closed her eyes in deep concentration. Not one of them expected it when both doors noiselessly swung open.

Thero and Tira both carried lanterns to light the way inside the dark, musty tunnel. Stefan removed an ancient torch from a niche in the wall. Tira exposed the flame of her lamp to set the torch ablaze. Stefan then took the lead, using the torch and his hands to push away thick dust webs. Tirani followed directly behind him, her youthful strength supporting her queen. Thero and Tira walked behind them, carrying lanterns and a large basket.

They walked through the eerie coolness of the tunnel until Alexa nearly questioned her sanity. Her head ached, and her knees trembled with weakness. Surely she must have been mistaken. Doubt assailed her until she turned her innermost thoughts to Val. Confidence returned. He had most certainly revealed this path. She must follow with faith. That thought entered her mind just as Stefan whispered they had reached the temple entrance.

Alexa gazed at the doors, the carvings of the sun within its pyramid covered with years of undisturbed dust. She stretched out a loving hand to wipe away some of the dirt. As she did so, the doors began to open, seemingly of their own accord. Stefan and Tirani looked at each other in startled amazement, then at Alexa. Both were dumbfounded. Tira smiled, growing suspicion lighting her sharp eyes. Thero only closed his in silent prayer. Val's time had come at last.

Alexa passed through the great portal, walking ahead confidently with renewed strength. The others followed, tentatively at first, then gaining confidence as great anticipation permeated each of them. Alexa approached the raised marble altar, her weakness growing less noticeable, purpose clearly defined in the square set of her shoulders. She moved toward her right to circle around to the front. There, directly above the center of the altar, hung suspended the symbol of Val. The sun was burnished gold and represented the warmth and light bestowed through Val's all-powerful love. The crystal pyramid that held the sun inside was symbolic of the three greatest of Val's gifts to his people: Love. Peace. Fidelity.

"Tirani, please bring the candles plus the flasks of oil and wine. Thero, assist me in placing the candles around the dais."

Alexa and Thero each took five candles. The massive dais was triangular and bore ten indentations holding ten silver-clad crystal cups. Alexa placed the first candle at the apex of the triangle that pointed at the great chamber where worshippers had gathered long ago. From the point, there were three candles for each side of the triangle.

Alexa silently indicated to Thero that he should have the honor of lighting the candles. As each flame began to burn, shadows dispersed, and the entire altar area was bathed in a glow far brighter than the tiny candles could cast on their own.

Tears shone on Thero's rosy cheeks. Throughout years of persecution and ridicule, he had struggled to guard his faith. He had continually promoted remembrance of Val in what had seemed a fruitless endeavor. He had persisted. He had believed.

Tira observed the old priest, his exultation almost tangible. Her heart swelled. Her mistress had promised that, despite the missing consensus of

Valiria, Tirani would certainly achieve her dream. To Tira's quick mind, Thero's tears were no enigma. Instead, they were confirmation that Val's deliverance was near.

Thero walked from the dais and down the altar steps. From Tirani, he took the bottles of wine and oil. Turning, he placed both flasks in Alexa's hands. She faced the dais, raised the flasks above her head, mouthed a silent prayer, and then set each on the altar. Thero removed an intricately crocheted golden shawl from the basket they had carried, which he draped over her head, smoothing it down around her shoulders. He turned to the others and whispered instructions for them to sit together along the front row of benches.

None of the three knew quite what to expect. Tirani was quiet with subdued excitement. Tira held her daughter's hand tightly, knowing only that she felt blessed to witness this incredible moment. Stefan, analytical as usual, studied every movement, every expression, every detail. Instinctively, he recognized that a momentous event was imminent but had not yet come to comprehend the magnitude.

Thero bowed his head and prayed over the bottles in the center of the altar. He offered the flask of sweet wine to Alexa, and she took a sip. Replacing the bottle on the dais, he took the bottle of oil and came to stand directly in front of her, one step above the level where she now knelt. She raised her hands to him, palms up. He carefully poured several drops on each hand. He turned long enough to place the oil beside the wine. Delicately dipping his index finger into the oil on her palms, he carefully touched the sweetly scented oil to her lips, her ears, her eyelids, and, finally, her forehead.

"Alexa Maraná, wife to Gregor of the Royal House of Toscano and King of Turand, you come before the altar of Val. Do you come to serve?"

"I come to serve my Lord Val with faithful heart and willing hands." Her voice was a lilting chant.

"Do you accept the challenges and responsibilities of service over and above the rewards?" Thero's eyes were intense as he gazed directly at her. Something within him was amazed that he remembered the simple ceremony that he had only read about so many years ago.

"I accept with grateful heart all that Val wishes for me."

"Do you accept his gifts, including that given to you in the matter of marriage?"

"I accept all his gifts with unparalleled thanks."

"Alexa Maraná, you are avowed Valiria, anointed in holy tradition and faith to our Creator. Have you been faithful, child?"

"My faith remains ever-strong and has never wavered, even when I could not comprehend the path shown to me." Her chanted replies filled the temple.

"Tell me, then, Alexa Maraná, what is it you seek within the hallowed Temple of Val?" Thero's voice rose and echoed against the soaring arched walls.

"I seek foremost to love and serve Val as he wills." Almost simultaneously with the end of this phrase, a tremendous blue-white light enveloped her entire body until her kneeling form began to rise from the stone floor.

Stefan gasped aloud, unprepared for the shock of watching her levitate and begin to hover just above the level of the dais. Suddenly, he felt compelled to acknowledge the truth of the old ways. Valkana was neither fairy tale nor legend. He questioned how he, neither believer nor disbeliever, had been chosen to witness the mystic marvel unfolding before him.

Tira and Tirani watched, too. While nursing her, they had whispered about what they had perceived as momentary flashes of light around her while she lay comatose. They had dismissed the lights as part of the secret, mystic gifts given to anointed Valiria. Now, the truth was far different from anything they had dreamed.

Meanwhile, Alexa hovered in midair, chanting ancient canticles. Musical essences penetrated the hearts and souls of those in her presence. Bells in the temple's carillon towers began to chime the melodies of her canticles. The swelling sounds of voices drifted in from the square outside. Until now, bells that had started ringing sporadically after Alexa's abduction had never rung in patterned melodies. People came from the palace and from the city to investigate this newest phenomenon. As yet, they were unable to approach the temple, which remained sealed by the energy field that had protected it from destruction by Sifiq invaders.

Stefan glanced distractedly at the heavy gold pocket watch he carried. In the distant reaches of his mind, he noted that the light and levitation must have begun precisely at midnight. Stefan returned his concentration to the surreal image of the queen suspended in midair. Seeing her motionless figure, listening to her song, and watching the glow of light that enveloped her perplexed him like nothing he had ever encountered. He decided he could not be dreaming. His exceptionally logical mind could never conjure up such a fantasy.

Clear notes of her songs began to slow and fade, drifting throughout the temple. Outside, the throng of Toraval citizens and early arrivals to Council remained in awe. Rays of light flashed from within the long-deserted temple. Bells rang out, and a sweet, melodious song hung in the night air.

From his bedroom window, Gregor peered out across the expansive square, watching the temple. The display of lights was fantastical, the voice hauntingly familiar. He wanted to go to Alexa to make sure she was all right. He wanted to investigate the strange sights and sounds beyond his palace. Instead, he closed the window and crossed the chamber to return to bed. His brain was too weary, his body too heavy to command. The tea Tirani had served him earlier continued to work its wonders. Again, he slept.

"Alexa, servant of Val, you are blessed by our great lord. Receive His blessing now," Thero called out.

Her light-encased figure drifted gracefully down to the same spot where she had first knelt. As she settled into place, golden beams radiated from different points above the altar, the shafts brilliant as they joined together at her heart.

"I acknowledge the blessings of Val. I shall serve him with love and fidelity, and to my life, he will bring peace and joy. This is the song of Val, bestowed upon his Priestess Valkana."

An array of multi-hued lights appeared to burst from her, and she rose to her feet. She turned to face Tirani. "Come to me."

Neither Stefan nor Tira could have prepared for the glow that emanated from Alexa's face. She had undergone an incredible transformation that radiated a sublime aura of peace. They stared, transfixed.

"Tirani, you say your heart desires to serve Val. In doing so, you must minister to his people. You must show them love, spirituality, and steadfastness. Is this truly your desire?"

Tirani's eyes shone. "Yes, Milady."

"Tirani, Val wishes to offer you a special gift, one which you may choose whether or not to accept. It is one that may bring you great physical pain and distress, but such pain will pass quickly. Val offers you his gift of Healing Graces so that you may help his people who suffer. What is your decision?"

Tirani glowed, her personal aura beginning to shimmer about her head before moving to surround her entire body. Her eyes closed. "I gratefully accept whatever path Val wishes me to follow."

Alexa proceeded to administer sacred vows to her young lady-in-waiting. Once complete, she pulled from within her bodice a golden chain entwined with purple silk rope, upon which hung a miniature crystal pyramid identical to the great symbol of Val suspended above the altar.

Tirani extended her arms to receive the marks she would bear for the remainder of her life. She flinched at the fleeting, burning sensation upon tender skin.

Alexa then turned to Tira. "You have perpetuated the teachings of Val in all you have done, Lady Tira. We know that your husband's death resulted from protecting you and your daughter as you escaped Sifiq, who murdered the Valiria prepared to receive your vows. Despite this tragedy, you remained faithful. If you so choose, you may complete those vows now. No matter your decision, you have found favor with our God, Val."

Tira rose and approached the Valkana, who offered resurrection for her long-forgotten dream. She, too, received her confirmation as Valiria.

Stefan observed the entire proceedings with unbridled fascination. Never once did the light diminish around the newly declared Valkana. Her demeanor was dignified and regal. She exuded a beauty that could only be described as ethereal. Her eyes, so deep in color, possessed a penetrating effect that caused him to shiver, though he felt neither cold nor afraid. His assessment was disturbed abruptly by the sound of his name.

"Stefan Sidano."

He rose automatically and bent his head. "Your Majesty."

"Stefan, come to me." It seemed she had issued him a command. He was certain this was so, but when he looked into her face, he wondered if he had ever in his life seen an expression so benevolent. He stepped forward to stand in front of her. Glancing downward, he watched her reach forward to take his hands into hers. He was stunned by the pulsating energy that flowed from her fingertips into his hands.

"Stefan, I trust you now understand the reason for secrecy and urgency regarding tonight. All will be revealed to our people in Val's good time."

"I do understand, Your Majesty." His voice sounded strange, almost foreign to his ears.

"Stefan, I know you are not yet a true believer in Val. Read. Learn. Feel. Remember all you have seen tonight. Know, too, Stefan, that I am personally grateful for the loyalty and friendship that you give to Gregor. Long have you been his sole anchor. You have ached for the sorrows he has known and the losses he has endured. I give you my solemn pledge that I, too, will stand by his side as we strive all together to achieve the dream of restoring peace to Turand."

Stefan smiled. His breath came rapidly with amazement at something newly sprung inside him. It was not a matter of knowledge that told him. He felt her words were truth. He would now serve them both. Optimism seeped throughout his being as he knelt before her in deep respect.

A trail of warmth caressed her cheek. Turning in bed toward the retreating touch, she lifted heavy eyelids only slightly. Her face softened with a drowsy smile.

"How can you possibly be so sleepy?" Gregor's resonant voice held a gentle tease. His lips curved in an indulgent smile. Black-brown eyes were warm and expectant.

"Gregor." His name was a whisper. "I'm so tired. I've hardly slept. Please. Just let me sleep a while longer." Unable to stay awake, she adjusted her position slightly as slumber claimed her once again.

Grinning to himself, he tucked the covers beneath her chin. Despite the circles rimming her eyes and the dark smudges remaining as testament to the abuse she had endured, Alexa had looked at him with incredibly happy eyes. Though she still had not said so, he felt convinced that she had come to care for him. He needed only to be patient.

He rose from her bedside and, after indulging in a final lingering glance, left to discuss remaining details for tomorrow's opening ceremony. How he hoped they would be able to reach an acceptable solution to his wife's inability to attend.

Chapter 13

The enormous assembly hall had been arranged with highly polished mahogany tables set in semi-circles. Ten rows of tables were set with twelve chairs each since each of Turand's twenty provinces had sent its full allotment of six delegates. Tables held crystal water pitchers and matching crystal goblets. Elaborate chandeliers hung from soaring ceilings. Through tall, broad windows poured early morning sunshine, its bright, natural light refracting through crystal prisms on the chandeliers.

Facing the semi-circles of tables was a raised platform carpeted in deep burgundy. Placed close together on the platform were two thrones with a carved table between them. The dark mahogany thrones were intricately carved. The backs and seats were padded and upholstered in burgundy velvet that matched the carpeting. A gold-leafed pillar stood at the side of one of the thrones, and upon it rested a golden cushion holding the gold filigree coronet belonging to the queen.

Brightly attired musicians led the initial procession of delegates into the hall. Delegates carried colorful flags or banners representing their home provinces. The representatives filed in and moved to their assigned tables. The hall was abuzz with greetings from old friends and last-minute, hushed negotiations and agreements as the assemblage awaited the king's arrival. Gossip and speculation were rampant since everyone knew of the queen's disappearance and that she had been critically ill since her return to Toraval. Some wondered if perhaps she had died or if Gregor now kept his reluctant bride a prisoner.

A hush descended on the congregation of delegates as Stefan followed a second procession of musicians who sounded notice that the king stood poised to enter. As the final notes faded, Stefan turned to address Council. His voice carried through the now silent hall. "Ladies, gentlemen, we embark upon a momentous occasion. I ask you to welcome Gregor, King of Turand, who has accomplished reinstatement of our distinguished National Council."

Gregor entered, his posture stately, his immense height providing an image of massive power. He wore a formal, royal blue tunic, edged at the neck, shoulders, and cuffs with wide bands embroidered with silver and gold threads. Simple black leggings tucked smoothly into low, cuffed boots. Upon his head rested the jeweled crown of Turand. Other than the royal gold medallion and his wedding band, he wore no jewelry. He appeared almost stark, especially when compared to so many delegates who had dared to wear long-hidden jeweled treasures to such an auspicious occasion.

Gregor graciously accepted the applause that followed his introduction. As clapping filled the room, his dark eyes scanned the gathering for friend and enemy. In the far right corner, in the ninth row, stood the delegation from Garogan. Indeed, Victor had claimed his ancestral right to represent Garogan Province. Only the most determined self-control had kept the king's eyes moving, thus preventing a visual duel between the two adversaries.

Gregor raised his arms high, and the applause abated. Anxious apprehension followed. Tradition held that the queen should have entered with him. Most suspected the king planned to request an exception to allow her absence. All knew that the southern provinces would obstinately oppose any such exception. Tension crackled in the air as all waited for the king to speak.

Gregor paused deliberately. When finally he spoke, his powerful speaking voice projected easily into every corner of the assembly hall. "My fellow citizens, I extend my personal welcome to Toraval and this palace. We come not only to create history but to reassert our rights to determine our own destiny."

As his brief and stirring welcome speech continued, he assessed the mood of the representatives. Mostly, there was great empathy and optimism. However, he observed stubborn resistance on the faces of provincial delegates from the south. Their barely concealed scowls left little doubt that it would be nearly impossible to obtain an exception for Alexa's absence. Somehow, he must find a way to succeed.

"As most of you are aware, our queen has been confined to bed after suffering severe, life-threatening injury." His preamble to the plea for an exception was interrupted as uniformed pages swung open the main doors to the hall.

Alexa stood in the center of the entrance, her pause deliberate as she glanced over shocked council members' faces. Her golden-brown hair hung in loose waves floating around her shoulders. Her lavender gown was velvet, trimmed with white lace insets and satin ribbons. She had chosen the color as an open declaration of her position in the Order of Val. Her face was exceedingly pale except for the remaining dark bruises. There was a slight unsteadiness, indicative of the effort required to stand unassisted. What no one missed were the intense fires in her eyes.

When she finally entered, she walked very slowly into the midst of the gathering. Her clear voice rang out above the stunned silence. "As my husband has explained, I have been very ill. I use this as my excuse to beseech your kind understanding and forgiveness for my late arrival."

She cast a brilliant smile that swept the room. Tremendous sorrow inundated Victor as he alone noted the excessive strain on her face. Alexa then stepped gracefully toward the center front where her husband stood. She slipped to the floor in a deep genuflect.

"I also ask your forgiveness, my husband, as I have come late to offer you the service and support of your queen."

Her face dropped in respect, as was the custom. Though she dared not look up, she could feel his startled eyes burning into her with near disbelief. Stefan, his expression reflecting admiration, calmly approached the pillar holding her coronet, removed it with stately ceremony, and then placed it in Gregor's hands.

With exceptional reverence, Gregor set the golden circle on her head. "Welcome, Queen Alexa." His voice quivered. She lifted her face to meet his gaze and was instantly moved by the tears glistening in his eyes.

He extended both hands downward to help her up. She suddenly trembled, fearful she would be unable to rise. With swift recognition of her plight, Gregor bent his knees and placed strong hands firmly around her waist as she moved her hands upward along his arms, grasping him with what little strength she could summon. Slowly, he lifted her to her feet.

Once she steadied herself, he took her left hand and raised it to his lips before turning to face the delegation. His voice shook noticeably. "Ladies and gentlemen, it is for me the greatest honor to welcome to National Council Alexa, my beloved wife and Queen of Turand."

Applause erupted, reaching a deafening level as Gregor pivoted on his heel to face her once again. Their eyes locked in a surge of connectivity, temporarily shutting from their minds the crowd of onlookers. Then, lovingly, in a gesture she was coming to cherish as a precious habit, he cradled her face between his hands. As his thumbs brushed away a few stray tears, he tenderly kissed her on the forehead. He then led her to the thrones where they would preside over the first National Council of his reign.

By early evening, Alexa felt weak and lightheaded, suffering from fatigue such as she had never known before. Earlier in the day, just as everyone was leaving for the midday break, she had risen and, accompanied by Gregor, had walked to the doors exiting the assembly hall. Overcome by sudden dizziness, she swayed, her knees collapsing. Gregor alertly caught her, gathering her into his arms to carry her upstairs to her chambers.

Lying in bed with Tirani holding a cup of herbal tea for her to drink, Alexa had listened patiently as Gregor stormed at her for even thinking to get out of bed, let alone attend Council. Remaining quiet until he finished his tirade, she already felt the strengthening effect of the herbal concoction. She whispered to Tirani to leave them. Once they were alone, she patted the bed beside her. "Gregor, come. Sit by me for a moment."

He hesitated, his anger vented. "Alexa, you mustn't push yourself this way. You must recover." He spoke more calmly as he lowered himself to sit at her side.

"Gregor, listen to me. The future of Turand depends on the outcome of this Council. No matter how dear the sacrifice, we must forge ahead. Failure is unacceptable. I know I frightened you, and I apologize."

He started to speak, but she shook her head at him. "We have almost two hours before the session resumes. Tirani will bring something for me to eat and prepare more tea before I return downstairs. First, I shall rest a while. I will be strong enough to attend the afternoon session. Be patient with me. Understand what I do and why. I must be there, and you know that. Help me so that I fail neither you nor our people."

Gregor stared at her, fighting a mad urge to hold her. He wanted to kiss her, to tell her how frightened he had been and how deeply he loved her just now but instead forced a terse smile. She was right.

"You must promise me one thing. You must let me know if you feel weak again. I can always call for short breaks. I cannot allow you to put your health at risk."

She patted his hand. "My health is fine. Of that, I can assure you. Only my strength is not yet restored. Go. I know there are people with whom you must talk. Tirani will stay with me."

He rose and went to the door, stopping as he grasped the handle. As he glanced back over his shoulder, his expression was serious. "Alexa, what you have done today, I will never forget. No man could ask more from a wife than you have given."

As the door closed behind him, she pulled a coverlet up around her, grateful for the healing sleep that came so swiftly.

Her reflection on the day's earlier events was interrupted by a gentle hand coming to rest on her shoulder. Gregor had risen from his throne and now stood at her side. Snapping out of her straying thoughts, she realized the first day's proceedings were being adjourned. She need only await a single-file parade of all delegates as they took their leave before going to prepare for the evening banquet.

Alexa's smile, though tired, was genuine and sincere. The ladies who approached kissed her on each cheek. Each gentleman knelt to salute her with a kiss on her hand. She graciously received wishes for a speedy recovery and warmly greeted various acquaintances, most especially Lady Lorinda Skanos, her mother's cousin. As she promised Lady Lorinda a private evening before the end of Council, she saw from the corner of her eye that Lord Anderon and his aides were approaching, closely followed by the Garogan delegation.

Gregor must have seen them at the exact moment as she. She felt his hand caress her shoulder and then gently squeeze in reassurance. Together, they could face this challenge. Although Gregor was not yet aware that Lord Anderon had planned her execution, he distrusted the man. As she glanced up at her husband, she perceived the icy expression and tension on his face.

She reached upward to briefly curl her fingers around his hand that still rested on her shoulder. He glanced down into emerald eyes offering him encouragement. He smiled into those eyes that he had come to love so dearly and prepared to welcome the delegates from the southern provinces.

Victor was the last to approach. He had not missed the exchanges between the king and queen and felt thoroughly sickened. He stubbornly refused to bow to the king in the traditional gesture of respect. Finally, knowing he dared not create complete scandal just yet, Victor extended his arm to shake hands with the man he hated so much. Gregor's grip was firm and strong, his eyes directly challenging Victor.

Moving with relief past Gregor to kneel before his queen, Victor took Alexa's fingers into his hand. His mind reeled from the shame and grief tormenting his soul. He had nearly killed the only woman he would ever love. He forced himself to look up into her eyes. How lovely she was.

"Your Majesty." Those words, the spoken acknowledgment of her place as another man's wife, were razor-sharp on his tongue. "We were all very concerned for your well-being today. It is great relief to see you so much improved."

"Thank you, Lord Garogan. Your concern is appreciated. I assure you that I am well on my way to recovery." Her response was so formal as to be an assault directly into his heart. As he solemnly kissed her hand, she felt the warm splash of teardrops on her skin.

Once the hall had emptied, Alexa closed her eyes, sighing in relief. The day was done. There was no requirement for her to attend the banquet. She could go to her rooms and lie down to rest. Gregor helped her to her feet and supported her as they slowly went upstairs. Standing just inside her chambers, she cherished the luxury of a private moment with her husband. His eyes were closed, thick lashes against his skin. Her fingers stroked a sensual line from his temple down along the line of his perfectly trimmed black beard.

"I need to ask a great favor of you, Gregor."

"Again? Tell me what favor you could need from me now. " His voice was a mere whisper as he reluctantly opened his eyes.

She smiled in amusement. "I know you'll be at the banquet until late, but…" She paused on a nervous sigh, unsure how to appropriately word her request. "I just wondered if you would return here to stay with me tonight."

Following a day filled with stunning events, he could hardly believe he had just heard her correctly. He studied her expression intently, noting the complete earnestness of her request. His lips formed a gentle smile. "Are you certain? It may be very late. I prefer not to disturb you so you can sleep."

"Please? Please grant me this request."

He drew her close to him, relishing the feel of her body, unspeakably gladdened by the mere fact that she was alive. "If that is your wish," he whispered. Following a brief kiss on the cheek, he left her so she could undress and prepare to rest.

⌒

Peacefully, she lay in bed. Earlier in the day, she had dreamed and had just awakened from that same dream. His image was clear before her. She saw his pain, his regret, and his internal battles. She felt the weariness in his soul—the need to find something missing, the powerful emotions stirring just beneath the surface. She concentrated on his eyes, the depth and darkness of their color.

She listened as the door eased open before closing again. She heard him move through the darkness. The sounds of clothing being discarded. The muffled thump of jewelry on the bedside table. Inhaling deeply, she heard him lift the covers and slide beneath them to lie on his back beside her. She rolled onto her side, her long fingers reaching out to lace into the heavy strands of his hair. She needed to be close to him, to touch him.

He was startled upon realizing she wasn't asleep. "I tried not to awaken you."

"You didn't. I've been waiting for you." She edged closer to him, the heat of his powerful body radiating against her skin. "I needed to talk with you. To be with you."

"You should be asleep," he gently chastised her.

Flooded with a torrent of emotions and need, she ignored him. He needed to know the truth of how she felt, and she desperately needed to tell him. "While I was in Garogan, I wrote you a letter. I was terribly afraid I might not live to explain to you the truth of what happened. Or all that I realized during my captivity."

By this time, he had turned on his side to face her. His hand had moved, seemingly on its own, to splay against her ribcage, his sensitive fingertips just beneath the swelling fullness of her breast. He was almost afraid to ask. "What was it you wrote to tell me?"

A tiny whimper escaped as she attempted to control the tremors racing through her body. She sought evasive words that she longed to tell him. "Today, in front of Council, you called me your beloved wife. Gregor, can that really be so?"

He held her closer, his heart beginning to throb within his chest. "Yes, Alexa, it is so. I do love you. My dearest hope now is that you might make my dreams come true. There is nothing I want more than for you to love me in return."

She shook—almost violently. Suddenly, she sought his lips, kissing every part of his mouth. Her hands moved over bone and sinew, across muscle and skin. "I do, Gregor. I love you more than I can say. Gregor, please make love to me. Let me be a part of you. I need you."

"Beloved, how can I? You've been so weak." Overcome with joy, yet struggling for self-control, he rained kisses upon her face and her silken hair. His lips caught hers briefly. "I cannot risk hurting you."

She felt a fevered pounding in her veins. "I hurt already. I ache for you, Gregor. Please? You cannot deny me. Not now." Her hands found their way beneath his nightshirt, wreaking havoc as they enflamed every nerve in his body.

Gregor, too, had suffered without her. Since her abduction, his heart had been dragged through nearly every conceivable human emotion. He had faced utter despair and hopelessness during the weeks following her abduction. Then, compelling fear had driven him during the desperate journey home from Garogan City. Overwhelming relief dimmed in comparison to the joy he had known when she had regained consciousness. Now, suddenly, she offered him fulfillment of his most precious dream. His body craved what only she could give him. Still, he was afraid to surrender to his personal desires, unable to bear the thought that he might hurt her.

To his surprise, he felt her rise above him, gently turning him onto his back as she moved to lie upon him. Her mouth trailed moist, hot kisses along the strong column of his neck as her cheek rubbed against the roughness of his heavy beard. He shivered at the warmth of her breath as her lips feathered velvet caresses along his ear, followed by the startling sensation of her teeth gently closing on the sensitive lobe.

"Gregor," she insisted, "I need for you to love me. I need for you to heal all the pain we've inflicted on each other."

His arms finally discovered strength to embrace her, his hands moving down to the incurve just above her hips and pressing her against him. Despite the worry that he might hurt her, his own passion swelled, unleashed by her deliberate attack on his senses.

He turned his head slightly, his mouth seeking hers. As their lips welded them together, he rolled her onto her back. She was so much thinner that he paused momentarily, her weakness a sobering concern. He lifted his face slightly away, breaking the bond their lips had formed. "Beloved, I can't."

She gave him no further chance to speak. Her fingers locked into his hair and pulled his face back, her lips demanding as they found his yet again. All fear, all resistance melted. His desire for her transcended every conscious thought.

Neither possessed any concept of the time that passed. Refuge sought became refuge found. They loved with words, with touch, with every sound, and every movement. They were joined in fire and in spirit and in soul. This night defined for them their destiny. They belonged together, to each other.

〜

Drugged by heavy slumber induced in the aftermath of their loving, Gregor turned and reached out to touch his wife. He was startled awake, finding her side of the bed empty. Fleeting panic flashed through his mind. Had last night's exquisite ecstasy been only another dream? He lifted his head from the pillow, seeking her through half-opened eyelids. She stood silently before the window, bathed in a soft glow of light. Partially drawn draperies permitted dawn's earliest rays to dispel some of night's dark mist.

He rose from the bed, shivering as chill air made contact with warm, bare skin. He snatched a soft woolen blanket off the bed and wrapped it around his shoulders. Bare feet padded as he approached her from behind.

Holding the corners of the blanket tightly, he stretched it around her and crossed his long arms possessively around the front of her shoulders. As he pulled her back against him, he felt against his skin the coolness of the thin, gauzy gown she now wore. He closed his eyes, savoring the feel of her chest rising and falling as his arms rested just above the generous curve of her breasts.

Her head fell backward, and his face immediately nuzzled against the side of her neck. He thought how perfect she felt within his embrace. If only this moment would never end, yet his own voice broke the silence. "How do you feel this morning?"

She rolled her head sensually against his shoulder. His closeness gave her such unbelievable joy. "Mmmm," she sighed. "This morning? I feel very well loved."

He couldn't help himself. It was impossible to suppress the laughter that erupted. "Of that, I am very well certain, my love. But that wasn't what I meant."

She giggled and turned within the protective warmth of the blanket and his embrace. Her palms flattened against his muscular chest. Her lips pressed tiny kisses against the smoothness of his skin. "I know very well what you meant. I tried to explain last night. I needed you. I needed your love to heal me."

Carefully stepping backward, Gregor led her toward the bed. Holding her tightly against him, he fell back onto the plump mattress, allowing her to land on top of him. Together, they squirmed underneath the covers, laughing and touching as if no other world existed beyond this one of their own creation. Finally, once they were settled, Gregor spoke, his tone quiet, almost solemn. "Alexa, we must talk. So many questions are flying through my mind."

She had known this moment was inevitable. "Ask," she prompted.

"First, tell me about last night. I must know."

She interrupted him with a kiss on his nose and a tease. "Yes, Gregor, as my lover, you were magnificent."

"Be serious," he chided, laughing again and finding it impossible to completely mask his pleasure at her lavish praise.

"I was being serious, but… All right. Since you insist, I'll try. Ask me your questions." She made an exaggerated effort to draw her features into a more serious expression.

"How is it you were so weak yesterday that you collapsed, yet last night you were so vital—so passionate? And now, this morning, you seem even stronger?" Curiosity was a driving force.

"You know that I came to you as Valiria. Valiria are, by nature, different. Everything for us is intense. Last night, I needed to share your love. It's complicated to explain, but it was the love you gave me, the bond we shared, that even now continues to strengthen me."

He considered her explanation for a moment, certain it was true even though somewhat puzzling. "I suppose I can only accept that response as given. I think my next question is perhaps not so easy to answer."

She leaned forward, touching his chin with her forehead, fully anticipating his next question.

"Alexa, two nights ago, the temple bells rang out at midnight, but they didn't just ring. They played beautiful melodies. While you were in Garogan, the bells rang every night at midnight until we brought you home. Last night, I was certain I heard them again."

"Did you check the time?" she asked. Her eyes gazed into his, reflecting not only her happiness but also merriment.

He cleared his throat and shook his head in mock annoyance. "I admit that I was too seriously occupied to check the clock. But I saw something else. Light. A glow. I find it impossible to believe it was just my imagination that we were surrounded by that light."

She smiled lovingly. The time had for him to know. With delicate fingers, she traced the sensuous curve of his lips, savoring the soft kiss he pressed against them. "Gregor, for years, you have relied solely on the steady support Stefan has provided you through unwavering friendship and the wisdom of his counsel."

"Yes, but what does that have to do with…"

She interrupted him with a brief kiss. "Gregor, Turand prepares to enter a new era. You have forces in the north, striking at the Sifiq when they are finally vulnerable. You have reinstated National Council. You face the painful probability of civil war. Your intentions are to usher Turand from the brink of total devastation in order to recapture the peace and prosperity of the past. Stefan remains your loyal adviser. You know you need additional backing. The light you saw last night was the harbinger of that support. Now, you have not only Stefan by your side. You have a loving wife." She paused. "And, for the first time in a century, Turand has the support of Valkana."

Gregor jerked upright in bed, her revelation an unexpected shock. "Valkana? Alexa, are you telling me you are…"

She smiled and sat up to face him, tugging blankets up around her. "Gregor, it's just one more unbelievable change. I feel awestruck that Val has chosen me for this honor. But, to answer you, yes. I am now Valkana."

He propped several pillows against the head of her bed and reclined back into them. Thoughts raced in rapid succession through his mind as he attempted to absorb the full import of her exalted spiritual role and what it would mean to him and to the people of Turand. Valkana had always been guides for Turandans—teaching them, loving them, healing them.

More than a century earlier, a movement had taken root, challenging traditional beliefs in Val. The Valiria had stubbornly persisted in preserving their order, but the last formally acknowledged Valkana had been of advanced age. Preparing for physical death, she had issued a dire warning, admonishing Turandans for allowing doubt to weaken their faith. She promised that no other Valkana would be sent to minister to them until they were once again ready to recognize Val's supremacy. He would continue to love them, but great tribulations would tear at the very fabric of their society. An age of suffering and want would assail them until enough Turandans were ready to accept and return to the God who had loved them and sustained them. They would exist in spiritual poverty and physical need until such time as enough prayers were turned to Val. Only then would he send them a new Valkana.

Gregor pondered the history and the legend. He remembered the teachings his mother had so lovingly instilled in him until the night of her untimely death. He reflected on the faith he had hidden and struggled to maintain along with the frequent, creeping doubts that his mother's dream-like image had continuously reminded him to disregard.

"Gregor?"

He looked at her, his eyes wide and childlike with undisguised wonder. "Valkana. My queen. My wife. How can this be?"

"It is as Val wills it to be. The time has come for our people to recapture the spirituality that once gifted Turand with peace, vitality, and creativity. I am Val's chosen guide. He willed our marriage, Gregor, so that you and I might come to accept and cherish his most precious gift. In our love, we can encourage and support each other through all that is sure to come. At the same time, we are a most visible example of how great are his gifts."

Gregor's huge hands enclosed hers as he gazed thoughtfully at her. "If you are Valkana, is it right that we love with such complete abandon as last night?"

The soft glow reappeared, surrounding her face, her shoulders. Her appearance transformed, and she seemed ethereal, almost otherworldly. He couldn't help but wonder.

"Gregor, our love is more than right. It is blessed. We have both suffered tragic losses and the burden of terrible sorrows. Sometimes, we have questioned and struggled. But always, whether obvious or not, our faith in Val was the strength that sustained us. It was our survival. This extraordinary love is one of those rewards about which you once challenged me."

The wry smile that crossed his face was quickly replaced by intense reflection. "Alexa, you have no idea how hard I prayed when they took you back to Garogan. At first, I prayed selfishly, wanting only to have you back. Later, I became frightened. What if you were happily reunited with Victor? Alexa, my very soul reeled in shock, but I began to pray that, whatever Val's will, at least you might be happy. The pain was staggering when I realized I loved you so much that I was willing to give you up." Tears eased along the side of his face.

Alexa shifted her legs around so she could lean against the expanse of his chest. "My beloved Gregor."

Her endearment wove itself into every thread of his being. Her nearness comforted him, diverting his attention from all the plotting and treacheries just beyond the haven of these chambers. He gathered her close as a whispered prayer of thanks sprang from his heart and crossed his lips.

Chapter 14

Committees formed to conduct many staggered sessions as representatives began to list actions and define directions for Turand's future. Some thought the affair no more than an elaborate distraction. Precious few had any idea that distraction was indeed intended for the relatively small Sifiq detachment still in Toraval. A secretly trained force of Turandans was, at that very moment, fighting Sifiq forces returning to the coast for voyages back to their homeland. The new rotation of Sifiq troops had been caught far out in the harbors by underwater traps that sank their ships. Those few who managed to reach shore in lifeboats were met by Turandan freedom fighters.

The following days provided a dramatic stage for subterfuge, negotiations, and plots. Throughout many emotion-packed sessions, Gregor remained attentive to the historical developments unfolding in Council. Despite all the disruptions and diplomatic finagling, he never failed to monitor his wife's condition.

Each day, she grew stronger, the natural, healthy blush returning to stain her ivory cheeks. Her smile was more frequent and spontaneous. Her expression was alert as she watched and listened carefully to everything around her. More and more, Gregor found himself discussing fine points with her to obtain her perspective. He was frequently surprised by her insight and impressed by her grasp of political issues requiring such diplomatic finesse. She quickly became a valued consultant and adviser. Still, she had not fully recovered her strength, so he frequently called for her to be excused from non-essential periods so that she might rest.

Evenings were hardest for them since she was usually exhausted by the end of each day's sessions. He insisted on personally escorting her every evening to her suite. Reluctantly, he left her to attend various delegates at dinner engagements or to meet privately with his supporters. Those hours apart were almost painful because of their personal needs to discuss and explore their newly acknowledged relationship.

Gregor returned to her rooms each night. Usually, he arrived so late that he would find her asleep. He understood that she was tired. For several days, that tiredness was complicated by her woman's time. Contented on those nights to steal into her bed and snuggle his massive frame as near as possible without disturbing her, he discovered a penetrating sense of solace that lulled him to sleep. As he inhaled the lilac fragrance surrounding her and listened to her rhythmic breathing, he found deep contentment in the certainty that she wanted him by her side.

Then, for two nights in a row, she had lain awake, awaiting his arrival. Her fingertips stroked away the day's fatigue and frustrations as she caressed his face and hair. He laughed as she promised she would never tire of touching him. Those were the precious nights when he had made love to her. The physical union between them was filled with passion and energy. Whenever he thought it impossible to reach a higher pinnacle, she inspired him to soar beyond any limitations he might have perceived. They loved with an intensity that inundated and surged through the very essence of their beings, merging them into a unique and transcendent force. Afterward, breathless and clinging to one another, they caressed and

232

exchanged tender kisses until they were calm enough to fall asleep in each other's arms.

At the end of the ninth day of Council, he arrived in her suite, surprised to find her still up, visiting with Lady Lorinda Skanos. The conversation he had intruded on had been noisy and animated. His arrival had caught the two women by surprise. Alexa rose immediately and glided into his arms, not hesitating to welcome him with a delighted kiss.

Lady Lorinda had knelt in formal salutation to the king. Enchanted by the vivacious expression on his wife's face, Gregor shocked the older woman by offering her his hand and helping Lorinda to her feet. He then bowed. "Lady Lorinda, anyone who can inspire such vitality in my wife after such a long, hard week deserves my personal welcome and my gratitude."

Lady Lorinda looked at him in disbelief. She had heard so much about him, both good and bad. She thought to gracefully accomplish her exit, just in case he was toying with her. "Sire, it appears I have stayed later than I should have. I really should say good night."

"Nonsense, Milady. It's not even ten-thirty. My wife has usually been asleep by eight or nine this past week. Please stay, if only for a few more minutes. You must realize it has been a very long time since she has enjoyed any time with family. I am also embarrassed to admit that, until now, I have had no opportunity to meet any of her family."

Lorinda directed a nervous glance at Alexa. Seeing emerald eyes twinkling with humor and pleasure, she was instantly reassured and resumed her seat. Gregor led Alexa to the longer settee on the opposite side of the small sitting room, where he sat down first. Alexa then sat beside him, picking her feet up and tucking them beneath her.

"So tell me. Why were you both laughing so hard when I came in? I've heard too little laughter recently." He dropped an affectionate kiss on the top of his wife's head, which rested comfortably against his arm.

The ladies exchanged glances, and Alexa burst into gales of laughter. Her sides ached in no time. Lorinda chuckled behind her hand, finding it nearly impossible to restrain herself in the face of her cousin's abandon but too well trained in decorum to laugh aloud in the king's presence.

"Will you not tell him?" Lorinda finally asked.

Gregor's eyebrows lifted high, arching in unaccustomed amusement at his wife's unusual outburst. "Yes, I would appreciate knowing what's so funny. Perhaps I might join the laughter?" He was teasing now, laughter already a soft presence in his wonderfully rich voice.

Alexa looked at him and only laughed harder. Untangling herself from his arms, she stood and went to pour herself some water. Each time she brought the glass to her lips, she broke into fresh giggles, unable to speak.

"You must excuse my cousin, Sire." Lady Lorinda felt sorry for the lost expression on his face as he watched his wife overcome with silliness. "We were discussing some of her victories at shots when you arrived. She had just started to tell me of her most recent tournament."

Gregor cast his wife an absurd expression that mixed amusement with mocking chastisement. He held a finger up, signaling for her to retake her seat beside him. Knowing she was lost, she obediently returned to sit down beside him.

"Tournaments?" he asked.

Lady Lorinda was all too proud to inform him of her cousin's accomplishments as a shots champion. Alexa had learned the skills in Garogan City and was one of only a few women proficient in the sport. She had won the entire field on three occasions, defeating women and men. Their great laughter had begun as they discussed the traditional downing of the Taca, remembering how each time she drank the foul ale, she had ended up practically unconscious for nearly twenty-four hours. Her final strategy was to lose the last rounds. She said she could never tolerate more Taca for the rest of her life.

Gregor nearly snorted his laughter. His face was alight as he remembered their own competition. "Then she hasn't yet told you of her most recent game of shots?"

Lorinda shook her head, her eyes puzzled at the laughter that rocked both of them now. "No, but it appears to have left quite an impression on the two of you."

Alexa finally rediscovered her voice, although it wasn't easy for her to talk. "Oh, cousin, it wasn't a pretty sight at all. Gregor and I had a bit of a disagreement."

Gregor interrupted her, snared by the spirit of fun. "She calls it a disagreement. It took weeks for our household staff to find and clear away all the remnants of crystal and porcelain that she broke in the library with antique silver coasters since renamed the Flying Disks of Toraval. Observing her technique, I innocently challenged her to a game of shots to resolve the dispute. She never informed me that she was a tournament champion." He shot her a glance of amused accusation.

"You, Sire, only asked if I had ever played shots," she replied with a giggle.

"And I clearly recall that you only said once or twice."

"Let me guess. She defeated even you at shots?" Lorinda asked, somewhat dismayed that her cousin would play to win even against the king.

"She most certainly did. It was the first time I had suffered defeat in shots since I was ten. But, alas, my revenge came when she downed the Taca."

"I can only imagine," Lorinda commented, relaxing slightly in the environment of comfortable humor that pervaded the room.

"Oh, Lorinda, I drank that horrible Taca, and I thought I was going to die. I was so lucky that here in Toraval, their tankards are so much smaller than in the south. I made it all the way here before I got sick." She burst into fresh giggles. "Gregor came to look for me, and I swear I could have died from humiliation when he found me sprawled on the bathroom floor. I took one look at him and started throwing up all over again. He practically had to carry me to bed. Then he gave me some vile-tasting medicine, and I slept only fifteen or sixteen hours."

"Your Majesty, I assure you. My cousin brought this child up with the most rigid training. She should have made you a more respectable wife." Lorinda was half-serious, barely suppressing the temptation to giggle as she tried to imagine Alexa's distress at being so sick in front of such a distinguished man as the king.

"Lady Lorinda, set your mind at ease. Your cousin makes a most delightful and entertaining wife." Gregor laughed and hugged Alexa close, his adoring affection obvious and reassuring to the older lady, who had prayed for years that Alexa might find such happiness.

They chatted for a short while longer before saying goodnight. Gregor and Alexa sat back down on the settee once they were alone. They cuddled and laughed, exchanging teasing remarks about the whole shots incident. For both, there was sweetness in the freedom of being themselves together. Laughter provided potent medicine, relieving much of the ongoing stress. Later, as they lay in bed, the same feeling washed over them. They were more relaxed together than either could ever remember in a marriage characterized by emotional extremes.

⌣

Three days before the scheduled close of Council, Gregor adjourned the morning session for the extended midday break. He rose from the table where he had studied documents and proposals prepared by the committee responsible for developing contingency plans for use in the event of national emergencies. He had already reviewed recommendations covering other aspects of the country's governmental needs. All proposals were now ready for final discussion and final approval during the last two days before closing ceremonies.

Delegates gathered around the king. Most offered sincere congratulations for the work accomplished thus far. Alexa made a path through the crowd and stepped alongside her husband, linking her arm with his. Pride in him shone on her face. He had taken substantial risks with the Sifiq to call and organize this National Council. That was success enough. Now, complex plans were developed to provide a shielding layer of protection against whatever lay ahead. Nevertheless, she felt confident that the sheer magnetism he possessed would carry the final processes successfully through ratification.

As delegates drifted from the hall, she caught his attention for a moment. "Gregor, if you have no objection, I would like to go outside for a little while. The sun is bright today, and I want to take a short walk."

"Is it not too cold?" he questioned, pausing to shake hands with two more well-wishers.

"I'll be fine. I'll join you shortly for midday." With that, she kissed his cheek and left the assembly. She moved purposefully past small groups of people who still lingered in the corridors. She paused only long enough to exchange a brief personal greeting or to graciously accept a congratulatory comment regarding her husband's continuing masterful conduct of Council.

She was relieved to reach the passageway leading to a small garden. Stepping out into brilliant winter sunshine, she allowed her head to fall back so that the sun could bathe her face in its glory. After several moments of such self-indulgence, she began to stroll through the stark leavings of summer's abundance. Wintry air was fragrant as an occasional light wind carried the rich scent of evergreens through the sanctuary. She breathed in deeply, expelling the air in soft, breathy sighs as she reached a bench she had claimed as her own. Slowly sitting on its penetrating cold surface, she slipped almost immediately into a light trance. A sense of overwhelming love permeated her very soul.

Following brief, silent prayer and centering, she rose. Without moving away from the bench, she stretched chilled limbs and shook off the coldness. She then turned to go in, startled as she ran directly into Victor.

"Alexa, I must talk with you." Hazel irises were surrounded by blood-shot veins. Facial muscles were tense, a faint twitch noticeable at the corner of his narrow mouth.

"Victor, there is nothing left to say between us."

"Alexa, too much enmity exists between us. I cannot bear it any longer. I still love you too much."

Alexa stared at him. She no longer felt secure in his presence. "You may escort me inside if you like."

He grabbed her hand, lifting it to his lips. "Alexa, please. You must understand. I never meant to hurt you in Garogan. I would sooner die than see you hurt." He was insistent, almost desperate.

"Then I fail to understand how you could have hit me when I was unable to defend myself. Or how you could agree to release me to Lord Anderon for execution."

"Sweetest, you know I would never have allowed him to hurt you. Considering your refusal to annul the marriage, I needed time to figure out how to save you. Damn it! I love you! I always have, and I always will!" He started to pull her toward him, but she quickly extracted her hand and sidestepped him.

"Victor, I must go inside. Now."

He grabbed her arms, restraining her. "Alexa, after all the tragedy we faced together... After everything we shared, can you honestly tell me you no longer love me?" His eyes gleamed golden, haunted desperation lurking in their depths.

She appraised him quietly, genuinely wishing to inflict no more pain upon him. "Victor," she began softly, "how can I deny the part of me that will always love you? You have always been part of my life. You brought light to chase away shadows and laughter to replace tears. Life has now led us apart. You must accept that truth sooner or later. I do not love you as a woman loves a man."

"Alexa, how can you expect me to believe that? How can you ever forget that day in Zenox Prison? The way you clung to me? The way we kissed? Your kisses promised me everything! We planned a lifetime of togetherness. I refuse to accept you no longer love me." His voice grew in volume until he nearly shouted at her.

Alexa inhaled deeply, her voice laden with sadness when once again she spoke. "Victor, you have no choice. I am deeply in love with Gregor." Her husband's name had barely crossed her lips before Victor's open hand came crashing against the side of her face, the blow catching her off-guard and knocking her to the ground.

Alexa was vaguely aware of footsteps rushing past her. She heard the scuffling sounds of struggle above her but was too stunned to look up. A pair of strong arms reached around her and supported her securely before helping her rise to her feet. Her breathing was rapid, and her left hand instinctively raised against her face. She looked into dark eyes filled with barely contained fury as they appraised angry red welts on her cheek and drops of blood oozing from an already swelling lip.

Alexa mastered her breathing, forcing herself to remain calm. The expression contorting her husband's face reflected a fierce desire for retaliation. She knew she had to maintain control. Violence of any sort was expressly forbidden by the ancient laws governing Council.

"Alexa?" Despite the almost tangible force emanating from his body, her name was uttered as a tender, frightened caress.

She moved her hand from her face and touched her husband's trembling jaw. She then turned around to glare at Victor, who fought against Stefan and two palace guards. Just behind him stood several Council delegates, who had been shocked onlookers.

Victor gasped when he saw her. Her face already showed signs of heavy bruising. Cold alone slowed the swelling. Worse, her emerald eyes seared into his soul with indescribable fires.

"Victor, you shame yourself and all you ever represented. I promise you one thing. You will never strike me again." She spoke quietly to him with an anger none present had ever seen from her. "My husband makes me proud with the restraint he now shows. I defer to his judgment as to how you will pay for this abomination."

Gregor glanced down at her. He knew she was in pain, yet she faced her attacker with strength. More than that, her wisdom provided compliment and reminder to her husband. He must address the matter in accordance with law.

Victor stared at her, his arms pinned painfully behind him. He could not believe he had hit her again. Unspeakable regret nauseated him. Still, he refused to show any sign of weakness in front of her husband.

Gregor stood stiffly erect, his immense height made more intimidating by the fury blazing within him. "Victor Garogan, you have defiled the sanctity of this National Council with violence. Further, you committed a disgusting act of violence by striking not just a delegate but my wife and our queen. You are to be bound and taken back to the assembly hall. I will call for Council to reconvene in fifteen minutes."

Gregor nodded to the guards, who dragged Victor, cursing and shouting, from the gardens. Stefan left wordlessly with the other representatives to summon all the delegates back to the assembly hall.

"Beloved," Gregor turned tear-glazed eyes to his wife. "Forgive me. I tried to reach you before he struck you." His hands held her shoulders, infusing her with much-needed warmth as her teeth began to chatter.

"Help me inside," she whispered. Then, with his arm behind her back, Gregor led her back inside the palace.

Entering the welcome warmth, Alexa leaned heavily against her husband's side. She wasn't seriously hurt. Instead, she discovered outrage she had not experienced since the Sifiq overran her childhood home. Hers was righteous anger, borne more of disgust that Victor would disrupt Council rather than the physical injury he had inflicted upon her.

"Are you certain you're all right? Alexa?" Gregor felt something change in her. He felt her lean weakly against him only momentarily before she straightened. She pulled away from him and ran to a lounge the ladies used.

Inside, she rushed past several women delegates who were already discussing details of the altercation in the garden. Her eyes burned through them, their subsequent silence instantaneous. She then went to a porcelain basin and ran cold water. Taking a freshly pressed linen towel from a woven silver basket, she dabbed the cloth in cold water and then pressed it against her injured lip.

She stared at her reflection in the gilt-framed mirror above the sink. She saw not the woman whose face was swollen and showing the fresh invasion of bluish-purple bruises. She saw Valkana, walking along the precipice of civil war brought ever closer by the act of violence she had just endured.

Gentle hands landed upon her shoulders. The mirror now reflected the faces of Lady Lorinda and the queen's two ladies-in-waiting. Alexa closed her eyes and swallowed hard. She turned to face them. Despite the fiery sting in her face, her voice was remarkably firm and restrained. "Ladies, there's no cause for undue concern. I needed only to gather my thoughts. Please accompany me to the assembly hall. My husband awaits me." She gave no chance for questions or sympathy.

Upon their arrival outside the room, Stefan awaited her. "Are you all right, Your Majesty?"

Alexa reached out and took his hand reassuringly. "I'm fine, Stefan. How is my husband?"

"Worried. Infuriated. Everyone is already waiting for you inside. Your Majesty, are you certain you are prepared to face this?" Stefan, who still addressed her formally in the presence of others outside the royal circle, was genuinely concerned.

Alexa nodded, then lifted her chin and squared her shoulders. An air of regal command, unusual for someone not raised as royalty, descended upon her. She linked her right arm in Lady Lorinda's left as she simultaneously laid her left hand upon Stefan's right forearm. Tira and Tirani took places immediately behind the queen as the dignified group entered the hall with great solemnity.

As they reached the center front where the king stood, Alexa's ladies-in-waiting fell back while Lady Lorinda gracefully moved aside to join her husband. Stefan, continuing with solemn formality, guided Alexa to stand directly in front of Gregor. Stefan's left hand crossed over in front of him to cover her hand and wrist as she dropped a graceful curtsy before her husband. Stefan then passed her hand to Gregor, who bade her rise.

Alexa's eyes rapidly assessed the anxious scene before her. Gregor's face was still flushed deep red, his anger boiling just beneath the surface. His eyes appeared black as onyx, glittering with reinforced wrath as he noted the extent of fresh bruising that already marred his wife's features. As she turned to sit upon the throne to which Gregor led her, she instantly saw Victor, securely restrained by two burly palace guards. Garogan delegates stood to Victor's right, and Lord Anderon stood to his left. Behind them were the remaining council delegates, some seated, most standing. Alexa steadied her breathing, knowing before a word was spoken that this represented a critical turning point in Turand's history.

Gregor chose not to sit. Instead, he paced several times in front of Victor, the physical activity somewhat abating the fury coursing through his blood. "Lord Victor Garogan, you have today committed serious insult and injury to Council and an act of unwarranted violence against not only a council member but against the Queen of Turand. Council Charter Laws have governed council proceedings for centuries and strictly prohibit any violence during Council. How do you speak concerning this matter?"

Victor's hazel eyes spewed hatred at the man before him. "What would you have me say, Your Majesty?" Victor answered, bitterly sarcastic.

"I would have you explain your actions, Lord Garogan." Gregor strained to control his temper.

"Then I would say that you have consorted with the filthy Sifiq to the detriment of the people of Turand. I would also tell you that you have stolen from me the woman who was meant to be my wife. I would tell you that my hatred for you is a flame that will most certainly burn you sooner or later. And, I would tell you that I regret striking the one love of my life. I only hoped to bring her to her senses."

Muted whispers followed shocked gasps from council delegates until Gregor lifted his hands for quiet. Gregor now stood rigid, fighting his own internal war. As king, responsibility was his to retain order and to enforce council laws. But, as a man whose wife had been brutalized by the man barely six feet away from him, he ached to lunge forward to inflict just punishment for the wrongs committed.

A hand slid firmly into place against the small of his back, snapping him from his inner turmoil. He was grateful for the support Alexa now provided him. Her mere presence provided a balm to soothe the raging within his breast.

"Lord Garogan, you disgrace the noble intentions of Council. Further, you are shamed by your acts of violence against anyone, most especially your queen. As Alexa's husband, I am physically sickened and appalled by your actions. However, my wife reminds me of my duties as king and leader of Council. Therefore, my decision is that you are to be returned to your quarters under guard. You will have one hour before you are escorted to the courtyard. You are then to be dismissed from National Council and Toraval under the shroud of dishonor. You will be returned to Garogan Province, bound if necessary."

Victor stared at Gregor in disbelief. He had not expected the severity of the penalty imposed, though it certainly could have been much worse. He honestly had believed that Gregor would not risk what such a decision would surely mean to Turand.

"Alexa, don't let this happen. You know what this means. Alexa, I love you! I never meant to hurt you!"

Alexa met his gaze, her expression intense. "Victor, as I told you earlier today, and not for the first time, I love my husband. That is why I stay, not because he exerts any force over me. I am here because it is my choice. At this moment, Gregor merits my respect more than ever. I alone know how great the cost of his outward calm. Val has given you choices. You chose violence in direct defiance of council law and tradition. My husband's sentence is both generous and merciful, considering the options available to him. Do not seek my intervention. It will not be forthcoming."

Gregor carefully studied Victor's blanched and shocked countenance. In a faraway corner of his being, Gregor could almost feel sympathy. He could only imagine how he would feel to lose her love. However, this was no time for a deeper analysis of feelings. He signaled his guards to remove Victor from the hall.

Upstairs, in her sitting room, her eyes begged his understanding. "Gregor, will you be able to forgive me if I do not accompany you to the courtyard?"

His gaze was loving as he studied the delicate lines of her face, the interlaced fingers in her lap contrasting against the dark violet gown flowing outward from her waist. There seemed an air of detachment about her. Perhaps it was resignation. "Beloved, I know how you once loved Lord Garogan. Is it too difficult for you to witness his final disgrace?"

She was touched by his honest concern, noting there wasn't the slightest hint of insincerity in his question. "I admit that it wouldn't be easy for me. I could never want something like this to happen to Victor. However, I am reconciled to what happened. In truth, I only wish to ask your consent for something I feel I must do instead."

"And that would be?" He knelt before her, his hands framing her face tenderly, mindful of the physical pain she must also be feeling. "If you have no objections, I wish to go to the temple." Her request was spoken softly, her need pressing.

"May I ask that Stefan escort you?"

She smiled and nodded, knowing he would feel better if someone he trusted accompanied her. She leaned forward and brushed his lips with hers. "Perhaps you might join us later. With Victor's exile sure to hasten hostilities, perhaps it's time for the remainder of Council to join us, too. The time has come for Turand to know the return of Valkana."

⇅

People filled the courtyard despite chill temperatures and biting winds. Lord and Lady Skanos joined Gregor as he waited on the front steps of the palace. As Alexa's only relative present, Lady Skanos had claimed the right to stand in the queen's place as justice was delivered.

Gregor's royal guards waited, prepared to escort Victor from Toraval. The other Garogan delegates had also hastily packed to return with Victor. Utterly defiant, Victor stood with hands tightly bound behind him. Gregor noted with puzzled surprise that Lord Anderon had joined the Garogan delegation. The Tasa Coast and Pitrand provincial delegates had also packed and prepared to leave Council in protest of Victor's dismissal.

"Your Majesty, I respectfully request permission to speak." Lord Anderon's voice was a high-pitched, nasal sound. A tall, thin man, his face was long and narrow. His eyes, a light brown color that almost blended with his pasty complexion, bulged slightly.

Gregor only nodded his permission.

"I plead with you, Your Majesty. Reconsider this matter. The consequences will most certainly be tragic. There must be a way to ease these tensions. The Tasa Coast and Pitrand delegations voice opposition to Lord Garogan's dismissal and prepare to withdraw from Council if you insist on this unadvisable course of action. You must consider an exception based on such unique circumstances."

Before Gregor could respond, Victor's voice called out. "Where is she, Gregor? Did you forbid her to come? Are you afraid she'll finally recover her senses if she sees me trussed and bound like an animal?"

Lady Lorinda stepped neatly in front of Gregor, blocking his way. She preferred risking his displeasure in order to keep him focused. She heard his voice low in her ear. "Cousin, impetuous action under crisis must be a family trait."

"Lord Anderon," Gregor replied at length, "your concern and your warning are received with due consideration. However, council law is specific and, as with my wife's earlier illness, allows no deviations and no exceptions." He then directed his attention to Victor. "Lord Garogan, you are officially banished from Council. You are to return to your home province with a decree of five years official dishonorable censure."

"Bastard! You still haven't the courage to answer me! Damn it, Gregor, I demand to see Alexa!"

Lady Lorinda stepped forward once again, the energy in her slender figure belying her age. Her features were more prominent than Alexa's, but their blood ties were undeniable. Her eyes gleamed with disgust. She called out in a sharp voice. "Lord Garogan, quiet! As Queen Alexa's only relative present, I hereby claim my right to speak in her absence. You and Lord Anderon shame us all with your deceit and treachery. I've heard you, Victor, shout obscenities at our king. I also heard you claim to love my cousin while showing no remorse for striking her. I spent last evening with her, and I think this is the perfect time for Council to know the sordid details of the queen's recent trip to Garogan.

"Tell them, Victor, how you kept her locked away in isolation, knowing full well such imprisonment is dangerous to Valiria. Or would you prefer to tell them how many times you shook her nearly senseless or struck her while she was alone and unable to defend herself? Or perhaps you could explain how you nearly killed her with the arrow you used in an attempt to assassinate our king?"

Lady Lorinda grew more inflamed than ever with all her cousin had told her. "And you, Lord Anderon, you vile and traitorous power-seeker! Why don't you explain how you watched as your men tried to beat her into agreeing to annul her marriage? Tell them that when she refused, Lord Garogan agreed to release her to you for execution. You are both shameful, disgusting examples of the worst that has happened to Turand."

Turning her attention to the council delegates, she continued, "Fellow representatives, what I have said is the truth from our queen's own lips. You all know that, as sworn Valiria, she dare not lie. With tears in her eyes, my dear cousin asked that I disregard whatever rumors I had heard. She truly loves her husband. She swore that he is her love and her happiness. Since coming to Toraval, I have spent time privately with both of them. I believe her."

Having vented her anger, Lady Lorinda was unaware that Gregor's face had drained of blood, his hands clenching stone balusters to steady himself when she had spoken of how Lord Anderon had abused Alexa. Until now, there had been little time to discuss details of her captivity in Garogan. When Lady Lorinda informed Council of the planned execution, Gregor had reeled, having no idea how severely his wife had been treated. Even now, the very idea threatened to overwhelm him with revulsion, his stomach pitching in protest. How close he had come to losing her forever! Gregor forced himself to breathe in and out, willing himself to do what was more necessary than ever.

"Lord Anderon, you and your delegates will not be permitted to leave Toraval until an appropriate escort is assembled." He then addressed the captain of his guard. "Captain, you are to escort the Garogan delegates back to their province. If they resist you in any way, utilize your own best judgment in dealing with them."

"Gregor, you will pay! I swear it! Alexa is mine! She always was and always will be!"

Gregor stared at Victor with an odd expression, disgust mixing with just a hint of pity. "Captain, have your men gag him and tie him to his horse. Then remove him from my sight."

Gregor stood rooted to the steps of the palace, watching the soldiers and the exiled council members fade into the distance. There was no shred of satisfaction in the punishment he had meted out. The fact that Alexa was safe from Victor was his sole consolation as he stood poised on the brink of war with his own people.

Euphonious chimes from the temple bells interrupted his somber contemplation. Music filled the air, and everyone turned automatically to face the temple's grand entrance. Twin spires towered above the central dome of the edifice and housed the carillons, now providing a beautiful symphony of sound. Sweet music beckoned to them all.

Gray-white stone walls gleamed golden in the afternoon sun and provided startling contrast to the soaring, arched doorways now swinging open. Gregor swallowed several times. Long before his birth, the temple had been sealed by an unknown force. This day would be the first occasion during his lifetime that a King of Turand had passed through its impressive portals. Butterflies flitted nervously in his stomach, leaving him feeling uncomfortably hollow.

Inviting Lady Lorinda and her husband to accompany him, Gregor started down the palace steps and crossed the square. Unsure what to do next, council delegates stepped back to clear a path. Upon Gregor's arrival at the temple entrance, he paused and turned to the crowd behind him, gesturing that they were welcome to follow.

Within the sacred walls of Val's temple, soft light illuminated wooden pews and intricately carved statuary. Tall, narrow, arched windows soared toward the heavens with filtered light shining through etched and frosted panes. At the front, Thero waited behind the altar, his balding head bent in prayer.

On steps rising from the main floor to the altar, a woman's solitary figure knelt. She was gowned in a simple robe gleaming with golden embroidery on golden fabric. Over her head, also bent in prayer, rested a plain golden band that held in place the intricately patterned gold-mesh veil that covered her face and her hair.

Gregor's heart skidded to a near halt. Already he physically felt the strong waves of vibrating energy emanating from her. He glanced from one side to the other, barely able to register the stunned expressions of Lord and Lady Skanos. They, too, were unmistakably affected by the flow of electricity.

Stefan rose from the front pew, his slender silhouette elegant and distinguished. He came forward to escort Gregor to a low-backed chair placed to the right of the altar. The chair was carved with ornate designs, its wooden arms and legs highlighted with the patina of gold-leaf accents. The back and seat were padded and covered with violet damask upholstery. This seat had been reserved centuries earlier for Turand's ruling monarch.

Gregor paused while Lord and Lady Skanos moved into the front bank of pews. Then, with stately composure, he walked to stand before his chair. No one spoke. The only sounds were the swish of ladies' gowns and the shuffle of many feet as delegates entered and filed into rows of long-empty seats.

As the last representatives found seating, the carillon bells slowed their melodious peal, and the front doors glided to a close, powered by unseen hands. Thero lifted his head, unashamed of the joyful tears streaking his face. No matter the solemn and heart-wrenching circumstances of earlier in the day, Val had finally chosen this moment to manifest the love and support he had promised to return.

"King Gregor and ladies and gentlemen of Turand's great National Council, I bid you welcome to the holy Temple of Val. I ask each of you to pause for brief meditation as I chant Val's loving welcome." Minutes later, Thero's voice faded as a soft echo. As his last notes receded into memory, the golden-clad figure before the altar began to emit a faint, unmistakable glow as it gracefully rose from white marble steps. Then, slowly, she turned to face the gathering.

Sighs, gasps, and muffled sobs were mere wisps of sounds filling the arched chamber. The woman who stood before them commanded with sheer presence since none could see even the tiniest part of her face. Some of those gathered were doubters who searched their souls to explain the undulating shivers moving through them. Others, whose spirituality and faith had been maintained despite every effort exerted by the Sifiq, wondered in amazement. Could this actually be happening? Could this possibly be Val's promise fulfilled at last?

The voice speaking out from beneath the golden veil was vibrant and melodious, tempered with indescribable gentleness. "Val is with us today. Give thanks and rejoice." She then turned and stepped up to the top level of the altar. Once again, she faced those gathered in the temple.

"The people of Turand are beloved by Val. Their prayers subsided in strength and numbers for too long. However, many once again seek the love and guidance that only God can provide. Challenges and tribulations still confront us. We will overcome them only through our re-alliance with the omnipotent force that is Val."

She patiently awaited an end to the hushed whispers that followed her declaration. Then, she shifted her focus to the king. "Gregor, only son of King Maxim and Queen Anlía, approach the altar of Val."

Gregor followed her instructions, awed by the power of the totally concealed figure before him. He knew no fear, yet never had he known such inexplicable anticipation. Without thinking, he knelt on one knee before her.

"King Gregor, do you know who I am?" Her intonation was so changed that he barely recognized her voice. He had no doubt the direction in which she sought his help.

"I know who you are, Milady. You are the chosen servant priestess of Val. You are Valkana." The rich timbre of his voice created a fresh round of awestruck whispers that swelled, then quickly diminished.

"King Gregor, you have come to the throne of Turand with faith in Val, which finds you in his favor. However, circumstances have initiated your reign without Val's blessing. You hold vast responsibility, not only to your people but also to Val himself. Declare now how you wish to continue your reign, knowing that you are blessed with the freedom to decide your own path."

Gregor's voice rose to the soaring arches above. "I desire Val's blessing for my people and his guidance to direct my reign. I also humbly ask his blessing upon my life and that of my queen and our marriage."

The figure remained motionless. "Are you absolutely certain this is the path you choose?"

"I am," he replied firmly and distinctly.

With arms outstretched, she approached him. He bowed his head as her hands came to rest upon it. What had been a subtle glow intensified and slowly began to pulsate until living light enveloped them both. After several moments, she removed her hands and, bending slightly at the knee, knelt to accept his hands into hers.

"Gregor, rightful King of Turand, rejoice in Val's great blessings upon you. Take comfort in the faith you have been given and guard it well. Your path is not yet cleared of tragic obstacles. Your love is your strength. Your faith will be your shield. Guide your people with wisdom, and you will surely prevail."

She allowed his hands to slide from hers as she rose again. Then, leaving Gregor in his kneeling position, she turned to Stefan. "Stefan Sidano, approach the altar."

Once Stefan had done so and knelt to Gregor's left, she continued. "Stefan, you entered manhood with great doubt and skepticism regarding our Lord Val. At the same time, you developed wisdom and integrity of the highest order. During these years, you have served your king as trusted adviser. Why have you asked to come before Valkana?"

Stefan trembled slightly with the powerful emotions coursing through him. "Lady Valkana, I have lived my life seeking means of survival for myself and our people. Although I have so much yet to learn, an undeniable truth has awakened in me. Each of us is precious in our own right as unique creations of the hand of our Lord Val. Survival alone is no longer enough. I desire life–life truly rich and fulfilling only when lived according to Val's teachings. Lady Valkana, I wish to declare newfound faith in Val. I request through his high priestess the blessings that will be the source of continued wisdom and perseverance as our nation faces the coming storm of dissent and potential violence."

The Valkana repeated her ritual with Stefan, identical to the way she had done with Gregor. She then gestured that both men should stand to face the members of Council.

"Behold the two men who lead this nation. Both have requested and received Val's blessings. Examine your beliefs, as well. Where is your faith? Are your hearts open to receive the love and blessings Val is prepared to give you? Contemplate the rapidly changing circumstances of your country and the needs of your people. Finally, I invite you to study the ancient writings and accept Val's invitation."

She fell into silence, her energy flowing into the gathering of delegates. Her voice was low when she spoke again, the tone soothing to the overwhelmed assembly. "I feel strong faith in most. A few are doubters. To the two of you who question so cynically, I declare that I hold no personal desire for your worship. Worship is not mine to desire. I am simply Val's servant, the guide he sends to you. I am your direct conduit to the forces he is willing to share with you. In return, he asks your love and devotion to what is right."

She allowed several minutes of contemplative silence before turning back to the altar. Lifting her arms high above her head, she gazed upward into the suspended crystal pyramid. From the golden sun within flashed dazzling shafts of light that immediately connected with her body. The connection persisted until she levitated. As she hovered high above the altar, her voice echoed throughout the temple. "Go from this place. Carry in your hearts and in your minds all that you have seen and heard. Accept Val's will and love him in return. Restore peace to Turand."

Shock was defined in every line of Gregor's face as Stefan literally pulled him to his feet and dragged him down the center aisle ahead of the other delegates. Valkana, strong and faithful, had been sent at last by Val to help his people. Gregor could hardly absorb the impact this would lend to accomplishing his dreams. Neither could he assimilate the dual roles Valkana played as his queen and his wife.

The energy subsided gradually as the priestess lowered to the floor. The Valkana leaned forward to lay her forehead reverently against the cool white marble of the dais. The temple was quiet once more, yet she sensed remaining energy.

"Lady Lorinda Skanos, why do you tarry?"

Lady Lorinda showed no surprise. After the impossible display she had just witnessed, the question seemed a simple matter for the woman whose back was turned to her. "I most respectfully request the honor to speak with Valkana."

The Valkana turned, still concealed beneath golden veils and robes. "Lady Skanos, your faith has never wavered throughout these many years of strife and oppression. Your desire to speak with me honors me."

Lorinda, unable to hide either her surprise or her pleasure, shifted her gaze downward. She breathed deeply to calm nerves jangled by more excitement in a day than she had known in a lifetime. "My Lady Valkana, I feel blessed to have been permitted to observe what occurred here today. To witness our king request and accept Val's way for Turand's future exceeds any dreams I ever entertained for my country."

"Then what thoughts intrude upon you with such sadness?"

Perception from the Valkana was instantaneous and somewhat disconcerting. "Milady, it is not my intention to question the wisdom of the events in the temple today. I only wish to express a certain sadness that my cousin, Queen Alexa, could not be in attendance. She suffered at the hands of an attacker today. I believe her husband sent her to her rooms to rest, so she could not attend. Surely her heart knows deep melancholy. She has lost so much in her lifetime and has asked for little. For years, she refused to submit to dangers inherent with her open declaration as Valiria and has resolutely practiced her faith."

Lady Lorinda's lips quivered as she recalled all the tragedy in her young cousin's life. "Lady Valkana, I only ask that my cousin be allowed to experience the joy of being here in your presence. To do so would be reward for her unwavering faith. I cannot describe to you the bliss she would have known had she been at her husband's side here today. Why was she denied? Why was she not allowed to be here today?"

The priestess beckoned Lady Lorinda forward. The Valkana's hands raised to the scalloped edge of her veil. As she began to lift the delicate, whispering mesh, the sound of her voice from beneath began to change. "Cousin, I've been here all along."

Lady Lorinda staggered and stumbled backward, only to be steadied by Alexa's quick embrace. Lorinda's smile of dawning recognition spread to brighten her entire face. "Alexa! Praises be to Val! Can I believe my eyes?"

"Believe, dear cousin, and keep the secret until Val chooses to reveal my identity. Promise me."

"You have my promise. Does Gregor know?"

"Of course, he knows."

"He seemed so astonished today. As we all were."

"Lorinda, just like the rest of you, he had no idea what to expect. Please, cousin, guard this confidence well, even from your own husband. This revelation must be made according to Val's will, not mine. Now, go. I must change and return to the palace. Gregor awaits me."

They hugged each other tightly before Alexa was left to change and consider how the day's events had unfolded.

Chapter 15

With his typical energy, Gregor bounded up the sweeping marble staircase, taking two steps at a time. Just as he reached the top, he watched Alexa glide toward him. She had changed into a dark green gown, fitted at the bodice, with brocade skirts falling from her waist into flounces swirling elegantly around her ankles. Wide cuffs caught full, puffed sleeves at her wrists. As usual, her hair fell into waves of curls just below her shoulders.

Her eyes appeared darkened to the shade of evergreens, lights sparkling from the depths of her being. Her smile curved wider the moment she saw him. He thought her beauty would be perfect just now were it not for the bruises darkening her cheek.

"I came to look for you. The delegates are all reconvened downstairs," he told her, linking their arms before escorting her down the stairs. Outside the assembly hall, he paused. Turning to face her, his expression was mystified. "This session should be quite interesting. We all experienced a rather unusual afternoon."

"Oh?" she responded, brows arched in feigned surprise. "How so?"

"Let us say you and I have some serious matters to discuss later. For the moment, Your Majesty, just know that I love you very, very much." He leaned forward to plant a brief kiss against her lips as the doors of the hall were opened for them. Without losing his composure, he whispered as they turned to enter. "Later, my love."

Two days later, Alexa stood before a mirror at the temple, adjusting the golden headpiece over her dark hair. Her breathing quickened, and her hands trembled slightly. With Val's presence intensified within the sacred confines of the temple, she pondered in amazement the continuously unfolding events. Since the confrontation with Victor, council delegates and Toraval's people had celebrated the return of Valkana to their midst.

Following Lord Garogan's expulsion and the departure of the southern provincial delegates, consideration and acceptance of most proposals proceeded rapidly. Many representatives also expressed the desire for personal consultations with the queen before departing Toraval. The queen, still known to them only as Valiria, could assist them in their search for the spiritual guidance that would fortify them during the coming months promising so much strife.

With golden robes smoothed into place and her face shielded by the golden mesh veil, Alexa knelt before the altar of Val. Her chant carried her into a deep state of meditation, her communion with Val vital to the success of bringing her people fully back to him.

So deep was her meditation that the sounds of delegates entering the temple did not disturb her. Thero waited at the altar, observing those early arrivals who gazed in awe upon the Valkana's intensifying aura. Gregor and Stefan entered last, taking their places in front. All present maintained respectful silence as they awaited their second encounter with the High Priestess Valkana.

Alexa began to center, her aura softening in intensity. Thero recognized this as the moment to initiate the meditative chant that would prepare minds and hearts for Val's newest message to be communicated via Valkana. Following completion of the initial chant, the figure before the altar rose, turning to face those in attendance. Again, the ethereal voice rang out, creating shivers in most, inspiring tears in many.

"Our Lord Val welcomes you once more to his temple. His message to you today is one of critical importance. War has come already to our beloved Turand. Few know that our king and his loyal advisers gathered other faithful Turandans in secret to prevent the arrival of Sifiq reinforcements. They have waged war against the Sifiq, who brought their evil upon us. Val grieves for the loss of life, both Turandan and Sifiq. However, this tragic period in our history approaches its end. Sifiq domination of Turand is over. Pray in thanks to Val for the courage and determination of Turand's secret warriors and for the leaders who planned their victory."

The delegates rose to their feet as one. Great shouts of joy mingled with tears of happiness and prayers of gratitude. Astonished by her knowledge of the events, Gregor clutched at the precious dispatch he had received less than an hour earlier.

The Valkana raised her arms in a request for silence. "My people, our victory over the Sifiq, which is nearly complete, is only part of what remains for us to overcome. We now must surmount the most painful challenge of all–that of imminent civil war. Still existing within our midst is evil that we must address as a people before we can merit Val's full forgiveness and the restoration of our nation. Join me in the ancient prayers. We must not lose that which Val is so willing to bestow upon us."

She turned to Gregor and reached out to him. He stood and approached her, his bearing respectful. She took his hands into hers and lifted them. Holding them close together, she leaned forward and placed her forehead against the backs of his hands. She stood motionless, her aura once again intensifying as she drew him into the presence that flowed through her. Both levitated, suspended above the altar by the unseen force that again filled the sacred temple.

The King and Val's priestess were joined in communion with the God they accepted. Val communicated his desire that they be seen by all as united in their service to him and his people. He also willed that their commitment to one another be a sign of his love and an example to be emulated.

The Valkana gradually lifted her head to speak as the two began to descend. "Gregor, King of Turand, Val's blessings are upon you even as he reminds you of tremendous challenges yet to come. He sends me as guide and teacher to your people. He also instructs that I support and counsel whenever needed and that I provide you the comfort and love that all Turandans should offer one another. Do you accept my role as willed by Val?"

Inside his mind, Gregor heard other words as clearly as the ones she spoke. He reverently touched the edge of the golden veil and, with careful fingers, began to lift it from her face. "I accept Val's will in my life, Lady Valkana, just as I accept his greatest gift of all—a loving wife who stands by my side as companion and helpmate, that we may serve our people and strive to restore peace to Turand."

Gregor's eyes reflected the wealth of emotions awash in his soul at that moment. He felt relief that, at long last, the Sifiq were being driven from Turand. There was also distinct gloom in the near certainty that war would pit Turandan against Turandan. Rekindled and revitalized faith in his God created confidence to confront any challenges that remained. Above all, love and pride burned fiercely in his heart, inspired by the woman before him.

He finally drew the veil fully up and away from her face, but his raised arms concealed her face from those watching spellbound from the temple seats. The very air was charged with excited anticipation as everyone realized King Gregor was about to reveal the Valkana's identity.

In his heart and in his mind, Gregor was sure Val would forgive him if what he was about to do was wrong, but his need was compelling. He bent his head forward and placed quivering lips against her delicate, smiling mouth. The contact was warm and infinitely tender. He was faintly aware of the taste of salt on his lips as he withdrew from her, wondering if he had tasted his tears or hers.

Together, in a single, synchronized motion, they turned to face the Turandans present inside the temple. There had been shock when he had kissed her. Now, with the revelation that their long-awaited Valkana was also their queen, everyone dropped to their knees in prayerful outpouring.

Too many years had been filled with too much tragedy and too little hope. No one had known quite how to react to the first startling news of the reinstatement of Turand's National Council. The illustrious event prompted an unprecedented air of excitement and anticipation. The occasion was overshadowed by all the drama and intrigue of the queen's mysterious abduction and then complicated by speculation whether or not an exception could be negotiated to excuse her from council sessions. No one, including the king, had been prepared for her stunning entrance to the opening session. Neither had anyone expected the heart-wrenching confrontation with Lord Garogan. Then, the appearance of the first Valkana in more than a century provided an exciting climax to this first National Council in decades.

Now, beyond any possible imagination, came this newest series of revelations. Gregor, the king whose loyalty had been doubted for years, was proven a shrewd and cunning monarch who had succeeded in orchestrating the defeat of the Sifiq. That he also bore the blessing of Val was manifested by his queen, who stood by his side not only as wife but also as Valkana, ultimate servant to Turand's people.

Sobs and prayers mingled into an indescribable hum filling the temple. Gregor and Alexa waited patiently, hand in hand. They understood.

Complete comprehension of all the events now in motion was staggering. They recognized better than anyone the precarious nature of so much occurring almost simultaneously. The sheer force of history unfolding during this National Council would ripple like tidewaters throughout this generation and many yet to come.

Part 2

Fingers of darkness resist the release,
Their vile grasp they seek to maintain
Throughout the night, so grim and so fearsome.
Yet the shaft of my light pierces the pain.
My light did I send to you, My children.
Give in to its glory; bask in its warmth.
That merciful light, sign of My covenant,
Embodied in love, dispelling the dark.

My servant, she comes,
Her heart filled with joy,
My children to serve, her faith to profess
My wisdom to share,
Your leaders to guide,
My hymn long silenced, sung by My priestess.

Lift high your voices, raise up your song
Sing with her, sing with My servant child,
As the darkness retreats,
Its sorrow dispersed,

Song of Turand

My light she does bear,
My promise revealed,
With lives so precious lost to war
And through your sacrifice dear,
The tyrants are banished,
The just have prevailed.
Now her song sounds true, bearing love in the light
Lift high your voices, raise up your song,
Sing with her, sing with My servant child,
The covenant shines in the midst of that light,
Take in its glory, gather heat from its glow,
For my children, My love have I sent to you.

Verses…from the Great Book of Val

Chapter 16

Along with several advisers, Gregor and Stefan pored over the latest dispatches from provinces bordering southeastern Toravalia. It was growing apparent that at least one Sifiq regiment had avoided the Turandan guerrillas who had blocked routes to the port cities. Several raids had been launched against isolated Turandan villages with the usual Sifiq penchant for bloodletting. The king sought to determine a pattern that would lead him to remaining enemy soldiers.

"Gentlemen, it's late. Why not try to get some rest tonight? You can review this again in the morning. Fresh minds might see things in different light." Alexa, who had entered Gregor's spacious office without even being noticed, spoke firmly.

"She's right, Gregor. We've all looked at these so long that nothing makes sense any longer." Within minutes, everyone gathered their things and left for the night. Stefan, who was last to leave, stood and reached up behind his neck to rub tired, aching muscles.

Gregor sighed heavily and began straightening the array of papers spread across his desk. "Try to get some rest. I'll see you in the morning."

With Stefan gone, Alexa walked across the carpeted floor and perched on the only edge of the massive desk not cluttered with maps, papers, and books. "Do you search for Sifiq or rebels?"

He looked at her with a dry, taut smile. "Sifiq. I prefer to concentrate first on that plague."

"Come to bed, Gregor. You've been up until one or two o'clock in the morning for more than a week. Then, you're back here before eight in the morning. Listen to me, my love. I promise. If you just get a decent night's rest, you'll feel much better and think more clearly."

He nodded slightly, knowing her advice was sound. He unfolded himself from his leather chair and stretched. A spark of humor flashed in his eyes. "Dare I hope you've been missing me?"

She laughed softly and slid off the desk, moving into the inviting circle of his arms. "Always, my love. But right now, I intend to take you up to bed and put you to sleep."

He kissed her forehead and hugged her close. "You have no idea how much I appreciate your patience. I believe I could not cope with all this without you."

The following morning, she got up quietly to go to morning meditations. She paused, smiling adoringly at Gregor's sleeping face, musing over how much she had come to love him. Immense satisfaction filled her that she had been able to massage away his stress until he had relaxed and fallen asleep. She was determined that he get to rest this morning as long as he needed.

Later, returning from the chapel, a whim prompted her to enter her husband's office to study maps that had been propped up on easels and meticulously plotted with every reported Sifiq raid. She felt convinced there was a missing piece to the puzzle. Closing her eyes, she pulled into her mind memories of the times she had traveled through the areas suffering the most frequent raids. Holding her open hands out in front of the maps, she passed them slowly from side to side. In her mind, she clearly saw the Sifiq, wearing their turban-like headpieces with the long, dangling tassels at the sides.

Stefan had entered without her hearing and stood motionless behind her. In the bright light of day, the faint shimmer of her aura was barely visible. He remained silent, praying her sensitivities would be more successful than all the hours he and Gregor had devoted to these maps. Stefan had learned in a very short time to trust her implicitly.

Without moving, she suddenly spoke. "Stefan, the plague to be dealt with lies to the south. I believe the Sifiq are in a unique cooperation with the rebels. Most likely, those from Tasa Coast and Pitrand. I cannot obtain a clear sense if Garogan is involved or not."

She turned around and gestured for Stefan to come closer. She described the region's topography to him, explaining how easily the Sifiq could have a base in Tasa Coast from which they could strike any of the areas that had been raided. They were exchanging observations and opinions as Gregor entered.

"It appears the two of you are resolving all the problems we left behind last night." He walked toward them, patted Stefan on the shoulder, and leaned forward to kiss the cheek his wife offered him.

"Your wife seems to be our best strategic weapon. I hope someday to be forgiven for ever doubting the powers of mysticism."

"And what have you two discerned so far from all this?" Gregor was curious. He felt much better after a full night's sleep, although his frustration still showed.

Stefan began to point out details Alexa had discussed with him. Gregor considered every point with great care. "You have reached a logical and very disturbing conclusion. As deplorable as the idea is, the only plausible explanation is that this band of Sifiq has native support. There must be some sort of agreement between them and the revolutionary leadership."

"Gregor, I believe you need to shift all efforts to the south. Arrange for the eastern provinces to assist. I believe this Sifiq regiment never left for the rotation in the first place."

Gregor looked at his wife in puzzlement. "Why would you think that?"

"When I was in Garogan, I spent a long evening in Lord Anderon's company. I read something ugly in his life force. At the time, I was already too weakened to make much sense of it. I can say only that I know this is somehow linked to him."

Gregor's eyes met Stefan's. Her instincts had so far proven solid. "If that is the case, we will have to assess a completely revised strategy. Stefan, let us take the morning off and meet again after midday."

Stefan was somewhat surprised when Gregor chose not to attack the problem immediately. However, he decided not to question his reasons. Instead, he thought he might use the free time for other matters that he had recently neglected.

Once Stefan left, Gregor took his wife by the hand and pulled her into his arms. He brought his lips down to hers, delighting in the instantaneous response he received. "I believe I've neglected you too much lately," he whispered huskily, moving his face only inches from hers.

She smiled, her eyes fluttering beneath his hot, steady gaze. "You have critical issues to deal with," she muttered, trying to appear understanding. She certainly had missed his intimacies. Her youthful body had awakened to his loving, and she wanted him badly at this very moment.

He laughed low in his throat, recognizing the spark of desire alight in her eyes. "Shame upon me if I ever let anything interfere with reminding you how much I love you. Come. Let's go back upstairs."

Once there, they undressed each other with shaking hands as their mouths moved together in tantalizing unison. Gregor picked her up and laid her on the bed, his mouth leaving searing trails along the length of her body. Her hands reached for him, trying to guide his face back to lips desperate for his kisses.

Sandra Valencia

His eyes devoured the intensity of desire on her face, and he languor-
ously moved toward her waiting lips, pausing to create sweet torment as
he caressed each breast with the moist warmth of his tongue. When she
was able to lace her fingers through the thick, black locks of his hair, she
tugged him back, her mouth hungry for his.

Their passion was fully ignited as their bodies merged. There was
nothing in the world beyond their combined effort to assuage the demanding needs they had for one another. With each stroke, each fiery touch,
they gave and received joy and satisfaction.

A little later, bathed in the afterglow of their lovemaking, she sighed
heavily, content to savor a few peaceful moments with him. She snuggled
closer, wishing they could spend the entire day together. He was right.
The past weeks had successfully kept them separated. She missed their
walks and the lively conversations she enjoyed so much. The very thought
that he would leave her shortly to go downstairs filled her with sudden
melancholy. Unexpectedly, she found herself biting her lip, restraining an
urge to weep.

"What's this?" he asked tenderly, lifting her face when he felt teardrops against his chest.

She emitted a kind of half-laugh, really a quiet and embarrassed
sound. "I was just thinking how much I've missed our time together. I
know how difficult and consuming your work is and how essential. I try
not to interrupt you. I think I've just been feeling a bit lonely."

"Alexa, beloved, you know that if you need something, I'm always
here. You should have told me how you were feeling. I didn't realize. I
thought you were occupied with your consultations and classes. I had no
idea you felt so badly."

She sat up and gave him a shaky smile. "You make it sound so melo-
dramatic. It really isn't as bad as all that. I just have no real friends here,
and sometimes I feel… To tell you honestly, I'm not exactly sure how I

feel." She paused a moment as she watched the bafflement on his face. She leaned forward to kiss him lightly. "One thing I can tell you. I am extremely happy for this morning with you."

He tilted his head to one side, eyes sparkling, lips pulled into a gentle smile. "But?"

"But nothing. Now, if you don't get up to dress, you're going to be late. Stefan will be waiting." She started to climb out of bed, but he pulled her over on top of him.

"Your Majesty, I need to be certain that you are happy. You must not let me fail you."

His sincerity touched her heart, and she playfully planted a hard, noisy kiss on his mouth. "And I love you, too, Your Majesty. Now, I'm starving. Let's go get something to eat."

He laughed heartily, following her as she scrambled out of bed. They dressed quickly, and, with him hugging her close, they teased and laughed all the way downstairs.

As servants moved around the table serving the midday meal, Gregor took generous portions of deliciously prepared dishes. His size and level of energy always assured a healthy appetite. However, he watched his wife serve herself unusually small amounts. "I thought you were starving," he commented observantly.

She glanced up at him and sighed. "I was, but I seem to have lost my appetite." She looked back at her plate, forcing herself to lift a forkful of vegetables to her mouth. Her face was pensive as she chewed the bite.

"Alexa, look at me." He addressed her seriously. "Are you certain everything is all right? I couldn't help but notice that you are thinner. I want you to tell me if you are melancholy or if you don't feel well."

She smiled in response and reached over to touch his hand. "I told you. I'm fine. There is nothing for you to worry about." She then took another bite to drive home her point.

After they were finished, Gregor escorted her through the corridors leading toward the suite of palace offices. "What are your plans for this afternoon?" he asked once they reached his office door.

"I have a class to teach this afternoon. Since the day is pleasant, we decided to go outside to the east meadows for our readings."

"Would you mind if I join you one day for a class?"

Her face beamed. "I would love to have you join us!"

"Then make sure Stefan knows your schedule. I promise to surprise you one afternoon." He kissed her cheek and watched thoughtfully as she practically skipped the rest of the way down the hall.

Later, bright sun cast its yellow glow over the broad green meadow on an afternoon that was unusually warm for early spring in Toraval. The grass was lush, the air particularly fresh and clean. Alexa's class sat on blankets and mats scattered in a large circle around her. Unfortunately, there weren't enough meditation books to go around, so many shared two or three to a copy.

Alexa held her own book in her hand. Her voice commanded the attention of her students. Many closed their eyes to more fully absorb the readings describing spiritual connectivities and means to achieve the precious bonds allowed to priests and Valiria. She walked around slowly, her words alive, infused with the dynamics of her faith. She studied the faces of her students carefully. Some were older priests who attended for a sort of spiritual renewal. Others were young and spiritually connected to Val, exploring the possibilities of furthering their commitments to his service. Her readings touched hearts and souls, bringing her a sense of deep fulfillment.

Upon finishing the readings, she opened the session for discussion. The free dialogue was her favorite segment of the classes because it allowed her to observe the flow of ideas and reactions to the readings. She could then address each student's more personal directions during individual meetings. Alexa stood with her eyes closed, listening carefully to the exchanges. Suddenly, an odd sensation washed over her.

"Milady, are you all right?"

She opened her eyes and sought the source of the concerned inquiry. Her face tensed. "I'm not quite sure." She then swayed and crumpled to the grass.

～

An insistent rap at the door disturbed the intense strategy session in progress inside the king's office. Complex plans required exceptional attention to every minute detail. Gregor glanced up in irritation. Explicit instructions had been given not to interrupt the meeting.

The knock sounded again, only more loudly. Stefan rose impatiently from his chair and left his place to answer the knock. He stepped just outside the door, holding it open only slightly as he spoke to the servant. "What? Are you certain? When?"

Gregor's head snapped up at the sharpness in Stefan's voice. He stopped the discussion with the other advisers, wondering what had prompted Stefan's reaction. When Stefan finally returned, Gregor immediately noticed the troubled look on his face.

"Gentlemen," Stefan addressed the others, "please excuse me. I have an urgent matter to discuss privately with the king."

Gregor indicated to his advisory staff that they should continue as they were and got up to follow Stefan into the adjoining office. "Stefan, tell me. What's wrong?"

Stefan closed the door between the two offices. "Gregor, they just sent word that Alexa is being taken to the physician's clinic. She collapsed near the end of her class."

"What! What happened?" he demanded, his face blanching as three long strides carried him to the main door of Stefan's office. Stefan followed close behind.

"They said the class was nearly over when, suddenly, with no warning, she just fell to the ground."

By the time the two men reached the palace clinic, Stefan was breathless from running to keep up with Gregor. The king's entrance was so abrupt that the doctor's assistant jumped from his chair, knocking it over.

"Where is my wife?" he demanded, unaware that his tone of voice caused the already startled attendant to shake nervously.

"Your Majesty," he stammered, "she's in the examining..."

Before the young man could finish, Gregor brushed by him and burst through the door to where the doctor leaned over Alexa's still form.

"Doctor Korodi! What happened? How is she?"

Doctor Korodi looked over his shoulder impatiently. "Sire, please keep your voice quiet. I will answer all your questions as soon as I know something." The elderly physician had known Gregor as a child and showed no qualms about his stern admonishment.

Gregor quickly rounded the examining table where Alexa lay. Leaning forward, he gently touched the side of her face. She was so pale and still that his heart missed a beat. His voice trembled as he bent over, whispering into her ear. "I'm here, my love."

"Sire, please. Wait outside while I finish my examination. I promise to call you the minute I finish." He stopped and waited while Gregor reluctantly backed out of the room, never taking his eyes from her face.

Several minutes later, Alexa began to stir, blinking with heavy lids, unable to remember what had happened, not knowing where she was.

Drawing in a deep breath, she let it out slowly and then twisted her head around several times as if trying to pull herself from the dark abyss into which she had plummeted. Although hearing someone nearby, she could not focus enough to know whom.

"Where am I? What happened?" she asked in a muffled voice.

"Milady, you're in the palace clinic. Apparently, you fainted. As to the cause, I hope you might help answer that question."

She started to sit up, but gentle hands pushed her shoulders firmly back. "Not yet, Milady. I want you to rest a bit longer."

Feeling disoriented, she didn't resist. "Fainted? I've never actually fainted in my life. I was fine all day, but I suddenly felt so strange outside. Now I'm here."

She lay quietly, clearing her mind while he looked into her eyes, checked her pulse, and listened to her heart. Finally completing his examination and feeling satisfied that nothing serious was wrong, he helped her sit up. He watched her closely as she breathed very slowly, deliberately measuring her breaths. "Now, let us discuss how you have spent your day. Perhaps we can figure out what caused this peculiar fainting spell. Have you eaten today?"

"Yes, doctor. Not until late, but I did eat."

"And what were you doing that caused you to eat so late?"

Her eyes glittered merrily. "I spent the morning with my husband."

"You spent the morning doing…" He looked up at her amused expression and smiled. "Oh, I see. And how did you feel afterward?"

She giggled. "Wonderful, of course."

Dr. Korodi chuckled and shook his head in admonition. "Milady, that is not exactly what I meant. This could be serious. I want to know if you felt headache or lightheaded or nauseous."

She grinned at him mischievously. "No headache. No nausea. But he always leaves me quite lightheaded."

"Your Majesty, please be serious. Have you experienced any unusual symptoms lately? Any kind of headache or body aches? Any nausea or other illness?"

She thought for a moment. "Gregor complained this morning that he thought I'd lost weight. I haven't been sick at all, but I don't seem to have much appetite, either. I've also never been so sleepy in my life. I think it's because I have so much to do, and often it's so difficult to keep up with my schedule."

The doctor looked at her curiously. "No sickness at all? And you are absolutely certain you've had no nausea or vomiting?"

She shook her head. "Nothing."

"Your Majesty, would you lie back? I wish to examine you a little further. Would you mind pulling up your skirts?"

She shrugged and gathered her skirts, sliding them up as she meekly lay back. Gently, the doctor began to push and prod at her from all angles. He glanced up at her with a kindly smile and pulled her hand down to her abdomen. "Do you feel this?"

She looked at him with eyes full of curiosity as she felt a small mass beneath her fingers. "Yes. What do you think it is?"

"Your Majesty, when did you last have your monthly courses?"

"During National Council." The moment she finished the words, she sucked in her breath, and her heart began to beat faster. "That was over three months ago! Doctor, do you think...?" Her face lit up, and her eyes widened in wonder.

"Frankly, I'm quite certain. I estimate you're approximately two months into your pregnancy, my dear. Fainting spells like this occasionally occur in the early weeks."

She smiled tremulously, not quite able to believe the news. "I never even dreamed... Oh, Doctor Korodi, you mustn't say anything to my husband. Let me tell him in my own time."

"Your Majesty, we must tell him something right away. He's waiting outside, and I am sure you know as well as I how impatient he can be."

"Outside? Oh, no. I fear we're both in for trouble. Promise you'll help me, though. Please?" Her voice was irresistibly charming as she pleaded with him.

He grinned as he went to open the door to admit Gregor, who, as soon as he saw her, rushed to her side and tightly grasped her hands. "Alexa, you nearly frightened me to death! What happened? Are you all right?"

"Sire, slowly, please," Dr. Korodi cautioned him as he placed a calming hand on his shoulder. "She should take things slowly for a little while, just until she recovers from this fainting spell. I suggested she rest for the remainder of the day. I'll check in with her again in the morning just to be certain everything is all right."

"Gregor, please don't worry. Truly, I'm fine. I think I've tried to accomplish too much lately. I just encountered a weak moment."

"A weak moment? A weak moment!" he repeated, unwilling to accept such a feeble explanation. He turned to the doctor. "Did she tell you how tired she's been or about her lack of appetite? I was already concerned something might be wrong, but now."

"Sire, trust me. Your wife appears to be a very healthy young woman. However, you must consider her recent experiences and all the major changes she has undergone. I firmly believe that several days of rest will serve her best."

Gregor shook his head nervously, gripping her hand tightly. Ever since he had brought her home from Garogan, he had been unreasonably fearful that something might happen to her. "Doctor Korodi, are you certain?"

The physician smiled benignly. "Certain enough to promise you that she's all right. She simply needs to take a slower pace for a few days. Trust me."

Still doubtful, Gregor had no other alternative than to accept the doctor's diagnosis. After thanking Dr. Korodi, he helped Alexa down from the examination table. He was noticeably relieved to see that she was steady on her feet. "Come, my love. You are going to your rooms for the rest of the afternoon." His expression was no-nonsense, and she meekly yielded to him.

～

A week later, Alexa still had not told him about the baby. Gregor continuously maintained a grueling schedule with Stefan and his other advisers. She wanted so much to create a special moment to share the news, but it seemed an emergency dispatch or a provincial official interrupted every private moment they got together. By the time he was able to retire for the night, she was sound asleep.

Finally, she got up earlier than usual one morning to complete her meditations and return to their rooms before Gregor usually awoke. When she walked inside the door, she sighed in relief to see that he was still there, although he was already up and nearly dressed. Crossing the room to where he stood, Alexa finished buttoning the side opening of the snowy white linen shirt he wore. There was cherished intimacy for both of them as she patted and straightened the fabric until it was perfectly smooth.

"You have a solemn look in those eyes of yours," he told her, a playful glint in his eye as he tugged at his cuffs to straighten his sleeves.

"I came early so that I might have the chance to ask you to do something for me." She smiled her most charming smile and gave him a look so flirtatious that he laughed in response.

"And what is it that I can do for you?"

Her hands fluttered along the sides of his shirt, continuing to smooth and pleat, the act one of exaggerated nervousness. "Do you remember the day I fainted?"

His eyes darkened, his humor fading instantly. "I could hardly forget being frightened that badly. Have you had another fainting spell and not told me?"

She grinned at him. "No, I haven't. I just wanted to remind you of something. You told me that day I should never let you forget about showing me how much you love me." Her eyes were wide and innocent. Almost.

He chuckled, shook his head, and kissed her lightly. "Later, my love, later. I promise. Right now, I have a meeting I must not miss."

"That isn't what I had in mind."

"No?" He sounded disappointed.

"No," she replied firmly. "However, you have spent all your time with Stefan, your staff, and everyone else who is helping plan this offensive. You need a respite, and I need you. I know your itinerary today is impossible, but tomorrow I thought I would prepare a special supper for just the two of us. We could eat here in private. I just want a little time with you. Is that too much to ask?"

The appeal in her face was irresistible as she breathlessly expressed her request. He tilted his head sideways, the sensual fullness of his lips drawn into an indulgent smile. "Supper? Alone together? What a wonderful idea! What time do you want me here?"

"Seven. Precisely. And don't be late. I shall have no time to remind you." She linked her arm with his and accompanied him down to his offices. She constantly chatted, her voice cheerful, her step light. As he kissed her on the forehead before going into his meeting, she smiled mysteriously. "I promise something very, very special tomorrow night."

His gaze was affectionate and amused. "Then I shall look forward to a perfect evening."

～

The long, thin match sent tiny swirls of blue-gray smoke into the air as she blew out its blue and yellow flame. Tall candles cast a lovely, flickering dance of lights that reflected off spotless crystal and gleaming white porcelain dishes. She had gone to the glass gardens early in the day to cut flowers for several arrangements that now graced the table and the sitting room. The food she had prepared sent mouthwatering aromas wafting throughout the suite. Looking around, she felt satisfied that every detail was in perfect order.

She then slipped into her room for one final inspection of her appearance. Despite her striking features, she had never been vain. Tonight, however, she wanted to look her best for him. Her golden-brown hair was pulled back from her face and held in place by a satin headband, white in color and wrapped in silver cord. Curling tendrils framed her forehead and temples while her hair cascaded past her shoulders. Her gown was also white, fashioned in the simple, high-waisted design she now found to be more comfortable.

Gazing into the mirror, she smiled at her image. Even she could see the gleam in her eyes. Laughing to herself at the thought, Alexa realized she had never been so happy or felt so beautiful. She sighed, anxious for her husband's arrival.

The tall, walnut clock in the hallway chimed the half-hour. Gregor looked up distractedly. He had been studying the most recent dispatches delivered from the embattled province bordering to the north of Tasa Coast. "What time is it?" he asked Stefan, who had spent the entire afternoon poring over the dispatches as well.

"Half-past eight. Do you wish to stop for tonight?"

Gregor, deep in thought, was stroking his beard when his mind registered the time. He rolled his eyes backward and grimaced, jumping to his feet. "Eight-thirty! I cannot believe what I've just done!"

"Is there something I can do to help?" Stefan asked, startled by Gregor's rapid shuffling of papers to leave his desk somewhat organized.

"I think not. I was supposed to meet Alexa at seven for dinner. I have the feeling she's not going to be happy with me."

Stefan grinned at him, his expression a friendly admonishment. "I warned you to start making more time for her. She deserves your attention as much as Turand does. Go. I'll clear things up here. And good luck."

Gregor cast him a rueful look and hurried from the office to rush up the main staircase, his long legs taking three steps at a time. Arriving outside their suite, he calmed his beating heart, praying she would not be too angry with him. He eased open the door. "Alexa?" He spoke her name tentatively into the dimly lit room.

Receiving no answer, he slowly entered. Atop a marble-topped side table, a single oil lamp shed faint, golden light across the room. The table was still set, and the faint aroma of food lingered in the air. Candlewax had dripped down onto crystal bobeches, but the flames had all been extinguished.

He walked through to the bedchamber and found it also deserted. He inhaled and exhaled heavily, frustrated that he had allowed himself to get so caught up in meetings that he had forgotten time and their dinner. Guilt mingled with slight worry. He still had not completely recovered from the shock of the day she fainted. He feared the possibility of upsetting her sufficiently that she might suffer a recurrence.

Gregor left the suite and walked dejectedly through the corridor, wondering where first to look for her. Heavy steps carried him downstairs. His first inclination was to check the chapel. Arriving there, he was disappointed to find it dark and empty. He paused, trying to think where she might have gone.

He decided to look for her outside at her favorite spot in the gardens. The bench where she often sat was bare and gray beneath silver moonlight. His next thought was to cross the central square to look for her in the temple, her most cherished retreat. He didn't even notice the lively gurgling of the great fountain that had filled with clear, sparkling water upon the public acknowledgment of the return of Valkana.

Stepping into the echoing halls of the temple, he felt a heaviness in his heart. Alexa was not there either. No sounds save those of his own breathing and footsteps were to be heard. Gregor walked all the way to the front of the temple and knelt a moment, prayerful that he would find her and that she would forgive him.

With each minute that passed, his guilt compounded. He considered how undemanding she had been. Her patience and understanding provided him an anchor of support as he struggled to set in motion the offensives that he hoped would quickly and effectively deal with the insurrection. How could he have been so insensitive to her needs and the only request she had made of him?

Head hung low in shame, Gregor walked back to the palace. He asked himself over and over where she might be. After checking her suite, the chapel, the library, the kitchen, and now the temple, he was beginning to feel a little sick himself. He wondered once again if perhaps she had fainted somewhere.

Having wandered through the palace one last time, Gregor grew more and more worried. None of the servants had seen her. Tira and Tirani had exchanged surprised looks, having thought her to be dining with the king. Finally, he shuffled back to the library, his own favorite retreat.

He pushed open one of the double doors and walked into the depressing darkness. Gloom inundated him as he walked toward a window to stare out into the night. His was a forlorn figure, hands clasped behind his back and shoulders slightly hunched. Over and over, he asked himself where she had gone.

Gazing into shadowy darkness beyond the walls of his palace, his eyes fell upon a figure in motion. Someone was walking alone about the garden pathways. "Alexa," he whispered and turned to run from the library. Outside, his shoes crunched on stone and brick walkways as he approached her.

"Alexa!" he called out her name.

She continued to walk away from him, seeming not to have heard him at all.

Finally, he reached her and took her by the arm. "Alexa, please. Wait. I've been looking everywhere for you." His heart ached as she jerked from his grasp and rapidly put more distance between them.

"Go away, Gregor. Just leave me alone." She choked on the words.

With long strides, he quickly caught up to her. "Please, my love, don't send me away. Talk to me. Please?"

When she turned to look at him, pale moonlight revealed cheeks shiny and wet with tears. Her chin quivered despite the taut set of her jaw. Her eyes were sad and accusing. "I said, go away. I prefer to be alone."

Gregor half-closed his eyes in frustration as he reached for her.

She jumped away from him as though his touch had burned her. "Don't touch me! I told you! Leave me alone!" she shouted at him as she lifted her skirts and ran from him.

Helplessly, he watched her distance herself from him. The hurt in her eyes had been dreadful, and he swore at himself for being the source of such terrible sadness. Again he ran, his long, powerful stride no match for hers. He grabbed her once again and spun her around to face him. Wetness stained his cheeks as he tried to wrap her in his arms. She fought half-heartedly against him, his strength easily subduing any efforts to break free. He felt her chest rising and falling quickly against his own, and he tightened his embrace.

She pulled back against his arms, sobbing softly at her inability to escape him. "Why can you not just let me go? Please, Gregor. Just go back inside, and let me be alone."

He nuzzled his face into the fragrant silkiness of her hair. "I cannot do that, beloved. How can I leave you out here alone when you're so upset?"

She steeled herself against the invasive tenderness his words were meant to convey. "You apparently had no difficulties breaking your promise to me tonight when you left me alone in my suite to look like a fool," she accused.

He gripped her tightly, refusing to give her the chance to run from him again. Instead, he kept his face buried in her hair, his breath hot upon her neck. "I was the incredible fool tonight. You have every right to be angry with me, but you must believe I had every intention of being there. Please, my love, try to understand."

"All I understand is that you never have any time for me, and I'm tired of spending so much time alone! Gregor, you're hurting me. Let me go. Now!"

He immediately loosened his hold on her, and instantly she jerked away from him. His eyes pleaded for understanding and forgiveness. He filled his lungs with a deep breath and forced himself to remain calm. "Don't pull away from me that way, Alexa. You wound my heart when you do so."

"Your heart? Wounded? At least you have Stefan and your loyal staff to fill your hours. What do I have? A husband who says he loves me but cannot spare even a few hours out of an entire week to dine with me? Do you think my heart doesn't also ache?"

He shook his head from side to side. "I failed you, my love. I know, but…"

"You know nothing!" she exclaimed, stepping even further away and turning her back to him. She crossed her arms tightly in front of her, confounded by torrential emotions crashing through her. A part of her heard his regret, but her own hurt was too intense for her to consider his feelings.

He walked up behind her and tentatively rested his hands on her shoulders. "You know in your heart how much I love you. Can you find no mercy for a man who made a terrible mistake and wants to make up for it?" His tone was intensely persuasive.

She choked back a sob. "You don't understand. Tonight was supposed to be special. I planned everything to be perfect. Everything is ruined now. You just don't understand."

Gently, he turned her around to face him. His eyes roamed over her face, and he bent his head to kiss her forehead. "Tell me, my love. Exactly what is it that I don't understand?"

She dropped her face, not wanting to look at him, needing time alone to resolve and pacify the raging, irrational emotions churning inside her.

He used his fingers to tilt her face back up to him. "There is something here much more important than a cold dinner. Am I right?"

She only sniffled in response.

"Alexa, I love you. I'm asking for your forgiveness. Please?"

She wanted to say something to him. Words only stuck in her throat. With some effort, she managed a whisper. "You wouldn't understand."

"I realize there's something I don't understand. I also know that I cannot hope to understand if you refuse to tell me. Let us begin with something else. I want you to repeat after me: Gregor, you are an insensitive fool, but I love you anyway, and I forgive you."

She looked at him in total consternation and shook her head.

He held her chin firmly and gazed deeply into her eyes. "It really isn't so difficult. Now, listen carefully because I am your king, and you may consider this a royal command. Repeat after me: Gregor." He saw her irritation and held her chin more firmly. "Say it. Gregor."

"Gregor," she repeated defiantly.

"Good," he said, satisfied he was beginning to reach past the barrier she had thrown up between them. "Now the rest of it. You are an insensitive fool. Say it."

She stammered, knowing she was succumbing to the warmth of his nearness and the charm of his approach. "You are an insensitive fool."

"My love, that sounded much too convincing," he teased. "The rest now?"

"But I love you, and I forgive you," she blurted out impatiently. "Are you satisfied now?"

He drew her closer, feeling the trembling in her body as she resisted complete surrender. Whispering against her ear, he denied being satisfied. "You still haven't told me the real reason why you're so upset."

She moved away again, needing space between them. She stared at the ground for a few moments, her weary mind struggling for words. She felt his gaze upon her, worried and questioning. After what seemed an interminable silence, she spoke very quietly. "I planned for tonight to be special. We've had so little time together, and I needed to talk with you about something extremely important."

He kept his distance even though it pained him not to touch her. He struggled as he faced the difficult acknowledgment of how his thoughtlessness had hurt her. "What is so important that you're still so upset?"

She glanced up at him, biting at her lower lip. "I didn't want for it to happen this way. It was supposed to be so perfect."

He took one step toward her, then stopped. "Alexa, I don't understand. You talk in circles. What are you trying to tell me?"

Sniffing again, she wiped her eyes and surprised him by walking toward him. Taking hold of his hand, she slowly pulled him closer until she could place his palm against her still-flat abdomen. She looked up at his puzzled expression and smiled sadly. "I had planned to tell you about our baby."

He blinked in startled bewilderment. Sucking in his breath, he exhaled sharply. "Baby? Alexa, are you certain?"

With lips pressed tightly together, she swallowed nervously and nodded. Abruptly, Gregor dropped to his knees. With his left arm snaking behind her hip, he pulled her forward and rested his cheek and the palm of his right hand against her abdomen. His eyes were closed, his posture reverent. As if by their own volition, her hands came to rest on his coarse-textured hair.

Gregor knelt for several long minutes until she grasped his shoulders in silent signal for him to stand. When he rose, tears streaked his cheeks, and his dark eyes revealed a depth of feeling that reached into her soul. His arms wrapped around her, enclosing her in an embrace that was both gentle and protective.

His voice was thick when he finally discovered words to speak. "Beloved, I never would have guessed. I feel even worse than before knowing that you planned to tell me such extraordinary news. Can you ever forgive me for ruining this for you?"

She could not reply. Instead, she just rested her face against his chest. Her head ached, and suddenly she felt drained. "Can you just take me inside?"

He smiled into the darkness, his arms contracting around her. He then led her back to the palace, intent on loving away her sadness in celebration of the joyful gift she had just shared with him.

Chapter 17

Dispatches arrived daily from the embattled regions bordering the southern provinces. Although a good portion of Garogan Province bordered Toravalia, so far, only sporadic fighting had spilled across its provincial boundaries. None of the hostilities had, however, spread near the capital.

Gregor and Stefan adhered to a strict daily regimen in order to contend with the continual parade of provincial representatives requesting additional aid and protection. Mornings were reserved for strategic reviews and briefings. All meetings with visitors were scheduled for the afternoons. An evening session occurred daily with all staff advisers to summarize the day's events and review the schedule for the following day. Often, days seemed to run in a blur from dawn until dusk.

Upon learning of his wife's pregnancy, Gregor faithfully scheduled time with her each day. They usually ate their midday meal together and took time for a leisurely walk through the gardens. He constantly reminded her of how remorseful he felt about the night she had told him about their baby. He never wanted to repeat the experience of her rejecting him the way she had that night. Whenever he mentioned the subject, she usually laughed, reminding him that they had both agreed he had been an insensitive fool but that she loved him to distraction anyway.

At least every other evening, Gregor adjourned all meetings by seven-thirty. This gave him uninterrupted time to spend with Alexa. In the beginning, he struggled with pangs of guilt for leaving too much to his advisers to attend to his personal life. However, within a week, he acknowledged the skill and aptitude of those in his inner circle. Besides, the breaks reduced his stress, allowing him to think more clearly. But, most importantly, time spent with Alexa provided them both rare happiness neither had ever known.

Very early one morning, a knock sounded at the door of their suite. Alexa turned over in bed, stretching sleepily and yawning. She tried unsuccessfully to open her eyes, having sat up late into the night listening to Gregor talk about current problems at the battlefronts. Usually, he avoided the topic with her, but he had needed to sound out his thoughts. She had listened attentively and asked thought-provoking questions that, in turn, prompted him to consider different possibilities.

The knock came again, slightly louder. Gregor, sound asleep, heard nothing. Reluctantly, she forced herself to get up, wrapped a floor-length robe around her, and went to the door. "Who is it?" she asked quietly.

"Alexa, it's Stefan. I must speak to Gregor. It's urgent."

She opened the door and invited Stefan, already fully dressed, into the sitting room. She questioned him with her eyes upon seeing that his expression was so grim.

"I apologize for disturbing you so early. A messenger just arrived. He has ridden almost without stopping for two days and nights. I need to discuss the matter with Gregor."

"Stefan, you need not apologize. Let me awaken him." She disappeared inside the bedchamber and gazed down into Gregor's face, peaceful and relaxed in sleep. She hated to awaken him, but she had no choice.

Lowering herself onto the edge of the bed, she reached out and gently shook his shoulder. "Gregor? Gregor, wake up. Stefan is here. He says it's urgent. Wake up, my love."

Dark eyes fluttered open, not quite willing to focus so early in the morning. "What time is it?" he muttered groggily, pulling himself to a sitting position.

"Not yet five o'clock."

Gregor fell backward and groaned into a pillow that he pulled over his face. If Stefan was here so early, there must be an emergency. Still, he was not ready to leave the comfort of bed. Alexa grasped the pillow and tugged it out of his hands. He rolled his eyes at her, and she chuckled in response.

"Lady Valkana, can you not summon all your mystic powers to make this damnable war go away?" he muttered as he slid out of bed.

Her expression softened. "If only I could. You know I can only offer guidance, insight, and spiritual support. War is an evil, human act. Only humans can stop it."

"My love, the hour is much too early for philosophy. All I want right now is to sleep," he commented dryly as she helped him into his robe.

In the sitting room, Stefan waited with the papers the courier had delivered into his hands so early. As Gregor sat down to review them, another knock sounded. Stefan glanced up at Alexa. "I took the liberty of requesting that breakfast be brought up."

She nodded and moved to the door, opening it and allowing a servant to carry the heavily laden tray inside and place it on the round table by a bay window. As soon as the servant had gone, she proceeded to pour tea. She then handed plates to the men and offered them savory sausages, sweetbreads, and fruits from various covered dishes. After serving them, she prepared her own tea and curled up in the corner of the settee where Gregor sat, bent forward to study the reports Stefan had handed him.

As was his habit, Gregor raked long fingers back through his hair, creating soft, leafy layers. His jaw was set, his mouth tightly closed. His eyes watched intently while Stefan explained the verbal details related by the courier.

Gregor stood and paced the small room. "With General Gordino dead, our leadership in the field will suffer tremendously. Kohira is the only officer out there who has a genuine sense of strategy. We must act quickly, Stefan. Let me get dressed. Summon the others for an emergency staff meeting."

Stefan left without another word. Alexa got up and went to where her husband now stood, lost in thought. Her arms circled his waist, and her hands clasped together in front of his stomach. She rested the side of her face against his back and felt his hands cover hers. She could feel the muscles in his back begin to tighten.

"Gregor, I'm so sorry about General Gordino. I know how much you respected him." She felt him shrug.

"Respect is only half the matter. I needed Gordino and his understanding of military strategy. There are so few left who understand because of all we lost to the Sifiq. I relied heavily on Gordino's judgment. Filling the void he leaves will be nearly impossible." He separated her hands and turned around to hold her. "I fear what this may do to our efforts to reunify Turand. I have no idea how to begin reassessing our position."

"I have faith in you, Gregor. You and Stefan together are a formidable force in this struggle. You are both determined and creative. I shall also pray for guidance and inspiration. I am confident that the two of you will discover some way to resolve this."

Gregor kissed her lips lightly. "What I want is peace for our people and for our baby to grow up without the constant threat of violence. And I want time with you."

She smiled gently into his troubled eyes. "You will succeed. I'm sure of it," she encouraged. "You are too strong and too stubborn not to."

His smile revealed the doubts floating so near the surface of his psyche. He felt desperate to believe her, but real war had not been waged in Turand for over five hundred years. Just to defeat the Sifiq occupying Turand had been costly in time and preparations, not to mention the lives of men unaccustomed to such violence. He sighed heavily, kissed her once more, and went to dress for the day.

Late that evening, Gregor and Stefan remained alone in the king's office. Their other advisers had already left for the night; however, Gregor continued to explore different options. He had analyzed every possible alternative, and one idea repeatedly entered his mind as the only logical possibility.

"Gregor, I'm not sure I like the look on your face right now," Stefan remarked. "Every time I've ever seen that expression, you've had some wild and crazy scheme in mind."

"Stefan, crazy schemes may be our only escape from this mess. First, we must pull our armies back together. Then we must discover and strike at the insurrection's weak spots. To do that, I need someone out there who can make fast analyses and then change directions in a heartbeat."

"There's no one yet available. I sent for Kohira, but it will take nearly a week for him to reach Toraval and then almost another week before he gets to the battle zones."

"I know of only one person who might be able to accomplish what needs to be done. Admittedly, his experience is light, but I trust his judgment and his determination."

"Who?" Stefan asked, unable to think of anyone who might be up to the task. "I can think of no one you might have in mind."

"Are you quite certain?" Gregor asked, his countenance firm, his mind already decided.

Stefan stared at him and gasped. "Gregor, no! You cannot do this! You must not! The dangers are too great! If you fall, so falls all of Turand!" Stefan's features had turned pallid. He could not bring himself to accept such an idea. There must be another alternative.

"Gregor, listen to me. Turand has survived these past ten years more because of the strength of your character than any other reason. We need your leadership to guide us through this crisis. There must be someone else who can lead our forces. What happens if you are killed the way Gordino was? Then what happens to Turand?"

Gregor's gaze was stoic as he looked at Stefan. "Then I leave my wife as queen and you as her chief adviser. She is stronger than even she realizes. The two of you will lead Turand out of this civil war, and you will then teach my child to lead our people."

A heated argument ensued, with both men raising their voices. Stefan grew more and more agitated as he found it impossible to reason with Gregor. He finally stopped and lowered his voice. "Gregor, I think you have every right to be confident in Alexa's abilities. Every day, she shows flashes of brilliance, which do help us. But I also believe you misjudge one critical aspect regarding your wife. She has lost too much already. How dare you even think to ask her to face the very real possibility of losing you! Especially now! Are you really being fair to Alexa?"

"What's this about being fair to me?" Alexa asked as she carried a tray of light finger foods and a pot of tea into the office. "You two look far too serious. Since neither of you bothered to show up for dinner, I thought I might bring you something to eat."

Deliberately, she ignored the obvious tension in the room and began to pour tea and hand them plates. Finally, she spoke. "Well? Must I wait all night to hear about what is fair to me?"

Stefan set his untouched cup of tea on the desk with a clatter. "I'm retiring for the night, Alexa." He placed his hand on her shoulder. "I shall let the king explain to you his latest idea." He left abruptly, slamming the door shut.

Alexa stared at Gregor in surprise. "I've never seen Stefan so upset. What did you say to him?"

Gregor swallowed his tea and set his cup aside. "He disagrees with my decision regarding new command leadership to replace General Gordino."

Her green eyes studied him intently. A hollow sensation struck in the pit of her stomach. "Please, Gregor, tell me you don't really plan to do this."

He knew her too well to be surprised by her quick perception. "I have no choice. Going into the field, I can make immediate assessments without making decisions based on days-old information. I'll have the flexibility to command and change direction as needed. I see no other options."

Alexa's hands shook as she sat down on the edge of a large leather chair. Color drained from her face, and her hands, as if by instinct, laid a protective barrier over her abdomen. "You cannot do this, Gregor. Our people need you too much. We cannot risk losing the king of Turand. Not now."

"Alexa, I must do this. I ask men to go out daily to fight and kill, knowing that many of them will also die. I must prove myself worthy to ask so much, and I must assume a more active role to expedite an end to this rebellion. Please try to understand." A faraway look dulled her eyes that were, as yet, dry, and he had to strain to hear her when she again spoke.

"Gregor, don't do this to me. I've already lost nearly everyone in my life whom I ever loved. Childhood friends, aunts, uncles. My parents. All killed at Zinzan by the Sifiq. Since then, I've lost so many friends in Garogan because of all that has happened. Even Victor. How can I ever forget the very real loss I suffered with Victor?" She saw him grimace at the very mention of Victor's name.

"The point is that I cannot possibly face losing you, too. I've never loved anyone as much as I love you. What happens if you are killed? What happens if something then goes wrong and I lose our baby? Gregor, no. Please, no."

He rushed around his desk and dropped to the floor in front of her. He grasped her hands and rubbed their trembling coldness between his own. "Beloved, you mustn't say such things. You mustn't even think about losing this baby. You're strong and blessed as Valkana. Right now, I need your confidence more than ever. With Stefan's help, you are more than capable of leading this nation back to peace."

"Gregor, do you not understand? My faith is strong, but even I have my weaknesses! I've lost too much already. I cannot do this! I cannot!" She jumped to her feet and bolted from the office. By the time he rose to follow her, she was already running up the stairway to their suite. Reaching their rooms, she entered and slammed the door behind her.

He arrived to find her stretched out, face down, on the enormous bed they shared. Lying down beside her, he ran his fingers through the silken length of her hair. Although she didn't acknowledge his presence, neither did she move away from him. Tentatively, he slid his arm around her waist and pulled her onto her side and against him.

"I love you, Alexa. Even if I told you a thousand times a day, I could never tell you how much. I want our baby to grow up in a country that is peaceful and prosperous. I don't want this child to know the sorrows you and I have faced. That is why I believe I must do this. Try to understand."

"I cannot even bear the thought," she whispered. "I'm terrified of losing you. I'm sorry. I cannot face this. Not now."

His long fingers caressed the cherished curves of her face. Although she did not cry, he could feel the tremors shaking her body. His hand floated down to spread across her stomach. "I love our baby so much already. I want a secure life for it. I can think of nothing I would not sacrifice for you and this child of ours. Not even my life."

With his words, she only shook harder, and so he held her tightly until she finally fell asleep.

⌐

Stefan personally oversaw preparations of the king's belongings to be taken along to the battlefields. He willingly accepted advice from Alexa, who had spent much time outdoors in Garogan. Lightweight white shirts would be best in the heat, and he would need several for the time he would be gone. Extra stockings and comfortable boots would be necessities. She inspected all of his personal belongings to be transported in the large trunk he would take.

Stefan seriously worried about her. When she returned from morning meditations at the temple, her movements were mechanical, her expression wooden. Her skin appeared almost colorless, and her typically bright and expressive eyes looked dull and remote. He could only imagine how she must have reacted two nights earlier when Gregor had announced his decision to lead his army.

"Alexa, you look so tired. Why don't you rest a while? Palace staff can finish this," he told her kindly.

When she looked up into concerned gray eyes, he instantly felt the hurt in her. Her attempt to smile failed. "Stefan, how can this be happening? It took so long for us to reach one another. Now, when I need him most, he plans to leave me to go to war. Am I so wrong wanting him to stay here with me?"

Stefan placed an arm around her shoulders in a brotherly fashion. "The truth is that I want him to stay, too. And, no, it isn't wrong for you to want him here. His rightful place is with you, especially now that you carry his child. I have tried to see things from his perspective. I also tried to convince him not to go, but we both know his passion as well as his stubbornness."

"Stefan, the whole idea of his leaving for war is more painful than I can explain. I'm so frightened that I even found it impossible to meditate this morning."

"Alexa, go upstairs. Rest. I shall try again to reason with him. You know I can promise nothing. However, I can certainly try to convince him to change his mind."

She reached out and briefly held his hand. "Thank you, Stefan."

⌐

A light supper had been served. Stefan sat silently in his chair and toyed with the succulently prepared fish filet on his plate. He had no appetite. He had argued with Gregor several times during the afternoon. Uncharacteristically, Stefan had finally lost his temper and launched into a boiling tirade against his old friend.

Gregor now sat at the head of the table, his expression sullen. His deep coloring made his ominous mood appear even darker. He, too, only shoved his food around from one side of his plate to the other. Finally, he pounded his fists on the table, causing plates and silverware to rattle. "Where is Alexa? She should be here by now!"

Stefan cocked his head to one side. "For what? To present a pretty face at dinner for a husband so ready to desert her?" His sarcasm was scathing.

"Stefan, what is wrong with you?" Gregor lashed back. "I am not deserting her! I am leaving her safe and well guarded. You have always been my most loyal and trusted friend, and I leave her in your care. Why is it so impossible for you—of all people—to understand that this is my only choice?"

Stefan lifted a bite to his mouth, the morsel seeming dry and taste-less. His expression revealed the conflicting thoughts troubling his mind. "Gregor," he spoke after several long, tense minutes, "I do understand. As much as I prefer not to admit it, you're probably right. It's just that, for once in your life, I wish you could set aside your responsibilities as king just to be Gregor."

"Who is Gregor if not the man nurtured and taught to be responsi-ble as monarch?" Gregor's eyes revealed the torment his own decision had created.

"Gregor, she needs you. She feels so lost already. I fear more for her than I do for you. You asked where she is. Go to the temple."

Gregor's face was grateful. "Thank you, Stefan, for all you have ever been to me and for all I must yet ask you to do for me." He then rose and left for the Temple of Val.

A single candle burned on the altar. Bluish light glowed from the crystal pyramid. The sound of quietly echoing sobs knifed into his heart. He saw her at the front, sprawled on the steps of the altar. Her shoulders shook, and her face was buried against her arms that lay on the cold stone.

With each step he took toward her, he questioned more and more the wisdom of his decision to take charge and personally lead his forces against the rebels. Her outpouring of grief was a powerful force slicing through his resolution. How could he bring himself to leave her now? She had brought him sunny days, thoughtful inspiration, loyalty, and devo-tion. In the depth of her love, she had nearly given her life to save his. Now, she was vulnerable, pregnant with the child he wanted more than he ever could have imagined.

He sat down on the step by her side and gathered her against his chest. He held her possessively, his rich voice whispering soothing words of love. He rocked her gently back and forth. Within the refuge of his embrace, she quieted. Her arms wound around him as her mind registered the strength of his body. She wanted to speak, but words were trapped somewhere within her choking emotions. Instead, she huddled herself tightly against him. They sat together before Val's altar for a long time. Each was lost in thoughts of the other. Both recognized their commitments to the people of Turand. Both wondered where within those commitments they might fit their promises made to one another.

Finally, Gregor spoke softly. "Let me take you home."

She did not resist as he helped her to her feet. Drained and lightheaded, she concentrated on the task of placing one foot in front of the other. His body provided the support she needed to make it back to the palace without collapsing. She was so glad for his presence, his closeness, as he guided her up the staircase to their rooms.

She thought she remembered going to the bathroom to wash her face and get ready for bed. As if in a dream, she allowed him to remove her clothing and slide a nightgown over her head. Now, she only stared dumbly at him as he sat on the edge of the bed, waiting for her. When her head finally came to rest on the thick, soft pillow, she realized how little energy remained to her. Lying down provided unimaginable relief.

Gregor gently tucked the covers around them and pulled her into his arms. With full, sensual lips, he covered hers in a lingering kiss meant to convey the magnitude of his love. "I love you, my dearest Alexa," he whispered raggedly after pulling his mouth slightly away from hers.

"I know you do," she responded simply.

"Beloved, I truly believe that we can end this war faster if I lead our armies at the front. You must know, though, that you are more important to me than anything else in this world. You and this baby of ours. If it means so much to you, I will do everything I can to find another way. I will not leave you this way. I cannot."

She closed her eyes in the darkness. He had conceded, yet she felt no sense of victory, no overwhelming satisfaction. Perhaps she was just too tired. She wondered if it even mattered. So long as he was here with her tonight, she would just push the rest of the world from her mind. "Gregor, I love you. All I want is for you to hold me. Please."

He found no difficulty in honoring her simple request. He wanted her close to him—for her to feel safe and protected. He wanted her to rest in the comfort of his embrace so that she might feel free of the burden of fear he had forced upon her.

⌒

Autumn skies. Woven baskets overflowing with ripe, luscious fruits. Sweetly fragrant steam rising from giant copper pots on an enormous wood-fired stove. Cheerful chatter from kitchen maids as they washed and cut fruits for more waiting pots.

The sounds of shouts in the distance. The shrill cries of Sifiq soldiers in full gallop toward her house. The terrified expressions on her parents' faces. Victor's voice singing children's songs to her in the dank darkness of a cellar.

She tossed and turned in her sleep, moaning softly against horrible memories relived in her dreams. "No! Please! Don't let this be!" She rolled over again, clutching desperately at sheets and pillows. "Mama! Papa! Don't leave me! Please! Don't be dead! Mama! Papa!"

"Shush, my love, it's all right. I'm here. You're safe. I love you, Alexa. I love you."

Several long moments passed as the warmth and richness of his voice created the connection that soothed away the distress of her nightmare. Then, without ever waking, she turned over one last time, pressing herself as near to him as she possibly could. He gazed grimly into the darkness. His mere presence had chased away the demon memories haunting her. He was grateful that, even in the vulnerability of sleep, she felt safe with him. Yet, at the same time, he questioned if he would ever be able to escape as easily should the ghosts of his people ever come to haunt him.

~

With feathery-soft strokes, she ran her fingers through the thickness of his hair. She found it impossible to resist touching him. His features appeared so much softer in repose—more reflective of the sensitivity she had come to admire and love.

He stirred beneath the fluttering sensations she created. Reaching for her hand, he dragged it to his lips. A hint of a smile lit his face. "You kept me awake half the night. Do you have to wake me so early?"

"It's not as early as you think. It's already well past nine o'clock."

He opened one eye to peek at her. She was dressed and appeared to have been up for some time. "How do you always manage to get up before I do and yet never disturb me?"

"That, dear sir, is a secret of Valkana. Now, you need to get up. I have breakfast on the way up, so you have about twenty minutes. Hurry. We have too much to do for you to spend the entire day in bed."

He grinned wickedly and pulled her on top of him. "Hmmm. I think that might be a perfect way to spend the day," he whispered suggestively, just before he playfully nibbled at her earlobe.

She laughed and wriggled out of his grasp, then rolled out of bed. "Fifteen minutes. Hurry, or your breakfast will be cold."

While he was in the bath, she prepared his clothes for the day. She ran her fingers along the fabric of his sleeves, smoothing any wrinkles and thinking how much she would miss this daily intimacy. When the servants carried in the breakfast trays, she sent them away as soon as everything was set down. Quietly, she set the table herself, lovingly touching each dish and utensil that she laid at his place.

"You look lost in thought," he observed quietly as he leaned against the polished wood doorframe.

She glanced sideways at him, and the corner of her mouth twitched in a smile. "There's so much to do that I'm not quite sure where to start. Breakfast is ready if you're hungry."

"When have you known me not to be hungry?" He walked over to the table, pausing long enough to kiss her and pull out her chair before he sat down.

She poured tea, then settled herself in the chair across from him. He offered a brief prayer of thanks for their meal before they began to eat. As he ate, he studied her closely. Her face was pale, her eyes underlined with dark smudges from where she had cried the evening before. She ate slowly, frequently staring out the window. She appeared distinctly distracted but, at the same time, different somehow.

"Do you not feel well?"

She raised her eyes to meet his. Her face was calm yet solemn. "I have a slight headache. Other than that, I feel fine."

"Then tell me what you're thinking," he urged, wishing so very much that he could see the brilliance of her smile.

She set her napkin aside and stood up to walk around behind him. Her hands ran down either side of his shoulders. Leaning over, she pressed kisses along the exposed column of his neck. As a reflex, he tilted his head away from her, simultaneously inviting and savoring the erotic shivers her lips created. She then moved her mouth just in front of his ear. Her soft breath deliciously teased him.

"I was thinking how very much I love you and how very much I'm going to miss you."

Gregor pulled her by the hand to his side. He then scooted his chair back from the table and drew her down onto his lap. "I thought we settled this last night. I told you I would stay."

Her arms slid around his neck, and she rested her head against his shoulder. Perched on his lap with his hands clasped snugly around her waist, she could think of nothing she wanted more. Still, last night's terrible dreams continued to haunt her. "I understand why you must go. And I'm sorry I caused you so much trouble." Her apology was almost childlike.

He held her away from him so that he could gaze directly into her eyes. "You had a nightmare last night. You cried out for your parents. I'm the one who is sorry I upset you so much. You were right when you told me you had lost too much already. You've lost more than anyone should have to face in a lifetime. That is why I said I would stay. I love you too much to risk hurting you more."

She stood and moved across the room to a small desk she used occasionally. She stared with unseeing eyes into the vividly painted landscape that hung above it. "The dreams are what finally helped me understand."

She slowly spun around to face him. "If you lead your armies, there's a much greater likelihood this will end sooner. If only one family can avoid the sorrows and heartbreak we've known, then our sacrifice will be worthwhile. Besides, you were right about something else. I also want our baby to grow up in a peaceful Turand. I don't want this child to know the threat of violence and death that we have."

Gregor's heart swelled with pride as he recognized the immensity of the effort she had just expended. His napkin fell to the floor as he rose and went to her. As he clutched her close, his eyes tightly shut as he concentrated fully on the feel of her body next to his.

"You don't have to agree to this, Alexa," he whispered. "You know that I never wanted to leave you."

"You must go, Gregor. I understand that. No one else in Turand has your fire or your determination."

He led her by the hand to the settee, and they cuddled close together. "I know of at least one other person who does. I shall leave her in charge at the palace during my absence. Stefan will stay to help you in any way you need."

She only nodded, blinking against the unwelcome threat of fresh tears. "You must promise me one thing."

"And that is?"

She sat up straight and forced a nervous grin. "My husband makes such an enormous target. Promise you will be very careful with him. I need for him to come home to me."

"That is a promise gladly given," he answered, surrendering to the urge to kiss her soundly.

~

"There," she pronounced with satisfaction. "These are the last of the bandages. I think this finishes all of the medical supplies to go with Gregor."

"Alexa, I'm amazed at how quickly you organized all this. What's your secret?"

Stefan's praise was received with appreciation. Since talking with Gregor the day before, she had directed a whirlwind of activity. Stacks of boxes, all neatly marked and labeled, filled the enormous assembly hall. Medical supplies, blankets, and personal care items had been gathered and packed in record time. Workers were moving crates out to load into wagons bound for the southern battlefields.

"It appears that a logistical genius is at work here!" Gregor's voice called out from the doorway.

"Your lovely wife is the guilty genius!" Stefan called back from behind a stack of boxes he and Alexa were listing on packing manifests.

She darted her head quickly around the corner to respond. "Perhaps His Majesty would care to lend a hand…" Her tease came to an abrupt halt as she dropped her pencil and writing pad to the floor. She stepped out from behind the tower of crates with a stunned expression. "Gregor?"

His dark eyes twinkled mischievously. "What do you think?"

She walked toward him with a dazed look on her face. She stretched out her right hand to touch him but stopped just inches away. "What have you done?"

"You don't approve, do you?" he asked ruefully.

Tentatively, she reached up and touched a stray lock of hair that tumbled onto his forehead. "Your hair is so short! And your beard! Gregor, I don't understand." Her eyes widened with amazement. A disbelieving grin threatened to disintegrate into uncontrolled laughter as she shook her head back and forth.

"I thought it best since you told me the southern provinces will soon be so hot. You aren't happy with the change, are you?"

She allowed her fingertips to stroke the smooth line of his jaw. Without his beard, his face seemed rounder, almost boyish. His lips looked fuller, their curve more sensuous than ever. Even his eyes looked different beneath dark, arching eyebrows. At long last, she swallowed and smiled, her eyes sparkling merrily. "It's been such a long time since I kissed a clean-shaven man. I'm not sure I remember what it was like."

He grabbed her playfully by the arms and, ignoring Stefan and all the servants milling around, planted a noisy kiss on her mouth. "That comment, Your Majesty, was totally unnecessary since you have never before seen your husband without a beard."

She laughed aloud. "Well, it's true! I seem to recall having fallen in love with a black-bearded giant of a man! If it weren't for those wonderful brown eyes of yours, I might not have recognized you!"

"Let me refresh your memory," he teased. This time, his mouth covered hers in a kiss that imparted so much passion that Alexa felt dizzy and breathless when he released her.

"Mmmm," she mumbled dreamily. "Do you think you might possibly spare one more of those reminders? You don't look like my husband, but no one else has ever kissed me that way!"

It was his turn to laugh out loud, the sound carrying through the busy hall. "Milady, you are impossible! Especially when I come to inform you that I wish to enjoy your company for the remainder of the day."

She laughed softly and hugged him. "Stefan, will you have someone else finish this? It seems His Majesty requires my presence."

Late afternoon sun cast dappled plays of light and shadow as they walked hand in hand through the palace gardens. He glanced at her repeatedly, memorizing her profile, the distinct rose shade of her cheeks, and the curling waves of her hair. The sound of her voice, sweet and gentle, imprinted on his mind. Already, he felt the creeping loneliness that would be his companion for longer than he cared to imagine.

They shared ideas about what she could do during his absence. She reminded him to pray and meditate. He warned her to eat properly and rest. She suggested he should walk hunched over to avoid making such a large target. He told her a dozen times how much he loved her and his baby that she carried beneath her heart. They laughed and touched and kissed.

Much later, she lay in his arms. His mouth carried scorching fires along every part of her body. Her breasts, fuller with her pregnancy, swelled beneath his questing touch. His breathing grew rapid as she begged him to make her part of him. He delayed the sweetness of their union, wanting her never to forget his kisses or his touch. When finally he joined with her, she shook violently and sobbed against his neck. "Love me, Gregor. Love me as if you'll never stop."

Their passions exploded, soaring to heights undreamed of as the anticipation of prolonged separation drove them to a frenzy for which neither could have prepared. As climactic surges pulsated throughout their bodies, their embrace took on a kind of desperation that left them trembling and fighting for breath.

~

She spoke little the next morning as she helped him dress. Her body still throbbed in reaction to the sheer intensity of his lovemaking, a bittersweet reminder that there was no way to know when she might experience such passion again. Or if... Thrusting the unwelcome thought from her mind, she stood back for a final inspection.

"Your Majesty, you are incredibly handsome this morning."

"Even without my beard?" He was determined to keep at bay as much gloom as possible from their parting.

She grinned and patted his smooth cheek. "Even without the beard," she responded, unnecessarily starting to fuss and straighten the collar of his uniform tunic.

"We need to go, Alexa. The men are waiting for me." He spoke gently, saddened by the shadows that crossed her face.

She sighed softly before hooking her arm through his. "Lead on, Your Majesty."

Upon stepping down from the last curved stair of the central staircase, she stopped suddenly. "Gregor, you go ahead. I forgot something. I'll meet you outside!" She turned and hurried back upstairs.

Outside, a small force of nearly two hundred men stood by their horses. Royal banners, carried high, fluttered in a light breeze. The symbol of Val gleamed golden against backgrounds of white and vivid purple. Wagons laden with fresh supplies formed a long line. Citizens of Toraval had gathered to show support for their king, who would personally lead the struggle for reunification.

When Gregor emerged from the palace, his bearing was regal, exuding confidence and resoluteness that permeated the very air around him. The men under his command stood at attention, their uniformed appearances enhancing the ceremonial atmosphere. Gregor raised his arms in greeting to all who awaited him. Toravalians cheered his courage. His soldiers saluted smartly.

Stefan walked up from behind and stood to his left. "You leave us to sounds of cheering optimism. I pray you can return to cheers for peace." Before Gregor could respond, Alexa came running up to him, breathless as she took her place to his right.

Gregor stepped up to a permanent stone podium and surveyed the scene before him. Despite the sea of bright colors and the now fading cheers, he wished this day had never been necessary.

"Good people of Turand," his voice rang out powerfully across the square. "I ask for your support and, most of all, for your prayers. I go with these men to join other brave Turandans who have united to drive the Sifiq from our nation. We must end the insurrection threatening to perpetuate the suffering and violence that have tortured our country and our people for so many years.

"I leave my beloved Toraval with a heavy heart, knowing that I lead our forces against fellow Turandan citizens. Your prayers are needed for all of us on both sides. In my absence, I leave our queen to fulfill my duties. Alexa will serve Toraval and all of Turand as queen and blessed Valkana, providing spiritual guidance and stability until I return. My longtime friend and adviser, Stefan Sidano, will continue as Royal Chief Adviser. I pray that you will give them your loyalty as we face the challenges awaiting us.

"To you who stand ready to accompany me to distant battlefields, I offer my gratitude and my respect. It is entirely probable that some of us will never return home."

He paused, allowing the impact of his last statement to strike home. He then stepped down from the podium, took Alexa's hand, and guided her to the front. "It is with love and tremendous pride that I announce that our queen honors me by carrying our first child. I remind all of you that this is the reason we must fight this war. We must restore Turand to a state of peace and renewed prosperity for the sake of our children."

The gathering erupted into cheers, which Gregor acknowledged with smiles and sweeping waves. Mingled were feelings of optimism, concern, and excitement. A sense of destiny hung in the air.

With his wife and Stefan accompanying him, Gregor strode toward the golden stallion that awaited him. A groom held the magnificent animal's reins as the king prepared to bid personal farewells.

He gazed intently into Stefan's gray eyes. "I entrust to you everything that is most precious to me, Stefan, most especially my wife and my unborn child. Take care of her. And yourself."

The two men embraced. "Be careful, Gregor." Stefan choked against rarely displayed emotion.

Gregor then turned to Alexa, who stood silently beside his horse. His eyes feasted on every delicate detail of her appearance. He dreaded the time that would crawl by until he could see her again.

"I brought you something. I want you to wear this as long as you're away." She stood on her toes to reach high enough to place the sturdy, elegant gold chain over his head and around his neck. Suspended from the chain hung a small, solid crystal pyramid with a golden sun embedded in its center.

He looked puzzled as he held the pendant between his fingers. "What is this? It looks familiar."

"It should. Remember the first time you took me to Lindaval? You told me I could use anything I found if I wanted to. I found this inside a drawer. It belonged to your mother."

Gregor shut his eyes, cherished memories of his mother's image floating before his mind's eye. "Yes, I do remember," he said softly.

"Did you not know she was Valiria?" Alexa asked, her eyes a deep evergreen hue as they roved over every beloved feature of his face.

His shock was evident. "I had no idea. Are you sure?"

She smiled and nodded. "You, too, are blessed."

Gregor lovingly cradled her face between his large, warm hands. Tears stung his eyes. "I do love you, Alexa, and never more than right now. Promise me again that you will take good care of yourself and our baby."

She refused to surrender to the desire to cry, not wanting his parting memory to be one of her overcome by tears. Instead, she forced herself to smile. "You have my promise. Gregor?"

"Yes, my love?"

She could only whisper. "Come home to me. Please. Just come home to me."

Gregor kissed her lightly at first, but the emotions he had dammed up overflowed the control he thought he could maintain. His mouth covered hers, desperately seeking to convey all the love and anguish that filled him as he prepared to leave. Forcing himself to drag his lips from hers, he held her tightly against him, swaying to a slow, internal rhythm borne from the depths of his soul.

She was the first to move away, knowing that if he held her one moment longer, she would likely beg him to stay. Instead, she lifted his hands to her lips and kissed the palms and tops. She then bent her head to touch them. "May Val's blessings go with you, my husband."

Assuming her role as High Priestess Valkana, she stepped up to the podium, her arms outstretched to the crowd. "Hear me, brave people of Turand. Val's love is with us all. We must not fail in our devotion to him. Neither can we fail in our prayers for these men who leave for war. Pray for them all. Keep them in your thoughts and in your hearts. They carry with them our hopes for a new era of peace."

All bent their heads in prayer. Only the occasional soft whicker of a horse or the call of a bird in flight broke their silence. Soldier and citizen alike united in a single prayerful entreaty. May peace return to Turand.

Alexa stepped down from the podium and back to the horse her husband had just mounted. She lifted her hand to touch his. "I love you, Gregor." She only mouthed the words that he would never have heard amid the clatter and noise of wagons, horses, and harnesses.

His gaze lingered upon her, his eyes mirroring the sorrow that filled them both. He then straightened in his saddle and signaled the beginning of the journey southward.

Chapter 18

G regor's forces established a central command center in the remote northeast corner of Garogan Province. The encampment covered acres of land at the base of a range of foothills. Those foothills swept into a mountain range stretching from Garogan Province across Tasa Coast Province all the way to the sea. Several enormous tents had been erected, including two as hospital tents, one as a protected area for dining, and one for use by the king when he consulted with his military advisers. A smaller tent had been set up as quarters for Gregor's personal use.

Crackling campfires dotted the encampment where Gregor stood outside his tent, surveying the scene before him. Firelight created a play of eerie, ghost-like shadows. Men sat in front of the blazing fires. Some talked while others inspected their weapons. Somewhere, someone sang to the accompaniment of stringed instruments. The ballad was a mournful melody that suited Gregor's mood. They planned to launch a major offensive the following morning, and everyone expected the fighting to be fierce.

Gregor turned and bent forward to enter his tent for the night. An aide had already been in and left a lit lantern on a small table. Gregor sat down on a chair, his long legs banging into the table legs. He grinned wryly to himself. Battlefield accommodations were not the most suitable for a man of his proportions. He laid out pages of stationery and set quill to paper.

My beloved Alexa,

Four long weeks have passed since I left you in Toraval. I hope you can forgive me that this is only the fourth time I write since then. Our days have been so filled with wearisome travel. Occasional skirmishes have been successfully routed, and we have lost only eight men. Can you imagine? Only eight lives lost on our side. The loss of even one life is too much and sorely grieves me.

Nights are, by far, most difficult for me. My mind sorts through dozens of reports from our scouts, and I think on how best to utilize the information. Each night, I hope that I will tire and fall asleep, but my thoughts always drift home. I lie awake often, my arms aching to hold you again. I knew that this separation would be difficult. What I never expected was the enormity of the emptiness I suffer without you.

Words escape me, my love. I can only tell you that I feel as though I left my whole heart behind with you in Toraval. Think of me often at night. I promise to touch those thoughts as I lie thinking of you and loving you.

Gregor

With deft fingers, he folded the paper quickly and sealed it. He wrote her name in flourishing penmanship on the front and placed it on the table. He reverently touched the letter and traced her name with his index finger, thinking sadly that she would touch this insignificant piece of paper before she would him.

Sighing heavily, he shifted in his chair to pull off tall, leather riding boots. He kicked them aside and stood to yawn and stretch. He extinguished the lamp on the table and lay down on the cot, tossing his blanket aside. The air inside the tent was thick and hot despite the late hour.

Lying on his back, Gregor stared into darkness. Wondering if she also lay thinking of him, he tried to picture how the passage of a month in her pregnancy might have affected her body. A single tear slid from his eye, and he whispered into the night, "I love you, Alexa."

~

Ever since that final, horrible day in Toraval, Victor had grown obsessed with devising means to obtain revenge against Gregor. He spent hours each day on drills and practices conducted with recruits he would lead against the king's forces. He drove himself until late most nights, preparing intricate plans for the Garogan and Tasa Coast revolutionaries.

He fell exhausted into bed each night, but sleep was always a long time coming. He tossed restlessly from one side of his bed to the other. He pounded pillows. He stretched and curled and stretched again. His body ached. His head throbbed painfully. Often, he cried.

Memories sank insidious fingers of despair that contracted around his heart. Her laughter had been infectious. Her perseverance had been inspirational. Her loyalty had been the foundation for his aspirations. All his hopes for the future had been connected to Alexa and the love he blamed Gregor for stealing.

He constantly berated himself for letting his political ambitions distract him from marrying her when he had the chance. So many times had he rationalized the delays and kissed the disappointment from her face. How often did he now think himself a complete idiot for not making her his instead of embarking on that fateful journey to Toraval?

Sometimes, he slept. Frequently, he awakened from dreams that only added to the clouds of depression that enveloped him. Sleep brought with it images from the past to flash through his mind. Alexa's expression when she informed him of her impending wedding. The forlorn look in her eyes the morning he was set free from Zenox Prison when she had told him that she belonged to Gregor.

Then there had been his elation when she had finally returned home to Garogan. He had touched her and kissed her in complete certainty she would be his again. He had entertained brief elation the morning he had gone to the chapel, expecting her to arrive to sign papers to dissolve her marriage so that he could make her his bride. Then Adrina had come, announcing that Alexa had refused to leave her rooms.

Guilt became his constant, hateful companion. He cringed, quaking with renewed terror as his mind replayed the image of his own arrow striking her in the back. He remembered the mindless furor that had driven him to shake Alexa in utter frustration. He despised himself for having lost control of his temper for hitting her several times.

The rhythm of his memories marched relentlessly. First, Alexa's dramatic entrance to National Council's opening session and her collapse later that day. His total helplessness as he watched the king cradle her possessively in his arms and carry her away. His own complete shame and despair after he had struck her in the garden. Her resolute rejection of him before Council followed by her adamant declaration that she loved Gregor.

Adrina, her heart aching, watched helplessly as her brother grew more and more remote and withdrawn. She tried to talk with him, to reason with him. Convincing Victor that he had to relinquish any claims on Alexa met with hostile demonstrations of anger that she had never seen. He exploded with rage, his face growing livid, his voice hoarse from shouting.

She always withdrew until he exhausted his anger. She would then return to him in silence, rubbing his shoulders and neck. Invariably, he would start to recount happier times when Alexa had lived in Garogan. Without fail, he would succumb to tears.

By the time Victor was finally ready to leave for Tasa Coast Province, he had assumed an icy cold demeanor that frightened his sister even more than his explosions of temper. Haunted by the unexpected change in Alexa, Victor retreated within himself. He was convinced that Gregor's death was the only way to restore Alexa's sanity and her affections. That obsession assumed powerful and ominous control of his every waking thought.

As Adrina stood outside the walls of Garogan Castle to watch the departure of the Garogan militia, she fretted that her brother had become a stranger. There had been no warmth in his farewell. Neither had there been any of his usual fond regard. She feared that his singular obsession with Alexa would prove a disastrous distraction. Praying, she dabbed her eyes with a lace-edged handkerchief.

~

Dearest Gregor,

Since you left for the southern provinces, Toraval has faced the newest challenges in our fight for freedom with a renewed sense of purpose. Without the presence of Sifiq military, the return to worship strengthens our people. Although we all share worry for our army and concern for the strife dividing our country, we offer concentrated prayers for reconciliation and peace.

As your queen, I hope that I will be strong enough to encourage this path. I hold many meetings, and city leaders bring wise, well-prepared advice and options. The same is true of most provincial representatives who come. Stefan is a master at helping me organize and proceed with steps that ensure the city's safety. His abilities dealing with the provincial leaders are extraordinary.

As your wife, my heart aches each day as I contemplate our separation. My great consolation is that I carry your child. This is the strength and the bond making these long days and nights bearable. You would probably laugh to see me. After nearly six months, I am beginning to look like I swallowed an entire melon. The baby moves often, and I suspect it will be as active and lively as you.

I long for the rich sound of your voice and the comfort of your touch. I read your letters every day, and they do help. Sometimes, during evening meditations at the temple, I comfort myself with the thought that you, too, are thinking of me. I tell myself that it is our love that forges these fleeting connections.

Gregor, please let us know if there is anything more we can do to aid you and our forces there. We are finally reuniting as a people, and we all know that if the southern provinces can be restored to our fold, we can be completely healed. You know that Victor carries tremendous influence with those not only in Garogan but also in Tasa Coast and Pitrand, as well as with sympathizers in other provinces.

Victor could be key to achieving peace if only he can move past the hatred he bears toward you. I don't know how we can reach him. I shall pray and meditate. Perhaps I can touch the essence of good that still lingers within him. But, my husband, do whatever you deem necessary. I trust in you, and I am confident your judgment will be best.

Please, my love, be careful. You face so much danger. I shiver at the thought of what may yet happen. My vision is not always clear. I suppose this could be due to my condition, or perhaps the occasional lack of clarity results from the fact that I miss you so much. Know that I support

you with all that is within me. And I need you.
May our God bring you safely home very soon.

I love you.
Alexa

⤸

Great clouds of choking, yellow dust swirled thickly above the ground. Hooves beat wildly against the ground, and the snorts and squeals of horses provided chaotic background for the harsh clang of steel ringing through the air. Desperate shouts combined with the agonized groans of injured men. Bloody bodies lay strewn across the battlefield. Horses tumbled. Men ran. Mass confusion prevented any clarity of vision as to who was who.

Alexa turned uncomfortably in bed. The burgeoning evidence of her sixth month of pregnancy slowed her ability to change positions. The chaos of the battlefield enveloped her mind. It was as if a part of her consciousness hovered in flight—searching, seeking.

"Gregor? Where are you?" She heard the words inside her head as perspiration began to wet her brow and soak her hair. Then, a familiar voice claimed her attention. Her sleep-bound consciousness swept toward the sound.

"I told you! She's mine! She always was and always will be!"

"Victor! No!" Shrill screams reverberated through the palace in the hour just preceding dawn.

Tira and Tirani rushed into her chambers to find her sitting upright in bed. Her chest heaved, and her eyes stared blankly into the darkness.

Stefan ran in behind them, terrified by the blood-curdling screams that had been unlike any he had ever heard.

"Your Majesty, are you all right? What happened?" Tira asked as she quickly sat on the bedside, rubbing Alexa's trembling hands between her own.

Alexa looked up at Stefan, who carried a small lamp. Her face shone with a thin film of perspiration. She blinked several times. "Stefan, you must help me."

"Alexa, of course. Just tell me what it is you want me to do."

"Stefan, wake the staff. Have them prepare provisions. I want twenty men from my personal guard ready to leave no later than nine o'clock. We ride for the south."

Stefan shook his head in bewilderment. "What? What are you talking about?"

She ignored his question. "Tira, prepare for travel as many of the herbs as you can for Raija and Kirmaya teas. You are to remain here in Toraval." She turned her attention to Tirani. "Tirani, the choice is yours, but I want very much for you to accompany me."

Tirani gazed at her mistress in the semi-darkness and felt her unwavering intentions. "I will accompany you, Milady," she responded without hesitation.

"You must understand. This trip could be dangerous. You will likely encounter requests for your assistance as Valiria. Some of those requests could cause you great physical pain."

"I understand, Milady, but I'm not afraid. I will go with you."

Having regained his composure following the shock of being awakened by the queen's screams, Stefan approached the edge of the bed. "Alexa, am I to understand that you intend to ride into the battle zones?"

"You understand correctly, Stefan. Now, please leave. I must get up to dress." The breathless, near hysteria of only moments earlier had been replaced with clear purpose and calm command.

"Alexa, there's something you don't understand. I will not permit you to make such a dangerous journey. Certainly not in your condition." His face was set as he crossed his arms, creating a stern image that emphasized his earnestness.

Alexa gazed at him, her face a mask of defiance. "Stefan, I know that Gregor asked you to take care of me, and I appreciate your intentions. Know this. Even if you tie me to this bed and lock me inside this room, you will find me gone within a matter of hours. This, I swear to you. Only I warn you. Do not allow those hours of delay to cost my husband's life."

"What are you saying?" Stefan asked, stunned by the intimidating way she had spoken to him.

She closed her eyes and drew in several calming, cleansing breaths. When she spoke again, her voice had regained its characteristic gentleness. "Stefan, sit down." When he refused, she ignored the fact and continued, "I had a vision. A terrible, terrible battle is imminent. Many men will be injured, and many will die. Tirani and I can save most of the injured who otherwise will surely die. If I do not make this trip, Gregor will be one of those dead."

"Alexa, what if it was only a dream? A nightmare?"

"Stefan," she ground out impatiently, "I know the difference between my dreams and my visions. I cannot let Gregor die. I will not. No one will stop me—not even you."

He had seen similar expressions on her face before, but experience had shown him that she could be even more stubborn than Gregor. "What about the baby? How can you take such a risk with your baby?"

"Stefan, I'm barely six months pregnant. Fortunately, I am tall enough to carry this child well, and I am not too ungainly. I will ride. I will go to my husband, and I will not lose his child. You must believe in me."

Having observed so many strange incidences involving her, he stared at her. His heart told him to trust her. His mind, however, presented a different matter. How could he possibly allow her to ride into hostile territory? Even if she didn't get killed or lose the baby, Gregor would definitely be enraged with him for allowing her to place herself in such danger. "Alexa, please. Don't ask this of me."

With patience waning, she flipped the covers back and slid out of bed, completely ignoring the fact that she wore only a thin, summer-weight gown. Her eyes glittered in weak lamplight as her aura began a shimmering dance that encased her pregnant figure.

"Stefan, you are my husband's closest friend and a good man. I thank you for your concern. I know you think only of my safety and my husband's request of you. Consider the matter this way. I ask nothing of you. I assume full responsibility and full command of this mission as Queen of Turand. If you wish to accompany me, you may. Otherwise, leave and assemble my guard as instructed." She turned away from him, walked into the adjoining bathroom, and closed the door.

He stared after her, unable to register the power or authority contained in her orders. Tirani, who had remained silent during the exchange, came to him and took him by the arm.

"Stefan, you must realize that you have no choice. I assure you. She means every word she says. She will go exactly as she plans, and I would not dare to walk in the shoes of anyone who would try to stand in her way."

Stefan glanced down into Tirani's dark eyes, his face tight with tension. "You know I cannot let her go alone. We may all be killed."

"None of us will die. None except Gregor if she doesn't. I felt the remnants of the vision in her. She is utterly afraid for him. The vision was a warning." She paused, her eyes serious. "He will die."

"Tirani, are you so certain?" His light eyes gazed at her with heart-wrenching indecision.

320

"Stefan, go with us. Trust her as I do."

Stefan reached backward, massaging the muscles pulling in the back of his neck. "It seems our king has come to love a most strong and stubborn woman."

Chapter 19

Hot sun beat down on the wide, dusty road leading southward to where the northernmost borders of Tasa Coast and Garogan Provinces met the corner of Toravalia. The morning had been a mad scramble getting soldiers ready to travel and preparing supplies the queen had insisted they should carry with them. The party left Toraval quietly, drawing as little attention as possible. Following hours of riding, they made steady progress.

Alexa pointed out a rippling stream off to the right side of the road and indicated they should stop. After Stefan and the lieutenant in charge helped her dismount, she stretched before walking the short distance to the gurgling water. Kneeling carefully, she dangled her hands into the coolness before splashing her face.

Taking a few minutes to walk around, she spoke personally to each man who had volunteered to accompany her. She asked each one his name before embracing him. Smiling at Tirani, her eyes revealed her gratitude for the devotion and courage of her young lady-in-waiting. She then approached Stefan, whose face remained stony and distant.

"Stefan, you're still angry. Your anger will only make the trip seem longer and more trying." Her eyes were kind as she solemnly appraised his mood.

"Your Majesty, with my life, I dread the idea of explaining to your husband how I could have permitted you to make this trip."

She smiled knowingly. "Please don't worry. Stefan?"

He looked directly at her for the first time since the morning. "Yes, Your Majesty?"

"First of all, dispense with the formalities. You will surely make me crazy if you persist. Second, I want you to think. I know how much you and Gregor love each other. You are more like brothers than friends. If you were absolutely certain that he would die if you were not there to save him, what would you do?"

He sighed heavily. "I would risk my own life to save him. I know that I wouldn't even hesitate."

"Bearing that in mind, can you understand why I must go? The battle has not yet occurred, and still, I fear we may not arrive in time. I must try. Gregor is more than my love. He is my life."

Stefan contemplated the remote expression that draped her features. He wondered what she saw in the distant fields of her mind. Was it a past, treasured memory? Or was it the horror that had been so clearly etched in her features that morning?

"Are you ready to ride again?"

Her face revealed her appreciation for his change of heart. "Help me to mount."

That evening, campfires crackled and snapped, sending sparks flying into the air along with plumes of swirling, gray smoke. Stars twinkled merrily above breaks in the forest canopy. Alexa and Tirani had placed their sleeping gear side by side. The queen's guards and Stefan had all discussed contingency plans in case of trouble. The women only exchanged knowing glances, understanding after meditation that their mission had been willed by Val. They both lay down wearily and fell asleep, firm in their faith in Val's protection.

Early the next morning, they both awoke before the men. They quietly walked a short distance into the woods to pray and meditate. They knew they must limit their time. The men would rise soon, and they would all need to eat before resuming their journey.

On the fourth day, the travelers maintained a driving pace. Alexa steadily grew more agitated and was willing to pause less frequently than the days before. By dusk, everyone showed signs of weariness and irritability. Suddenly, Alexa turned her horse from the main road onto a narrow, rutted wagon path.

Stefan nudged his mount quickly forward. "Alexa, what are you doing? Where are you headed?"

"I remember a farmhouse used to be back here. It will be a good place to spend the night. Rain is coming."

The soldiers brought up the rear. Minutes later, they reached a broad clearing containing an old, well-maintained barn and a small, tidy farmhouse. At a covered well alongside the house, an elderly woman stopped her task of drawing water to stare at the arrival of the unexpected party. Alexa immediately signaled one of the soldiers to help the woman with the bucket of water.

Stefan and the lieutenant dismounted and helped Alexa down to the ground. She slapped some of the dust from her riding skirts before stiffly walking toward the surprised woman. "Mrs. Kadrani, do you remember me?" she asked, her hands outstretched in greeting.

The old lady studied her in the fading light of dusk before smiling her recognition. "You are Alexa, the Valiria who graced us with your visit so many months ago."

"You do remember! I am grateful. Mrs. Kadrani, I come to you once again to request the gift of your hospitality."

Mrs. Kadrani cast a questioning glance toward Tirani and the detachment of soldiers, who still waited to dismount. She then looked back at

Alexa, noting her pregnant figure. "Lady Valiria, I can offer only my barn as shelter for so many men. My home is ready to receive you and the other lady. Surely a woman in your condition should not be out riding."

Alexa thanked her and, after issuing instructions to Stefan, followed Mrs. Kadrani into the house. Tirani and the soldier who carried the pail of fresh water followed close behind. As Alexa and Tirani passed through the door, they sensed something not right. "Mrs. Kadrani, your husband—is he ill?" Alexa inquired.

Mrs. Kadrani turned to her with eyes full of sadness. "Yes, my dear. I'm so glad you've come. His heart is as broken as his legs. With our sons gone to fight alongside the king, he tried to fix a hole in the roof. He fell and broke both legs. They are useless now, and he is confined to bed. He grows weaker and weaker, and I think he will die soon. He seems to have lost the desire to live because he feels so worthless. Perhaps you will pray with us."

Alexa and Tirani exchanged concerned glances and entered the small room where the old man lay quietly in bed. Mr. Kadrani's face was pale and drawn beneath thin wisps of snowy white hair. His cheeks were gaunt, his eyes sunken. As he dozed, a foul smell of sickness hung in the room.

Tirani sidestepped past both women to go to his side. She laid one hand upon his forehead and the other upon his heart. She closed her eyes for several moments, then glanced up at Alexa. "It does seem he has lost the will to live. I believe we have come in time."

Alexa wrapped her arm around the older woman's shoulders. "Tirani here is also Valiria. Let her stay with your husband for a while. In the meantime, I'm going to plead with you to share some of that wonderful stew I smell."

At the dark trestle table in the kitchen, Alexa spooned a bite of thick stew into her mouth. "Mrs. Kadrani," she said appreciatively, "your food is every bit as delicious as I recall."

Mrs. Kadrani smiled her thanks, continually shifting her eyes to the bedroom door behind which lay her husband. "I'm sorry there is not enough to serve the men. Who are they, Milady? They look like soldiers."

"They are. Since I left you, my life has changed. I married shortly after I reached Toraval. I now ride to where the king has taken his army."

"Then these are the king's soldiers? I'm not sure I understand. I remember you spoke of your betrothed being from Garogan and imprisoned at Toraval." The woman placed a mug of cold milk in front of Alexa before sitting at the table to eat her own meal. Her attention was divided between practiced listening for her husband and her curiosity regarding the lone woman traveler her family had sheltered barely a year ago.

A knock sounded at the door, and the lady started to rise. "Please stay seated, Mrs. Kadrani. Come!" Alexa called out, knowing it was Stefan who waited outside.

He entered the inviting atmosphere of the kitchen, his eyes rapidly surveying everything to assure himself of the safety of the women in his charge. "Your Majesty, the men are already set up in the barn and secure for the night. Is all well here?"

"Yes, Stefan. This is Mrs. Kadrani. She has graciously offered me her hospitality in the past."

Stefan took the lady's work-roughened, age-spotted hand and brushed it with his lips. "Mistress, we thank you for your kindness in allowing us to stay here the night."

The woman, unaccustomed to Stefan's formal manners, actually blushed, her wrinkled cheeks turning a delightful shade of pink. "Sir, you are welcome. I only wish I could offer better accommodations."

Stefan's smile was charming. "Mistress, you provide the first roof over our heads after three nights of sleeping beneath the stars. With rain threatening, we are made more than happy by that which you so kindly offer." He then spoke to Alexa. "Guards are posted outside. I will be in the barn if you should need anything."

"Thank you, Stefan. Try to rest. Tomorrow's trip will prove much more trying."

After he had gone, Mrs. Kadrani stared into her guest's face as Alexa finished her stew and a thick slice of bread spread with freshly churned butter. "Lady Valiria, the gentleman referred to you as Your Majesty."

Alexa smiled and nodded. "Mrs. Kadrani, when I went to Toraval, King Gregor made me his bride."

The lady rose stiffly, nervously beginning to clear away the dishes as Alexa sipped fresh, creamy milk. "I cannot believe that the Queen of Turand dines at my simple table," she muttered. "I heard at the market that our new queen is also Valkana. Is that also true?"

Alexa stood and rested her hands on Mrs. Kadrani's shoulders. "Calm yourself, dear friend. You have offered your kindness to me twice now. I am forever indebted to you. To answer your question, the news you heard is correct. Your queen is also Valkana. She is also the same woman you took in not so very long ago. The only difference is that she is no longer so lonely or so sad."

Mrs. Kadrani gazed thoughtfully into Alexa's face. Faded blue eyes were still expressive enough to reveal her amazement. "I never dreamed even to know of such things, let alone to have someone like you in my own house."

"Milady," Tirani beckoned from the rough-hewn bedroom door.

Her face glistened with perspiration, and she looked exhausted. However, she smiled serenely. "Please come."

Mr. Kadrani slept peacefully. It was evident that a tremendous change had occurred. Color flushed his cheeks, and his shallow breathing had become deep and regular. Mrs. Kadrani moved to his side and took his hand in hers. In awe, she turned tear-glazed eyes to the priestesses standing at the foot of the hand-carved poster bed.

Tirani walked back to the side of the bed and drew aside the colorful, loomed coverlet. "His legs were nearly black. The bones had been splintered, and the tissues were dying. Now, all is healed. You can see that fresh blood circulates and restores the natural color. The bones have also healed. He will need to sleep the night through and to rest for perhaps two weeks, but he will be fine."

Mrs. Kadrani ran her hands along her husband's sturdy legs in disbelief. Her lips pressed tightly together as she sought words sufficient to express her feelings. Her eyes told them what her voice could not.

Just before dawn, Alexa awakened to the sound of raindrops on the roof that had subsided from the angry pounding she had heard upon first drifting off to sleep. Placing a hand against her pregnant belly, she smiled briefly when she felt her baby move. Lying in the darkness, listening to the pat-a-pat of the rain, she knew that Gregor was also awake. She felt the weight of his anxiety upon her chest, sensing not only his dread but also his commitment to what he must do.

Their baby shifted positions again as she heard her husband's voice inside her mind. At this very moment, her name was upon his lips. She wished she could magically shift time and space to reach him faster. She balled her hands into tight fists. "I'm coming, Gregor. Live, my husband, until I can reach you."

As dawn's misty light began to penetrate the small window, Alexa silently climbed from the narrow bed in which she had slept. Tirani still rested, her slumber deepened by her first encounter with the Healing Graces in a life and death situation.

Alexa had laid out clean clothing the night before and now dressed quickly in semi-darkness. In sock-clad feet, she padded out to the large kitchen and found a cup for water. She slipped on the shoes she had left by the door and went outside. The rain had stopped, causing relief to seep through her. She walked to the well and drew up fresh water, dipping a cool drink to raise to her lips.

"Who is there?' a voice called out in the morning's gray shadows.

"It is I, soldier. Your queen," she responded, recognizing the voice.

He approached her quickly. "Your Majesty, you should not be out alone in the dark."

She shook her head at him. "I am not alone. I have brave young men like you to protect me, and my Lord Val is ever-watchful."

He smiled, her confident reply enhancing his pride in being afforded the honor to participate in this mission. "Your Majesty, may I ask you a question?"

"Of course," she replied, forcing herself to listen to this young soldier instead of her husband's voice echoing in the far recesses of her mind.

"I was told you make this trip because of a major battle to come. My brother left with the king's army, and I know there has already been fighting. Is there a way to know if he is still alive?"

"Come closer. Let me touch your face. What is your brother's name?"

He did as she instructed and allowed her to place her hands upon his face, covering his eyes. "He is called Tristo."

"And you are Tirstan. I remember." She closed her eyes and allowed herself to touch his energy. He was a kind, thoughtful young man and very idealistic. She stepped away from him. "Your brother is well as we speak. I suggest you pray for him and all the others. At this moment, they prepare to march into a dreadful battle."

He saw great sadness and apprehension line her face. Spontaneously, he took her hand into his. "Your Majesty, if I have to carry you myself, I will deliver you to your husband. I swear it."

She nodded solemnly, grateful for his show of devotion. "Thank you, Tirstan. Please. Go awaken Sir Sidano now and send him to me in the house."

Back inside, she lit a candle on the table and an oil lamp in the center of a large sideboard. Grateful that embers still glowed brightly in the massive iron stove that dominated the kitchen, she pushed in fresh wood, built up the fire, and set a kettle of water on to heat. She needed a cup of tea and a moment to organize her thoughts.

The door creaked as it opened. Stefan entered, his eyelids heavy, his voice husky with sleep. "You sent for me. Is something wrong?"

"Sit, Stefan. I'm fixing tea. Will you have some with me?"

He nodded, wondering at how rested she looked when the rest of them felt worn out by the pace she had kept.

She served them both tea and sat down across from Stefan. Her face was grave. "As we speak, Gregor prepares for battle. Stefan, I can feel how apprehensive he is. His men are ready, but Gregor knows this battle might easily be a major turning point. Stefan, he's afraid."

"How long before we reach them, Alexa?"

"I think not before tomorrow. I fear we may already be too late." Her mind replayed the scene that had driven her these past few days.

"What will happen?" Stefan asked softly.

"Fighting will be fierce. Worse than any they've faced until now. I saw Turandans and Sifiq, but I believe very few of our people realize they fight alongside Sifiq. Victor is also there."

"Is he the one?" Stefan had not meant to ask the question but had been unable to stop himself.

"Yes," she whispered. She swallowed several times before speaking again. "He is determined to destroy Gregor. How ironic that I was the one who saved Victor's life because of my love for him and now…" She blinked back tears and abruptly stood up. "Come, Stefan. We must hurry."

Chapter 20

Gregor surveyed final reinforcements set up around the camp. Humid air already hung over his army in stifling, oppressive heat. Acrid smoke lingered from the previous night's campfires. The pungent smell of sweaty men and horse dung wafted on a hot breeze that promised yet another miserable, sweltering day. The king knelt to pray. His men followed his example. They all knew this battle would be critical. They called on Val for protection and mercy in the face of their enemy. They prayed that those who would surely die this day would not lose their lives in vain.

When Gregor rose to his feet, he gave a signal, and his horse was led to him. As he mounted, he took the reins firmly in hand. Glancing at all around him, he then paused before placing a hand against his chest, over the crystal pyramid tucked snugly inside his tunic. His glance then fell to the wedding band on his finger. "I love you, Alexa. Now and forever," he whispered, just before calling out the command to advance.

His forces had proceeded barely three miles before they encountered the initial thrust of the rebel army. Gregor and his officers shouted out orders, galloping back and forth through confusion and chaos. Wounded and dying men soon lay everywhere. Horses shrieked as they toppled to the ground with their riders.

Gregor redirected his soldiers numerous times, taking advantage of openings and weak spots breaking the insurgent lines. Through an intricate system of signals, his carefully coached army made rapid changes where necessary. His troops responded immediately. Still, the opposition fought tenaciously.

The day was nothing less than maddening pandemonium. Sounds of battle created a cacophony that was a constant, deafening crescendo of sword against sword, shouted commands and counter-commands, screams, cries, and agonized moans that seemed to have no end. When it appeared the Royal Army would gain an advantage, a redirected wave of attack would necessitate urgent reassessment and counter moves.

Gregor sent Kohira forward to command the front lines as he backed up with two other officers to protect a group of wounded soldiers struggling to return to camp. His horse's hooves barely missed striking a man who, still alive, lay pinned beneath a fallen horse. He shouted for the officers to continue with the others while he quickly dismounted and ran to free the injured soldier from beneath the animal. He had just pulled him loose when he heard someone call out his name. Spinning around, he came face to face with Victor Garogan.

"So, the mighty King Gregor has come to lead his army to defeat," Victor sneered, his eyes flaming with hatred.

Gregor backed up a step, drawing his sword from its sheath. "Garogan, help me put an end to this madness! These are all good Turandans!"

Victor held his gleaming steel blade at the ready, his voice cold and menacing. "The only thing I intend to stop is you, Gregor. I swore back in Toraval that you would pay for the atrocity you committed against Alexa. That day has finally come."

Victor advanced, grim confidence etched into every line of his face. The two men dueled, their swords clashing and clanging. The battle they fought was far removed from the fight being waged by others on the battlefield that afternoon. Theirs was a personal war, spiteful and vicious, especially with Victor so obsessed by his consuming desire for vengeance.

Although Gregor was a skilled swordsman, Victor was more experienced. Further, he was inspired by a fury that had taken precedence over every other aspect of his character. With every thrust, every turn, and every sweep of his weapon, Victor was set on punishing Gregor for taking the only woman he would ever love.

He taunted Gregor, trying to break his concentration. "She belongs to me! You know that! She was always meant to be mine. You are mad if you think she will ever forget me or what we shared. You may use her like your whore, you bastard, but she will be mine again!"

Gregor fought wordlessly, refusing to yield to Victor's tactics as the duel seemed to go on endlessly. Both men sweated profusely, their breathing rapid and labored in the afternoon heat. Gregor continued to parry every thrust until he tripped over debris left behind in the battle. Losing his balance, he stumbled backward.

Victor, alert and ready for even the slightest mistake, lunged forward. "Die, son-of-a-bitch! I told you! She's mine! She always was and always will be!"

$$\backsim$$

Rain from the night before created heavy mist in hot summer air. The entire party was miserable as Alexa pushed men and horses to their limits. Crossing early into the far northeast corner of Garogan Province, they now skirted the border of the Tasa Coast Province. Heat and the driving pace, combined with the need for increased vigilance, set every man's nerves on edge. They had pressed forward for so long that it was with great surprise when, in mid-afternoon, Alexa harshly jerked back the reins on her horse, stopping abruptly.

"No!" she screamed. "Stefan!"

Stefan immediately halted his mount and swiftly dismounted, running to her side. "Alexa! What's wrong? Are you all right?"

Tirstan, the soldier she had spoken to early that morning, also dismounted and was almost instantly at her side. He helped Stefan carefully lift her down to the ground.

Stefan immediately recognized that something terrible was amiss. Her breathing was fast and irregular. Her hands were cold and trembling despite the heat. "Come, let's sit in the shade," Stefan said, leading her to the side of the road and out of the sun.

Alexa sat on a large boulder, covering her face with her hands. By now, Tirani was at her side, wetting a handkerchief with water from a leather canteen to wipe Alexa's face. "Stefan," Tirani spoke quietly, tears swimming in her own eyes, "have the men rest here a short while. They should eat, too. There will be little chance for rest from here on."

"Tirani, I don't understand," Stefan replied in confusion. "Is she all right? What's happening?"

Alexa's hands fell away from her face, revealing the most excruciating sorrow he had ever seen. Except, perhaps, the day Gregor had held her unconscious body outside Garogan Castle. "Stefan, it's Gregor. He's dying."

Stefan stared at her and dropped to his knees on the damp ground in front of her. "Can there be no doubt?" His words were strangled as his eyes searched her face with quiet desperation.

She shook her head and drew in a shuddering breath. "None. Tirani, help me up. I must go where it's quieter. I must meditate."

Tirani helped her to her feet, and they walked a little farther into the woods. They found a shady spot where they could sit on a thick, soft mat of evergreen needles.

"Tirani, I need your help, but I must also explain what I hope to accomplish," Alexa began, her voice still quiet and tremulous while regaining a tone of purpose. "Unless we manage to accomplish the melding of three serving spirits, we will never arrive in time. My husband…" she paused, more afraid than she had ever been in her life. "Gregor's body has been pierced through by a sword. He bleeds, his insides torn apart."

"Milady, we are only two spirits who serve Val. How can we hope to call together three?" Tirani gently reminded her.

"Tirani, join hands with me. We must maintain our circle, no matter what. Gregor's mother was also Valiria. I carry her grandchild within me. My only hope is that enough of her life force infuses this child that we might summon sufficient energy to sustain Gregor until we arrive."

Tirani's eyes revealed understanding. With fingers tightly interlaced, the two women began a prayer to Val for protection. In unison, they chanted ancient passages that swept them into a profound state of meditation. The trance was far deeper than any Tirani had yet experienced.

The surrounding forest, alive with animals and busy sounds of woodland life, receded. Time grew insignificant. The sensation of freedom from body and ground carried them through unknown space without boundaries, without gravity or any other kind of constraint. There existed nothing beyond an infinite tranquility that swept gently over them and through their spirits until a sweet voice called out from somewhere beyond.

"Welcome, Alexa and Tirani. You summon the spirit of Anlía from her home with our Lord Val. Why?"

"Dearest Anlía, Valiria and servant of Val, I call upon you from my heart as Valkana, serving Val's people in Turand. Join us, Anlía, to save the life of your son, Gregor. I go to him, but I am still too far away. You are our only hope as you are spirit not fettered by time or worldly bonds. I am his wife and blessed to carry his child, your grandchild. It is this precious thread of life that we use to call upon you. Please, sweet spirit, help us."

Near the road, Stefan and the queen's guards stood with eyes turned skyward, each and every one awestruck. Hovering just above the tree line,

Alexa and Tirani held hands and spun in a clockwise direction. A slowly pulsating globe of light enveloped them. Sweet, musical sounds unlike anything they had ever heard filled the air.

On a quivering breath, Stefan whispered to the men around him. "To those of you who know Val's Prayer of Life, let us begin to recite it now." Their voices joined together, calling upon Val for his love, mercy, and succor.

The phenomenon continued for nearly a quarter-hour. Alexa and Tirani finally descended to the ground, their circle unbroken. Alexa centered first, roused by the shifting motion of the baby within her womb. Her eyes opened slowly, and she watched until Tirani also emerged from her meditation.

Stefan had come to look for them and observed in silence as they slowly pulled their fingers apart and began to flex and stretch. Tirani stood first and glanced over to Stefan, wordlessly beckoning him to her side. Then, together, they helped Alexa rise to her feet. Both noticed renewed energy in her as she led them back to the waiting soldiers.

Alexa forced herself to eat. She explained how their mission had taken on new urgency. Many good men lay suffering and dying, including their king. "We shall ride until we can ride no further, and then still we will ride on. We progressed quickly this morning. We must advance faster now."

The military detachment reassembled. Weary soldiers checked saddles and bridles. They made sure that provisions were secured on the pack animals. Each one committed to serve his queen to the point of personal collapse. There existed among them a single-minded vision that drove them on. Their queen was Valkana—guide and inspiration. Not even one could imagine failing her.

Major Kohira had issued commands for senior officers to initiate a renewed advance that successfully began pushing the insurgent forces into retreat. Accompanied by several mounted soldiers, he had fallen back, searching for his king. He scanned the dusty battleground strewn with the bodies of men and horses. He had spied Gregor just as he stumbled backward.

Kohira and his men spurred their horses forward but were too late to reach the king in time. Some chased Victor, who hurriedly leapt onto his horse and galloped off with a group of waiting rebel officers. Meanwhile, Kohira dismounted and raced to his fallen leader's side. He desperately ripped away Gregor's tunic, shouting at nearby soldiers for anything at hand to cover the wound to stop the profuse flow of blood.

Other men came running to assist. A litter was rushed over. The king's limp body was lifted onto it and urgently carried back to the royal encampment. Kohira ran alongside, doing his best to keep the pads in place to hold back some of the dark blood, carrying with it the precious force of the king's life.

⤳

The early nightfall of the south enveloped the countryside within its pervasively obscure blanket. Unsettling quiet accompanied riders who were forced to slow their pace as they proceeded along unfamiliar paths that might conceal enemy attackers behind their wooded boundaries. Finally, Alexa lifted her hand and signaled her intent to stop.

Stefan, riding alongside, looked at her questioningly. "Do we camp here for the night?"

"No," she replied. "Help me dismount, Stefan."

He climbed down from his horse and requested assistance from one of the soldiers to help her down.

"Tell everyone to take a few minutes to stretch their legs. Stay here and wait for me."

"Alexa…"

Before he could protest, she turned to him with eyes that glittered eerily beneath faint moonlight. "Stay."

He obeyed but watched protectively as she walked purposefully ahead, her back ramrod straight, her face tilted upward. He could barely see the reflection of her clothing when she stopped. Tirani had come to Stefan, allowing herself to lean tiredly against him as he placed an arm around her shoulders.

Stefan wanted to ask what Alexa was doing but feared interrupting the apprehensive silence that gripped those who awaited their queen. As they kept vigil, they listened to a softly chanted prayer drift upon the night air. She had slipped once again from her role of queen to that of Valkana. The unmistakable blue-white glow appeared just above her head and cascaded downward, intensifying in brightness as did the volume of her chant.

After minutes that seemed an eternity, she turned and appeared nearly to float back to them. When she reached her traveling companions, she touched the faces of each one, infusing them with a refreshing flow of energy. She did the same for each of the horses. Her face was solemn, concentrated. "We must proceed quickly. Our destination is much closer than I thought."

After helping her mount, Stefan brought his horse up alongside Tirani's and flanked the Valkana. The Valkana had become a guiding beacon, the source of shimmering light that led them ahead with unquestioned certainty. Half an hour passed when she stopped once again. Stefan drew closer to her and realized she had been riding in a state of trance, eyes closed, her inner vision providing unfaltering direction for those who followed.

She remained silent, and it seemed that even all the woodland creatures observed her need. No crickets chirped. No night birds sang. Not even the trees dared whisper back in the cooling breeze that lifted and ruffled her hair.

Tirani sensed her mistress' summons. She guided her mount forward and awaited her instructions.

"Praises be to Val that we are almost there," Alexa announced. "There will be much confusion when we arrive. Tirani, be prepared with the pack animals. We need to prepare the herbs immediately. Have the lieutenant and Tirstan set right away to boiling water for the teas.

"Stefan, have someone tend to unpacking and taking clean bandages and blankets to my husband's tent. I shall require your assistance, so you must stay with me." She paused as if listening to some distant voice and nodded. "I understand, sweet spirit. Thank you. We are coming."

Stefan and Tirani exchanged glances, their faces illuminated by the soft glow emanating from the Valkana's still figure. Stefan vowed to question Tirani later regarding to whom or what Alexa had spoken.

"Tirani, I want you to bring both Raija and Kirmaya teas to me the moment they are brewed. You must also drink Raija yourself to reinforce your own energies. Then have someone start administering Kirmaya to the wounded right away. Hold firmly to your faith, dear Tirani, because you will need to concentrate your meditation as never before. You have my complete confidence. Many will most surely die without your call of the Healing Graces upon them."

Alexa breathed in slowly several times, exhaling just as slowly. Each time she did, the aura around her grew in breadth and brightness. "Now, we ride."

Unexpectedly, she dug her knees into her mount's sides and bounded forward. The others, caught off-guard by her sudden departure, quickly leaned into their horses and followed. She guided her horse rapidly up to the crest of a gentle rise. Upon reaching the top, they looked down over a much steeper descent and across a vast encampment dotted by the leaping orange and yellow flames of dozens of campfires. To their right stood a number of tents. Far off in the distance, a faint glow on the horizon indicated the location of the opposing camp.

Without hesitation, Alexa guided her horse along the crest of the hill until she found the well-worn path that led down. Her guards spurred their horses ahead of her. Taking the lead, they placed themselves between their queen and any potential threat of danger. They implicitly trusted her instincts. They also knew that unexpected riders galloping out of the night and into an attack-wary camp presented easy targets.

As they approached the line of sentries posted along the camp's perimeter, one soldier threw up the royal standard without dropping pace. The lieutenant forged ahead, calling out loudly, "Stand aside! The Toraval Royal Guard passes!"

Shocked sentries scrambled out of the way of the tight formation of horses that pounded its way directly toward the small city of tents dominating the backside of the camp. From wherever they were, men jumped to their feet, also shocked by the riders who had, without warning, intruded upon the mournful atmosphere pervading the camp.

The group slowed and halted as the heavy breathing of tired horses and men heralded the new arrivals. Stefan and Tirstan immediately went to the queen's horse to lower her to the ground. She shook herself slightly, her aura quickly dissipating. Then, without a word, she swiftly strode directly toward the entrance of the king's tent.

Major Kohira had risen to his feet, blocking the tent's entrance. His weary face displayed total disbelief when he recognized the queen. He then saluted her with a hasty bow. "Your Majesty, I never expected to see you here so near the battlefield," he muttered, distress evident in a voice usually strident with command.

"I have come to be with my husband," she informed him curtly, her figure erect and unwavering despite worry and fatigue. Kohira glanced nervously in Stefan's direction, his eyes requesting a moment alone with the king's chief adviser. He was surprised yet again when Stefan shook his head in refusal.

"She already knows, Major. That is why we're here."

"How?" His question faded into the night. For her to arrive now, they must have left days earlier. For a moment, Kohira had forgotten the legendary mystic insight of those anointed into the service of Val. He sighed, the sound filled with gloom, then turned to hold open the flap that served as the door to the royal tent.

Alexa acknowledged him with a reassuring smile as she strode past, bending slightly to enter. Inside, oil lamps cast eerie, flickering shadows against the tent's canvas walls. Near the center stood the wide cot where Gregor lay motionless with two aides by his side. They both looked up in astonishment, their expressions clouding to register both grief and sympathy.

Her breath caught in her throat. Her heart beat heavily within her breast. Her hands pressed against her abdomen as if to shield the tender life she carried within. Consciously, she willed away her fatigue, convinced she was not too late. Once again, she reminded herself that her inner vision would not have led her here if it were Gregor's time to die. She must reinforce that belief if she should have any real chance of saving his life.

She turned to Stefan, who had followed her inside. "These aides must leave. As soon as Tirani brings in the teas, you must help me with Gregor. Hurry. Bring that small table over here."

She began to issue curt, concise instructions. Reluctantly, the aides left the king they had served since leaving Toraval. Two of her own guards entered. The guard carrying blankets passed one to her and immediately placed the others on the far side of the tent where she had pointed. The other began to unroll bandages, putting them on the table that held the oil lamps.

Stefan studied her closely as he busied himself by folding bandages according to her directions. His assessment was filled with admiration at her efficiency. He paused a moment, thinking that, little more than a year ago, her expression had reflected disgust every time she looked at Gregor. Now, she demonstrated unparalleled determination born of a love he could not begin to fathom.

Once Gregor's aides left and the soldiers followed, Stefan continued to observe her. First, she washed her hands in a basin of clean water. Then, moving swiftly to Gregor's side, she gracefully lowered herself to her knees and, with her right hand, stroked perspiration-soaked locks of hair away from his face. With gentle fingers, Alexa caressed a line across his forehead to his temple and then along his lightly bearded jaw. His eyelids fluttered, opening slightly for a matter of seconds, revealing pain-glazed irises. Despite trauma and apparent agony, a momentary flash of recognition appeared to ease tension from his features.

Tirani noiselessly entered the tent, carrying two small pots filled with steaming, aromatic teas. She placed them on the table within easy reach of Gregor's cot. She then pulled a tin mug and a spoon from her pocket and set them down beside the pots.

Alexa motioned Stefan closer and mentally braced herself as she proceeded to draw aside the blanket covering Gregor's body. With delicate fingers, she plucked loose the sticky edges of the bandages from her husband's skin and removed coverings that were soggy with his blood. Revealed was the seeping, angry gash that had ripped through his flesh and completely penetrated his body.

Tirani's calm voice sounded just above Alexa's shoulder. "It is a miracle he still lives, Milady. A wound such as that should have claimed him hours ago."

Alexa nodded in grim accord. "It can only mean that our Lord Val does not yet wish him dead. I was summoned here that he might be healed. He must live, Tirani. Hurry. Soak two thick pads of clean bandages in the Kirmaya. Stefan, help me turn him enough that I can place one of the pads on the underneath side of the wound."

As Stefan turned him, Gregor groaned in agonized response. Alexa quickly and deftly removed the sodden bandages from under him and slid a long, dry dressing beneath him, draping the excess onto her lap. She then placed the first Kirmaya-soaked pad against the rear opening of the wound. She held the pad in place as Stefan gently lowered him.

Slipping her now bloody hands from beneath his back, she worked with rapid, sure motions to place the second warm pad over the larger front wound, covering that with a dry pad. Finally, she passed the long, wide bandage across Gregor's body and secured it as best she could on the other side.

She rose quickly to wash his blood from her hands. "I will need more clean water. For now, Tirani, you will need to hold the cup of Raija for me. Stefan, I want you to raise him slightly and support his shoulders."

She then sat as close to her husband as possible, cradling the side of his face against the cushion of her breast. With loving patience, she spooned tiny amounts of the warm liquid into his mouth, willing him to swallow its strength-giving essences.

When she was satisfied he had swallowed enough, Stefan settled Gregor back once more. Alexa smiled reassuringly at Tirani. "Go now. Drink a cup of Raija before going to the others. They need you." Turning to Stefan, she reached out to touch his arm. "You, too, may go. Rest if you can. First, post guards outside. Give explicit instructions. Absolutely no one may enter this tent. I must remain undisturbed. Completely undisturbed."

Once she was alone with Gregor, she rose to assure herself that everything she might need was within easy reach. For later, when she would rest to renew her own energies, she quickly arranged several blankets and a small pillow several feet away from where her husband now lay. She then took one last cover and gently spread it across Gregor's body, grateful the cot was wide enough that she could lie against his side.

She poured herself a cup of the fortifying Raija and began to drink. As the last of the warm liquid flowed down her throat, her eyes closed, and she began to focus her energies inward. She ended brief meditation on a fervent prayer of supplication. "Let me be strong enough to endure, oh, my Lord. Help me to transfer your Healing Graces to my beloved husband."

With all preparations complete, she removed her outer garments and then leaned over to place a kiss against his unresponsive lips. She breathed in deeply and stretched out on her side, pressing herself against his fevered body. Gently, she extended her arm over him. His body reacted to her touch with a weak tremor. Tears filled her eyes as she tenderly kissed his damp, feverish cheek. Within her, she felt their baby stir.

"Gregor, my love, listen to my voice. You must listen with your heart and with your soul. Our child needs his father. He will need your strength, your guidance, and your wisdom. I need you, too, my love. You are my life. Fight, Gregor. You must help me. Live, Gregor. You must live."

Quietly spoken words grew more fervent, their intensity penetrating the night in a flow of loving encouragement. As she continually talked to him, energy in the form of pulsating light began to emanate from her body. White light expanded into an ever-growing sphere covering and encircling the two of them. Once their bodies were entirely enveloped, the orb of light ceased its fluctuations and settled into a steady blue-white glow.

Outside, many watched the strange play of lights through canvas walls. Though tired to the bone, Stefan sat before the entrance, blocking it bodily. Though near exhaustion, he felt compelled to maintain his vigil, unable to bear the thought of losing his dearest friend. The mere sight of Gregor's hideous wound had physically sickened him. Amazed by Alexa's calm ability to tend the injury, Stefan felt intensely thankful for the mystic graces that had urged her to his side. Silently, he prayed for Val to strengthen them all.

As if the glow emanating from Gregor's tent were not sufficient to mesmerize the weary encampment, brightly colored lights began to dance above the tents sheltering the wounded. Earlier, Tirani had enlisted the aid of Tirstan and several medical attendants. They had administered Kirmaya tea to all injured men to fortify their life forces until she could call upon the heavens to dispatch the Healing Graces that would mend torn and broken bodies.

Tirani sat cross-legged between the various tents sheltering injured royal forces and rebels. The Raija she had drunk suffused her body with energy. The novice priestess reflected momentarily upon the encouraging words spoken by her queen and high priestess. If Alexa believed so firmly in her, then she, simple Tirani, would strive with all she possessed to prove herself worthy of such trust.

After brief, intensive meditation, Tirani lifted her arms heavenward, then lowered them to her sides. As she did so, lights sprayed down from the dark skies in flickering, darting motions until they expanded into a sphere-like dome fed from above until it encompassed the entire perimeter of the tents. Tirani's motionless figure belied the rapidly beating heart within her breast. The energies she had summoned began their blessed work, entering injured and dying men, spurring bodies to rebuild ripped and shredded tissue and to knit shattered bone.

Nearly five miles away, the retreated forces of the rebel provinces stared in stark astonishment at the fantasy-like display of lights shimmering and flashing around the king's camp. Those who impersonated Turandans were stunned. Fear insinuated itself along many shivering backbones.

Native Turandans grew wary, uncertain of what to think. Was it possible there was truth in the traditions of Val that so many had forsaken? Were legends describing the Lights of Val fact rather than myth? Soldiers looked to their leaders for explanation and reassurance. If Val indeed lived, then perhaps rebel leaders were mistaken about the corruption of the royal court. Otherwise, the Lights of Val, unseen for at least a century, definitely would not have appeared above the king's army.

Victor Garogan tiredly raised himself from a table inside the officer's tent. He followed other officers to investigate the disturbance outside. Each stopped abruptly, staring in shock at the spectacle in the distance. Victor gasped aloud.

Earlier, although physically weary, Victor had been smug and self-satisfied, convinced that the next battle would end far differently with Gregor now dead. He had experienced savage satisfaction when he had forcefully plunged his sword into Gregor's body. Withdrawing the bloody steel, he had savored the feeling of vindication, confident that Gregor was mortally wounded and the royal Toscano line ended. Revenge had been exacted. He would ride again to the capital to recapture Alexa. With the king gone, he would reclaim his love, by force if necessary. He firmly believed that, if only he could possess her, her lost sanity would be restored.

Now, he watched dumbfounded, acknowledging that the Lights of Val had returned to Turand after more than a hundred years, fulfilling the prophecy of the last Valkana. Solely because of Alexa, he knew the Valiria line of priestesses had not been destroyed. Undoubtedly, a mystic had surfaced and had been proclaimed High Priestess Valkana.

Alexa! Her name exploded inside his mind. His knees weakened. Blood throbbed savagely inside his temples. Alexa must be present in the embattled foothills of Garogan Province. For him, there could be no doubt. He had known her too long and loved her too well. Precisely as he had always expected, she had ascended to the position of Valkana.

Thoughts raced through his mind. So many times had he suspected her to be the chosen one who would restore the blessing of Valkana to Turand. Though she never believed him, he had seen what he always considered signs. Her steadfast adherence to the teachings of the Order of Val. The unusual instances when she knew things impossible for her to know. The odd occasions when he was convinced that he had glimpsed the legendary blue-white aura that belonged only to those chosen by Val.

Victor's questions swirled in maddening confusion. Why had she left the relative safety of the capital? Had she come to bury the husband who had forced himself upon her? Would she deliver the Turandan army to the rebels now that she was finally free of Turand's dark king? Did she genuinely love Gregor as she had insisted? If her love for the king were indeed real, would she herself lead the forces of Turand against the insurgents? What significance did those lights bear? What was happening there in the distance?

Victor inhaled deeply and exhaled very slowly, centering and focusing himself the way Alexa had taught him to do many years earlier. He forced himself to observe, to analyze. He studied the extraordinary scene that blazed in the distance and, upon careful scrutiny, determined that the brilliantly colored, dancing lights actually formed an enormous sphere.

Minutes passed before he differentiated a second sphere of light to the right, just beyond the multicolored lights. The second sphere was smaller, yet the light shining forth was more definitive in shape and hue. This light was single-hued, a soft, bluish-white that glowed with steady intensity.

"Oh, my God! Gregor still lives!" The words escaped Victor's lips in bewildered disbelief as he choked back bitterness that rose and burned sharply in his throat.

The officers around him turned and glared at him as if he had lost his mind. His exclamation was ridiculous. "Impossible!" one spat out.

Lord Anderon grabbed Victor's arm and shook him. "Control yourself, Victor! We all saw Gregor fall by your own sword. No man could survive such a thrust."

Victor gazed out over the forested horizon. "No ordinary man could," he ground out. "But Gregor is no ordinary man. He is King of Turand. Not only that, he is loved by the High Priestess Valkana and wed to her as well."

"High Priestess Valkana? What nonsense are you blathering, Victor?" Anderon grew increasingly angry, already agitated and nervous from observing the strange lights shining in the distance. "Valkana are long dead."

"Lord Anderon, do you see the third sphere of light forming to contain the original two? Send some soldiers to try to penetrate the boundaries of that sphere. Then, when they return, tell me again the Valkana are dead."

Victor's eyes challenged the hateful lord before he spun on his heel and stalked off into the trees, desperate to be alone. He must think, knowing how carefully he must consider what might happen next.

Alone in the woods, with the anxious voices of soldiers fading into the night, Victor stumbled over stones and tree roots. He wanted to run and scream at the top of his voice. He desperately needed to expel the rush of painful emotions raging through his body. The toe of his boot caught beneath a woody vine. Pitching forward, he broke his fall by throwing out his arms and landing against a tree. The rough bark scraped and burned his palms. Frustration and anger surged, and he pounded a fist against the offending tree, then cursed it in vehement, irrational fury. He kicked at it time and time again before falling heavily onto his knees. His head dropped to rest against the unyielding recipient of his rage.

Hot tears tracked scalding rivulets down sunburned cheeks. He nearly strangled on sobs wrenched from the depths of his soul. His stomach pitched in nauseating waves. Intense heat scorched his skin only to alternate with shuddering, icy tremors. He gasped for air to fill tensed lungs. All efforts proved useless. Excruciating grief gripped Victor's heart. Left with no other choice, he was forced to accept what he had truly believed to be impossible. All life's meaning fled in those tortured moments when he succumbed to sorrow that wracked his body and soul. He had lost her. His precious Alexa truly belonged to Gregor.

Hours later, Victor lifted his head from his knees. He had no idea how long he had sat with his back to the tree, his arms wrapped around his legs that were drawn up and tucked against his chest. His head throbbed with persistent, pounding pain. He opened eyes that were red and swollen. For the moment, he was grateful for the darkness that would not further offend.

He felt drained. In a matter of hours, he had gone from arrogant, elated confidence that he would finally reclaim Alexa to the total desolation and emptiness of knowing she was forever lost to him. What would he do now? Would there ever be any end to the terrible, aching loneliness that had overcome him? How could he ever reconcile himself to her love for Gregor? How could he possibly live with the hollow, purposeless soul he now possessed?

Wearily, he rose to his feet. His boots felt impossibly heavy, weighing him down as he walked back toward camp. He forced himself to look again in the direction of the royal encampment. He swallowed hard against the choking lump in his throat. The Lights of Val continued to shine brilliantly.

Chapter 21

Tranquil, rhythmic breathing brought tears of joy to Alexa's eyes. She rested her face against Gregor's upper arm, his relaxed muscles a comforting cushion. Smiling to herself, she breathed an earnest prayer of gratitude. Her husband's life was saved. His recovery would be nearly complete after a few hours of sleep.

That thought was deeply satisfying as she carefully left the cot. Delicately, she removed the tea and blood-soaked compress from his side. Her face held a hint of a smile as her finger traced the vivid scarlet line that marred his body and would forever remain as a scar. But, most importantly, the wound had closed, healing accelerated miraculously by the energies transferred by Val's Healing Graces.

Alexa placed clean dressings over still-raw flesh and tucked a fresh blanket around Gregor. She then used a soft, damp cloth to wipe his face. Her eyes lovingly floated from feature to feature. She suppressed intense longing to gaze into the dark eyes she so loved. In Val's good time, she thought. In Val's good time.

She leaned over and placed yet another kiss against his still lips. She straightened again, her hands straying to massage the dull ache in her lower back. She prayed in thanks once more before leaving the tent.

As she stepped out into the night, cooler air washed over her as she breathed in its cleansing freshness. A cool breeze blew from the north, promising a welcome respite from the heat. Alexa savored its flow against her skin as serenity seeped into the farthest points of her being.

When she felt strong hands tightly grip her arms, Alexa slipped from her reverie and opened tranquil eyes to meet Stefan's fearful countenance. Her heart was glad that her husband possessed such a friendship.

"Stefan, you need worry no longer. Gregor sleeps peacefully. Please go stay with him while I check Tirani and the others."

Stefan inhaled sharply, his heart welcoming the rush of relief her words delivered. "Should you not rest? You must be exhausted."

She responded with a nod of her head. "I am, but I must check the others first. Then, I promise I shall rest. Lend me your blanket."

Stefan pulled the lightweight blanket from around his shoulders and wrapped it around her. He was unable to suppress a smile as she snuggled into the warmth of its folds. "Go then. I'll remain with Gregor, but don't tarry. I prefer not to explain why I allowed you to wander out into the night should he awaken."

She only smiled before turning to Major Kohira, who had also maintained the vigil outside the tent's entrance. The major stood, offering his hand in support of his queen. He would accompany her to the light sphere surrounding tents that sheltered the rest of the wounded.

When Stefan knelt alongside his friend, he studied Gregor's face in the dim lamplight. The tense, pain-contorted features of hours earlier were now soft in repose. There was not even the slightest indication that, only a short time ago, Gregor had lain moments from death.

Stefan blinked rapidly, unable to halt a sudden flow of tears. His mind reflected back in time to early childhood when, as an orphan, Gregor's parents had taken him into their family. He and Gregor had quickly forged a unique bond that had thrived through many difficult years. Memories flooded him. He recalled two boys losing a mother. He remembered their anguish upon learning that Sifiq were drugging and controlling Gregor's father. Secret conversations during the middle of so many nights as Gregor and he grimly plotted strategies against the Sifiq. Days spent convincing the Sifiq that Gregor was a spoiled, self-centered man who made a willing puppet king.

Stefan's mind moved forward. For the first time in their lives, he had doubted Gregor's judgment with the manipulation of circumstances that forced Alexa into marriage. Stefan observed as that marriage began a strange battle of wills before settling into a wary truce. He watched Gregor's growing frustration as he tried to maintain cool detachment. He had admired Alexa's resolute determination as she attempted to develop the marriage into an amicable relationship. Although uncertain when the relationship began to transform, Stefan knew each had refused to acknowledge any substantive change until her abduction.

Stefan rested a hand on his friend's shoulder. Never would he forget Gregor's helplessness during that period. Scathing self-reproaches had been bitter scenes to witness. Soul-wrenching torment upon learning of her return to Garogan had accompanied weeks of silence while nervously anticipating an announcement that their marriage had been annulled and that she had married Lord Garogan. Then, in Garogan Province, there had been stark amazement upon witnessing Alexa's dramatic flight from the castle and her wild leap to save Gregor's life.

Afterward, with Alexa's guidance, Stefan had discovered personal faith and now prayed in thanks that Val had sent the mystic Valkana to love and save the life of his friend. Tears welled in Stefan's eyes, released by the torrent of feelings bound up with this sleeping man and the woman who was his wife. For the first time in his thirty-three years, Stefan believed he might live long enough to experience a peaceful Turand. Finally, real hope existed that the dreams he and Gregor had cherished and nurtured might be fulfilled for their people and their nation.

⌒

Major Kohira was surprised by his lack of hesitation as he allowed the queen to guide him directly through the wall of light separating the hospital tents from the main camp. As they stepped through the sphere's perimeter, the only trace of their passing was a momentary fluctuation of light that settled into a slightly brighter glow.

Tirani sat on a blanket spread on the ground between the hospital tents. Alexa walked past her lady-in-waiting and entered the tent to her left. Sliding her arm free of Kohira's, she held her hands out and closed her eyes. Her lips moved in silent prayer, and blue-white light surrounded her. As they proceeded to the next tent, Kohira shivered from the electrical pulses that raced through his body in an invigorating rush when she again linked her arm with his. After she had repeated her prayerful action in the remaining tent, he accompanied her back to Tirani, understanding her every intention without a single spoken word.

He helped her down to kneel directly in front of Tirani. He watched in fascination as the queen stretched her arms out from her sides and chanted a lilting song for peace. With slow, deliberate symmetry, she wrapped her arms around Tirani's shoulders. After several minutes, both began to center, and they exchanged warm smiles. Alexa's face glowed with gentle reassurance and praise as she looked down. "Go, my dear Tirani. Your work is finished. The Healing Graces will stay. You have done very well. Rest peacefully."

The queen then raised a hand to Kohira, who helped her rise to her feet. Alexa allowed Kohira to guide her back to the king's quarters. Before she entered, she raised appreciative eyes to the major. "I know that your quick reaction and cool head were crucial to keeping my husband alive long enough for me to reach his side. Major Kohira, I will be forever in your debt."

Kohira bowed his head to her, unable to utter a single word. His chest swelled, filled with loyalty and pride. His king's life and her praise provided unparalleled reward.

"Major, I'm going inside to rest. I want you to ensure that the entire camp rests now. If you look carefully, you can see a third sphere has formed as Val's blessing. You need post no sentries. Val Himself serves as our guard this night. The only other thing you must do is to send someone to the hospital tents. Those who do not rest easily or show no sign of healing must be secured as you deem necessary. They are Sifiq. You can identify them by the scarlet lightning bolts tattooed on their left shoulders."

Kohira's face registered shock, even though he had suspected Sifiq to be among the wounded. He did not doubt her, but neither could he comprehend how she knew so much within such a short time. However, once she disappeared into the tent, he acted immediately on her instructions.

⌐⌐

Gregor opened his eyes and stared upward at the canvas canopy peak above his head. The golden light of dawn barely filtered through the tightly woven fabric. His body felt weighted, unwilling to respond to his initial efforts to move. Pervasive quiet all around struck him as both unnerving and unnatural because he knew his army must be just outside.

Concentrating, he managed to pull himself into a sitting position. His hands flew immediately to his side, the tightness inside sore and painful. His breathing labored as sweat beaded over his brow. He remembered the piercing thrust and sharp twist of Victor's broad sword with sudden clarity. He briefly questioned how it was even possible that he could still be alive.

Tentatively, he stood and straightened, his hands pressing firmly against his side. He swayed weakly, then moved slowly toward the opening of the tent. He felt uncomfortable with a pressing need to go outside to relieve himself. Not bothering to put on shoes but with his blanket wrapped around him, he wandered out into the night. As far as he could see, campfires had burned down into glowing, orange-red piles while his army slept.

Gregor walked around for several minutes in the misty light, confused and disconcerted by the uncertainty of his surroundings. The camp was too peaceful, too calm. Still, he was too groggy to question or analyze. He decided all he really wanted to do was to return to his cot to sleep.

Back inside, he shuffled slowly to the long, bench-like table holding some of his belongings. At the end of the table was a basin filled with clean water. He washed his hands and splashed water onto his face. Exhausted from his exertion, he rested his palms flat against the table and leaned heavily forward. His brain fought for alertness. He desperately needed to comprehend what had happened since the bitter confrontation with Victor.

A muffled sigh and a rustle of motion from behind him disturbed his attempt to think clearly. Slowly, he turned and lifted his head to look beyond his shoulder for the source of the sound. He barely made out the shape of someone asleep on a pile of blankets on the ground. He shook his head as if by doing so, he could rid himself of clouded thoughts that formed like thick fog inside his brain.

Straightening, he turned and took two steps toward the sleeping figure just as it changed positions. The outline of a woman's pregnant body shocked him awake. Slowly, almost reverently, he approached her. Clutching his side protectively, he lowered himself to his knees. He stretched out a hand to touch her but stopped, certain he could only be dreaming or dead.

However, there was the definite, soft breathing associated with deep slumber. The outline of the face was achingly familiar, infinitely precious. Now that she lay on her side facing him, her swollen abdomen looked so different from his memories of her. Instead of touching her face, he stretched out his fingers, star-like, to lay against her body. His touch was met with an immediate bump.

Almost immediately, Alexa's eyes opened, her lips drawing into a surprised smile. "Gregor," she said sleepily, raising herself up on one elbow. "You're awake already?"

He only stared at her with astonished eyes, his full lips forming a curious, disbelieving smile. She laughed softly, realizing what must have happened. Then, twisting enough to lift the blankets behind her and scoot back to the edge, she held up her blanket invitingly. Her eyes glittered playfully. "I think we have room for one more."

He hesitated before shifting his weight and sliding beneath the cover she held up for him. He winced against momentary, piercing pain that shot through his side, then stared again into her face. With wordless wonder, he allowed his hand to sweep along the firm, swelling curve formed by his unborn child. Even in semi-darkness, his eyes sparkled with awe.

With loving fingers, she stroked the lines of his lightly bearded face and then kissed the tip of his nose. "Sleep, my husband. Go back to sleep."

The sound of her voice was a sweet caress laced with the effect of a narcotic. With her well-remembered scent filling his nostrils and the comforting closeness of her body next to his where it belonged, he silently obeyed her gentle command.

Hours later, she awakened again. The air within the canvas walls was warming beneath the fully risen sun. Voices from outside indicated the camp was up and fully awake, already tending to the day's routine.

Alexa shifted her position, hoping to ease minor stiffness in her back. Opening her eyes halfway, she realized her husband was also awake, watching her while she had slept.

She sighed softly. "How long have you been awake?"

He smiled lovingly. "A while. You looked so peaceful, and it's been so long since I last enjoyed having you by my side." Receiving a drowsy smile in response, he continued in a voice much more solemn. "I must ask a question of you."

"Yes?" She closed her eyes again, wishing she didn't have to wake up just yet.

"Alexa, is my assumption correct that, if you were not here right now, I would already be dead?"

A frown wrinkled her forehead. The mere mention of that narrowly avoided reality troubled her. "Yes," she replied, almost inaudibly.

His fingertips raised to brush across her cheek and through her hair. He placed his lips against the velvet smoothness of her forehead. The moist warmth tickled her as his lips moved against sensitive skin. "I love you."

Tears welled in her eyes. Speech failed her as his touch fulfilled every dream she had ever known.

Without further conversation, he got up and then helped her. With firm strokes, his long fingers smoothed the waving mass of her hair into some order. He traced the outline of her temple, cheek, and neck with his index finger. Then he moved his finger to mark the generous curve of her mouth as she gazed intently into his eyes. Slowly, with both hands, he covered the swelling declaration of their love. His fascination with the change in her figure was evident. Finally, he wrapped his arms tightly around her, breathing in the faint, teasing lilac scent that seemed always to accompany her. He reveled in the sensation as her arms returned his embrace. Words were unnecessary, their communication more a communion of two bonded souls.

Reluctantly, they drew away from each other. She slid her hand along the side of his face, testing the feel of his heavily shadowed beard. "It's getting warm in here. Don't you think we should dress and go get something to eat?"

She helped him into dark leggings and a clean, linen shirt. He dressed slowly, the stiffness in his body hampering his freedom of movement. As she rolled back the full sleeves of his shirt, she assured him that his pain would not last long. His wound had severely damaged him internally, and although the healing was virtually complete, tender nerves and tissues should be expected.

He grinned at her, happy merely to be alive. "I think I can manage to cope with some pain. I certainly don't find the alternative at all appealing."

She attempted to smile at his levity but turned away, pretending to concentrate on getting dressed. He walked up behind her and slid his arms around her. "It wasn't my intention to remind you."

She leaned back against his body. "I'm sorry. You have no idea how close I came to losing you. The mere thought still terrifies me."

She turned back and faced him, her fingers nervously fumbling with the pearl buttons on the front of her pale blue blouse. He took over the task with quick efficiency. "Then let us discuss it no further, beloved. Put on your shoes, and we'll go outside."

He lifted the flap for her, and she stepped out into blinding sunshine. Once her eyes adjusted to the bright light, she saw many curious, expectant faces turned to her. Smiling, she stepped aside to allow her husband to come out.

Gregor's army ceased all activity and rose almost as one to stand at attention. Respect was defined on every face. Many found it extremely difficult to control the genuine desire to cheer their king's miraculous recovery. However, Kohira had distributed orders early that Gregor be received quietly to keep their enemy guessing the status of his condition.

Gregor, deeply moved by the quiet tribute, executed a stately bow in salute to men who had followed him so courageously. A broad smile lit his features when he straightened, and he stepped forward to speak. "Gentlemen, I can imagine no greater honor as leader of this army than the respect I receive today from you, whose courage and loyalty were so well demonstrated in battle. Much hardship still lies before us, yet my confidence and optimism do not waver because of you. I tell you, as well, that I stand encouraged by the devotion of our beloved Valkana, who has joined us here. May Val grant us the means to end this war soon that we may finally know peace in Turand."

Those in front passed the word back to those who could not quite hear. Finally, both sides saluted each other with bows before resuming their activities. Alexa beheld the exchange with enormous pride in both her husband and her people. Such tremendous respect and devotion surely merited Val's blessings.

She then watched Stefan approach Gregor. The two paused, then tightly embraced each other. Then, without a word, she quickly disappeared, allowing them a few minutes together so that she could have a few private moments to herself.

When she reappeared, she felt refreshed and fully awake. She had washed her face and brushed the tangles from her hair. Arrangements were made to transfer her personal items and clothing to her husband's quarters. Instructions were given to air out the tent and to remove dirty blankets and the soiled dressings used on Gregor's wounds.

Standing in silence for several minutes, she watched as many of his officers lined up to greet him and express their individual satisfaction over his recovery. Never had she imagined his appearance as it was at that moment. Snug, black uniform leggings accentuated the firm, muscular build of his hips and thighs. His white linen shirt, tucked loosely into his waistband, billowed slightly in the light breeze. Fashioned with a straight, narrow collar, the shirt fell open from the side shoulder opening. Long sleeves were rolled up just below his elbows and revealed forearms darkened with hair. His beard was several days old and darkly shadowed his face. Never did he lose his distinguished air of authority, but neither did he exude the more regal demeanor she generally associated with him. Instead, his appearance impacted her as totally approachable and thoroughly, breathtakingly masculine.

Feeling her eyes upon him, he glanced in her direction. He cocked his head to one side, his left eyebrow lifting in question. She smiled thoughtfully, then moved toward a table beneath a large, shady tree where cooks were setting breakfast out for them.

Moments later, her husband, Stefan, Tirani, and Major Kohira joined her. They all linked hands while Gregor offered a heartfelt prayer of thanks, not only for the meal but for the many lives saved because of the safe arrival of the party from Toraval.

The men served themselves and talked incessantly. Alexa and Tirani sipped tea and ate crisp flatbreads, cheeses, and fruits taken from filled platters on the table. Tirani ate in silence, content to bask in the full approval of her high priestess. She felt genuinely gratified that her faith had earned her a gift that had helped save the lives of nearly a hundred men and healed many others who had been severely injured.

Alexa had awakened ravenous, having eaten little the day before. She now served herself several thick slices of smooth, white farmer's cheese, an apple, dark purple grapes, and two slices of flatbread. Eating quietly, she heard little of the conversation going on around her. Instead, her mind was occupied with details of various tasks she wanted to accomplish later in the day.

Gregor glanced over, an amused expression crossing his face as he watched her reach for a golden plum and take a small bite of the juicy fruit. "Alexa, my love, are you demonstrating what it means to eat for two?"

She raised surprised eyes to meet his teasing ones. As she chewed the deliciously sweet bite, she wiped a trickle of sticky juice from her chin with her napkin. Her face showed her lack of appreciation for his remark. "I was hungry."

"I can see that. I just can't ever remember seeing you eat so much at one time." He couldn't help but laugh at the look on her face.

She took one last bite from the plum and hurled the fleshy pit in his direction. He dodged and laughed aloud. "You, Sire, should be a bit more considerate of your wife. She deserves no such insults after riding the entire day yesterday and then nursing you through the night with only a bowl of porridge in the morning and a roll with cheese in the afternoon. For some odd reason, she thought getting here to save your life more important than taking time to eat properly."

Stefan laughed aloud. "She's right, Gregor. She drove us all like slaves yesterday. I risk being disrespectful when I say you deserved to get that pit right between your eyes!" Everyone laughed with him, good humor its own unique tonic.

Gregor pulled his chair back from the table and motioned for her to come to him. Drawing her face into a pout, Alexa stood and walked over beside him. She didn't resist when he pulled her onto his lap and wrapped his arms around her expanded middle.

"I beg your forgiveness, Your Majesty. Sometimes your husband can be…"

She leaned closer and whispered into his ear. "An insensitive fool?"

He grimaced painfully. "My love, you wound me deeply by reminding me of an even worse transgression. Please say I'm forgiven."

She relished this moment of lighthearted banter almost as much as he had needed it. She kissed his cheek lightly. "Forgiven," she pronounced, "but never to be forgotten."

Laughing together, they easily escaped into a world of their own despite the many people so close around them. He reached up to lift away a wind-tossed strand of hair that blew across her face and caught his breath when he saw the tenderness in her eyes. He then rested a hand upon her firm stomach. "I love you more than you will ever know."

Stefan grinned at the others, and all rose to leave the table. He walked around to Gregor and laid a hand on his shoulder. Gregor glanced up, his eyes alight. "I suppose I've been ungracious by ignoring all of you too much?"

Stefan chuckled. "Not at all. I only thought the two of you might enjoy a little time alone."

"There is much for us to do later, Stefan. Please allow me an hour. We can meet then with Kohira and the other officers to plan our next moves." Concern briefly shadowed his eyes.

Alexa saw the fleeting expression and wriggled her way free of his grasp. Selfishly, she desperately wanted that hour. The marvelous richness of his voice and the penetrating warmth of his touch had successfully chased away the aching loneliness she had endured these past months. "Gregor, you have important duties to attend. I have other things I can do. Go ahead with Stefan."

Gregor rose to his feet, emitting an unhappy sigh as Stefan walked off to assemble the other officers. Stefan already knew that Alexa would require the sacrifice from herself even if Gregor resisted.

"Alexa, I need you here. With me. Now. I cannot begin to tell you how terribly I've longed for you." His voice lost all trace of humor and softened to a somber tone.

She wrapped her arms around him. "The faster we resolve this insurrection, the sooner I can have you home. You know I cannot stay. I will not have our baby born on a battlefield."

He tightened his arms around her and rained kisses upon her hair and face. Tears stung his eyelids. "Beloved, you've been so patient with my leaving you behind for so long. Can there be no time at all for just us? Is it so wrong for me to want time alone with you?"

His plea tore at her heart as she remembered asking Stefan a very similar question not so very long ago. She swallowed several times, unable to answer him at first. "Gregor, do what you must with the others. Let me attend some things I must do. Then, I promise we can take some time for each other." Her voice caught for an instant. "I want time with you, too. And I want you to hold me but not with an army of lonely men watching us. Remember, they've also left loved ones behind."

He gazed down into her face, his expression dark and sober. "Will I ever be free to show you the love and attention you deserve?"

She pulled his arms from around her back and placed his hands once more over her rounded stomach. "It seems you must have done so at least once already."

He laughed spontaneously, her irreverent comment breaking through his tension. He kissed her soundly. "Thank you for reminding me why I love you so much."

Chapter 22

Taking the queen's advice seriously, Major Kohira had separated Sifiq soldiers from the Turandans, isolating them inside a separate tent. Those prisoners not critically wounded were securely bound and kept under close guard. Captured Sifiq cast hateful stares at any Turandan who walked through their midst.

Despite deep-rooted uneasiness in their presence, Alexa radiated an image of confidence as she checked the most seriously wounded Sifiq soldiers. Tirani, plus four royal guards, accompanied her. At Tirani's request, Alexa had come specifically to see two Sifiq soldiers. One, a young man, tended to another who was unconscious. "What is your name?" she asked.

He looked at her with anxiety-filled eyes. "I am Var-Tan. This is Lor-Tan, my brother." He was unusually soft-spoken compared to any other Sifiq she had encountered in her lifetime.

"Do you know who I am?" Alexa asked.

Var-Tan turned light blue eyes first to Tirani, then back to Alexa. "I am told that you are wife to Turand's king."

"Why are you here, Var-Tan? You show no sign of injury." Alexa's questions were curious, revealing none of her typical dislike for the Sifiq.

"I was seriously injured, Your Majesty. I was carried here with two arrows lodged in my back. Today, miraculously, my wounds are healed."

Alexa exchanged a questioning glance with Tirani. She had shielded herself carefully from evils she sensed in the Sifiq. However, this young soldier was strikingly different. Now, she found herself anxious, knowing she must open herself to understand the significance of what Var-Tan had told her. "Why do you think you were healed?"

He hesitated, then dropped his voice to little more than a whisper. "Your Majesty, I have studied much about Val, the God of Turand. He has touched my soul, and I have come to believe."

She concealed her amazement. Such a declaration from a Sifiq soldier seemed nothing less than miraculous. "Var-Tan, do you know the difference between Valiria and Valkana?"

He looked puzzled. "I know that both are anointed as priestesses to Val. The Valkana was high priestess and has been absent from Turand for more than a century."

"Var-Tan, I am going to touch you. You must relax and not resist." She placed one hand against his forehead and the other over his heart. Entering a meditative state, she read his life force, then that of his brother. She then studied Var-Tan's face. He appeared only slightly older than she. His hair was pale blond and cut very short. His complexion was fair, and his eyes the lightest shade of blue she had ever seen.

Several moments passed before she spoke. "Var-Tan, Tirani is my lady-in-waiting. She is also Valiria, and it was she who summoned Val's Healing Graces. You were healed because you have indeed accepted Val into your heart. Your brother lies unconscious because he has not yet fully acknowledged God. However, for reasons of his own, Val chooses to sustain Lor-Tan. Turand is again blessed with Valkana, and I have been chosen to fulfill that role. Tell me. What is it you wish to do?"

Var-Tan dropped down to one knee in solemn respect. "Your Majesty, I wish to serve Val in whatever manner possible. I truly believe my brother will follow my lead. We both tire of violence and killing. The ways of our people are wrong, and we can no longer live as warriors."

"Tirstan," she called to the young guard, fast becoming her favorite. "These two men are to be reassigned. Move them immediately to one of our hospital tents. I accept Var-Tan into our fold. If any Turandan objects or fails to respect them in any way, he is to answer directly to King Gregor." She then turned back to Var-Tan. "May the peace of Val go always with you and your brother."

She then left for the tent holding the Turandan rebels. Because of their close connection to faith in Val, the Healing Graces had healed most of them. As such, most were secured with heavy bonds. All were quiet, resigned to their status as prisoners, awaiting an uncertain fate. She walked among the nearly eighty men in the tent, pausing to speak here and there to some and constantly reminding them of the need to be faithful to Val. Upon recognizing Garogan-style uniforms, she stopped to inquire from which part of Garogan the soldier had come.

Finally, she stood silently among them. Closing her eyes and praying, she became absorbed in Val's loving presence. Most of the rebels gasped when they watched as she became enrobed within a sheath of light. When her eyes opened, she appeared more spirit than woman.

"Gentlemen, I understand that most of you are here because you desire freedom for Turand. However, you have also been misled. Your king shares your dream for peace and fights for the same goal. Pray. Open your hearts to Val. Let him guide you. Hear me and know that you came here wounded, many dying. It is Val who sent the means to heal you. It is he who asks me, Valkana, to remind you that your faith must be a living part of all that you are. Pray for understanding. Pray for truth concerning your leaders and the path you must now take."

As the light faded from around her, she found herself surrounded by kneeling men, except for a small group of doubters to her left, who were mainly Tasan and Pitrandan. And a solitary figure moving closer to her right.

"Alexa?" The voice registered shock.

Alexa quickly turned to glance at the man who stood apart from the others. "DiLeno? Is that you?"

On unsteady feet, he approached her, but her personal guards immediately closed around her. His face was stunned. "Alexa? Can it really be you?"

She pushed past her guards and rushed to her old friend, DiLeno Tarandá, throwing her arms around his broad neck in a welcoming hug. With his hands bound tightly behind him, it was impossible for him to return her affectionate embrace.

"Tirstan," she commanded, "free him."

Tirstan stepped forward. "Are you certain, Your Majesty?"

She nodded, her eyes reflecting delight. Once Tirstan's knife sliced through the ropes, she immediately grasped DiLeno's wrists and gently rubbed away the rope burns. "What happened to bring you here?"

Astonished, he watched her hands upon his wrists as the burning redness disappeared beneath her fingers. "I was struck in the leg by an arrow. Although my injuries weren't life-threatening, I was hurt too badly to stand. Today, it's as if I was never wounded at all. Alexa, you must explain what's happening."

She tucked her arm under his and led him outside, where they found a fallen log to sit on. "Oh, DiLeno, I'm so glad to see you. I have sorely missed so many of my friends from Garogan."

He sat quietly. She had changed so much from the last time he had seen her, which had been just before her departure for Toraval to find Victor. "Is what you said true? Are you really Valkana?"

She nodded. "One of many recent and dramatic transformations in my life."

"That I can see," he noted solemnly.

She rested her hands in front of her abdomen. "DiLeno, I wish you at least could be happy for me."

"Are you happy, Alexa? Really happy?" he asked, remembering times past in Garogan City.

Her smile revealed more truth than any words. "I am, DiLeno. I know it seems improbable at best. When I married, I did so for no other reason than to save Victor's life. My life would have held little meaning had he been executed. However, Val had already taken control by then, and suddenly my entire life transformed. At times, I still struggle to comprehend it all."

"When Victor returned from Council, he was devastated. One of the other delegates told me that you insisted that you love the king. Can that truly be?" His face clearly showed disbelief. He had been so close to both Victor and Alexa that he found it nearly impossible to accept the idea she no longer loved Victor.

She laid her hand upon his. "DiLeno, other than my faith in Val, my love for my husband is the greatest truth I know. No one could have been more shocked than I when I realized how much I had come to love him. I despised him for the longest time. Facing the changes in how I cared for Victor wasn't easy either. Even now, I love him in so many ways. But not as I love Gregor."

Her words held the same intensity he would always associate with her. "And the king? What does he think about this? How does he treat you?"

"DiLeno, you may judge that matter for yourself. First, I need to ask you a critically important question. You must answer honestly. You understand that I will know immediately if you do not."

"We have always enjoyed an honest friendship. What is it you wish to ask?"

She paused, considering the best way to phrase her question. "How is it that honorable Turandans from the southern provinces chose to include Sifiq soldiers within their ranks?"

His reaction was startled. "What are you talking about?"

"There is a tent over there. Inside are almost fifty Sifiq soldiers, all dressed as either Tasan or Garogan militia. Why?"

"Alexa, I don't know what to say! I have served as an officer, and I know nothing of any such thing." His mind reeled at the very idea. "Anderon. That can be the only explanation. As much as Victor hates…"

"As much as he hates my husband, even Victor would not knowingly fight alongside Sifiq?" She completed his statement for him. "I cannot believe Victor knows, either."

"Alexa, if this is true, then our fight against the king is without merit. Are you certain?" DiLeno struggled to grasp the impact of her shocking revelation.

"Positively. I can take you in to see for yourself if you doubt. DiLeno, I tried to explain to Victor that Gregor's dreams for Turand are as dear as his. Unfortunately, I believe Victor's judgment is so clouded that he can no longer see what is happening around him."

DiLeno agreed. "He's been almost maniacal for months now. I was visiting Katara when Victor brought you back from Toraval. When I came back, he had just returned from Council. He was someone different from the Victor we both knew. I even shudder to think of how he would react to see you now."

"You mean because of my pregnancy?"

DiLeno answered her with a solemn nod. "After all that has happened, your pregnancy is the one thing that I believe will be completely too much for him to cope with. He still clings to the idea that the two of you are destined for one another. He will always be in love with you."

Sadly considering his comments, she was convinced he was right. "DiLeno, come with me. I wish for you to meet my husband." She led the way.

DiLeno followed, just steps behind her, as they walked up an incline toward a group of men. Several officers leaned over a table, shuffling maps and in intense discussion. One looked up. When he straightened, DiLeno saw the tallest man he had ever seen. The dark features could only belong to the king. DiLeno observed the sudden transformation from utter concentration to incredible tenderness. With only a few long strides, he quickly approached Alexa.

DiLeno watched closely as the man's hands grasped and firmly held Alexa's upper arms. His smile was undeniably affectionate just before he tenderly kissed her. "I was getting ready to come to look for you. I don't want you to overtire yourself."

"I won't, my love. I promise." She beckoned to DiLeno. "I brought someone I want you to meet."

"Oh?" Gregor asked in surprise.

"Gregor, I want to introduce you to an old friend, DiLeno Tarandá. DiLeno, this is my husband, Gregor."

DiLeno bowed, not knowing what to expect when he straightened to face the one known in Garogan Province as the "Dark King of Turand."

"DiLeno Tarandá, I am most pleased to meet a friend of Alexa's." Gregor further surprised DiLeno by extending his arm to shake hands.

"Your Majesty, I am honored to meet you."

Gregor motioned for them to proceed to the table and chairs. Stefan had already cleared away maps and charts and dismissed the officers.

"Please let us sit. Stefan, would you have some tea brought over and then join us?"

"Gregor, DiLeno is Katara's brother. We've known each other for years," she explained. Then, instead of sitting, she walked around to stand behind her husband.

"So, you are brother-in-law to Lord Zephirás?" Gregor inquired politely, quietly appraising the man who did not hesitate to stare squarely back at him.

"Yes, Your Majesty, I am," DiLeno answered, offering no further comment as he performed a silent assessment of his own.

Gregor leaned backward for a moment, letting several seconds pass as he delighted in the feel of his wife's fingers gliding through his hair. It had grown back to fall past the nape of his neck, and her touch recreated delightful sensations that he had missed tremendously.

DiLeno did not miss the expression that crossed the king's face. That look had been filled with intense reverie. He also noticed that Alexa touched her husband almost without conscious realization that she did so. A strong, comfortable connection clearly bound one to the other. DiLeno immediately felt pity for Victor. The love he so tenaciously clung to would never be his again.

Gregor's deep voice interrupted DiLeno's thoughts. "It is obvious you have served with the rebels. Has my wife informed you of circumstances involving the Sifiq?"

DiLeno's mouth tightened into an angry line. "She did, Sire. I swear with a clean conscience that I knew nothing about it until today. I have no doubt that if the Garogan militia knew, they would be furious."

"Who do you believe is behind this insult to all of Turand?" Gregor's question was blunt and direct to the point.

"Alexa and I discussed that as well. I can only believe this to be the treachery of Lord Anderon. He has driven the Garogan leadership for over a year to prepare for insurrection. Most Garogans were more than willing to go to war to end Sifiq domination. However, most were reluctant to declare against you until…" He paused uneasily. "Until Victor allied himself with Lord Anderon after you married Alexa."

Gregor closed a hand around his wife's. "Please, beloved, sit down with us. You must rest."

Wordlessly, she moved from behind him and sat on the chair by his side. He adjusted the position of his seat so he could be closer to her and enclosed her hand within his own, holding it on his lap.

"Do you believe Lord Garogan has knowledge of this appalling abomination?" Gregor's question was sharp. More so than ever, the mere thought of Lord Garogan incensed him.

DiLeno inhaled sharply. "I cannot know for certain, but I find it difficult to believe. To be brutally honest, as much as I know Victor hates you, he hates the Sifiq even more."

Gregor's jaw moved tensely from side to side as he considered the response. "This situation is too horrific to be believed. I must find a way to end this damnable war. Too many lives are lost already. Had my wife not placed herself in a direct line of danger, even more lives would have been sacrificed. Perpetuating years of tragedy is unacceptable." He lowered his head, staring at the gleaming wedding ring he moved back and forth on Alexa's finger.

"Gregor," she spoke quietly, "you know the key is to reach Victor. Deep inside me, I'm sure he knows nothing of Lord Anderon's betrayal."

Gregor jumped to his feet, the jarring pain in his side an unnecessary reminder of how much he despised Lord Garogan. He paced rapidly, hoping to dispel this latest burst of wrath shafting through him. "If only I could believe he is innocent of such involvement! All I have ever seen from him is a penchant for deception and willful, violent behavior! He is uncontrollably vicious and a threat to all of us!"

"Gregor…" his name escaped more like a tiny whimper. Tears threatened in the face of her husband's building anger.

He stopped abruptly, realizing how close to the surface ran her feelings. The last few days must have been torturous for her, both physically and emotionally. Ignoring the presence of Stefan and DiLeno, Gregor dropped to his knees. For the first time in months, he reverted to his habit of cradling her face between his hands. His eyes roved over every precious feature, and he felt guilty for prompting the sadness he saw there.

"Alexa, forgive me, my love. I never meant to upset you. Try to understand how much I fear what he may yet do. I can never erase from my mind that day his arrow struck you or the day I saw him hit you and knock you to the ground. I now have so much more to lose. Please, beloved, don't cry."

DiLeno contemplated Gregor's reaction to Alexa and felt a different stirring within himself. The king before him was a man who possessed a side no Garogan would have believed possible. He possessed a unique intensity of body and spoken word that translated to the kind of love one might only hope to find in a single lifetime. Then, too, there was the king's staggering comment about Victor striking Alexa. DiLeno found the very idea revolting.

Suddenly remembering they were not alone, Gregor turned back to face DiLeno, who smiled grimly in return. "Your Majesty, I ask two things of you. One, that you accept the offer of my loyalty and my services, and second, that you allow me to speak to my fellow provincial soldiers. I am confident that they, too, will offer you their allegiance once they know the truth."

Gregor glanced worriedly at his wife's pale face. Seeing her nearly imperceptible nod, he rose to his feet to shake hands with DiLeno. "I welcome you to my ranks, DiLeno Tarandá." He turned to Stefan with instructions to accompany DiLeno and help him in any way possible.

Dismissing the two men from his presence and his mind, Gregor returned his full attention to Alexa. He regretted the silent teardrops sliding down her cheeks. "Come. Let us both go rest a while."

As she stood, he placed his arm around her shoulders, and they walked to his tent. Once inside, he wiped the tears from her face.

"I'm so sorry, Gregor. I don't know why I started to cry," she apologized uncomfortably.

Saying nothing, he began unbuttoning her blouse, sliding it from her shoulders, and hanging it across the back of the chair. Gently, he drew his finger across the lace-trimmed edge of her camisole, just above her breasts, and thought how incongruous the delicate fabric appeared within the stark interior of his field quarters. He proceeded to unfasten her skirt, supporting her as she stepped out of it.

As he began to undress, he never moved his eyes from the woeful face he adored. Finally, he took her by the hand and guided her to the cot now thickly padded with clean blankets. Smiling, he watched as she lay down and adjusted her body into a comfortable position.

"I haven't told you how beautiful you look."

"Now I know you must be joking," she replied skeptically. "Not only is my appearance a total disaster, I look ready to explode."

"Hush. You're lovelier than ever." He leaned over and kissed her just above the cleft of her breasts. "I want you to rest. After such a long trip and then taking care of me all night, I know you must be exhausted, even if you won't admit it."

Unexpected weakness pervaded her as if his saying the words had released emotions she had trapped beneath all the tasks requiring her attention. Again, she wept softly, and he lay down at her side, holding her close.

"Gregor, I left Toraval because I had a vision. I saw what Victor did to you, and I woke up screaming. I was so terrified I might not arrive in time. My mind reeled with the thought of raising our baby without you."

"Don't cry, beloved. We both must be grateful that Val did bring you in time. Now, I know I'm tired, and you are, too. Let's try to sleep a little. Later, we can talk or do whatever you want. All right?"

She sniffled and raised her index finger to draw down along the slightly rounded curve of his nose. "First, you must say you forgive me. I didn't mean to get upset over what you said about Victor. It just happened."

He closed his eyes. "There's nothing to forgive. Now rest." The air was thick around them but not oppressive. With his hand gently rubbing her stomach, she relaxed and fell asleep.

Hours later, they stood laughing and teasing underneath a make-shift shower. Water had been run down from a spring and was shockingly cold against warm skin. He twisted comically as she drew long, swirling circles in the soap bubbles she had lathered onto his back. He returned the favor and then pulled on the rope that showered them with more cold water. Gregor's laughter came in bursts as he tried to rinse her hair clean of the fragrant lather she had used to wash away grime from her trip.

They dried each other off behind a concealing curtain of blankets hung on ropes tied to trees. After helping one another dress, Gregor insisted that she sit while he combed her hair. The wet, heavy locks were harder than ever to manage, but he patiently worked through tangles and waves until her hair was neat and orderly. They both laughed when he remarked that, as soon as her hair dried completely, they would likely have to repeat the process of taming the curling masses sure to appear.

When she stood up and turned to face him, her smile was so bright that it nearly took his breath away. "You are so lovely. And I feel so much better now that you feel better."

Just as he started to kiss her, the sounds of hooves and harness approached, growing louder and louder from just beyond the hill. Gregor's face froze in sudden, fearful panic. The last thing he wanted was an assault on his rear with his wife in the direct path of attack. He heard Kohira shouting orders. Within scant minutes, the queen's guards raced toward her with horses following on lead. Other soldiers were swiftly setting up defensive positions.

Alexa grabbed Gregor's arm in all the confusion. "Gregor! Stop! It's all right!"

He swung around to her. "Stop? There's no time! Go with your guard! Kohira has already given them directions to evacuate you! Alexa, go!"

"Gregor, no! You don't understand! Wait! Listen to me!" As he ran, she clutched his arm tightly. While she tried to stop him, he literally dragged her along with him.

"Alexa, for the love of Val! What is it?" he desperately cried out to her.

She closed her eyes for barely a second, then gazed at him calmly. "Just before I left, I sent dispatches to Willem to try to assemble reinforcements. I feel his presence. He's bringing help!"

Gregor stared at her in stunned amazement just as the first riders crested the hill lying to the north. Indeed, lead riders carried banners bearing the royal standard and the Zephirás coat of arms.

"How?" He started to ask her how she had known they would need reinforcements and how she had known who the approaching riders were. "I may never grow accustomed to your doing things like this," he exclaimed in a tide of relief.

Gregor then ran to his officers, advising them that the approaching soldiers were reinforcements requested by the queen. With orders issued to resettle the camp, he ran to personally welcome troops led by Lord Zephirás himself. Upon seeing Gregor, Willem dismounted and greeted his old friend with a warm embrace.

"Willem, I cannot begin to tell you how much it means to see you here!" Gregor told him sincerely. "Thank you for coming."

"You should thank our wives. Katara had a dream that Garogan City would soon come under attack. She insisted it wasn't your army. Then I received Alexa's message, so here I am."

"Speaking of my wife." Gregor glimpsed her from the corner of his eye as she hurried toward them.

"Willem! You came! Thank you so much!" she exclaimed, throwing her arms around him affectionately. "You are a wonderful sight!"

When she stepped back, he stared at her. "You are the sight! I had no idea you were expecting! This is a shock!"

Gregor laughed heartily. "She shocked us all by arriving in camp last night. And just in time to save many critically wounded soldiers, myself included."

Willem shook his head in wonder. "I learned long ago to expect surprises from her. However, this is one time when I get to surprise her."

As he spoke, a roan mare broke through the lead line of Willem's troupe, and the rider dismounted. Alexa's mouth opened wide in astonishment, causing her to cry out in joy. "Katara! Dearest Val! Can it really be you?"

She ran to Katara, and the two women hugged each other in total abandon, alternately laughing and crying. When at last they parted, they still held hands. "Katara, I can hardly believe you've come! How could Willem let you?" Alexa asked, her face shining with delight.

"It was more a matter of how he could stop me! I had a powerful dream, Alexa. You may not believe me, but we were already on our way when we encountered your messenger." Katara's face was as lively as ever with its softly rounded features and smooth, rosy complexion. Her thick, white-blonde hair was braided and wrapped around her head.

"I am the least likely one ever to doubt a dream," Alexa reminded her. "I'm just so happy to see you, whatever the reason."

Katara's bright blue eyes flashed mischievously, and she lowered her voice. "Tell me, Alexa. Is that King Gregor?" She nodded directly at the king, who stood talking with Willem, Stefan, and Major Kohira.

Alexa grinned back. "That, my dear, is King Gregor."

Katara shook her head slowly, as if in shock. "Dear God, he is absolutely incredible! I would never have believed him to be so handsome! Or so tall! He certainly doesn't resemble the black-eyed monster king we used to tell stories about!" She then made one of the ugly faces they used to make whenever they had described their king.

Alexa burst into uncontrollable laughter, remembering the awful jokes they had made when everyone thought Gregor to be the black-hearted pawn of the Sifiq.

Gregor glanced in her direction and, smiling, excused himself to the others and strode toward the two women. Just as he reached them, he opened his arms and embraced Katara. "You must be the famous and beautiful Katara. What a pleasure to meet you at last!" His voice was filled with warmth and welcome.

Katara was speechless for probably the first time in her life. She stammered before responding to his greeting. "Your Majesty, I am honored to meet you."

"My dear Katara, I feel as if I've known you forever. My wife has told me so much about you. But, please, I ask that you not be so formal. You must call me Gregor." He then draped his arm around Alexa's shoulders and looked into his wife's sparkling eyes. "You told me to expect laughter whenever Katara is present. I see you were right."

"You will see even more. She's wonderful."

"Come then. Let's go back to camp. I think everyone is recovered enough to go for midday. May I assume you and your husband will join us, Katara?"

She smiled and nodded, intimidated yet enchanted by her friend's husband. "Thank you, Sire. We would be most happy to do so."

Gregor smiled broadly, his eyebrows arched in amusement. "Shall we practice a bit? If you say my name just once, you will find it's not so difficult. Gregor. Say it."

She looked into his dark eyes and instantly responded to his sincere good humor. "Gregor. Gregor? Gregor." She repeated it three times, intoning the name differently each time. "Of course, you're right. I can say that name. Now, if only I can remember to forget all the formal training my mother tried so hard to teach me for so many years. Yes, perhaps I can call you Gregor."

"See, Gregor? She's already teasing you. I think she loves you already."

His wife's smile was brilliant, her reunion with Katara unanticipated joy. Gregor observed the animated conversation between the two as they walked toward camp. He had never seen her interact with any of her friends except Willem. That had happened during the early days of their marriage when she kept so much of herself in reserve because of their strained relationship. Still, that glimpse of her devotion to her friends showed how much she needed them. He felt pangs of guilt at having forced her to stay separated from them, but he continued to rationalize to himself that he had needed to keep her safe.

As they reached camp, aides had started placing the midday meal on several tables pushed together. Alexa went to find Tirstan and whispered something to him. She then returned to those who were already preparing to sit and eat. "Katara, you've given me the happiest surprise I've had in a long time. Now, it's my turn to surprise you."

Katara looked at Alexa in puzzlement until she saw her brother's smiling face coming to join them. "DiLeno!" she shrieked. She ran into his arms, and he picked her up, swinging her around in an exultant hug.

⌣

Evening shadows hung across the camp like soft, deep blankets. Campfires were being built up for the night, and the smell of burning wood filled warm summer air. The atmosphere felt restrained as soldiers mentally prepared themselves for the day to come. Tomorrow, once again, they would march into battle.

Katara and Alexa sat cross-legged on a mat placed in front of an enormous bonfire. Their conversation had changed from the earlier light-hearted banter to more serious matters. "Are you not afraid of being out here now that you're pregnant?" Katara asked, concerned that Alexa's reduced mobility might place her in unnecessary danger.

"For myself and my baby, I am not. Val has willed that I be here. I place my faith in him."

Katara remained silent for several minutes. "You know, when our delegates returned from Council, I cried when I learned that you are Valkana. I always knew your faith set you apart from the rest of us. Victor always believed you were chosen. Everything that has happened to you seems so amazing."

Alexa stared into the fire, watching with fascination as yellow flames danced around burning logs. Comprehension of all those changes often eluded her. "There are times when I wonder if I'm going to awaken and find this all an elaborate dream."

"Alexa, at least you have the best part of the dream." Katara could not avoid thinking that Victor's dream had transformed into a nightmare. Dismissing the fleeting thought, she smiled again. "I feel so happy for you when I see you with Gregor. I cannot believe the way he looks at you or the way he touches you. He undoubtedly loves you. As much as I know Willem loves me, he is never so openly affectionate with me." Her sigh was somewhat envious.

Alexa almost smiled, her mind reflecting on the tenderness of her husband's fingers grazing her cheek briefly as they sat together or how often he stopped to drop a kiss on top of her head in passing. "He spoils me," she finally agreed. "I suppose it took us so long to find each other that we need the physical contact to remind us of the reality."

"You must have suffered terribly in the beginning. I was so unbelievably sad and angry when I learned how you had married the king. Victor came shortly afterward to visit us. He was already on the verge of a breakdown. I don't believe he'll ever fully recover from losing you."

"Katara, you know I loved him dearly. I will always owe him so much. Marrying Gregor was the single most difficult decision I ever made in my life. At the time, it seemed the only way to save Victor." She hesitated. "Katara, I've never mentioned this to anyone. Before I met Gregor, just before I went to the palace, I had a vision during meditation. Val showed me an image of myself—joining hands with Gregor. At first, I thought he was showing me how to save Victor. It was months before I realized Val was actually presenting me with the path to find my own happiness,"

Katara smiled. "And you are happy. I can see it all over you."

Alexa grinned humorously and patted her stomach. "All over me."

Gregor, who had completed final consultations with his officers and advisers, came to interrupt them. "Excuse me, ladies. Beloved, I'm tired, and tomorrow promises to be extremely difficult. Shall we retire?" His voice was quiet and gentle as he leaned forward to help Alexa up from the ground.

Katara stood up as well. "Alexa, your husband is right. We all face a long, hard day tomorrow. At least you now have extra willing hands to help. Good night." Katara kissed her friend's cheek and smiled at Gregor before leaving to join her husband.

Once inside their tent, Gregor and Alexa quickly prepared for bed. They lay close, tenderly stroking each other in the darkness. "May I ask you a question?" he asked curiously.

"Of course," she answered, her eyes closed as she luxuriated in the feel of his hand moving in circles over her rounded abdomen.

"Early this morning, when I was talking to some of the officers, I saw you watching me. You had such an odd look on your face. What were you thinking?"

She smiled to herself, her mind's eye retrieving the image that had so enchanted her.

"Well?" he prompted when she failed to answer.

"I was thinking I had never seen you dressed so casually as this morning. Even when we were at Lindaval, you always dressed with such formal flair. This morning, you looked so strong—so masculine and incredibly handsome that you took my breath away."

He chuckled softly. "I believe your judgment to be somewhat slanted, Milady."

"Perhaps, but Katara certainly agrees with me." She had barely spoken when a wide yawn overcame her.

"You need to sleep. I know you must still be tired from your journey." He kissed her forehead. "I love you, sweet queen of my heart."

Chapter 23

Katara and Alexa held hands tightly as they watched Gregor's army leave camp to advance once again against rebel forces. Willem and thirty of his men remained behind to augment Alexa's personal guard to evacuate the women and any injured should the camp be threatened.

Gregor's eyes had reflected tremendous anxiety as he issued commands to the remaining soldiers and then gave strict instructions to follow in case of attack. Kissing his wife farewell, he had been exceedingly proud of her courage. If they survived this war, he vowed to himself that he would never leave her again.

Alexa turned away first, shifting her focus from concern for her husband to preparations for casualties sure to come. Katara and Willem took charge of preparing bandages and dressings from the extra supplies Katara had insisted on bringing. Tirani and Alexa brewed the special herbal teas that would be administered to any wounded. With many willing hands, they completed the work rapidly. The most challenging task of all—that of waiting—began.

Alexa decided to go to the tent housing the Sifiq. As determined non-believers, many had died, untouched by Val's healing powers. Some remained critical. Despite all they had taken from her, she believed her responsibilities as Valkana required her to minister to them, too. Others, less severely injured, were restrained to prevent escape. Their antagonism faded as they wondered what fate the Turandans would impose on them.

She then went to the tent where only Var-Tan, the Sifiq convert, remained with his brother. Alexa studied Lor-Tan intently and placed her hand on his head. "I believe he will awaken soon. It seems Val has touched him, even in his coma," she reassured Var-Tan.

"Praises be to Val," the young Sifiq breathed, unspeakably grateful for the gift of his brother's life.

"Var-Tan, you do know that the soldiers have gone to fight again," she told him.

"I know, Your Majesty. You need only ask if you require my assistance in any way." His sincerity was deeply rooted in the loathing he had developed for the suffering his people were so intent to inflict on innocent victims.

"Thank you. I expect we will need every available pair of hands." Calm and composed, she returned to the table where Tirani and Katara waited with mugs of Raija tea. They knew they would need every ounce of energy for later.

The women spoke little as the morning dragged. Stefan and Willem were discussing the rebel forces' likely strategy when Stefan looked up to see the first of the injured being carried toward the tents. "Ladies, it appears the battle is well underway."

Katara, Tirani, and Alexa joined hands for a final prayer before hurrying to the receiving area they had organized earlier. The first arrivals were quickly assessed for the severity of their injuries and then assigned locations inside the hospital tents. Var-Tan, along with several other aides, began to administer the life-sustaining teas as the three women worked quickly to bind up bloody gashes and remove lodged blades and arrow tips from the flesh of injured soldiers. Meanwhile, Stefan and Willem maintained order and control outside to move the most seriously hurt soldiers inside first for care.

Groups of men limped in on their own, often assisting others with more critical wounds. Royal forces came as well as rebel. For a while, it seemed there would be no end to the gory parade.

A lull in the arrivals occurred mid-afternoon. Alexa and Tirani ate a quick meal at Katara's insistence. The priestesses then conferred on how best to proceed, deciding at last that Tirani should prepare for meditation to summon Val's Healing Graces. In the meantime, Alexa would prepare eight men to enable them to enter and exit the energy-laden sphere that would materialize around the Valiria and the wounded.

The light dome, barely visible in the bright afternoon sun, formed just as the newest arrivals entered the camp. Again, Alexa and Katara tended the wounded with gentle efficiency. They requested assistance from the men only when they needed to remove deeply embedded weapons.

Securing the dressings on the arm of a man whose hand had been severed just above the wrist, Alexa heard Gregor's voice shouting her name. She spun around, her heart leaping into her throat.

Katara's head shot up, and she saw the near panic on her friend's face. "Go!" she exclaimed. "I can finish here."

Quickly, Alexa wiped her hands and ran from the tent. Outside, she saw Stefan and Willem standing with Gregor beside her husband's big stallion. Sheer terror immobilized her. With every shred of will she could muster, she forced her feet to move in her husband's direction. The mere sight of him caused her insides to quake. His tunic jacket was gone. His white linen shirt was drenched with blood, and the scarlet-stained fabric stuck against his skin.

He looked up and called to her. "Alexa, hurry! Help!"

Without knowing how, she ran forward. In what appeared to be nothing but chaos before her eyes, Stefan and Willem were shouting at soldiers to fetch a litter.

"Gregor!" she cried out, her voice breaking with fear, tears streaming down her face.

Realizing how frightened she must have been upon seeing him covered in blood, he ran to meet her and grasped her shoulders. "Look at me, Alexa!" he commanded. "Beloved, I'm all right. I'm not hurt."

"But…" she let out a shuddering sob.

"Alexa, I've brought Victor. He's wounded and bleeding profusely. Come, my love. Hurry."

Fleeting relief shot through her only to be replaced with a different kind of panic. No matter what Victor had nearly cost her, she knew she had no choice but to try to save him. Hurrying to where his body was being lifted onto a stretcher, she knelt at his side. Quickly removing Gregor's blood-soaked tunic, she saw the enormous, gaping wound that slashed from just beneath the ribs on his right side across to his lower left side. Alexa held her breath for only a moment, willing herself to stay calm.

"Hurry!" she shouted. "I need dressings and lots of them! Someone bring me some Kirmaya! Now!"

She received the dressings without seeing who placed things in her hands and quickly soaked them with some of the Kirmaya tea. She packed them firmly against Victor's wound, then issued additional instructions. "Hold them tightly in place! Willem! We need to move him! Quickly!"

Thankfully, Gregor's hands firmly grasped her waist, helping her to her feet. When she turned to face him, she found his expression impossible to fathom. "He's dying," she whispered.

"I know. I brought him as fast as I could," Gregor assured her, his eyes searching her face. "Alexa, you must try to save him."

She could barely imagine the inner conflict he must have confronted in bringing Victor to camp. "Gregor, I'm not sure I can. He's lost too much blood. If there's any chance to save him, I need to be alone with him. I'll need to hold him, just as I did with you."

Gregor hesitated only seconds. If Victor should die, he knew in his heart how deeply she would grieve. She needed no more sorrow in her life. "Beloved, I know how much he means to you, and you know I trust you. Do what you must. Save him if you can."

She stood on tiptoe and brushed a kiss against his lips. "I love you." She turned to the others. "Take him inside the king's tent. Hurry!"

Gregor ran ahead and held open the flap, allowing them unimpeded entrance. Alexa followed, barking instructions at everyone, including her husband. He lit an oil lamp for her and snatched up clean clothing for himself. His firm grip on her shoulder conveyed all his love and confidence in her. "I will see that you are not disturbed."

Finally alone with Victor, she began a brief chant as her hands worked rapidly with the thick pads of dressings covering his wound. She sensed Victor's life force rapidly ebbing away. Grabbing a thick, wet towel, she quickly washed off her hands as best she could.

With her chanted prayer complete, she drew her fingers across his forehead. "Victor," she spoke firmly, "it's Alexa. I'm here, Victor. I won't leave you. I intend not to let you die. Hear me, Victor. You must not die."

Her voice broke. She lay down beside him, wrapping her arm around him, and felt the warmth of his seeping blood against her skin. She prayed again, slipping into the meditative state that connected her with the Healing Graces.

Just as before, her aura appeared, enveloping her first before expanding to surround Victor. She whispered his name, and, before long, her sweet voice was heard singing children's songs recalled from another tragedy many long years ago.

⌐

Gregor sat before a blazing campfire, elbows digging into his knees, his chin resting on his hands. Unseeing eyes stared into dancing yellow flames. The solemnity of his countenance belied the fact that his army had gained a significant victory in the costly battle waged earlier that day.

"Tea?" Stefan carried two mugs and offered one to Gregor, who reached up mechanically to take one.

"She's been in there so long," he muttered, struggling to cope with the fact that his wife now dedicated every shred of her energy to an attempt to save Victor's life. The absurdity and the irony of the situation twisted painfully into his mind and heart.

Stefan sat down on the log that held Gregor's pensive form. "I suppose it will take longer if she's able to save Victor."

"Why do you say that?" Gregor asked gloomily.

"She emerged a little more than four hours after being with you. She has been with Victor for more than six. My opinion is that her love for you is so deep that her energies were stronger."

Gregor's expression eased only slightly. "I question my own sanity as to why I went to such lengths to save him after all he's done. I never saw a man so intent on killing as when he fought me. And every time I remember what he did to her…" He could not continue as, in his memory, he saw her tumbling to the ground with Victor's arrow protruding from her body. The image was one he would carry forever.

Stefan breathed out heavily. "Despite it all, you know that, had it not been for Victor, you would never even have known Alexa. He alone saved her from the Sifiq massacre at Zinzan. In a convoluted way of thinking, he even led her to you. Now, she strives to save his life. I heard you tell her that you trust her. You must believe that."

Gregor glanced sideways at Stefan. "I do trust her. I also know her soul. I worry enough about her being out here in the middle of all this, especially considering her pregnancy. That alone makes things infinitely worse for me. In so many ways, she is the strongest person, man or woman, I've ever known. But you were right when you told me her sensitivities are just as strong. I don't want her hurt anymore."

"Believe in her, Gregor. Understand that the kind of love that so worries you right now is what strengthens her. Believe me. I've watched that love in action."

Both men fell silent, gazing into the blue and yellow depths of the fire. Gregor ached inside, tormented by the idea of Alexa lying by Victor's side, attempting to save his life. Although he knew how much she had once loved Victor, he did trust her without question. What troubled him was the intensity of his resentment. And, he admitted reluctantly, his own lingering jealousy. Part of him would always remain jealous that she still cared so much for Victor.

Slender arms wrapped around his waist from behind, disturbing the murky thoughts clouding his mind. He closed his eyes, savoring the feel of her face nestled against his broad back. He breathed a fervent prayer. She still belonged to him.

~

Sitting beside Victor, she gently wiped traces of battleground grime from his face. He had slept through the night. In sleep, his face was more like the man she so fondly remembered. Straight, dark hair framed a ruddy complexion. His smallish mouth, with its bow-like curve, was a deep blush color. And, asleep, there was none of the recent rage that had tainted her memory of him.

He rolled his head from one side to the other, a low groan rumbling in his throat. His eyelids slid open, but he shut them tightly again. Sleep was a dark, heavy veil to be drawn aside to reveal the day's light.

"Victor?" she spoke his name quietly, knowing he needed to be roused. "Victor, it's time to wake up."

His eyelids blinked open and shut several times before he could keep them open. He stared straight up, feeling disoriented and confused. He turned his head slightly until he looked directly into her face.

"Alexa. Sweetest." He smiled for only an instant before awareness of where he must be registered in his weary brain. "Oh, Alexa, why didn't you just let me die?"

"You know I could do no such thing. Whether or not you believe it, you will always be important to me. Besides, as I recall, there was a time when you refused to let me die." She spoke to him in a soothing, comforting voice, her eyes filled with empathy.

"Alexa, that was a different place and a different lifetime. We both dreamed of a future together. For me, no such dreams remain to live for," he told her, his voice husky with sleep and grief.

She reached over to a small table for a cup of Raija. "Here, let me help you raise up. You need something to drink." Her manner was serious, allowing for no nonsense. She knelt on the ground, lifted his head to rest against her shoulder, and held the cup to his lips.

He lay back, exhausted by nothing more than the effort to drink. Then, with eyes closed, he concentrated on his breathing, trying to focus away from the pain filling both his body and his soul. "What now?" he asked at last.

She stood and walked away from him to select one of Gregor's shirts to replace the ruined one cut away from Victor the night before. As her hands moved through her husband's things, she answered him thoughtfully. "What's next depends entirely on you. I can tell you there are some very grave matters we absolutely must discuss."

"Alexa, you don't understand. Nothing matters anymore. You were the foundation for all my dreams and aspirations. Without you, my life is pointless." He choked against the anguish constricting his throat, remembering how much he had wanted to die.

Her eyes glittered intensely when she returned, carrying the shirt in front of her. "Victor, you're wrong. You are a leader with great power in your abilities to reach far into people and inspire them to action. Your life can never be pointless when you are capable of so much good."

She handed him the shirt, which he instantly dropped to the ground. His hazel eyes swam with tears that he could not hold back. "Oh, my God. Not this, too." He had just noticed the swelling evidence of Gregor's total possession of the woman he would forever love. Shock sliced through his heart more surely than the steel blade that had split him open the day before.

She knelt to retrieve the shirt and shook the dust from it. Once again, she sat beside him. "Victor, you know in your heart I never planned to hurt you," she said, tears wetting her velvety cheeks. "I loved you so much, but Val chose a different destiny for me. You must know that a part of me will always love you. The difference is that my love for you, no matter how strong, is very unlike my love for Gregor."

He laughed cynically, his tone completely self-deprecating. "There's a peculiar irony to all this. When I thought I had slain him, I congratulated myself for ending the royal Toscano line. I was even wrong about that." He started to sit up but, unprepared for the sharp pain that assaulted him, fell backward, his breathing growing ragged. His eyes closed against the physical and emotional realities overwhelming him.

Feeling deeply sorrowful for him, Alexa reached out and ran her fingers along his cheek in what was, for him, a bittersweet caress. "Victor, despite everything, I want you to live. You have so much to offer those around you—and to all of Turand. Besides, I already mourned once over losing you. Please, Victor, please. Don't make me mourn for you twice."

When he finally reopened his eyes, their golden depths revealed unspeakable heartache. "It seems I have little choice. My great challenge now is that I face mourning my loss of you for the rest of my life. Alexa, I love you, and I will love you until the day I die."

She nodded, her face sad. "I know, Victor, but you must live beyond that. We need you if we are to bring lasting peace to Turand."

"Me? You need me?" he scoffed. "Do you forget that I'm the confirmed rebel who not only helped start this rebellion but also tried his damnedest to kill your husband?"

Alexa grimaced, still sensitive to Gregor's close encounter with death. "Victor, I must ask you something, and you must answer me honestly." Receiving his nodded agreement, she continued, "Why have the southern provinces allied themselves with Sifiq soldiers?"

He rose on his elbows and looked at her as if she had lost her mind. "You know better than anyone how much I hate the Sifiq! How can you imagine I would ever consider fighting with them? My goal has always been to rid Turand of their pestilence!"

She noted the spontaneous response and felt the veracity flowing through his life force. Her relief was immense that, at least in this, his integrity had not been compromised. "Victor, we have brought in wounded regardless of which side they represented. Among them were dozens of Sifiq soldiers. Each one was dressed as either Garogan or Tasan militia."

"Alexa, tell me you're not serious! You know I would never consider such an abomination!" His eyes glittered furiously.

"And you know that I am sworn to the truth! Beyond that, how can you imagine I would contrive such a story? No matter what else in my life has changed, I am still priestess to Val." Her words were not angry but, instead, a stern reminder to him of the essence of who she was.

He swallowed with difficulty. "I swear I know nothing of this. The only plausible explanation is that Lord Anderon negotiated some sort of alliance with the Sifiq garrisoned in Tasa Coast. That might explain some of his odd behavior and demands. In which case, I've been duped. Alexa, on this, you must believe me."

She smiled into his eyes. "I believed in you even before I asked the question. In fact, I've already defended you on this count, but I needed to hear it from you. The rebel forces were driven back in defeat yesterday. We also just received a dispatch from scouts who located a second force moving northeast from the coast. I believe the two groups will rendezvous and march first to Garogan City. If they succeed there, they will march to Toraval. We need you, Victor. Desperately."

He stared into her face. "You ask me to ally myself with a man I hate more than words can say?"

Her face changed, losing the warmth of only moments ago. "I ask you to channel your energies to fight for the dream we held so dear—the dream I refuse to believe is dead in you. My husband believes in our goal, Victor, and he fights honorably to achieve it. Put your feelings for Gregor aside. What about Turand? Our people? What about Garogan City? Your ancestral home there! Adrina! This war marches toward home, Victor! Can you actually mire yourself so deeply in your hatred for Gregor that you would reject him as the one barrier standing between continuing Sifiq evils and the destruction of your own home and family?"

Her words struck him with the fiery sting of a whip. They both knew he could never allow the destruction of his home without trying to protect it. He must possess the necessary shreds of strength to confront and manage his bitterness toward Gregor for the sake of Adrina and his home.

Pausing to gather his thoughts, he forced himself to answer her. "Alexa, I accept the truth of what you say. I will work honorably at the king's side for the benefit of Turand. However, you must understand one thing. You can never ask of me either friendship or long-term support. My feelings against him run too deep."

"Let me help you up, Victor." She helped him stand, holding him firmly as he steadied himself against invading dizziness. She then wrapped dressings around his midsection. "There will be no more bleeding. The bandages will provide support for tender tissues still healing," she explained. "You must be careful for a few days."

He picked up the shirt she had handed him. "This is his?"

She lifted stern eyes that intimidated him into silence. "There's nothing decent left of yours. We're going out to eat breakfast. Considering that we'll be joined by Willem, DiLeno, Katara, and my lady-in-waiting, I would hope you could at least make yourself presentable."

"And I suppose he will be there?" Victor's words were bitterly resentful.

"I expect he will be. I also expect that you can and will conduct yourself as a gentleman in his presence. Victor, you must make peace with what is. Otherwise, all the sacrifices we made and all the lives already lost will have been for naught. Please, Victor, I beg of you. Do not fail me in this," she pleaded with him.

He dropped his face and studiously managed the buttons on the finely woven shirt that was much too long for him. As he rolled back the cuffs, he looked up, his expression softening. "Is he really so tall?"

Her expression turned peculiar. "Yes, he is."

Victor reached out, stroking his fingers through her hair. "I will do whatever I can for Turand. And for you, Alexa. I want you to know I regret with all my heart all the times in the past when I failed you. Our lives would be very different if I had been sensible enough to marry you years ago. I swear to you now. No matter what happens, I will never fail you again."

She gazed into the golden irises of his eyes and felt reconnected to the Victor she had once adored. At that moment, she comprehended that their connection to one another could never be destroyed. With a deep sigh, she moved into his embrace and accepted the conciliatory promise he offered her.

He fought yet another private war as he held her close, her pregnant body a poignant reminder of the life he had lost.

Alexa left the tent first. Victor had requested a few minutes alone to prepare himself for the looming ordeal of again facing her husband. He held no false illusions. No matter the strength of Alexa's character standing as buffer between them, their personal enmity would be a smoldering fire easy to flare. Already, he almost regretted his promise to her.

Outside, she breathed in deeply of the fresher air. Although knowing everyone awaited a report on Victor's condition, she remained motionless, seeking control of her own thoughts and feelings. Sensing one pair of eyes intent upon her, she turned to see the inquiring look on her husband's face. Her response was a brilliant smile that sent an invasion of relief throughout his being.

He left the officer with whom he spoke and strode quickly toward her. When he reached her, he encircled her waist. Moving into his arms, she delighted in his strength, partaking of the refuge of his powerful embrace. He drew away from her enough to study her expression, which told him that she had reached Victor and that hope existed for collaboration for the benefit of Turand.

There was no need for him to speak words of love. Instead, his eyes and his smile conveyed all as he responded to quivering lips that clamored for his. And Victor, who had just stepped out into the sunshine, experienced the first of a lifetime of thrusts into his heart as he watched them together.

Later, around the breakfast table, Katara and DiLeno stayed close to Victor. As family, they felt protective of the cousin whom they loved dearly. His pain was evident, and both cousins wondered which was more acute, the physical or the emotional.

Once everyone had gathered, Gregor spoke, his voice subdued and tightly controlled. "We welcome you to our table, Lord Garogan. Would you be so kind as to honor us with prayer?"

Victor glanced at him in silent surprise and, after a short hesitation, recited an ancient prayer of thanks. Anxiety was evident as everyone sat down. No one was certain what to expect with Gregor and Victor sitting at the same table. No one could think of a way to break the strained silence.

The tension was finally dispelled when Alexa jumped, bouncing her fork off her plate. Her expression was a comical mixture of shock and delight as she pressed her hands against her stomach. Katara laughed aloud while Gregor, fork in mouth, stared at his wife in dismay.

Alexa sheepishly returned his questioning glance. "I apologize. It was the baby. He kicked me."

Gregor laid his fork down as a wide grin spread across his face. He leaned toward her and, placing his hand against her curving stomach, was instantly met with a firm thump. He tilted his head comically to one side, unable to disguise either his amusement or his amazement. "It seems, my love, you have quite a challenge to deal with."

She laughed happily. "Two of them! I'm afraid this baby is going to be as strong and energetic as his father!"

Everyone at the table joined her laughter—everyone except Victor, who lowered his head and squeezed his eyes tightly shut, fervently wishing that he could block out the image of her carrying another man's child.

Two days later, oppressive heat and humidity returned, making travel miserable as Gregor's army marched toward Garogan City. Many soldiers from the northern provinces, unaccustomed to the exhausting heat that drew rivers of sweat down their bodies, stripped to the waist as they plodded along the dusty road. Nearly all of the Turandan rebel prisoners had chosen to join Victor and DiLeno by pledging allegiance to the king and joining his army. They were more used to summer heat and trudged along quietly, bitter and aggrieved at having been tricked into fighting alongside the despised Sifiq.

Gregor rode in front, astride the golden stallion that had carried him through the entire campaign. DiLeno acted as guide. Stefan and Willem rode at his side. The king had organized his forces with wagons bearing the women, wounded Sifiq soldiers, and supplies in the center of the army. Major Kohira brought up the rear. Gregor intended to minimize risks for the women by having experienced officers at either end who could get them to safety in case of attack.

Gregor had also insisted that Alexa travel by wagon, fearful of her riding horseback under the scorching sun. By early afternoon, her stomach ached, and her head pounded. Too much noise prevented her from meditating. Heat, combined with the bouncing ride over rough roads, fast became more than she could tolerate. Katara, who had stayed with her, now fretted as she wet towels to wipe and cool Alexa's hot, sweaty brow. The damp towels made little difference. Finally, Alexa could take no more. "Katara, make the driver stop. I have to get out."

Katara scrambled forward and shouted for the driver to stop. Before she could move back again, Alexa had already pushed open the back and was climbing down. She ran to the side of the road and, partially concealed by trees, bent nearly double. Despite the heat, her skin crawled as chills shook her body. Finally, she heaved, overcome by nausea.

"Alexa!" Victor called out her name. He had seen the wagon's abrupt stop, then watched as she bolted from the back. Victor then immediately spurred his horse in her direction, pulled it to a jolting halt, and dismounted in one quick, fluid motion. Running past Katara, he rushed straight to Alexa, securely placing his arm around her. The violent quaking of her body frightened him even more than the wetness soaking through her clothing.

"Alexa, breathe. Breathe deeply and slowly. Breathe, Sweetest," he instructed.

She looked up at him and began to weep. "Victor, I feel so sick. Help me back to the wagon." She took a step but swayed unsteadily.

Realizing how much the heat inside the wagon had stressed her, he lifted her into his arms. Her head fell weakly against his shoulder, and her sobs were barely audible. "My sweetest Alexa," he whispered gently, "you're going to be fine. Trust me. I'm here to take care of you."

"Victor," she sobbed softly. "I'm so sick. I'm afraid. My baby. I don't want to lose my baby."

"I won't let anything happen to you or your baby. Just stay calm and breathe." He glanced up at Katara. "Get some towels, Katara. Soak them. We need to lower her temperature."

Victor carried her beneath denser shade, then carefully lowered himself to the ground while still holding her in his arms. He lifted her hair away from her face and neck to allow freer flow of air. Bending one of his legs up and planting his boot solidly on the ground, he eased her back against his leg and supported her head on his arm. With his free hand, he unbuttoned her sleeves and pushed them back while Katara bathed Alexa's face with wet towels.

"Katara, take off her shoes and anything else you can remove. She needs to cool down quickly." The pounding of hooves approached, but he didn't bother to look up. Gregor must have noticed something was wrong and come to investigate.

The instant Gregor saw Alexa lying in Victor's arms, he jumped from his horse and raced toward them. "In Val's great name, what happened?"

he thundered, his heart skipping a beat upon seeing her pallor and Victor's frightened features. "What's wrong with her?" Then, almost by instinct, he reached to draw her away from Victor.

Victor glared at him angrily before responding with barely contained fury. "Heat sickness. She doesn't need to be moved. Help us get some of her clothes off so we can cool her down."

For a moment, Katara feared the flames burning in their eyes would erupt into a full-fledged explosion. "Gentlemen," she admonished sternly, "your ego clashes can wait until later. I think we need to concentrate on what Alexa needs right now."

Shoving aside his misgivings, Gregor helped Katara by pulling Alexa's skirts up as far as possible and opening her blouse. While Katara bathed her legs, Gregor placed wet cloths against her chest and shoulders, just above her camisole.

"Katara, have someone summon Tirani," Gregor whispered, terrified by the limp way Alexa lay against Victor.

While waiting for Tirani to reach them, Gregor began to speak to his wife in a soft, comforting voice as he stroked her hair. "Beloved, listen to me. Pray, my love. I'll pray with you." His voice faltered as he initiated the beginning of a traditional prayer for Val's blessing on the sick. Although her face was ghostly pale, her lips moved in unison with those of her husband. He glanced up, seeing that Victor, too, prayed along with them.

Once Tirani arrived, she instructed Gregor to move aside so she could sit on the ground beside Alexa. Gregor helplessly watched as Tirani told Victor to change positions so that she might place her hands more firmly against Alexa's forehead and over her heart. Tirani prayed a barely audible chant as she slipped into a light state of trance.

In less than ten minutes, Alexa began to stir. Gregor's heart lurched as he saw her nestle her face against Victor's shoulder. Victor's face held an expression so transformed with loving tenderness that Gregor discovered new appreciation and sympathy for his former enemy's anguish. Even so, he felt disconsolate and impotent watching his own wife in the arms of his avowed personal enemy.

Alexa's eyes were barely open, but she knew that Victor was the one who held her, and she placed her hand against his cheek. "Thank you, Victor. Thank you for helping me." Her words were just a whisper.

He smiled down at her. "I promised I'd take care of you. You're going to be fine now." He spoke tenderly as, for just a moment, he pretended this was the way it would always be for him—watching out for her and taking care of her in times of need.

"Victor?" She paused, trying to clear the haze from her mind. "Yes, Alexa. What is it?"

"Gregor? Where's Gregor? Is he here?"

Victor's eyes closed. His momentary fantasy shattered, leaving him emptier than ever.

As Tirani moved away, Gregor was instantly by her side. "I'm here, beloved."

She turned toward the direction of his voice and looked into her husband's face. Her arms stretched out to wrap around his neck. Gently, he pulled her against him and away from Victor. His heart responded joyfully to her reaching out for him as he chided himself for his momentary lapse of confidence. He cradled her against his chest and whispered adoring endearments against her ear.

They made camp for the night. With the intense, energy-draining heat, everyone was grateful for the early end to the day. Plans were made to break down camp at dawn to march during the cooler morning hours. Once Gregor had communicated orders to his officers, he expressed his gratitude to Katara and Tirani before settling himself to take care of his wife.

She napped until early evening, waking hungry and in good humor. Hers was a special happiness at finding her husband sitting by her side, reading scout dispatches by the light of a small lantern. She laid her hand upon his firmly muscled thigh to gain his attention.

"So, I see you've decided to rejoin us." He laid aside the reports and twisted around to gaze down at her. "I hope you realize that you nearly scared me to death today."

"I warned you this morning I preferred not to ride in a wagon. I feared this stage of pregnancy, combined with riding in a wagon in this heat, would make me sick. I just didn't expect it to be so bad."

"I would have thought that being Valkana would protect you from such things," he teased.

"Being Valkana does not change the fact that I am subject to the same kinds of maladies as any other person." She laughed softly as she pulled herself into a sitting position.

"And what do you think you are doing?" he asked.

"I think that I'm going to get up," she responded with a smile. "My body is complaining that I've been lying down too long, and I'm starving. I want to go outside."

"All right, all right. I refuse to argue with you because I know who will lose. Let me help you." He picked up the lantern, scooted to the end of the wagon, and climbed out. He then helped her down, holding her firmly for a moment until she gained her balance.

Minutes later, Gregor excused himself, leaving Alexa in the care of Katara and Tirani. Spending much of the last few hours mulling over those long minutes watching his wife in Victor's arms, he reluctantly recalled the agonizing weeks after she had been taken to Garogan. Except by the grace of one of Val's greatest gifts, he could so easily have been the one suffering the tremendous heartbreak he had observed earlier on Victor's face.

He finally found Victor alone, brushing a horse. Seeing Victor's posture so lonely and forlorn, Gregor wavered a moment before quickly recovering his resolve. "Lord Garogan, may I speak with you?"

Victor paused, then continued to run the brush along the horse's flanks. He nodded slightly, unable to muster words to answer.

"Lord Garogan, I wish to thank you for what you did for Alexa today." Gregor searched for the right thing to say in the face of the malice existing between them. "Tirani told me that your reaction probably saved her from a more severe case of heat sickness. I have no words to express my appreciation."

Victor stopped what he was doing and turned slightly. "You should have listened to her this morning when she tried to explain to you. She is priestess to Val. None of them can be closed in for long. Considering the way the wagons magnify this damned heat, you could have caused her to lose her baby or, even worse, killed her." He resumed grooming the horse.

Gregor remained quiet, uncomfortable with the truth in Victor's angry admonition. At length, he replied, "I made a mistake. I was only trying to protect her. Still, I do not argue your point. I'm just grateful that you were there to help her. Despite the differences that exist between you and me, I am learning to accept that she will always care deeply for you. The fact that you can set aside all the enmity you feel toward me for her sake is something I respect. I just want you to know that." When Victor said nothing else, Gregor turned to leave.

Suddenly, Victor's voice sliced through the tension that crackled in the air. "I honestly wonder if you have any idea how much she really loves you. No matter. I tell you as I told her. I will love her until the day I die. Because of that simple fact, there is no challenge that will deter me if it is for the sake of her happiness or well-being. That includes conducting myself civilly with you. I accept your thanks. I also ask you to be more careful with her in the future. I may not always be around the way I was today." He then dismissed Gregor's presence, returning in silence to his task.

Chapter 24

E arly afternoon sun was shrouded in gray clouds that threatened Garogan Castle with a late summer thunderstorm. Adrina watched the skies as dense cloud cover raced by and hoped the coming storm would bring relief in the form of lower temperatures to break the unusual heat wave that had plagued Garogan. A strong breeze already blew through the trees and hinted that a welcome change lay behind the storm.

Adrina stepped outside and let the breeze blow against her perspiration-dampened face. The inbound storm felt in utter harmony with her thoughts. She constantly fretted about her brother. She had never seen anyone change as much as he had just before he left for the fighting. Neither had she heard from him even once since his departure and would have been desperate had it not been for the occasional wounded soldier or courier returning with word that Victor was well.

She also continued to wrestle with her memories of Alexa's disastrous return to Garogan. Her emotions were a tangle of conflicts. In the end, she admitted to herself that she had most probably driven away the best friend she had ever known. Adrina's guilt was compounded by the acknowledgment she had done nothing to try to understand her friend's feelings. Too, she remained appalled whenever she remembered how she had slapped Alexa out of sheer frustration.

Later, Adrina was stunned upon learning that Alexa had been beaten. She had intended to apologize the night of Alexa's escape. Even now, Adrina could close her eyes and find herself haunted by the bruises and swelling that had distorted Alexa's face. Waiting up until dawn for Victor to return, she had shouted at him for the first time in her life. A temper she had never known erupted as she screamed at him for having allowed Lord Anderon to abuse Alexa so brutally. Victor's reaction had been just as shocked, and he immediately ran to see for himself. Arriving at her rooms, they discovered she had escaped.

The breeze quickly strengthened into powerful gusts that whipped stinging bits of dirt and grit against Adrina's soft cheeks. Tears stung her eyes. She would forever wish Victor had never decided to go to Toraval. The calls of an approaching rider interrupted her melancholic contemplation.

"Lady Adrina!" the rider, a girl in her teens, cried out as she galloped up. "An army rides in from the south! They're almost at the edge of the city!"

"Could you tell who they are? Do they appear ready to attack?"

Adrina, now clutching the horse's reins, questioned her. "No weapons are drawn, Milady, nor do the mounted troops appear ready to launch an attack, but they do bear the royal standard!"

"Then go! Warn everyone to stay inside and lock themselves in! I'll sound the alarm to the garrison."

Adrenaline pumped through Adrina's blood as she ran to the rear of the castle, where a contingent of Garogan militia remained to defend the castle. The garrison was small but exceptionally well trained. Adrina shouted to the commander about the approaching army and then ran inside the castle. She called out to her household staff, urging them to hurry to their practiced positions.

She then ran back outside, where townspeople were beginning to crowd in, seeking protection within the castle's tall fortress walls. In the frenzy of so much commotion, she barely heard the commander shouting her name. When she finally heard him and looked up, he waved frantically, urging her to come up to the observation turret where he stood.

Lifting her skirts, she rushed up the square stone steps that led to the tower. Looking out in the direction where he pointed, she saw a lone horseman riding toward the castle.

"Victor!" she shouted in disbelief. "It's my brother! Open a gate!" She hurried back down the steps and ran out through a back gate where guards had just removed the massive beam used to secure the rear entrance.

Adrina's feet skimmed out across the uneven ground to meet her brother. Nearing his horse, she stretched her arms out to him. He dismounted and dragged his sister into his arms, hugging her tightly. Just seeing her again lifted his spirits, and he simultaneously regretted all the grief he had caused her. This reunion with her meant more than he could say.

When they drew apart, Adrina looked up to him with questioning eyes. "Victor, I'm so glad you're home, but I don't understand. Why have you come back bearing the royal standard? What's happening?"

He forced a smile and gently brushed tears from her cheeks. "I'll explain later, sister. First, we must get people inside as fast as possible. This storm is going to be bad, and it's almost here."

Turning, he signaled Gregor's army to advance before proceeding with Adrina through the gates. Since not everyone would fit under roof within the castle compound, he instructed garrison officers to guide many soldiers to shelter inside the city.

Once his officers had taken everything well in hand, Victor prepared to break the news to his sister. He knew her well and could only guess at how disturbed she might be. "Adrina, we're going to have house guests. DiLeno is with me, and so are Willem and Katara."

"Katara?" Adrina interrupted in amazement. "What in heaven's name is Katara doing out there with the army?"

Victor held Adrina by her arms and gazed solemnly into her face. "Adrina, she came to help with the wounded. But there's something even more important I have to tell you—something that is likely to prove extremely difficult for both of us."

"What?" she asked, uncomfortable with the haunted look in his eyes.

"Adrina, King Gregor will also stay here." He clenched his jaw, his teeth grinding together. "Alexa is with him."

"What!" she exclaimed. "Victor, you can't possibly be serious!"

"Adrina, I promise to explain everything later. But, right now, you must prepare everything inside to receive guests. Hurry, sister!"

Just as the first raindrops began to splatter, Gregor dismounted his horse in front of the wide castle doors. Assuring himself that someone would help Katara and Tirani, he was immensely grateful for the arched roof overhead that provided protection for disembarking guests and went to his wife. She had refused to ride another day in a wagon and now accepted his help as he effortlessly lifted her down from her mount.

Victor had come through the castle and swung open enormous double doors to allow his guests to enter. Adrina waited just inside, her nerves shattered. She had no idea how she would summon sufficient courage to face Alexa again.

Katara entered first, greeting Adrina affectionately. It had been almost three years since Katara had married Willem and left Garogan. She commented on how wonderful it was to see her cousin. Adrina responded with a nervous smile and clasped Katara's hands. Katara, ever-sensitive despite her vivacious nature, hugged Adrina once again, whispering into her ear that there was no need to fret.

Tirani followed Katara and was introduced to Adrina as both Valiria and lady-in-waiting to the queen. While Adrina welcomed Tirani, Victor watched disconsolately as Gregor clearly offered words of encouragement to Alexa, whose face revealed her own anxiety. Deep inside, Victor suppressed a fresh surge of unwelcome jealousy as he watched the possessive manner in which Gregor ran his hands up and down her arms.

Finally, Gregor placed his arm around his wife's shoulders, and they started toward the entrance. He permitted Alexa to precede him, and Victor forced a smile as she passed by. Her eyes fixed on Adrina's pale, anxious face. Alexa sensed the battle of nerves and remorseful sadness that churned within the soul of her old friend. That sense presented itself as a kind of spiritual bond. Hope existed to recover that which had been lost.

Alexa sighed and smiled serenely, moving toward Adrina and wrapping her arms around her. She spoke very softly. "Adrina, my dear friend, how good it is to see you. I hope this visit fares better than our last."

Adrina drew back, tears brimming in her eyes. "Welcome home, Alexa." She glanced down and then back up to meet Alexa's sparkling green eyes. "I had no idea you were expecting a baby."

The smile that lit Alexa's face was a delight. "Approaching seven months now." She paused tentatively. "Adrina, I want you to meet my husband."

Gregor had remained standing in the doorway, his tall figure imposing as he dominated the entrance. Alexa beckoned to him, and he entered, extending his hand to her.

Adrina was dumbstruck by the sheer height of the man, let alone the idea of receiving Turand's king into her home. She dropped a deep curtsy and wished she could have had more time to prepare for this unexpected event.

"Lady Adrina Garogan," Gregor greeted warmly, "thank you for granting us the privilege of staying in your home."

She rose and faced him, trying not to reveal how unnerved she was by his presence. "Your Majesty, my brother has invited you into our home. I assure you that I will do everything possible to see to your comfort."

He acknowledged her greeting and graciously allowed her the opportunity to avoid additional conversation until she could relax more in his presence.

Half an hour later, Gregor sat on the bed in rooms that had belonged to Alexa during the years she had lived at Garogan Castle. He watched as his wife gazed out the windows facing the meadow and forest that had been the scene of her mad escape from the castle.

"It feels so strange being here with you," she remarked thoughtfully, turning her attention away from the turbulent storm outside. "I feel completely turned upside down with all that's happened over these past few days."

"I can only imagine," he remarked sympathetically. "Perhaps this is a chance to achieve some sense of reconciliation. You've been forced to contend with one life-altering event after another, and most have been nothing less than traumatic. Maybe this is Val's way for you to recover and rebuild some of the relationships that were so precious to you."

She turned around slowly, her expression pensive as she came over to the bed to sit beside him. "I hope you're right."

Placing his arm around her, he eased her back onto the bed before allowing himself to collapse backward. "Mmmm," he muttered in ecstasy. "A real bed with a real mattress! Oh, this is going to be one wonderful night!"

She giggled and dug her elbow into his side. "What happened to my personal philosopher?"

He ignored her question and pretended to snore. She rolled onto her side and tickled him without mercy until he finally sat up, his face alight with a wide grin. "Come. We need to clean up and change for dinner. I heard Adrina say to be down by seven, and it already grows late."

Alexa went downstairs ahead of Gregor, who begged a few extra minutes to luxuriate in a tub of hot, sudsy water for the first time in months. Before leaving, she lathered and rinsed his hair, scrubbed his back, and then laid out clothing for him. Then, automatically, she headed toward the kitchen. Just as expected, Adrina was busy, personally overseeing meal preparations.

Leaning against the stone archway, Alexa watched quietly. This was how she remembered Adrina. Always efficiently in charge of her household. Always directing others, always keeping herself occupied. It was easier than combating her shyness in broader social settings. When Adrina looked up and noticed Alexa was watching her, she froze, faltering for words even more so now that they were alone.

Alexa went to the long, brightly tiled counter where Adrina added finishing touches to a decorated cake-and-crème dessert to follow dinner. Alexa took the utensils from her and placed them on the counter. She then laid her hand along the side of Adrina's face. Her eyes searched, finding treasure lost.

Adrina spoke first, more than ready to release a tide of long-suppressed emotions. "Alexa, you have no idea how sorry I am for everything that happened when you were last here. I have prayed constantly that you could forgive me—and perhaps even Victor."

Alexa's face held a shaky smile. "Adrina, all of us were stretched beyond our limits. It took me a long time to recover and longer to understand. The one belief that helped me most is that you, Victor, and I love each other dearly. I know that not one of us could ever want to deliberately hurt the other."

Adrina turned back to finish her task with the desserts, using the activity to regain her composure. "Life has been so hard since you first left for Toraval. I truly believe my brother will never be happy again. I only hope that you and I can be friends again. I've missed you terribly."

Alexa put her arms around Adrina. "You and I have always been more than just friends, and nothing can ever change that. As for Victor, he's learning to accept reality."

Hopeful, Adrina nodded. "The kitchen staff can finish now. If you'll excuse me, I think I'll go upstairs to wash my face and quickly change into something else." Hesitating, she embraced Alexa tightly once more. "I do love you."

Tall white tapers burned in two ornate, wrought-iron candelabras gracing the oak table inside the castle's informal dining room. As master of the house, Victor stood at the head of the table with his sister behind the chair to his right. Gregor was at the far end of the table with his wife to his left. Everyone else had taken places in between, and all had joined hands to pray.

Victor felt little satisfaction that he managed to maintain a steady, unemotional voice as he invited the king to honor the gathering by offering the mealtime prayer. Gregor responded graciously, giving thanks for bonds of friendship and family, and for blessings of hearth and sustenance for body and soul.

They all sat quietly to eat. Katara took the lead, trying to dispel any animosities with bright and lively chatter about her baby girl. Achieving limited success, she proceeded to relate some of her triumphs in adapting to life in Willem's home province with humorous embellishments. She described how her naturally effusive nature created many challenges in an environment characterized by a more sedate and conservative society than in Garogan. Her energy was irresistible, drawing everyone into the conversation. By the time dessert was served, the atmosphere had brightened tremendously.

Gregor remained relatively quiet throughout the meal, although he smiled frequently and interjected sporadic comments. He mostly savored a finely prepared dinner for the first time in months while enjoying the intense pleasure of having his wife close by his side.

When a servant placed Adrina's delectable cake-and-crème dessert before him, Alexa grinned wickedly. "I warn you, my love, this dessert can be deadly—especially for someone with your love of sweets." She watched closely as he lifted the first chilled bite into his mouth. His dark eyes closed as he allowed the lusciously smooth combination to slide across his tongue. The flavor was especially sweet after months of camp food. She stifled the urge to laugh at his expression of sheer ecstasy.

When he was nearly finished, he stood up with grand ceremony to address the other diners. His eyes sparkled, and his smile was broad and genuine. "Ladies and gentlemen, I ask you to pardon me for interrupting this delectable dessert course, but I have something I must say. My wife has frequently extolled the talents of our hostess and her unique culinary abilities. I now personally know what she meant. This meal has been a delight from the very beginning. Lady Adrina, I hope you will accept my sincerest appreciation for a delicious meal and this most divine dessert."

He then bowed, and Adrina's mouth dropped open in self-conscious surprise. "Your—Your Majesty, I thank you for your praise," she stammered.

"It is praise richly deserved, Milady," he replied, bowing once again and leading everyone at the table in a lively round of applause in honor of their hostess.

Gregor and Stefan excused themselves after dinner, requesting that someone escort them to the quarters lodging Major Kohira and the other officers. Gregor needed to assure himself all was in order before retiring for the night.

He had been gone only a few minutes when Alexa decided to walk outside beneath a covered walkway, wanting to watch the storm that continued with pelting rains and jagged bolts of lightning that split the night sky and rumbled the ground with roaring thunder. Such storms were almost unheard of in Toraval. Occasionally, she longed for the vibrating force of a Garogan summer storm. After a while, she leaned against a stone pillar and stared pensively into the violent skies.

"I see you've never lost your fascination for storms."

She had been so engrossed in watching the storm that she was startled at first. Sighing in relief, she turned to face Victor. "Storms unleash powers that never fail to draw me out. I never understood why."

He placed a gentle hand on her arm. "Alexa, why don't we walk back to the patio? I would like to talk with you if you will allow."

The pleading in his voice touched her heart. She permitted him to link her arm into his, and, together, they slowly returned through the covered corridor that ran the length of the rear of the castle. They sat at a round, wrought-iron table with four chairs. Sitting in silence for a while, each examined inner thoughts to the dissonant cacophony provided by the waning storm.

Victor's voice was solemn as he finally broke that silence. "Alexa, I'm not even certain where to begin or how to say what needs to be said."

Her expression was encouraging. "I always believed it best just to let words flow as they come to mind. Remember, you are talking with me."

His heart lurched as she stated the essence of his problem. He ventured ahead. "I wish I could tell you without making you feel uncomfortable. It's only that I know myself too well. Well enough to know that I can never stop loving you. That is a simple, unavoidable fact of my life. In saying that I love you, I also comprehend how important your happiness is to me.

"Alexa, I cannot describe to you how painful it is for me to watch you with him. I feel more than simple jealousy. There is a sorrow inside of me that…" He paused, searching for words. "I meant it when I told you how much I regret all the times I disappointed you. When I think of how much I always loved you, it's unbelievable that I could have failed you so many times. I also want you to know that I honestly had no idea of what Lord Anderon did to you."

Nearly strangling on the words, he averted his face from her. He fought against emotions threatening to spill over, and his voice cracked. "I swear I was gone when it happened, or I would never have allowed it. Adrina absolutely exploded at me when I came back. That's when I went to check on you and discovered you were gone."

She reached out and took his hand. "Victor…"

He shook his head, rejecting the forgiving tone in her voice as she spoke his name. "Alexa, my entire life fell into shambles in little more than a year. To have lost you because of my own actions is torment enough. To think that I descended into such a deplorable state that, not only did I hit you, I almost killed you." His voice trailed off. "Later, as much as I hated Anderon, I hated your husband more. After that, I honestly didn't give a damn about anything except retribution. Right now, I find every hour a struggle to live with the guilt and misery that I alone caused."

"Victor," she began gently, "I never intended to hurt you, but I know I did. When I first went to Toraval, there was very little I would not have done to save you. I loved you that much. I understand now that you only lashed out because I was the one who caused you so much pain. I know it's no help at all when I tell you how much I always loved you or how much I still do. I never expected it, but that love changed."

"Alexa, I know all that. I know you as well as anyone does. Probably even better than your husband. But the pain doesn't get any better. Every time I see him touch you, I only feel worse. Every time I remember all our plans and our dreams. Or when I think how this baby of yours should have been mine."

"Victor, you mustn't torture yourself. You accomplish nothing except more misery. Nothing can change the events since I went to Toraval. I wish I could magically erase your grief, but I cannot do that anymore than

I can stop loving Gregor." She hated seeing him so distraught as well as her helplessness to comfort him.

After a prolonged silence, he rose from his chair, reluctantly releasing her hand. "I think I'll go in now. Perhaps we can find a few minutes to talk again before you leave. Will you go in?"

"No. I think I'll stay outside a bit longer."

He leaned forward and placed a lingering kiss against her cheek. "Good night, then. Sweet dreams."

Once he had gone, she sat back and folded her hands on top of her stomach. The rain had slowed to a drizzle, and the air had cooled to a much more pleasant temperature. She contemplated Victor's emotional plight and her role in his misery. She felt no guilt, only deep regret that he continued to suffer so.

"I doubt that even time will ease his sorrow." The richness of her husband's voice carried through the darkness. She listened to his footsteps as he walked over to where she sat. He stopped behind her chair and began to gently knead the muscles along the back of her neck. "You should go inside and take advantage of having a real bed to sleep in. I want you to rest."

She smiled at his concern. "I will. I just find it so hard to stop thinking about him. You've never known the gregarious, fun-loving side of him that I do. He was always so good to me. Gregor, I ache for him."

"Alexa, you must accept that you cannot solve this problem for him. Whether or not you believe me, I sympathize, too. I remember only too well my own taste of what he's suffering. However, you are my most important concern, and I don't want to see you upset. Let's go in now."

He spoke firmly to her, then guided her inside, where they wished everyone goodnight before going to bed.

⌐

Gregor pulled the smooth cotton sheet more tightly around him. He was comfortably nestled into the soft depths of the mattress, where he had fallen deeply asleep with his arm draped over his wife. Faint trails of sensation floated along his back and shoulder, and he resisted waking to discover and stop the cause.

Alexa grinned mischievously and continued her morning assault. She raised up and leaned over to run the tip of her tongue along the shell-like rim of his ear. He shivered in response, pulling the covers up over his head. She whispered teasingly. "You may as well wake up, Your Majesty. I refuse to allow you to escape."

He groaned and pulled the covers back just enough to peek at her with one half-opened eye. Half-asleep, he mumbled, "What am I escaping?"

Her laugh was low and seductive. "Not what. Whom." She slid her hand beneath the covers and, with just her fingertips, traced light circles against his bare chest, then down to the sensitive plane of his stomach. When she felt his muscles contract beneath her touch, she knew she had begun to achieve her goal.

"What do you think you're doing?" he muttered, clutching the covers back over his face.

"Trying to rouse you enough to seduce you, of course."

Her touch had begun to incite chaos in a body that had been too long without her. He slowly removed the covers from his face and appraised the concentrated expression in her eyes. He quickly reached down to grip her hand as her fingers probed along yet more intimately. "Stop, my love. You are nearly seven months pregnant. The last thing I want to do is to hurt you."

She pursed her mouth into a mock pout. "You'll only hurt me if you refuse to make love to me right now. Unless, of course, you find your own handiwork repulsive and undesirable."

He rolled over and pulled her close, his voice sternly scolding her. "I never want to hear such a thing from you again. You have never looked more beautiful than you do right now."

Her hand roved freely over the firmness of his chest. "Then love me, Gregor," she begged. "I need you."

Her touch had already aroused him, and his passion flared, a quickly rising flame fueled by their long separation. He kissed her forehead, forcing himself to control his desires. "Are you positive I won't hurt you or our baby?"

She nipped his earlobe playfully and teased again. "Not so long as we avoid any acrobatics."

He tightened his hold on her and laughed. "Have I ever told you how impossible you can be?" he asked, sliding his mouth down from her neck and shoulder to capture a firm nipple between his lips.

"Many times," she gasped breathlessly, tangling her fingers into his hair and pressing him tighter against the cushioned mound of her breast.

With hands and lips, he reacquainted himself with the fragrant smoothness of her skin, the sweetness of her mouth, and the even fuller curves of her feminine body. With every touch and every kiss, he grew more intoxicated. With her body responding instantaneously to his every move, he suddenly comprehended how incomplete he had been without her.

His fiery touch sent shivers of delight in rippling waves across every nerve in her body. She had ached for him, and their intimate reconnection promised fulfillment beyond description. She moaned with sweet abandon as his hands erotically stroked sensitive skin, stirring her body to renewed life.

She cried out his name as their bodies finally reconnected, receiving him with unspeakable rapture. With her hands covering him in sweeping caresses, she sought to deliver to him the same level of passion that he gave her. She occasionally scraped her fingernails into his back as he raised the height of her arousal to new plateaus. Their loving was a powerful force unto itself, a symphony that swept them from one dynamic crescendo to another until they reached explosive climax.

Breathless and sated, they clung to each other. They whispered endearments and exchanged showers of sweet kisses. Physically, they had manifested the transcendent nature of a love that truly made them one.

⌒

Victor was noticeably absent from the breakfast table. Thankfully, Adrina appeared much less nervous as she ensured her guests received the finest hospitality her household could offer. Soufflé, thinly sliced smoked meats, a selection of hot breads, and fresh fruit were served for a substantial and satisfying breakfast. Adrina found herself blushing more than once at Gregor's continuing lavish praise of her culinary talents.

Amused, she accepted his hearty thanks for what he referred to as her overnight miracle of clean and freshly ironed laundry. She laughed to the brink of tears as he vividly described trying to get used to river-washed clothing. He embellished the description with animated gestures of his reactions to clothes that always seemed stiff, wrinkled, and perpetually gritty, no matter what his aides did.

Gregor and Alexa enjoyed high spirits as they held hands throughout the breakfast conversation. Katara was quickly drawn into the infectious good humor, and even the more staid Willem and Stefan fell prey to their lively mood.

Once breakfast ended, Stefan, DiLeno, and Willem decided to accompany Gregor to the quarters housing his officers. Alexa walked her husband to the door, clinging to his arm and smiling radiantly. His heart was intensely satisfied to see her looking so lovely and so happy. Ignoring the presence of the others and showing no sign of reluctance or embarrassment, he kissed her passionately. More to him than just his wife, she had become his primary purpose for living. His dark eyes shone as he touched his index finger to her lips. "Save this for later. I thought we might spend the afternoon together so you can show me around."

She said nothing, her face aglow with loving acceptance of his invitation. She kissed his finger and then watched as he resumed his role as king and commander of an army at war before following the other men, who were waiting outside.

From behind, Katara's arms circled her expanded waistline. "My friend, you could at least try to hide that smug, satisfied look on your face. What did you two do to each other?" Katara hissed into her ear.

Alexa giggled uncontrollably and bit her lips together in an attempt to avoid bursting into outright laughter. After several moments of silent shaking, she hissed back at her old friend. "Must I really explain?"

Both surrendered to laughter until Katara, shaking her head back and forth, managed to speak. "All I can say is that man you married is magnificent! And if Willem ever kissed me like that, especially in front of someone, I would surely die from shock!"

"All right, I think it's time for you two to settle down and behave," Adrina interrupted them with barely suppressed laughter. "Let's go outside for a while."

More than an hour sped by as they sipped fruited tea and shared news about all their old friends. Adrina and Katara chatted about who had married and who now had children. Alexa listened in quiet contentment, delighted just being with them again. Katara was the first to rise, excusing herself to go inside. She wanted to be sure everything would be well organized for the next day when she, Willem, and Stefan would escort the queen back to Toraval.

"Your eyes filled with shadows when Katara mentioned your return to Toraval," Adrina remarked thoughtfully. She had always been closest to Alexa and found it a simple matter to discern her friend's thoughts and feelings.

"I almost dread going home tomorrow. Leaving Gregor will be incredibly hard," Alexa replied, her eyes darkening. "For more than three months, we've had barely a week together."

"This war has been short, but it has brought loneliness to many of us."

"Adrina, Toraval is so beautiful, but I feel lost and empty without him there. Other than Stefan and an elderly priest, I have no real friends. Not like here."

"Considering everything you've gone through, I find it hard to believe you still feel that way." Adrina's expression revealed that she continued to cope with a keen sense of remorse despite her conversation with Alexa the day before.

Alexa leaned across the table and placed her hand over Adrina's. "What happened resulted from unimaginable circumstances. You were torn between love for your brother and your feelings for me. Adrina, how can you imagine I would allow a single emotionally-charged moment to ruin years of loving friendship? I treasure you too much to lose you."

Their eyes met, and Adrina's heart rejoiced at what she saw. Getting up, they embraced one another. Adrina cried while Alexa, smiling through a veil of tears, offered a silent prayer of thanks for yet another precious gift from Val.

Sitting down again, a flash of inspiration seized Alexa. "Adrina, with the rebel army coming, no one really knows how long hostilities will last here or how bad they will be. Katara has to return home to her little girl. Why don't you come to Toraval with me? It would mean so much to have you there, especially with the baby coming. I know I wouldn't feel so alone if you were with me."

Adrina stared at her in astonishment. "Alexa, I don't know how I could! I mean, to leave when I may be needed to help with injured soldiers. And Victor…" Her face expressed her doubts.

"Oh, Adrina, please think about it. I've already spoken with Tirani. She will stay to tend to the wounded. Val has blessed her with the Healing Graces. She can do so much more than you can imagine. Besides, there will surely be others to help her."

Adrina wasn't quite sure what to say. "I had almost forgotten that she is Valiria. But that still leaves Victor. In his state of mind right now…" she stopped, unable to continue.

Alexa's face softened. "I know how much you worry about him, but DiLeno is his best friend, and he'll be here. I also have no doubts that Gregor will also watch out for him."

"Your husband? After all that's happened?" Adrina asked in disbelief.

"Adrina, I know Victor told you that he would have died had I not been near the battlefield. There's something else that I doubt even Victor knows. He was too near death to remember. I would never have had the time to help him had it not been for Gregor. Gregor is the one who bound up his wounds, and he personally carried Victor back to camp. He's as much responsible as I am for Victor being alive."

Adrina's eyes were clearly incredulous. "But why? You can watch them just glance at one another and see sparks fly."

Alexa shrugged her shoulders. "I really don't know. I never questioned Gregor. He brought Victor back, shouting for me to come help." She shook slightly, the remembered image of him drenched in Victor's blood sufficient to frighten her anew. "Gregor was so covered in blood that I thought he was the one who had been wounded. Adrina, Gregor actually urged me to stay with Victor to save him. I know that wasn't easy for him, but he did. That is something I will always respect about him. In truth, I'll always be grateful. Victor still means so much to me."

Adrina saw her friend swallow hard. "So I also owe my brother's life to your husband. And you honestly have no idea why he saved Victor?"

"I suppose it's because he knows I still care for Victor. He also knows that Victor saved my life in Zinzan. Whatever his reasons, I know they must be complicated."

For several long moments, Adrina silently considered the strangeness of her brother's life being saved by his greatest rival. "Nothing has been simple for so long. I need to go in now to check on some things." She rose, placing her hand on Alexa's shoulder. "Let me think about going to Toraval."

⌒

Following a lively midday meal, Gregor and Alexa left the castle. Hand in hand, they walked through the narrow, red brick streets of Garogan City. The many homes, built close together, were constructed predominately of white stucco with red tiled roofs rising above tree lined streets. Most windows and doors were arched and then trimmed and painted in vivid shades of blues, reds, or greens. Swirling floral patterns and elaborate geometric designs were wrought in iron to decorate balconies and gates. Glazed clay urns and pots sat everywhere, holding well tended plants boasting flowers in bright purples, pinks, and reds. The provincial capital was bright, clean, and charming.

The couple occasionally encountered someone Alexa had known during the years she had lived in Garogan. Reactions varied from reserved to cautiously friendly. Alexa took it all in stride, understanding the loyalty to Victor and the nervous apprehension of being introduced to the King of Turand as he strode casually through their streets.

By mid-afternoon, they left the city streets to stroll across the broad, sloping meadow in front of the castle compound. Gregor's hand tightened around his wife's as he unwillingly recalled the morning he had watched her ride out of the shadows of the castle's stone walls. He would never forget that day as long as he lived.

She glanced up, noticing the tensing of his jaw. Instinctively, she recognized the memory playing through his mind. She pulled her hand from his and slid her arm around his waist. "Don't remember if it upsets you so much."

He drew her around in front of him and gazed into the depths of her emerald eyes. His own eyes misted as his mind relived what he would forever consider the most horrific moments of his life. His heart pounded, and his face reflected remembered terror.

She spoke again, her voice soothing. "My love, it's over now."

"I know." He inhaled a deep breath. "I know it is, but I will never forget that day. When I saw you riding away from the castle directly toward me and then…"

"I remember practically nothing."

His lips pressed together in grim recollection. "That is probably a blessing in itself."

He led her across a narrow point in the stream and then walked to the spot where they fell from their horses. He let go of her and crouched close to the ground. "This is just about where it happened. After you knocked me over, I couldn't see you at first because you fell between your horse and mine. I remember Stefan ran to help me up while someone led horses around to shield us from any more arrows. When I saw you lying face down with that arrow lodged in your back … "

She stood above him, saying nothing as she watched the faraway look in his eyes. Today was the first time he had ever really discussed any details of that day with her. That memory seemed a burden he needed to release.

"There was so much confusion that I don't even remember who removed the arrow. Someone told me you were still alive. I do recall that Stefan helped bandage the wound. When we turned you over, I received the worst shock of all. Blood was gushing from the side of your head. And your face, Alexa. Dearest Val, when I saw your face so swollen and covered in bruises." He squeezed his eyes tightly shut against the terrible, disturbing image.

"Gregor, you can leave it in the past now," she said, deeply moved by the play of emotions on his face.

He glanced up at her, teardrops sparkling on his long lashes. "You don't even recall that you woke up for just a moment?"

She shook her head. "No."

"That is something else I'll always remember. When you looked up at me, I was never quite sure if you smiled or not. You whispered my name. Then you said, 'You came for me. You came.' That was all before you fell into the coma. I spent days trying to understand what you meant by that."

She extended her hand to him, and he stood up. She raised up on tiptoe and lightly kissed him. "As hard as it is to think of it, that single event brought us together as much as any other we've ever known."

Beneath the turquoise skies of Garogan, he drew her against him. His lips moved sensually along her face. His mouth covered hers, and his tongue plunged past her lips, seeking and partaking of all the sweet, sustaining love she had to give.

As he slowly withdrew from her, she smiled at him in adoration. "Look around, my love. This is such a beautiful place. I bear no regrets for what occurred here. It is here that I finally came to understand how much I love you, and it was here that we were reunited."

His throat constricted, rendering him unable to speak. Instead, he wrapped her again in a tight, possessive embrace. They started to walk again, but they frequently paused to embrace or exchange kisses. Often, he would stop just to gaze lovingly into her eyes as he stroked his hands over the pregnant curve of her abdomen.

Upstairs, inside the castle, the door to Victor's master suite stood ajar as Katara walked through the wide hallway on her way downstairs. Glancing inside, she saw Victor standing in the shadows beside a window. There was a sorrowful melancholy in his posture that struck her, and she couldn't avoid going inside. She stopped directly behind him. He was so lost in his contemplation that he never heard her. Katara glanced outside. In the distance, Gregor and Alexa were bonded together by the passion of a lover's kiss.

"Cousin," Katara whispered with intense concern, "why do you torture yourself so?" She placed a comforting hand flat against the small of his back.

The fact that he cried was apparent from the thick sound of his voice that he made no effort to conceal. "They look perfect together. And so very happy. Tell me, Katara. Did she ever look that happy when she was with me?"

"Victor, you know as well as I how much she always loved you." Katara's heart ached for her cousin.

"Katara, I want her to be happy. I honestly do. I just can't escape from the idea that if I had only married her years ago, the way she wanted—if I had never been so stubborn and never gone to Toraval." He choked back a sob, unable to continue.

Katara found it impossible to restrain her own tears as she searched for something to say that might offer some small measure of consolation. "Victor, I believe as Alexa does. This can only be Val's will. Otherwise, the ifs you mentioned would have been a different reality for you both. You must accept that if you are ever to have any peace."

"I love her, Katara. I always have. I don't know how to escape that reality. I try to console myself with the knowledge that she's finally happier than she's ever been. Take a closer look at them, Katara. The love you see out there is extraordinary—the kind of love that inspires ballads and legends. That is exactly how I once envisioned my love for her. Now, I am completely, utterly lost."

Katara realized that there existed no possibility to comfort him. She patted his shoulder, knowing the gesture was ineffectual to console a soul torn by such grief. There was nothing more she could do other than leave him alone with his thoughts.

"Thank you for caring, Katara. Please. Close the door when you leave." He heard the click of the door closing and resumed watching out the window. He observed intently as Gregor appeared to lead Alexa in some sort of flowing, romantic dance across the bright, verdant meadow. Their faces glowed with brilliant smiles. Unwillingly, he recalled earlier that morning when he had stopped outside her door for reasons he could no longer remember. Victor's shoulders shook violently as he sobbed into the darkness of his suite, recalling the muffled sound of her voice crying out Gregor's name. Never in his life could he have imagined any greater torment.

Intensive discussion regarding preparations for the following day preceded supper. Victor had spent much of the morning working with various Garogan officials to arrange a gathering in front of the city's main temple for seven-thirty the following morning. Final details had then been organized with Stefan's assistance.

The king would speak to Garogan City's citizens to explain the details of all that had occurred with the Sifiq and the menace of Lord Anderon's advancing army. Victor and DiLeno would appear at the king's side in a demonstration of unity. The temple would then open for the formal introduction of Valkana to Garogan's populace. The plan allowed an hour and a half so that the queen's party could be ready to leave for Toraval by late morning.

Supper was a more solemn affair than the night before. Laughter was more subdued despite efforts by everyone, including Victor, to maintain a cheerful atmosphere. Victor and DiLeno suppressed substantial worries about the army advancing on the city they loved and called home. Although looking forward to returning home to her daughter, Katara dreaded leaving family and friends behind to face the impending attack. Gregor and Alexa did their best to buoy the spirits of their friends.

Just before dinner ended, a messenger arrived and handed a sealed envelope to Victor. Casting Gregor a grave look, Victor nodded toward the door. The two men excused themselves, rising simultaneously to leave the dining room. Stefan, Willem, and DiLeno all followed quickly, gathering in the grand foyer at the front of the castle.

Gregor carefully read the dispatch and looked grimly at Victor. "It appears Lord Anderon's armies advance faster than anticipated. If they continue at the pace indicated in this message, they could easily reach Garogan and be set to launch an offensive within four days."

Victor's thoughts raced, mentally auditing the status of the city's defenses and reserves. "Garogan City can certainly withstand a siege, but I think it much more advisable to aim a thrust at them before they advance this far."

"I agree," Gregor stated quickly. "Stefan, would you go with me? I want to discuss strategy with Kohira and start preparing the men. We must move troops out tomorrow to intercept Anderon."

DiLeno and Willem left with them. Victor remained behind to retrieve area maps and diagrams that would prove useful in drafting plans to defend Garogan City. Inside his study, he quickly rolled up the papers he had pulled from the castle archives. A quiet sound interrupted his task. When he glanced up, Alexa stood in the doorway.

"I know Gregor needs those right away, but I thought you might send them by messenger. I had hoped you would walk with me outside for a bit."

He looked at her in puzzlement. Her face was tranquil, but he saw that her eyes were troubled. He cursed himself for his continuing sensitivity to every nuance of her expressions. Instead of answering her, he nodded and pulled a brocaded bell rope to summon a servant.

After the messenger came and was entrusted to deliver the assembled documents, Victor crossed the study to where she waited. Gazing into her eyes, he could almost delude himself into believing nothing had ever changed.

She linked her arm with his, and they walked through the corridor and out the front entrance. They strolled together in silence for nearly ten minutes before she finally spoke. "Victor, I want you to know how worried I am about you."

He sighed heavily. "I'll be all right. Eventually." He lied to her and fully expected to be admonished.

"I wish I could believe that. Victor, I don't want you to be careless if you ride back into battle. Promise me you'll be careful." She stopped and gazed into his eyes, her lower lip quivering.

"After everything I've done to you, can I really believe you're asking me to be careful?" Her concern was genuine, touching and warming a part of his heart that he thought might be eternally frozen. He received a fleeting smile.

"I told you before—when we were in camp. Part of me will never stop loving you. You must promise you won't do anything to make me mourn for you again. Please?"

"Are you using my most serious weakness against me?" he asked quietly.

"Weakness? I'm not sure what you mean."

"You. You always were, and always will be, my greatest weakness. How can I possibly deny you?" Something in her manner had, at least for the moment, soothed away some of the sharp pain that had become his constant companion.

"Weakness or not, I want you to be careful. Remember that. Now, may I have your promise?" A slight sparkle of restored calm returned to her eyes.

"If it's so important to you, then you have my sincere oath that I will be as careful as possible," he promised. "Does that satisfy your request?"

"It satisfies so long as you remember your promise. Now, I must ask you something else." The tone of her voice, almost a whisper, filled with an intensity that washed over him like the first warm breeze heralding the coming of summer.

"Alexa, you know you can ask me anything. I cannot promise an answer, but I'll try." Once again, he felt a stirring inside and believed only she could be the source.

"Victor, I have to know there can be peace between us. Never will I be able to express in words how much a part of my life you'll always be. I need to know that, someday, you can forgive me for having caused you so much sorrow."

Victor drew in a deep, shaky breath, and his head fell back abruptly. He could never have consciously prepared himself for such an entreaty. Yet, this was the Alexa Victor had always loved, always turning everything to a new, unexpected direction. Would he never be able to comprehend the intricate workings of her heart and mind?

"My sweetest Alexa, because of my own stupid, misguided actions, you married a man you didn't love or even know. You gave yourself to him that I might live to fight for the dreams you and I shared. How can you possibly think you should be the one asking forgiveness?"

Every line on her face showed a solemnity that even he had never seen from her. "Still, I hurt you, and I never wanted to. I never dreamed how my life would change. Regardless, I want to know that you can at least try to forgive me for whatever part I play in your unhappiness. Victor, you deserve better than this." Words caught in her throat, and she could go no further.

Victor placed his hand tenderly against her cheek. "Alexa, I saw you with him in the meadow this afternoon. In all the years I've known you, I've never seen you so completely free and blissful. In all honesty, I cried when I saw the two of you, and I've thought of little else since. Call it forgiveness or whatever you want. I want you to accept this truth." He paused and placed her hand over his heart. "As impossible as it sounds, nothing is more important to me than your happiness. So long as he is good to you and you are happy, then you can be assured that peace already exists between us."

The pain had not disappeared from his eyes, but she noted a subtle change. She smiled tenderly, confident that someday he would recover part of the robust vitality that her love for Gregor had snatched away from him. Spontaneously, she kissed his cheek. "Thank you, Victor."

They slowly began to walk again. The night grew darker, and the hour was late. Just before they reentered the castle, Victor stopped her once more in front of the enormous wrought-iron lanterns that lit the way inside. Their golden light bathed her face in a soft glow. He lightly caressed her cheek. His hazel eyes glistened with love, and his voice filled with emotion. "Be happy, my sweetest." He then opened the door for her to go inside.

Upon entering the castle, Alexa found the downstairs deserted. In a way, she was glad. A part of her was free of a ponderous burden now that she and Victor had finally reached a kind of reconciliation. Still, there was tomorrow. Thankfulness filled her that she would start the day in communion with Val inside a hallowed chapel. She would pray for Val's blessing to strengthen her in the face of renewed separation from her beloved husband.

Her footsteps dragged as she pushed open the door to her room. Just the thought of returning to Toraval without him already weighed down her spirits. She was crossing the room toward the dressing table when Gregor emerged from the bath, startling her from her dismal thoughts. Without saying a word, she moved straight into his arms.

He placed his arms loosely around her, his head tilted to gaze down into her face. "Are you all right?"

Unsuccessfully, she tried to smile. Unable even to speak, she pulled away and went to sit before the mirror on the dressing table. She began to undo the braids that Katara had worked into her hair earlier in the day.

Gregor sensed her melancholy and went to her, working long fingers into the thick braids looped at the back of her head to loosen them. He had returned early from his meeting with Kohira, knowing this would be his final evening with her before she departed for home. Disturbed to find her neither downstairs nor in her room, he went looking for her. Upon seeing her walking arm in arm with Victor, it had required every bit of willpower Gregor possessed not to interrupt them.

"I saw you outside with Victor. Was there any problem?"

"No," she replied quietly. "In fact, I think we finally managed a sort of resolution."

"Good." He leaned forward to pick up a silver-handled brush from the dresser. As he drew it in long, firm strokes through her hair, he studied her reflection in the mirror. With her eyes closed, she looked somber and distant. After a while, he slowed the pace of his brushstrokes. When she leaned her head back against his body, he saw that a few crystalline teardrops eased down her face. He reached around her and wiped them away. "What's this?"

She rose from the vanity chair and moved into the haven of his arms. "I already dread leaving you tomorrow. It hurts so much, and I'm afraid you won't be home with me when the baby comes and… Oh, Gregor, hold me. Please."

With her body tightly enfolded in his arms, he felt tremors run through her. He wanted so much to keep her with him, yet he dared not expose her to such imminent danger. Tilting his head down, he buried his face in her silken hair. "Do you know how much I hate the idea of sending you home like this? I ache, too, but I have no other choice. How can I make this easier for you?"

She backed slightly away for a moment and stared at him. Every nuance of his presence revealed the sadness filling him. She could feel inside herself that he dreaded this newest separation as much as she.

Returning to his embrace, she found his closeness her only possible consolation. Placing her hands against his chest, she slid them down to where his shirt tucked into his waistband. She tugged at the fabric until she had freed it. She slipped her hands underneath, circling her arms around his muscular back and touching the warmth of his bare skin.

"Alexa? Will you not talk to me?" His voice was low. Her present melancholy so painfully contrasted with her earlier high-spirited mood. He would give anything in his possession not to put her through tomorrow's parting and to retrieve the joy of the afternoon that had been theirs.

Her eyes were dry as she looked up into the face she cherished so much. The state of her emotions was too precarious for speech. Instead, her body became her means of communication. She lifted herself on her toes to place her lips against the fullness of his. Her mouth opened slightly, begging him to give her the arousing pleasure she always found in his kisses. She swept her hands downward to cup them over the fullness of his masculinity. Satisfaction filled her as she noted the immediate surge beneath her touch.

His mouth slid from hers for only a second in an involuntarily gasp. Her unexpected intimacy had sent shafting impulses through every fiber of his being. His eyelids lifted, revealing eyes darkening with passion that rose swiftly in response to her body demanding union with his.

He guided her to the bed, maintaining the deep connection of their kiss while lowering her to sit on the edge. With shaking fingers, he unbuttoned her blouse. Impatiently, he pulled away the rest of her clothing as she reciprocated with his. By the time he settled her back on the mattress, the forces of his desire hammered through him. Knowing he would again be without her drove him with a kind of insanity, especially as he felt her smooth skin in motion against his. Overtaken by desire, he had little control when he took her.

She clutched him frantically as though she would never again have him close enough to fulfill her need for him. Her lips transferred heated, sensual paths along his neck and shoulders as she desperately sought every touch and taste of him to sustain her through the lonely days and nights to come. Her soft moans provided a stimulating rush against his ear, and she reveled in the quickened pace of his possession. They moved together in unison, their bodies reconfirming the love that must endure yet another forced separation.

When finally their desires culminated in fiery bursts, they both shook violently. Satiated passion left them bonded together in bittersweet gratification. Their very souls cried out against the injustice of the war that would use time and distance as weapons of torture against them. Pressed tightly together, they surrendered to sleep for their final night together in Garogan Castle.

Chapter 25

Gregor turned over in bed, awakened by a series of firm knocks on the door. Glancing over at where Alexa had lain next to him and realizing she had already awakened and gotten up, he reluctantly dragged himself from bed, wrapped a blanket around his naked body, and went to the door. "Yes?" he called out in a sleepy voice.

"Gregor?"

Opening the door, Stefan entered. Gregor's first thought was that another urgent courier dispatch had arrived, and he shuddered at the idea of more bad news. "Has something else gone wrong?"

Stefan shook his head. "No, nothing has changed. Before she left, Alexa sent me a message to wake you up in time to go to the temple."

"Before she left?" he asked, dropping the blanket to the floor alongside the pile of clothes they had discarded so hastily the night before. He immediately went to the armoire for one of the clean uniforms that Adrina's staff had left yesterday.

"From what I understand, she came downstairs just after dawn. Tirani helped her get ready before they left with Lady Adrina for the temple."

"Did no one else go with them?" Gregor asked worriedly. The idea of Alexa walking the streets of Garogan City, accompanied only by two other women, left him extremely uncomfortable.

"As far as I know, they went by themselves. I dispatched two of the queen's guards to check on her."

Stefan left. Gregor dressed quickly. Rushing out into the corridor, he collided with Victor, who was already dressed and had apparently been up for some time. "I came to look for you, Sire. We're ready to leave."

"Lord Garogan, I was informed that my wife left for the temple much earlier with her lady-in-waiting and your sister. Do you know if they arrived safely?" Worry etched furrowed lines into his otherwise smooth brow.

"I do believe Alexa is still safe in Garogan City. However, I have already sent someone to look for them. They were all safely inside the temple." Victor, his emotions still raw where Gregor was concerned, answered in a voice filled with cool reserve.

Conversely, Gregor was too relieved to care what Victor thought one way or another. "All thanks be to Val," he uttered on a heavy sigh. "I wonder if I will ever grow accustomed to these impetuous and reckless impulses she has to go out on her own."

Victor's face tensed when Gregor's words stung a long-open wound. His words were bitterly ironic when he spoke. "My advice is that you never accustom yourself to that aspect of her character. That is exactly how I managed to lose her."

They had started down the stairs, but Gregor stopped abruptly. Victor's comment was not made in anger. Still, it struck a sensitive chord. "Lord Garogan, I offer you my apology. No matter what else you may think of me, I am not an insensitive man. My comment was a sincere expression of my own personal concern. It was never meant to…"

Victor interrupted him. "Sire, when speaking of Alexa, nothing you can say can cause me any more pain than I already know. You have my sworn support as a loyal citizen of Turand. As long as you take care of her and she is happy, you will have my gratitude. Never expect more from me." Victor turned, his boot-clad feet clicking against carved stone stairs as he left Gregor standing alone at the top of the stairwell.

⌒

A park and public square marked the center of Garogan City. At one end stood the ancient temple constructed from rose-colored granite. Wide stone steps rose five levels to the massive arched doorway opening to a softly lit interior. A single carillon tower rose above the right front, and its bells chimed strains from an ancient hymn.

The city's citizens crowded in front, their voices a hushed murmur as they watched Lord Garogan and DiLeno Tarandá escort King Gregor to the top step. Because Garogan's people prided themselves on their hardiness and typically robust physical characteristics, the king's presence would leave a lasting impression. His finely tailored uniform accentuated his unusual height and his well-defined physique. His black uniform leggings revealed muscular legs. The pale gray tunic, belted in black leather, accented his narrow waist. Leather straps slid over wide shoulders, crisscrossing his broad chest. Their king exuded a powerful image to behold. Quiet descended as everyone intently watched him, waiting to hear him speak formally for the first time during his reign.

Victor addressed the crowd first, the expectation that the traditional loyalty afforded to members of the Garogan family would alleviate any lingering reservations regarding Turand's king.

"My fellow citizens, I trust that, over the years, you have all grown to appreciate my personal love for Garogan Province and its people. I dedicated myself to activities that I believed would counter the deterioration our nation suffered under Sifiq occupation. I admit to you that I, along with many others, thought the only way we could make lasting changes was to start with the elimination of what appeared to be the corruption of our own leaders in the Royal Palace of Toraval."

He paused a moment, unable to completely suppress the grief in his next words. "Most of you are also well aware of the personal tragedy I suffered as the result of going to Toraval in my attempt to address that situation. Since then, many astounding events have occurred throughout the past year, completely altering my assessment of our future. First, I learned that our king was not the selfish and cruel puppet of the Sifiq, as we thought. Instead, he and a small group of loyal advisers played a desperate game that has resulted in the defeat of the Sifiq throughout most of Turand. However, there remain other dangers we must confront. To explain further, I now present to you our King, Gregor of the Royal House of Toscano."

Almost hesitantly, Gregor extended his hand to Victor and was surprised to receive a respectful bow and a firm handshake in return. Gregor then turned to face Garogan's people, who waited in spellbound silence for him to speak. His voice was powerful, vibrant, and clear as it projected across the vast square.

"I am more than honored to have this opportunity to address loyal citizens of Turand who call Garogan Province home. I consider it proof of the extraordinary character of the Garogan people when I can stand here before you in the company of brave Turandans like Lord Victor Garogan. Despite personal conflicts with which he and I contend, I have come to respect his courage and his intense love for Turand and its people. This love for our nation is the driving force behind efforts to restore peace and prosperity to our country. This is a love that I confidently say he and I share with you.

"Citizens, the weeks just ahead promise to be more difficult and painful than most Garogans have ever known. An army approaches this city from the south. I am disheartened knowing that Lord Anderon, a fellow Turandan, commands this army. Worse yet is that many of his soldiers are dedicated Turandans who believe they fight for our country's freedom. This is a tragedy of which Lord Garogan and Sir Tarandá bear direct knowledge.

"With his goal to secure personal power, Lord Anderon has secretly built his army in an alliance with Sifiq soldiers who disguise themselves as Tasan and Garogan militia." Gregor paused as the crowd let out a shocked gasp. Murmurs of their reaction rippled through the square.

"Lord Garogan and I now combine our efforts, as well as the experience and dedication of Turand's Royal Army and your own Garogan militia, to defend Garogan City. And, if Val so wills, we will put an end to this tragic war. To achieve this goal, we require patience, support, and courage from each of you here today. What we all face is death and destruction in a part of our country that has so far escaped the worst devastation wrought by the Sifiq. Therefore, I pledge to you my life in defense of Garogan. At the same time, I beg for your help.

"I want you to know that, although this is my first trip to Garogan, your province commands a special place in my heart. As you know, our queen was born in Garogan Province, in Zinzan. Many of you knew Alexa and even loved her when she lived here. For years, your province was the only one in all of Turand blessed enough to have a Valiria within your midst. Now, I am blessed to have her as my wife, and we await the birth of our first child.

"In this time of great turmoil, the gift of her presence provides valuable lessons to us all. She remains steadfast in her faith. She reminds me daily that, by believing in Val and following his teachings, we are assured of promised rewards and blessings. Val's blessings are with us, now manifested through Alexa's anointing as Valkana. Our Valkana stands ready to lead us spiritually and to guide us toward those rewards Val offers us all. Inside this temple, our High Priestess Valkana awaits with Val's message that, through faith, prayer, and unity, we can achieve the peace of Val for the good of all Turand's people and for the futures of our children."

Jubilant cheers and thunderous applause erupted. There was a unique sense of pride that Alexa, beloved daughter of Garogan Province, was now chosen to lead Turand back to spiritual wealth. Despite the dangers lying at their doorsteps, they also discovered a newfound sense of pride and confidence. Following years of chaos, they could believe in a leadership devoted to re-establishing the splendor that long ago had been Turand.

Smiling and waving to the crowd, Gregor silently prayed, thankful for the welcoming acceptance that flowed from them. He had suffered profoundly through years of unwarranted contempt and personal sacrifice for a dream that had most often seemed unattainable. This moment gifted him with a gratification he would savor for years to come.

❧

Gazing into the mirror above her dressing table, Alexa secured the braided loop of hair that had fallen to her shoulder. She managed a faint smile, appreciative of the morning's meditation in the temple and the encouraging comfort of Val's presence as she tried to prepare herself for later. During her presentation to a filled temple, she had felt Val's words inside her mind as she translated his message to the people. The resulting wave of adulation and praise directed to Val had filled her heart with joy. She also felt encouraged to define and develop her own unique style of serving as Valkana.

On the way to the temple, Adrina had told her of her decision to accompany her to Toraval. Alexa was glad beyond words at the prospect of having the solace of Adrina's presence because she already doubted she could face today's parting without breaking into tears.

She readied herself to go downstairs for breakfast with her husband and the others who were more like family than friends. These few moments alone in the privacy of her rooms provided much-needed time to compose herself.

She was the last to arrive in the dining room. Somber eyes acknowledged those who awaited her and whom she adored so much. Despite her underlying despondency, the smile she exchanged with them was warm and affectionate. Without saying a word, she walked to the empty chair beside her husband. After Victor offered grace, they all sat down to breakfast.

There was none of the lively humor or conversation that had characterized other meals they had shared since coming to the castle. Even Katara was unusually quiet. All worried about news of how swiftly Anderon's army was advancing on Garogan City. Solemnity descended more heavily yet as not one could ignore the sadness showing so plainly on Alexa's face.

Gregor watched as his wife took a few small bites from a meat-filled, golden-brown pastry. Her manner grew more remote with each minute that passed until she aimlessly pushed food around on her plate. Finally, Gregor reached over and took the hand that held her fork. She glanced up at him.

His voice was quiet when he spoke to her. "You have a long journey ahead of you, my love. You need to eat."

The tender expression in his eyes shattered the fragile control she had struggled to maintain. Abruptly, she jumped up from her chair and ran from the room. Gregor released a heavy sigh of frustration and rose to follow her. He returned within minutes, his face pale with concern. "I have no idea where she went."

Victor glanced up immediately and rose from his chair at the head of the table. "I think I know where she went. I'll go talk to her."

Gregor's initial inclination was to object. She was upset, and he wanted to console her. He also faced dejection that Victor knew her so intimately that he was confident of where she had fled in her distress. Still, some instinct told him that it might be better if Victor was the first to go to her.

Victor found her in a tiny room that could be accessed only from his private study. Years ago, he had transformed the space into a secluded retreat where she could meditate in peace without going to the temple. The room had a single window opening onto a well tended rose garden. He had personally chosen the oval floral oils hanging on the walls and the two rose-colored, wing-backed chairs that faced the window. With his own hands, he had crafted an oval table set between the chairs. Upon the table stood a porcelain oil lamp and a small crystal pyramid.

Alexa leaned against the wall by the window frame. Her arms lay against the gray stone of the outer wall, and her face was hidden against them. Her entire body shook. The sound of her crying tore into his heart, even though her tears were shed for another man. Victor crossed the room and rested his hand against the back of her shoulder. "Alexa?" he said tentatively.

She slowly turned around and moved into his arms. Crying so hard that even the top of her blouse was wet, she buried her face against his shoulder, helpless to check the deluge of tears that had overcome her.

He stood patiently with his arms around her. Whispering into her ear, he tried to calm her. "It's all right, Sweetest. Cry it all out. You've been so brave, traveling first all the way to the battlefield to nurse so many of us away from death's edge. It's just like it always was—you caring for everyone except yourself. This is one of the few times you need us to take care of you. You know we're all here, and we're doing our best."

Her sobbing slowed, and he felt her hiccuping against him. She turned her face slightly, never leaving the solace she had sought in his arms. "I'm so afraid, Victor. My vision isn't clear right now. I'm terrified knowing that Anderon brings an army augmented with Sifiq soldiers."

"More than anyone else, you have to believe in us, Alexa."

"I do, but I…" she hiccuped on another sob. "Victor, this isn't fair to you. I am so sorry."

"Shush. Don't think about that. Right now, I only want you to think of your own good and that of your baby. It is surely no good for you to be this upset. Besides, you know you'll be much safer in Toraval, especially because of the baby,"

"I know, but I can't help myself. Every time I think about going home without him, I feel sick all over. And what if something happens to him? Or if he isn't home when the baby comes? I know I sound terribly selfish, especially when all of Turand is at stake."

He interrupted. "Alexa, he's your husband and the father of your baby. There's nothing selfish about wanting him and needing him to be with you." He was finally able to lead her to one of the chairs and get her to sit. He knelt in front of her, cupping her more delicate hands in his and gazing into her eyes.

"How can I do this? How can I just leave, not knowing when or even if I'll ever see him again? Will I never stop losing everyone I love?"

Victor lowered his head and kissed her fingertips. "You mustn't think you're losing him, Alexa. You're just facing a separation. Listen, I have an idea. If you stop crying, I'll make two promises."

Looking into Victor's face, she sniffled in response, her eyes red, her lips taut and swollen from biting into them. She breathed in deeply several times, forcing herself to calm somewhat.

"That's better. Now. The first thing I promise is that I will stay close to him wherever he goes, and I will do everything in my power to see that he doesn't get hurt. Then, when it comes closer to the time for the baby, I will personally escort him to Toraval, even if it means DiLeno and I have to wrestle him down and tie him onto his horse. "

"Victor, as much as I wish I could, I can't ask that of you. I know how you really feel."

"Alexa," he said firmly, "Gregor is our king. Every good Turandan is bound by honor to help him. As for bringing him to Toraval—I can manage my own feelings. The question is, do you trust me on these promises?"

She managed a weak smile and slid her arms around his neck. "I don't know what I ever would have done without you in my life. Thank you, Victor. Thank you so much."

After a few quiet minutes passed, Victor eased her against the back of the chair. He stood and looked down at her. "Your husband was nearly frantic before I came in here. I'm going to get you something to drink and a wet washcloth for your face. Do you want me to bring them back, or should I let him?"

She shook her head. "Victor, if it isn't too much to ask, would you? I need a little more time before I can face him."

He left her, going directly to the kitchen for a glass of water and cold cloths for her face. He returned through the dining room, where only Gregor and Adrina now waited. Adrina immediately rushed to his side.

"Is she all right, Victor?" she asked as Gregor looked up wordlessly, his expression despondent.

"She will be. She just needs some time to regain her composure. Except for a few rare occasions, she has spent her life taking care of everyone around her. She knows exactly how vulnerable she is right now, and that makes her afraid."

Gregor felt helpless as he forced himself to speak. "I've tried every way I know to reassure her. You know I have no choice but to send her home—only because she'll be safer there."

Victor's voice revealed none of his usual resentment when he responded, "She knows that. She's especially fearful that something will happen, and you won't be with her when she really needs you. Her pregnancy makes her feel helpless."

When Victor returned, he dragged the empty chair around so he could hold the water glass to her lips. She sipped slowly, her hiccups almost gone. Tenderly, he wiped her face and used a second cloth to lay against her eyes. Her wobbly smile showed her appreciation for the relief of the cooling compress against swollen eyes.

Perhaps another ten minutes elapsed before Victor helped her up. "Come. You need to help him through this, too. He feels as unhappy as you about your leaving today. He's waiting."

She looked at him with just a faint smile touching the corners of her eyes. She leaned forward and placed a brief, gentle kiss against his lips. "Thank you, Victor," she whispered.

Adrina was waiting in the foyer. She had sent Gregor upstairs to wait for Alexa, thinking they needed to be where there was no chance for interruptions while they sorted out their farewells. Adrina gave her a hug for encouragement and sent her up.

Alexa suffered an almost physical jolt when she pushed open the bedroom door. Gregor, his head hung low, faced the window. His posture alone revealed the burden of responsibility and anxiety bearing down on him. Alexa crossed the room in silence and rested the side of her face against his arm. Neither moved for several long moments.

At last, her voice trembling, she said, "Please forgive me, Gregor. I never meant to worry you so."

He turned around, revealing a face wet with tears. He clenched and unclenched his teeth, his mind seeking something to say to ease the pain of this parting for both of them. He tried to speak, but words got lost somewhere in a throat too tight to speak. Instead, he pulled her tightly against him, his body swaying from side to side in slow, steady rhythm. Finally, he stilled and drew away just enough to gaze into her eyes. "Alexa, you cannot know how hard this is for me to send you home to Toraval."

She lowered her face, unable to bear the grief in his eyes. "You carry the responsibility for so many lives right now. I feel guilty that I only add to your burden."

He lifted a finger to her lips. "I don't want you to feel guilty. In fact, considering how I've left you alone to face this pregnancy with our baby, I am the guilty one. My place should be at your side, yet either I leave you, or I send you away. Beloved, you must believe that what I do is what I honestly believe best for our future." His voice trembled and faltered.

Within her chest existed a hollowness that held a leaden weight at its bottom. It hurt to push air into the depths of her lungs, and speech seemed an impossibility. Part of her wanted to scream. Another part wanted to dissolve again into tears. Somehow, she held tears at bay and, instead, grasped his hands tightly together and placed them against her cheek. Her eyes closed, and her expression broke his heart.

Again, he wound his arms around her tightly, surrendering to his own heartbreak as a sorrowful sob shook his powerful body. Tears flowed freely from his eyes as he clutched her close. He melted into her embrace that he knew he would miss to the point of physical pain. He realized how much of his strength she had become. Her looming departure was already draining him.

She held him tightly, feeling his grief as her own. She was almost surprised when she found her voice calmer than his. "I love you, my husband. I love you more than life itself. You must be strong. Not only for all of Turand and for me but also for your son. He will need his father."

Gregor lifted his head, tears still streaming from his eyes. The corners of his mouth lifted the tiniest bit. "My son? You say that with such certainty."

"Have you forgotten your wife is Valkana? She knows such things," she told him tenderly, just before lifting her face in an unspoken request for his kiss.

Outside, Victor's spacious, comfortable travel carriage waited to transport Adrina, Katara, and Alexa to Toraval. Adrina and Katara had already said their farewells and seated themselves inside the carriage. They waited for Alexa as she hugged both DiLeno and Victor. Stefan stood by the open carriage door with Gregor, who prepared once again to entrust his wife's safety to Stefan's care.

Alexa forced herself to walk steadily toward the brougham and her waiting husband. Gazing up into his face and seeing his tears, she could no longer restrain her own. "I love you, Gregor," she whispered, weeping softly while leaning against him with her arms stretched around him.

Helping her into the carriage, he leaned inside to ensure she had settled next to Adrina. He grazed her hand with his lips in loving tribute and then, with great reluctance, withdrew from the carriage. He secured the door and watched Willem and Stefan wave goodbye as the women started their journey back to Toraval. Gregor's lips moved in silent prayer, begging Val to take her safely home and to give him the strength to withstand this newest and most heartbreaking separation.

Chapter 26

The Royal Army rallied behind the unified leadership and brilliant strategies developed by King Gregor and Lord Victor Garogan. When the revolutionary militias learned that Lord Garogan and DiLeno Tarandá had sworn allegiance to King Gregor and that much of the Garogan Militia had followed suit, questions arose that Lord Anderon refused to answer.

Anderon's lead officers demanded brutal punishment for those who refused to fight without explanation. Dissent mushroomed into chaos until the insurgent army fell apart. Facing the Royal Army's determined advances, Lord Anderon finally surrendered. Most of his remaining command officers were Sifiq. As a group, many committed suicide rather than suffer the humiliation of capture and imprisonment.

With the surrender accomplished, the king grew more anxious than ever to return home. Kohira had already earned a field promotion to general, so Gregor left him in charge of his victorious forces and charged him with orchestrating the triumphant return of the main army to Toraval. That return would bring Anderon, his collaborators, and all remaining Sifiq prisoners to face justice before a Council Tribunal that would be specially convened with representatives from each of Turand's provinces.

Civil war had reached its official end. Destruction at the hands of invaders and power-seeking Turandans would cease. A courageous king had devoted the efforts of a lifetime and established an order in which Turand could rebuild and recover past prosperity. He had persevered, fought hard, and won the loyalty of other dedicated Turandans. Together, they had combined knowledge, skills, and fidelity to achieve a precious, collective dream. Renewed and growing faith had brought about the blessed return of Valkana. Peace had finally returned to Turand.

⤴

He glanced several times at the king as they picked up the pace of their ride toward the capital. Throughout the past weeks, Victor had gained rare insight into Turand's king. For many years, circumstances had forced Gregor to reveal little of his true self to those around him. The king's character was complex. He could be cool and calculating whenever the need existed. He could change instantaneously to praise a determined soldier or encourage a wounded man. The fiercely courageous commander of a morning battle transformed in the evenings to a sensitive, anxious husband spending the night worrying about his pregnant wife so far away.

Gregor had not made it easy for Victor to keep the first promise he made to Alexa that final day at Garogan Castle. The king had ridden directly into fierce battles, paying no heed to dangers or risks. As an officer, he was single-minded in his concentration and determination to force the enemy into defeat. Victor often exhausted himself just trying to maintain the pace forced by Gregor, let alone attempting to protect his back as they fought together for a united cause.

The man now at his side looked strikingly different from the warrior king. Gregor's face was intense, almost as if he focused every breath in an effort to will time to stand still until he could arrive home. Victor considered how Gregor had shared personal thoughts with him on only a few recent occasions. Each time, he had been seriously troubled about not being home when Alexa needed him most. His voice had quivered, leaving Victor with the undeniable certainty of his love for her.

Those were the most difficult moments. Gregor's expression immediately became apologetic that his laments always gave rise to fresh grief for Victor. Despite their growing mutual respect, Alexa remained a barrier between them. Victor felt disheartened and realized that, under different circumstances, he and Gregor might have shared a strong friendship. However, that friendship could never be, just as his consuming desire for Alexa would never be fulfilled.

Vivid autumn reds and golds splashed the trees lining the road to the royal palace in Toraval. The air was cold and fresh, scented with rich soil, fallen leaves, and autumn flowers. Birds called noisily from overhead as they journeyed toward warmer climes to avoid the cold Toravalian winter. Occasionally, a furry woodland creature scampered across the road as it carried food to store for the coming months. A chill wind blew, announcing that winter was not long away. With each mile they passed, Gregor's heart beat just a little faster. He was almost home. He prayed fervently that his arrival would come before that of his baby.

Afternoon was nearly over when two silent riders neared the front steps of Toraval's palace. Palace guards standing duty at the grand entrance bowed in respectful welcome to their king. Then, with Victor following close behind, Gregor himself pushed open one of the enormous doors to go inside.

Stefan was on his way to his office when the opening door permitted a mighty whoosh of cold air to blow into the grand entrance hall. The air carried a burst of crackling leaves that scattered across polished marble floors. Stunned by Gregor's sudden appearance, Stefan dropped the portfolio he had held and ran to embrace his friend. The two men hugged tightly, patting each other heartily on the back.

Gregor stepped away. He removed black leather gloves and then pushed the hood of his winter tunic back from his bearded face. His cheeks were ruddy from the icy wind, and his hair fell in untidy waves. "Stefan, I cannot tell you how good it feels to be home! How are you?"

"Actually, better than I've ever been in my life. And a good deal happier knowing that you're finally home safe." Stefan's blue-gray eyes sparkled as he smiled.

"Alexa? Is she all right?" he inquired anxiously. "And the baby?"

Stefan shook his head and grinned. "Fortunately for you, the baby has not yet come, although Dr. Korodi told us yesterday that it could be any time."

"Where is she?" Gregor's eyes were bright and expectant.

"I'm not really sure, but she has been taking a nap in the afternoons. You might try her chambers."

Gregor immediately hurried toward the marble staircase leading to the upper floors. "Lord Garogan, please inform Stefan about the surrender while I go to my wife."

Minutes later, he returned downstairs to interrupt Victor and Stefan as they discussed events surrounding the last days of the conflict. "Stefan, she wasn't there. I looked around down here and didn't see her either."

Stefan excused himself to Victor and went to a small office where the housekeeper reviewed accounts with her staff. When he returned, he had his cloak with him. "Carlo said that Corporal Fratino escorted her a while ago to the temple. I'll walk along with you."

Gregor quickly slipped his hood back over his head and pulled on his gloves. The two men left, bracing themselves against stiffening winds. "I see my wife can still create more trouble than anyone I know. With the advanced state of her pregnancy, how in Val's name could she think to come out in this cold air?"

Stefan laughed heartily. "She loves to be outside. She insists she needs to go outside, and every time I try to reason with her, Adrina takes her side. I can negotiate with any politician you send me, but since we returned, I have yet to find a way to win against the two of them."

Gregor glanced up and laughed heartily. "Other than that, how has it been having Lady Adrina here with Alexa?"

Stefan's face transformed momentarily. "Your wife needed Adrina. This latest separation has been a real ordeal for her. Adrina's presence has made all the difference in the world."

"And?" Gregor asked, sensing something left unsaid.

Stefan looked at him with a sheepish expression. "She's made all the difference in the world for me, too. Adrina and I have fallen very much in love."

Gregor stopped abruptly, his expression turning incredulous. "You? And Lady Adrina? Are you serious?"

Stefan laughed, his eyes glittering happily. "Absolutely. She is sweet and lovely and... What more can I say? She captured my heart. My good fortune is that she has given me hers in exchange."

Gregor hugged Stefan again. "Unbelievable! I think I need time for this one to settle in!"

Reaching the temple, Gregor bounded up the steps to the front entrance. Opening the door, he was quickly disappointed to find the temple deserted. He came back outside to where Stefan waited. "You don't really think she's out walking in this, do you?"

Gregor's anxiety was growing. He desperately ached to see her again. Stefan shrugged his shoulders and suggested they go around the palace in case she was walking outside. By the time they reached the rear, they shivered with cold and hurried in the door to the kitchen.

Celia, the chief palace cook since Gregor's childhood days, looked up in surprise. "Your Majesty! Praises be to Val, you've come home!" she greeted in delight. "I'm preparing a tray of tea and cakes for the queen. She will be so happy to see you!"

Gregor laughed as he removed his gloves and held his hands in front of the enormous corner fireplace. "That may be. Now, if only I could find her! Where is she, Celia?"

Celia cackled humorously. "She came in only a few minutes ago, Sire, and asked me to send a tray to the library. She insists on going to your library because she says she feels closer to you there. Go! I will send this in as soon as the water is hot."

Gregor glanced at Stefan with a grin before running from the kitchen. He rushed through palace corridors until he arrived at the double doors leading to the library. One door stood open, and he peeked in. In front of the massive fireplace, Alexa leaned against the mantel, reading from a letter in her hand. He wanted to laugh as she balanced precariously, holding first one foot, then the other, to warm in front of the blazing fire. Instead, Gregor stayed quiet, cherishing this private moment to gaze at the woman he loved and who was so near her time to give birth. There was an infinite sense of beauty surrounding her that he was sure he had never seen before, and he resolved to record every detail as a masterpiece portrait in his mind.

Finally, he said softly, "I cannot tell you how very glad I am that you decided to wait for me."

She paused from her reading without moving, then shook her head slightly as though she thought she had imagined the sound. As if in slow motion, she looked up and around, her eyes shocked at first, then widening with disbelief. Suddenly, her face transformed from disbelief to absolute exultation. The letter fell from her hands and floated to the floor as her arms stretched out to receive him.

He moved quickly to encircle her within his arms. His hands roved upward from her waist to where his fingers entangled in the silken curls swirling lovingly around her shoulders. He leaned his face forward and captured her mouth to share a kiss that erased at once all the aching loneliness they both had faced since her departure from Garogan. Their lips moved ecstatically from mouth to cheek, then back again as there seemed to be no way to satiate the driving need spawned by their reunion.

He felt her wet tears on his cheeks. He moved feverishly, burying his face into her scented hair, whispering how much he loved her and how much he had missed her. Yet again, he dragged his lips back to her trembling mouth, allowing himself to partake of the intoxicating joy he found there. He was home at last, and this woman, his beloved wife, was drawn back into his arms where she belonged.

Much later, they sat close together on the leather sofa in front of the fireplace. Tea and cakes were consumed as he asked her one question after another about the progress of her pregnancy and how she felt. Just as he had done in Garogan, he began to rub her stomach in fascination. He laughed softly, amazed by the hard roundness low in her abdomen. Occasionally, feeling a moving lump beneath his fingertips, he was unable to hide his astonishment as she explained that he was touching a tiny foot, an elbow, or a knee.

That evening, they joined Stefan, Adrina, and Victor for a delicious celebration dinner. Gregor watched Stefan with Adrina, newfound romance lighting their faces and brightening their eyes. Outwardly, Victor participated in the happy occasion, but his eyes held even more in reserve than usual. Gregor felt a peculiar sadness for him, knowing that seeing Alexa had to be hard enough. Facing the probable loss of his sister in marriage had to make matters even worse.

Alexa retired early, and Gregor went upstairs with her. There would be plenty of time to discuss details related to the end of the conflict and the implementation of actions to revitalize Turand. At the moment, nothing else mattered to him except being with her. He took time to bathe, and by the time he crawled into bed beside her, she was more than ready to cuddle with him.

"Mmmm," she sighed. "How I've missed having you here to keep me warm." She turned clumsily onto her side to face him and placed a small cushion beneath her swollen stomach for support. He snuggled as close to her as he could, only to receive a solid thump against his stomach.

"How do you sleep with that?" Gregor asked, starting to laugh as she giggled in amusement.

"Often, I don't. Now you get to stay awake with me and share the fun!" she teased, happily floating her fingers back and forth along his arm.

He pressed his lips against her forehead, smiling against the smoothness of her skin. "I will take great delight in sharing with you, my love. Already I've missed too much of this experience."

"Gregor. Oh, Gregor." Her voice trailed off, catching in a thick blanket of emotion. "I've missed you every hour of every day. How I love you."

"I know, beloved." He lifted a hand to caress strands of hair away from her face, finding such sweetness in just being able to touch her again. "There's something I've dreamed of telling you."

She rested her hands against his chest, comforted by the heat of his body penetrating the soft flannel of his nightshirt. "What?" she asked dreamily.

"You sound sleepy," he whispered, planting fresh and tender kisses on her face. "Perhaps I should wait until morning."

"Unacceptable, my love. You have something to tell me, so I'm listening," she prompted curiously.

His mind reverted to the final night he had spent alone in her bedchamber at Garogan Castle. He had felt miserable, recalling the piteous look in her eyes as he had backed out of the carriage. He hadn't cared that Victor, DiLeno, and dozens of soldiers had seen his tears as he watched her leave. His departure from Toraval had been painful enough. Sending her away from Garogan had been agony.

"Gregor?" Her voice lovingly called him from his thoughts.

"I apologize. I was just remembering. After you left for home, I spent another two days in Garogan City. I'm almost ashamed to admit that, on my last night there, I drank a little too much. By the time I went up to bed, I was wallowing in self-pity."

He emitted a short laugh. "I wasn't drunk, but almost. Melancholy overwhelmed me, and I started walking around the room. I touched your things. I opened closet doors and drawers. I have no idea why. Anyway, I eventually sat at that desk in front of the window and pulled out the top drawer. Inside, I found a letter. Some of the words were smudged, but I was still able to read it."

Tears pricked her eyes. "My letter? The one I wrote when I was captive?" She asked, even though she already knew the answer.

He sighed and lightly kissed her lips. "I've carried that letter with me everywhere. As much as I read and reread all your other letters, that one letter is more precious to me than any other. I'm not even sure why."

She moved her face closer to his and kissed him slowly. As their lips reluctantly parted, he rested his open hand over her stomach. Whispering to each other, they fell peacefully asleep.

⌇

Gregor devoted all of the following day to his wife. They enjoyed a light breakfast together in their suite before he escorted her to the Temple of Val. There, they prayed together in gratitude for the joy of their reunion. They also prayed for wisdom to guide their nation into an era of recovery and restoration. Later, with the sun out and cold winds diminished, he gave in to her insistence for a walk.

"You seem restless," he observed as she ambled beside him. "Are you sure you're feeling well?"

She flashed him a brilliant smile and stepped quickly in front of him. She clasped her hands in front of her stomach and acted as if she were holding it up. With exaggerated motions, she imitated every pregnant woman she had ever seen. Her laughter bubbled up and suffused him with warmth despite the cold temperatures. "I feel wonderful, but I doubt you could walk as gracefully with all this weight hanging inside your belly!"

"My dear queen, you continue to be impossible!" he scolded comically, reaching for her hands and pulling her to him. His lips descended to hers, and they kissed noisily.

"Stefan, if you ever do that to me in public!" Adrina's voice, deliberately loud, carried throughout the garden. Gregor looked over, pretending to be embarrassed.

Stefan raised his hands in mock surrender. "Not I, my dear. Our king and queen are silly enough romantics for all of us."

Adrina looked at him with feigned consternation. "That wasn't what I meant. I intended to tell you that I would be more than happy to return the favor!" She caught the more sedate and conservative Stefan off-guard as she threw her arms around him and kissed him soundly.

Gregor's amused laughter filled the gardens. Alexa held her stomach and shook with giggles. Stefan looked confounded only momentarily before being caught up in the spirited moment. He quickly grabbed Adrina around the waist and hauled her into his arms, kissing her breathless.

"Now, Lady Adrina, I hope you see what an apt student I can be. I only hope our king realizes that all this romance is apt to slow down his work ethic as well as mine. When we start back to work. If we ever start back to work."

Meeting where their paths intersected, they strolled and chatted a while longer until Alexa asked to go inside. She laughingly complained about ankles that were determined to swell despite the fact her feet were freezing.

That evening, she went up to bed even earlier than the night before. She had eaten little at midday and almost nothing at supper. Since the afternoon, she had grown very quiet, and her eyes reflected a gentleness that Gregor watched with increasing fascination. He excused himself to Stefan and their guests to go up with her. Adrina said nothing, convinced it must be time for the baby.

During the night, Alexa tossed restlessly, holding her stomach as she rolled into a new position every few minutes. Gregor turned several times with her and massaged her back or stroked her hair.

"What's wrong, my love?" he asked at last, concerned that she was getting no rest.

"I know I must be keeping you awake. My back ached all evening, and now I just cannot seem to get comfortable. Maybe you should go to another room so you can sleep."

"Absolutely not. I'm staying right here beside you." He kissed her on the cheek and squeezed her hand comfortingly.

"Then be a good husband and help me up. One of the delights of being nine months pregnant is having to go to the bathroom constantly."

They both chuckled as he climbed out of bed and came around to help her up. She remained long enough that he had begun to worry when he heard her call his name nervously from inside the bath. He jumped to his feet and hurried in to her. She stood in front of the basin with her hands out to her side. Her nightgown was drenched, and the floor was wet. A shaky smile spread across her face.

"Alexa, are you all right? What happened?"

"Gregor, you need to call someone up. My water just broke."

"I don't understand," he told her, having never been around anyone having a baby and not familiar with the process.

She laughed despite her discomfort. "My darling, your son is about to be born. First, you must send for Dr. Korodi and have someone clean this up. Then get me a dry gown and help me to the birthing room."

He remained completely motionless for at least a full minute, his mouth open and his eyes wide. Somehow, the immediacy of the moment was lost in his shock.

"Gregor," she prompted again. "I need you to help me."

Snapping out of his stupor, he handed her several towels. He then ran to pull the bell chord to summon servants on night duty. Returning, he placed additional towels on the floor so there would be no risk of her sliding on slick tiles as he carefully led her from the bath. He removed her wet gown, then quickly slipped a dry one over her head and wrapped her in a warm robe.

By the time he finished, a light knock had sounded at the door. Gregor gave the servant instructions and then, with his arm snugly around Alexa, led her to the room already prepared for the baby's birth. Gregor lit lamps as Alexa placed a mountain of pillows at the head of the bed.

Suddenly, she grasped the bedpost with one hand and clutched her stomach with the other. She breathed rapidly in and out, sighing heavily afterward. Gregor had rushed to her side, holding onto her tightly. Her voice was shaky when she caught her breath enough to speak. "Help me out of my robe and into bed. I think my backache was actually labor."

When Dr. Korodi's voice greeted them from the doorway, Gregor was busy arranging pillows behind her back. "Good morning, Your Majesties," he said with a drowsy smile. "I will never understand why babies insist on being born in the wee hours of the morning. How is Mother doing?"

She couldn't answer as another strong contraction overtook her. She recalled the times she and Adrina had attended births in Garogan and utilized breathing techniques that helped ease the powerful, vise-like contracting of muscles. She was extremely grateful for Adrina's recent coaching and their practice as she concentrated on her breathing.

Dr. Korodi's hands rested on her abdomen as he watched her intently. "How long have you been having contractions, my dear?" His voice was calm, instilling a sense of confidence that Gregor needed far more than his wife did.

She drew in a sustaining breath. "They started early in the evening, but I didn't think anything about it. Over the last few hours, I haven't been able to sleep because my back hurt. When I got up about twenty minutes ago, my water broke." She grabbed Gregor's hand and squeezed tightly as another contraction began.

Dr. Korodi had started timing and smiled at her, waiting for the contraction to end. "Had you waited much longer, I believe you might have caused your husband to have a serious panic attack. Sire, go awaken Tira and ask her to come quickly."

"Gregor?" His name escaped her lips just as another contraction came.

"Beloved, don't be afraid. I'll be right back." He ran from the room to fetch Tira. He made so much noise pounding on Tira's door and calling her name that he woke up everyone on the floor. Soon, Stefan, Adrina, and Victor were all up and heading downstairs to wait together.

When Gregor returned to the birthing room, Dr. Korodi looked at him sternly. "Sire, I suggest you go downstairs to wait with everyone else you woke up. We will send for you as soon as the baby comes."

Alexa's eyes pleaded with him, and he took her hand firmly. He leaned over and kissed her cheek. "Don't worry, my love. I have no intention of leaving you."

She squeezed his hand tightly as she breathed her way quickly through yet another contraction.

Dr. Korodi scowled, his face clearly showing disapproval. "Fathers are quite useless during a birth, Sire. They usually faint or some other such foolishness."

Gregor's voice sounded determined. "Doctor, I've been at war for six months. I am certain the birth of a child cannot compare to what I have seen on battlefields. Besides, this baby is mine, too. I refuse to leave my wife."

The old doctor shook his head impatiently. "Then you must do exactly as I say, and you will stay out of my way." He looked up and saw as Tira entered. "Tira, I am glad you're here. We're going to have to work around a very stubborn king. I want you to help Alexa while I go wash my hands and prepare my things."

Tira smiled at Gregor, revealing that she did not share the doctor's opinion regarding the presence of fathers at the births of their children. Within minutes, Gregor supported Alexa's shoulders as they adjusted pillows behind her. Alexa insisted on experiencing labor according to Garogan tradition that adhered to the idea that if a mother assumed a semi-upright position, her delivery would be more comfortable. Tira and the doctor helped position her legs apart, and the doctor began a closer examination.

Through several contractions, she concentrated on her breathing while Gregor whispered words of encouragement into her ears. Following each contraction, he discreetly flexed his fingers, astonished by the strength she exerted as she squeezed his hand.

"Milady, this baby is in quite a hurry to be born. Focus on your breathing. As the contractions grow stronger, breathe faster. Pant like a dog if it helps." He looked up at Gregor. "Are you positive you wish to stay through this?"

Gregor laughed, his initial case of nerves having subsided. "Absolutely. If she can do this, I can stay with her." He glanced down at her with loving eyes. "I told you I would be here."

She smiled briefly until yet another contraction left her breathless. The overwhelming power fascinated her even as it required every ounce of her ability to concentrate. She applied meditative techniques to enhance her concentration. Soon, the contractions came so fast she couldn't tell when one ended before the next began.

Tira placed clean, damp cloths in Gregor's hand, and he gently mopped away the sweat beading on her forehead. He continued to encourage her, and she nodded in response, having no time to form words between contractions. The whole event assumed a dream-like quality as every word and every sound occurred with an intensity that seemed to magnify with each passing minute.

"Gregor!" she gasped when an irresistible urge to push overtook her by surprise. "The baby!"

Doctor Korodi glanced up quickly, but his voice stayed even and calm. "You're right, Milady! Push! I see the baby's head. Push! Push!"

Gregor's arm held her shoulders firmly as she pushed hard, gasping for breath between pushes. Within moments, a lusty cry filled the room, and Doctor Korodi lifted the newborn infant boy for his parents to see. Alexa's smile, though tired, was joyous. Tears filled Gregor's eyes upon seeing the tiny, precious life the doctor held in his hands.

The doctor tied and cut the cord, then proceeded to tend to Alexa. Meanwhile, Tira took the wailing infant to clean him and wrap him in soft, warm blankets. She then placed the still protesting baby into his father's waiting arms. Cradled against his father's chest, he quieted. His tiny, round face immediately enchanted Gregor, who carried his son to his wife's bedside so that she, too, could see him.

Tears shone in her eyes, and she dropped a gentle kiss on the baby's forehead. "He's so beautiful! And so perfect! Look at all the hair! He's going to look just like his father. I can tell already!"

Gregor sat on the side of the bed so that she could take their baby and hold him close to her breast. He watched as she lovingly touched tiny fingers and traced the softly rounded features of their baby's face. In the mellow glow of lamplight, the baby's eyes were open, and he appeared very alert, even curious. Deep within his soul, Gregor etched this moment into a memory that he would never let fade.

She gazed up into her husband's eyes and touched his face. "I think I have never loved you as much as I do right now."

He smiled through tears of wonder and happiness. "Thank you, my sweet Alexa. Besides your love, you could give me no greater gift than this child. You should rest now. Would you mind if I take him downstairs to introduce him around?"

"Not so long as you take good care of him. And don't forget to support his head." She kissed her baby again. "And you, my tiny darling, take care of your father. It will be good having help with that job."

Gregor laughed lightly as he leaned forward and kissed her on the lips. "I love you, Your Majesty. Now, I want you to get some sleep." He then stared down into the dark eyes of his son. "I love you, too, my little one. I think your mother wishes to call you Nikolai. Prince Nikolai. That is such a powerful name for such a tiny baby."

Her eyelids grew heavy as she listened to him, murmuring to their baby as he left the room and walked down the hallway. Doctor Korodi finished packing away his things while Tira helped Alexa into clean, dry clothes and rearranged the bed for her. Once fresh blankets were tucked around her, Alexa whispered a prayer of thanks before instantly falling asleep.

Downstairs in the family sitting room, Adrina and Stefan sat on a sofa that faced a roaring fire. Adrina leaned her head against Stefan's shoulder, and the two held hands. Victor stood by the mantel and stared into the depths of the dancing flames. Together they maintained a quiet vigil, waiting for news about the baby.

Adrina was the first to hear the sound of Gregor's voice, and she practically leapt to her feet. Stefan rose after her and turned toward the door. Gregor walked very slowly, talking continuously to the tiny bundle he carried in his arms. Adrina hurried around the end of the sofa and ran to him.

He lifted a proud, smiling face to her. "Lady Adrina, may I introduce you to our new prince, Nikolai?"

She nudged the edge of the blanket aside and smiled at the sight of the baby's wide-awake face. His tiny fingers tightly encircled his father's index finger. "What a darling! He's wonderful!"

Although she wanted so much to hold him, she didn't try to take him from his father. Judging by the fiercely possessive look on Gregor's face, she sincerely doubted he would have let her. Having been present at many births, she could never remember seeing a father so thoroughly enthralled with a newborn infant.

Stefan now stood at her side and craned his neck over her shoulder to glimpse the baby. "I thought all babies did was cry when they were born."

Adrina laughed and poked him with her elbow. "They don't cry constantly. Besides, he's warm and happy right now. Look at him."

Victor lifted his head but did not approach them. "Alexa? How is she?"

Gregor raised his face and saw the raw ache in Victor's eyes. "She did beautifully. She's resting now. Doctor Korodi told me her labor and delivery were unusually fast and easy for a first child, especially considering the baby's size. He weighs over nine pounds."

Adrina reluctantly let Stefan get closer to see the baby while she went to her brother. She was sure she saw traces of tears on the lashes of his closed eyes. "Do you want me to go check on her?" she whispered, understanding how worried he had been.

He shook his head before forcing himself to cross the room to see the new prince. As he gazed into the baby's face, he was amazed by how small he was. He was sure he already saw signs of Alexa's bone structure in his little face. Victor couldn't hide a smile. "He is quite a handsome young prince. I suggest you take good care of him."

Gregor gazed thoughtfully at Victor. "I assure you that I have every intention of doing so. However, I expect there will be times when I will very likely need help. Alexa wants me to ask both you and Stefan to consider sharing dual roles as godfathers to Nikolai."

Victor was shocked. Alexa's request wasn't nearly as much a surprise as was Gregor's apparent concurrence. He wasn't sure how to answer. Beyond the responsibility, he wondered if the role was one he could assume with a clear heart. Still, that tiny baby was as much a part of her as he was part of the father. Knowing how much he would always love Alexa, he acknowledged to himself that he would forever be bound to Nikolai.

"May I hold him?" he requested tentatively.

Gregor nodded, and Victor gently removed the baby from his father's arms. He cuddled Nikolai close to his face. "You are every bit as precious as your mother, aren't you? Would you like for me to be your godfather?" The baby stretched and yawned. "Yes? Well, I suppose you give me no choice, Prince Nikolai. Tell your father and your mother that Lord Garogan will be honored to be your godfather. All right?"

Part of Victor ached as he returned Nikolai to his father's waiting arms. Yet another part felt suddenly less lonely. Deep inside, he knew that he would come to love that child dearly.

After everyone laughingly wished Nikolai a happy birthday and congratulated Gregor, the beaming father excused himself to return upstairs.

Nikolai was falling asleep. Gregor wanted to put him to bed and to check in on Alexa before going back to bed to get some sleep for himself.

⌒

Late the following afternoon, Alexa awoke from a brief nap and, glancing at a clock, thought it must be nearly time for her tiny son to be demanding to nurse. Feeling rested, she decided to get up since the cradle by her bed was empty. Putting on her robe and slippers, she slowly walked downstairs and then went straight to her husband's library and stood silently in the open doorway.

A fire blazed in the grate and radiated velvety warmth into the room. Gregor sat, snuggled into the corner of the leather sofa, holding their son and singing a beautiful, old lullaby. She smiled to herself, rejoicing that she finally had both of them with her. She entered and walked up behind her husband to run both hands through the thickness of his hair. "I knew you had to be the guilty one."

He looked up over his shoulder. "And what do you think you're doing out of bed?"

"I came to search for my missing baby. I thought he might be getting hungry. May I join you?" Not waiting for an answer, she moved around the end of the sofa and sat next to her family.

When Gregor looked up, his face revealed inconceivable tenderness. "He fascinates me. Every sound. Every movement. Eyes. Ears. Nose. Hands. I find it so hard to comprehend that he lives simply because we loved. My mind refuses to grasp the magnitude of that simple fact."

She slid closer to her husband and laid her fingers against her son's downy-soft cheek. "He is Val's gift to us. Just as I consider you to be Val's reward to me."

Gregor nodded in agreement. "How thankful I am that Val presented us with our son now that peace is accomplished, and I was finally able to come home. Beloved, after all that has happened, never, never let me forget to make time for the two of you."

"I promise to remind you every day if necessary. I've lived without you long enough to last me two lifetimes."

"You know that we have years of extremely hard work ahead of us to rebuild Turand. I expect that it will rarely be easy."

"I know. So long as we're together through those years, I'll be happy. Besides, Nikolai will help us as he grows." She reached over to hold the baby's hand in her fingers. "For some reason, I believe our Nikolai will grow up to be a wise and loving man and a great king, just like his father."

Gregor chuckled, trying not to startle Nikolai. "I won't ask how you know, Lady Valkana."

"Being Valkana has nothing to do with that bit of knowledge. Knowing that Nikolai is a blessing from Val—and that he has an exceptional father to guide him—tells me everything."

Positioning the baby carefully on his lap, Gregor turned so that he was able to gaze directly into her shining emerald eyes. He lifted his hands to cradle her face, pulling her forward to receive his kiss. That kiss united them together physically just as their newborn son whimpered and started to awaken. They both glanced down simultaneously, knowing that Nikolai manifested the loving bond that would eternally link their souls.

Epilogue

Song of Turand
(Gregor's Song)

Bringing great gifts by your courage and grace
To Turand, you came as guide and as spirit.
In all who received those gifts from your heart
Linger the glow and the warmth of the fires you lit.

Of Love and of Light you were born for this land.
Sing the Sweet song, the Song of Turand.

As our universe marches through curtains of time,
And our world soars through the vastness of space,
Forever my love will remain yours alone,
My soul now conquered by your beautiful face.

As the oceans eternally embrace the shore
And the far-flung horizon kisses limitless skies
So shall I cherish the smiles that you gave
Forever and longer, I'll adore your emerald eyes.

Song of Turand

Of Love and of Light you were born for this land.
Sing the Sweet song, the Song of Turand.

I pray in Thanksgiving that you are made mine.
To be source of my strength sprung from your love,
For your song dispelling those years of my grief
My prayer do I send to our God above.

Together we fought to restore freedom and peace
To defend life so precious, so no more would be killed.
Now our people cry out with joyous release
For your faith was my guide, your wisdom my shield.

Of Love and of Light you were born for this land.
Sing the Sweet song, our Song of Turand.

My love, you exceed bound'ries measured in time.
The soul that you are and ever shall be
Will give wings to my heart and flight to my being
And our love so wondrous will soar gloriously free.

Forever reveling in the fragrance of spring
Beneath golden sun we'll walk hand in hand.
Together at last by the warm flowing waters
Our souls bound as one,
For you are my Sweet Song of Turand.